KOKORO

"I'm a huge fan of books that send me on spiraling internet searches, digital walkabouts that start in one place, and wind up somewhere completely different. *Kojiki* is one of those books, spinning away from a neat, accessible introduction into an exploration of a myriad of creatures and the worlds to contain them."
Barnes & Noble SciFi Blog

"A win for Keith Yatsuhashi."
The Silver Words

"I am a big fan of Anime and any book that makes me feel like I'm watching an Anime movie… well, it gets the immediate thumbs up from me!"
Fiery Fantasy

"If you're looking for a unique spin on fantasy, a space where dragons and elementals war with each other over broken Tokyo – then this book is worth your time."
Sci-Fi & Fantasy Reviews

"In many ways, *Kojiki* is a metaphor for discovering your heritage and engaging with your roots, especially as a second-generation immigrant. Rooting the novel in Keiko's real world, relatable struggles gives the story depth and helps anchor its wonderful flights of fancy."
Fantasy Faction

"Recommended."
The Curious SFF Read

KEITH YATSUHASHI

KOKORO

ANGRY
ROBOT

ANGRY ROBOT
An imprint of Watkins Media Ltd

20 Fletcher Gate,
Nottingham,
NG1 2FZ
UK

angryrobotbooks.com
twitter.com/angryrobotbooks
Guardians of the galaxy

An Angry Robot paperback original 2017

Cover by Thomas Walker
Set in Meridien and Montserrat by Epub Services

Distributed in the United States by Penguin Random House, Inc., New York.

ISBN 978 0 85766 618 5
Ebook ISBN 978 0 85766 619 2

Printed in the United States of America

9 8 7 6 5 4 3 2 1

For Caitlin

1
AFTERSHOCKS

Keiko Yamanaka hovered in space. Her burgundy shield lit the darkness, dimming stars, banishing night. Only the breathtaking planet below, the one Takeshi hid in a pocket within the Boundary, outshone her. Silver and gold marked its wide continents, blue and turquoise coloring its glistening oceans, rivers, and lakes. Lush, verdant forests abutted the much larger desert wastes in the west, while in the east, green gave way to fields and plains, the transition too abrupt, the woods too small. Higo. Takeshi Akiko said the ancient Japanese fable about a man whose love brought a willow tree's spirit to life was a hauntingly appropriate name. The world was supposed to draw Roarke, Kami of Earth, from his seclusion.

Keiko smiled sadly. That hadn't happened. Roarke remained locked away, unwilling to venture out, unwilling to do anything but grieve the loss of his wife. As if catching her thoughts, Takeshi's shield appeared against the velvet sky to Keiko's right. The Kami of Spirit stopped over a solitary mountain and motioned Keiko to join him.

"How long has it been?" he asked as Keiko slid her shield next to his.

"Long enough." Keiko worked her face into a disbelieving frown. "I can't believe you haven't heard anything."

"Not a word." Takeshi sighed. "Roarke's as silent now as when he left Earth. I thought he'd found closure. I was wrong."

"You really didn't think this would happen?" Takeshi's admission meant this was more serious than Keiko thought.

"Never confuse caution with certainty, Yamanaka-san," Takeshi said. "I was simply taking precautions, something I should have done with Vissyus."

"You should have done that with Seirin. She's the one who started everything." Seirin Bal Cerannon, Queen of the Oceans and Kami of Water had craved a child, circumventing kami law to make that dream a reality. The results were devastating: the ancient Earth nearly destroyed; Vissyus, Kami of Fire, insane and burning the world to cinders; rifts, battles, and uncountable deaths, Roarke's lover, Botua, among them. Apart from a short reappearance a few Earth years ago to help his friends defeat Vissyus, Roarke remained in seclusion.

"Higo was supposed to give him a chance to start over. Apparently, he didn't see it that way."

Keiko rubbed her cheek. "I guess. But what does that have to do with us?"

"This has everything to do with us." Takeshi turned to face her. "Without a kami's influence, war has come to Higo, a war that will spread to other worlds unless we stop it."

"What? How? Higo's sealed off in its own section of the Boundary. I watched Gaiyern do it. I helped."

Takeshi nodded patiently. "True," he said. "Unfortunately, none of us knew that, intentionally or not, Roarke left his Gate between Higo and Earth open."

Blood drained from Keiko's face. "And because he still controls the Gate, you can't close it."

"You are learning, Yamanaka-san. Higo is Roarke's world now; his will, or lack thereof, controls everything that happens here. Which is why we can't prevent his people from moving from one civilization to another."

"But…" Keiko sputtered. "That doesn't make any sense. How are we supposed to do something, if we can't actually *do* anything?"

"Carefully." Takeshi smiled grimly. "*Very* carefully. First, we'll remove Higo from the pocket and bring it back into real time."

"And then?"

"And then we fix this."

Keiko rolled her eyes. "Have you told Yui? If this involves Earth, she needs to know."

"She has enough to worry about with rebuilding Earth and letting its people adjust to her existence."

"And if the fight spills over? What then? She'll *have* to step in; she won't have a choice."

"Then we'll just have to stop that happening, or at least contain it if it does."

"Okay," Keiko sighed. "I get it. When do we leave?"

2
THE REFUGEE

Earth: Guilin City, China
The Present

Baiyren Tallaenaq pulled his battered jeep to the side of the road and looked uneasily into the sky. He'd assumed a new start would change him, would ease his anxiety and bring him the peace he'd never had on Higo.

He'd been mistaken.

Instead of peace, fear stalked him wherever he went; he jumped at shadows, saw danger where none existed. Even here, in a remote corner of China's Guangxi province, he imagined the worst. The rational part of his brain told him that the speck of silver light knifing through the sky was nothing to worry about, but his emotions refused to listen.

"It's just a plane," he said aloud. The odds of it being anything else were astronomical. He closed his eyes and drew a long, slow breath. *Your brother hasn't found you. He wouldn't know where to look.*

In desperation, he pulled a pair of binoculars from the

passenger seat, set them to his eyes, and focused. One look would dispel his fears, one glance to confirm. He found the vapor trail a little to the right, catching a thin sliver of white mist. Adjusting his aim, he worked his way up the streaks. Dread clawed at him. He lurched farther right and zoomed in on the object. A pair of silver tail fins appeared at what he knew were the heels of two chrome feet. Both fins swept upward and merged with what could only be thick metal legs that met an armored torso above which sat a cruel, hawklike helm.

The sight knotted his stomach. Mah-kai. Higo's forces had come for him. Any doubt he had fled; no matter how badly he wanted to deny the truth, he knew he couldn't. Cursing, he leaped into his vehicle and slammed the accelerator. The camp! He had to reach the camp, get his things, and leave as fast as he could. He pushed the car hard, the wind whistling around him. The radiation detector he always wore in China whipped from his shirt and flittered on its lanyard. He knew the simple card didn't do anything other than make him feel better; no one knew where China ran nuclear tests or disposed of nuclear waste. To make matters worse, his team shrugged off his concerns, leaving him feeling foolish. The thing was cheap after all, and looked more like the plastic forehead thermometers his colleagues used on their kids.

Grumbling, he shoved the lanyard into his shirt, worried its flapping might distract him from the road. The last thing he needed was to lose control and end up in a ditch. Fortunately, the road was long and straight, and he made good time. A mile on, he glimpsed a slender figure waving at him by the side of the road.

Recognizing the girl, he pulled over, cursing the delay. "What are you doing out here this early?" he asked, trying to sound casual.

"I'm sorry, Baiyren," the girl said. "I went out for a run and lost track of time." A burgundy band pulled her dark silky hair from a decidedly Japanese face. Her smile was light if mischievous, almost as if she'd been caught doing something wrong.

"You must've gotten up early to make it this far. What're we, ten miles from the dig?" Ten miles. How long would it take her to run this far? She was young, maybe twenty, but her hair, face, and running clothes were as dry as a desert.

"Yeah, well," she said, dabbing at her sweat-free forehead. "You know how it goes. I was trying to work out a problem and lost track of time." That mischievous smile was back, almost as if she found her words funny.

"I guess I do." Baiyren threw the vehicle into gear. "Hold on," he said, flooring the gas pedal and speeding off down the road.

A light chuckle sounded over the roaring wind. "It's different for you. You're in charge." The girl pulled her headband off and let her short, layered hair blow in the breeze. "I'm Keiko, by the way," she said, holding out her hand.

Baiyren took it and shook. Her palm was soft and warm and as dry as the rest of her. "How'd you know – that I didn't remember your name, I mean?"

"You had that look about you." Keiko shrugged. "Like you were fishing around in your head to remember something." Her smile vanished and her face became serious. "I know how it feels when people don't know the real you."

Baiyren coughed and nearly swerved onto the grass. Was Keiko messing with him or was he just getting paranoid? He forced a smile. "Being the boy genius does have its advantages." He glanced over this shoulder. The sky was still clear.

"You mean like getting your team together in half the time it takes everyone else, not to mention convincing the top-level Chinese officials to issue permits in less than a day? That's pretty incredible. Of course, finding fossils of new species does have that effect on people, especially ones as unique as you've uncovered."

That disconcertingly knowing look was back, and though Baiyren only glimpsed it as he fought to keep the car on the road, he thought she knew way too much about him.

"I read your first find looked like a giant ape, something fifty to sixty feet tall. I saw pictures of the second – a kraken if I'm not mistaken. The last one, the one that got you into *Smithsonian* magazine, was like a pride of huge saber-toothed tigers." She snorted. "I remember when pictures of creatures like these showed up in tabloid newspapers. They were always fuzzy and out of focus." She sighed wistfully. "Cameras have come a long way."

Baiyren grunted something he hoped sounded like agreement and glanced into the sky again. Nothing. He clutched the steering wheel until his knuckles whitened. Damn them! He'd made a home here. He had friends and colleagues who respected him for who he was, not because he was born into the right family. He wasn't Higo's prince any more, and that was fine by him.

"Is something wrong?" Keiko asked, sounding neither surprised nor concerned.

"What? No. I just have a lot on my mind."

"Yeah," Keiko agreed. "But why the rush? The find's not going anywhere, right?"

Something in Keiko's tone set off warning bells in Baiyren's head. Was she testing him? How much did he really know about her?

A second road cut across the fields, a precisely tiled ribbon of mortared stone that shot straight as an arrow toward a wall of jagged mountains. He turned onto it, the faux archeologist in him noting its age, the fugitive watching for danger. Without trees or buildings, he was alarmingly exposed. His gaze alternated between road and sky. The mountains, despite their size, looked so far away.

"What about you?" he asked, gunning the engine and speeding ahead. A tunnel cut through the wall, and he aimed for it. "You joined us in Japan right? You were at Tokyo University?"

Keiko swallowed uncomfortably. "I was studying there when I heard about your dig." She curled her shirt around her finger and twisted. "I had to take a class in archeology, and the professor was all over what you were doing. Anyway, even though I'm majoring in history, I knew I had to join you. You're making history, not teaching it. No way was I going to miss out on a chance this big. So... I sent in an application for an internship through my professor, and that was that."

"We don't take many interns," Baiyren said, suspicious now. They hadn't taken any. Researchers only. Keiko looked even more uncomfortable, so much so that Baiyren barely saw the two people blocking the tunnel entrance ahead.

Swearing, he slammed on the brakes and fishtailed to a stop. "What the hell's the matter with you?" he shouted through the windshield. "I could have killed you."

"I doubt that," a strikingly beautiful young Asian woman said in fluent if accented English. Her voice, though light and musical, was as hard as steel. Her flowing kimono rippled in the light breeze, the athletic figure beneath coiled like a stalking cat. Her eyes moved to the passenger seat. "Keiko," she said, nodding her head. "Is there something I need to know?"

Baiyren tried to hide his shock. His head swiveled from Keiko to the woman and her companion, up to the sky, then back. "Who are you?" he demanded of them both. "What do you want?"

The woman's companion, a lean and powerfully built man in periwinkle blue robes, stood beside the driver-side door. He hefted a long, elegantly carved staff in his right hand which he lowered to block Baiyren's way, the concentric rings at the tip clinking in the morning air like a jailer's keys.

The woman cocked an eyebrow. "Your Zhoku doesn't mention me? I'm insulted. I'm this world's kami, Yui Akiko." Baiyren's soul plunged into the ground. The Zhoku. Kami. "I've left you alone out of respect for your lord. That stops here. I know why you've come, and I won't let you disturb Botua's grave."

"Botua was Roarke Zar Ranok's wife," Keiko whispered. "She's the reason he hasn't appeared on Higo. He's still in mourning." Keiko shifted in her seat. "I'm fine too, Yui. Thanks for asking." Keiko turned to the man. "How's she doing, Father?"

The man shrugged noncommittally. "You know I can't

tell you, Keiko." He smiled. "It's good to see you. I think your training agrees with you."

Baiyren sank into his seat. "Will someone please tell me what's going on?" He shot a glance into the sky.

"You don't need to worry about them yet," Keiko said. "Father and I are holding you out of time to give us a chance to talk."

"I don't want to talk; I want to *leave*!" Ignoring the remark about time, Baiyren stomped on the pedal, but the car stayed where it was. He fidgeted. "Look, I don't really care who you think you are or what you can do; I certainly don't care about this grave you're talking about. I just want to go. The sooner the better."

Yui's expression turned glacial. "And I'm perfectly happy to see you go, young prince. Unfortunately, you've shared your knowledge with too many people. If you disappear, they'll finish your work for you, probably in your name." She stabbed a finger at him, her lacquered nail glinting under the sun. "I need you to tell your team you haven't found anything and should move to another site."

Baiyren shook his head frantically. "You don't understand; they'll be here any minute. I can't let them find me!" Sweat soaked his shirt and beaded his forehead. He felt as jittery as a cornered rabbit.

Keiko held up her hands. "Whoa, whoa, whoa. Let's all calm down for a minute. We all want the same thing." She turned to Yui. "Higo's forces are coming through a Gateway, what Baiyren calls a Portal. Their scout's already passed over once. I need to get Baiyren out of here as fast as I can. You know he has a guar... a mah-zhin with him, right?"

"I felt it," Yui acknowledged. "Given its current state, the sooner it's gone the happier I'll be."

Keiko nodded. "Good. Now, Baiyren," she said, turning. "You have to go back to your base. When you get there, you can do what Yui's asking. Let the team know you need to do more research before you can start digging."

Baiyren's head was a confused jumble. He didn't know what to think, let alone say. This was all happening so fast. Another kami: a friend of Lord Zar Ranok, an intern who was *far* more than she seemed. He couldn't process the news. "What will I tell my researchers?" he panted. "We've put so much work into the expedition."

Keiko waved her hands around in the air. "I don't know. Make something up. You're the expert. They'll listen to you. Once you've done all that, get to the mah-zhin and go. Just remember: I'm holding you in time now; I can't do that with the mah-zhin. It's too independent. That means time starts as soon as we're done here. I won't stop it again for you." Keiko looked from Baiyren to Yui. "Agree?"

Yui nodded, but Baiyren couldn't bring himself to agree. "I don't know," he muttered. "I can't... I don't know what to think."

"Bzzzt. Wrong answer." Keiko's breezy tone and whimsical expression contrasted sharply with Baiyren's predicament. "Look," she continued. "Yohshin *knows* what's coming. It's going to wake up, Baiyren."

Baiyren swallowed fear. His world was unraveling at an unbelievable rate. He drew a breath and let it out slowly. "Why should I trust you? You've done nothing but lie to me. I don't even know who you are."

"Fair point," Keiko conceded. "But from where I'm sitting, you don't have much of a choice. As for who I am: I'm exactly who I said I am. Keiko Yamanaka."

"Just not an intern."

"You could say that. I'm a kami's guardian. You do know what a kami is?" Baiyren nodded, and Keiko continued. "I'm here to help you." An odd calmness settled over Baiyren. He found himself believing everything Keiko told him. Truth or no truth.

"All right," he said, a part of him not at all sure of his decision. "But we have to be quick."

"Well, all right then." Keiko sat up and straightened her shoulders. "I'm glad that's settled. As for speed, lucky for us my father and I can reintroduce you to the time stream just about when the scout came by." She looked at Yui. "Okay by you?"

Yui studied Baiyren for a moment. Her blazing eyes cut into him with predatory intensity. Nodding, she moved out of the way. "For Keiko's sake, I agree." She glanced at the man behind her. "Give him the time he needs, Matsuda. Not too much – enough to keep Yohshin from reacting."

"As you say, mistress." The robed man drove his staff into the ground. An aura of periwinkle blue surrounded his body. A similar orb surrounded Keiko, hers of deep burgundy.

Blinded, Baiyren threw his arms over his face. Sound and movement halted. The odd sensation of time winding backwards filled him.

Keiko placed a steadying hand on his. "The first time's always the worst. Take a few deep breaths; the disorientation will pass." He sat up in his seat and reached for the gears only to have another wave of dizziness wash over him. "Deep breath," Keiko repeated, and this time he listened.

When he felt like himself again, he nodded, slipped the car into gear, and plunged into the tunnel. The echoing engine assaulted his ears as he pushed the car as hard as it would go. The road cut through slim karst hills. Baiyren didn't know who had built the passage or why, only that – judging by the aged paving stones inside – it was at least as old as the Great Wall itself. He considered asking Keiko but quickly dismissed the idea. Even if she knew, which she probably did, he wasn't sure he could handle the answer. Baiyren shook his head and drove on.

Growing sunlight signaled the end of the tunnel, and in seconds they hit the mouth without slowing. Baiyren fumbled for his sunglasses to compensate for the bright summer sun, grasped them, and threw them on. He followed the road past the banks of a large cenote that, according to local legend, a water goddess had blasted into existence before filling it with tears.

Yohshin filled the pool now, a weapon that brought tears to millions. Beyond the water, Baiyren spied a collection of tents, Quonset huts, and generators in the middle of a green meadow. Juno Montressen, the youngest member of his team, stalked about the camp with a tablet in her hand.

As if sensing his approach, Juno turned, lifted a hand to hood her hazel eyes, and stared down the road. Under ordinary circumstances, her sensing his presence would have pleased him. This time it brought a mixture of pain and regret. Suppressing both, he angled in her direction, brought the jeep to a juddering, dust-lifting stop, and climbed out.

"You're late, Doctor Tallaenaq," Juno said in a rich and husky voice. "You told me you'd be here early." She wore a pair of khaki short-shorts over a white linen blouse, short-sleeved and somehow unwrinkled despite the heat, and a pair of clunky tan work boots that she still managed to handle with the grace of a ballerina.

Vivacious and idealistic, Juno rekindled the passions Baiyren lost long ago. A former student turned researcher, she'd spent the last year with him. She made him whole, made him forget his past on Higo. He was a different person when he was with her; he was happy, optimistic, and, according to his colleagues, someone who lived life to the fullest.

"I had a couple of things I needed to do," Baiyren said climbing out of his seat.

"I see," Juno said in a tight voice. "Morning, Keiko. You're up early."

Keiko muttered something that sounded like, "That's all we need," and stomped off to another part of the site muttering to herself about women and jumping to conclusions.

"She certainly is...unique," Juno said after Keiko had gone. She spun then, punched Baiyren's shoulder, and smiled broadly. "Anyway, let me show you what I found while you were out. I've been babysitting your equipment and came across something really interesting." Juno looped her arm through his and led him into a large tent where rows of computers were plugged into portable generators.

Baiyren kept casting furtive glances skyward. "I really

don't have time for this, Juno."

"Make time." Juno was young, just twenty, and her infectious personality and easy charm put Baiyren at ease. She still had the innocence he lost when he was seven. At fifteen, he fought in his first battle. A few years later, he brought tragedy to his family and his people. Everyone around him had a way of getting hurt. He should go; going now was for the best, better for him, better for Juno. She wouldn't take it well. They were in the earliest stages of a relationship they'd started during their last expedition.

Baiyren watched her make her way to a command station, rearrange the piles of papers blocking a small monitor, and point at the screen. "Here's our sleeping beauty." She traced a finger over the fossilized body of a tall woman. "And this..." Juno tapped a few keys and stepped back. "This is what was waiting for me when I checked the computers this morning."

For one heartstopping moment, Baiyren thought she'd found Yohshin. Holding his breath, he waited for the screen to shift, but when it did, instead of cold, dark water, he saw gray rock framing an incredible figure. Judging by the notations floating along the righthand margin, the fossil measured nearly two hundred feet from head to toe. It was bipedal with long, sinuous arms that looked more like thick vines than animal appendages. A vaguely human head sat between narrow shoulders, withered leaves running up and down the length of the body. For some unknown reason, the figure reminded him of Yohshin.

"I need to get a better look," Baiyren said, rolling back the desk chair and sitting.

Juno leaned over him. Her light red hair brushed his neck. She smelled of sweet apple and fresh summer flowers. The touch of her hand on his back tingled; her breath caressed his cheek, bringing goosebumps. He tried to focus, found it difficult. The glint of silver and gold drew him back. The necklace he'd given her swung from her neck like a hypnotist's watch. He swallowed fear, fought for a way to remove it before he left; she wouldn't be safe unless he did.

"I don't know, Juno," he said. "I'm starting to think I've made a mistake."

"A mistake?" Juno's face flushed in anger. "Did Keiko help you come to this *conclusion?* She's just an intern, Baiyren. She doesn't *know* anything." This time the jealousy was unmistakable.

"It's not like that," Baiyren said quickly. "Keiko was out running and asked for a ride back. That's all." That wasn't all, and Juno caught the lie. She crossed her arms and fell silent. "The Chinese will be here in a couple of days," Baiyren said into the conversational lull. "When they see all we've found is a woman and what looks like a redwood, they'll be pissed. We need to get out of here before they ask us to refund their grants."

A distant rumbling brought him up short. He was out of time. They were coming and nothing would stop them, nothing but a larger threat. He swore, not wanting to wake the weapon he'd taken, hating the killer it made him. If only there was another way.

There wasn't.

He cleared his throat. "My notebook's in the trailer. Can you get it for me?" An innocent request, and believable. He tried to estimate how long it would take.

"Where'd you leave it?" she asked irritably. He heard the crunch of gravel as she headed out.

"Next to my laptop; you know where that is?" A muffled acknowledgment wafted back to him along with the rustle of tent fabric and retreating footsteps. He waited until he heard the clang of an aluminum door before standing and rushing back to his jeep.

The booms came again, louder this time and more insistent. Over and over they echoed, the sound like incoming thunder. Throughout the camp, he heard doors slamming and the rush of confused voices.

Across the basin, a small mountain collapsed in an avalanche of smoke and stone.

Baiyren stood, his hands gripping the chair to keep him from falling. Guilt, fear, and regret wrapped his chest in iron. His temples throbbed violently, and he was vaguely aware of his body slumping to the ground. Hands touched the side of his face, lifting it until his eyes met Keiko's. She crouched beside him; her lips moved, but he couldn't hear the words. A second voice called out to him to drown out hers, this one deep and strong and vibrant.

Mah-kai! the voice cried inside his head. *Our enemies are here. You should have told me sooner.*

No, Baiyren thought. *Not again. I won't let you. The last time... The last time...* The last time he'd enjoyed the power – and the chaos.

An unseen force hauled him from the camp. Wind whistled in his ears, smoke passing him, a strip of sandy earth swirling up to meet him. Beyond, clear water lapped noisily at a rocky shore. Bubbles broke the surface as waves swirled around a perfect eye. An immense shadow appeared in the depths and raced upward. Burgundy light brought tears to his eyes, and the force lessened. He knew it was only temporary. Looking up, he found Keiko beside him. Her eyes met his. "Don't fight it," she said. "Go do what you have to do."

He pushed himself from the ground, clawing at it to keep the force from dragging him away. "Juno. My team. They're going to die."

"I'll take care of them. You have my word."

"And the others?"

"They'll be fine once the Heartstone leaves. The Riders aren't after them."

Their gazes locked, and Baiyren saw confidence and determination in Keiko's stare. "She'll be safe with you?"

"I'm a guardian, Baiyren. If I protect the kami, I can protect Juno too."

Slowly, reluctantly, Baiyren put Juno's life in Keiko's hands, released his grip, and let the golden light tear him away.

3
TO THE SOUND OF GUNS

Takeshi Akiko stood in a cavernous hall looking up at the stone giant kneeling before him. Like the kami hidden in its closed fist, the guardian remained silent. *Your people are suffering, Roarke*, he said evenly. *They need you.*

Roarke didn't answer, not that Takeshi expected him to. Sighing, he let his body dissolve and shifted his mind to a study several thousands of miles to the east. There, he rematerialized and walked to the room's only closet. Inside, he found the lightbending robes of the Nan-jii and put them on. A large wooden desk dominated the middle of the room. He walked over, manipulated its communication systems with a thought, and opened a channel.

A woman's voice answered. "We're five minutes from leaving the Portal. Do you have anything for me?"

"I'm afraid the prince no longer has the Heartstone," Takeshi said calmly. "Ignore its call and head for Yohshin. That's where he'll be."

"He gave it away? You're sure?"

"I'm sure, Regan. Let the Riders chase the stone; use

what time you have to reach Baiyren. The succession depends on his coming home."

"And what about Yohshin? That thing is a menace. It sees everything as a potential enemy. Bringing it home is a mistake."

"One will not return without the other. Just bring them back as his father commanded."

"As the king commanded," Regan said with an edge to her voice. "The king, Nan-jii, not you. You don't command me. I report to the throne."

"And yet you need the intelligence service to give you information. Let me help you, Regan. You're newer to your post than I am."

"I doubt the king even knows when you took over," Regan said angrily. "As our head of security and information service, I'm sure you can recall exactly when the king made me captain of his guard. I've been in the position for years." The Nan-jii fell silent, a tactic he'd perfected. The quiet made Regan uncomfortable. She'd know he was using it against her, but she couldn't help herself. "I'll think about it," she said finally.

"As you say." Takeshi clicked off and sat back, a grim smile splitting his face. He had her; now, he just had to mold her into what she was supposed to be.

Regan Sur-ahn, captain of the Royal Guard, pondered the Nan-jii's words as she burst from the Pathways and entered a world of blue and green. Striated walls gave way to jagged mountains and lush fields. Black smoke was everywhere, thick and oily and impossible to penetrate. Blasts swept in from the right to mix with what already blotted half the sky.

She surveyed the area in one sweeping glance, braced herself against the cockpit seat, and sent her mah-kai, her mechanized, robotic armor, into a dizzying dive. "I need a report, Seraph," she said to her armor's AI.

"Enemy mah-kai ahead," Seraph answered. "Two clusters – one in the upper atmosphere and closing, the other skirting the northeastern mountains."

Kaidan, the king's elder son, was always one step ahead. "Can you identify them?"

"Riders, mistress. Kaidan sent his elite forces through the Pathways ahead of us."

Regan swore. "What about the crown prince? Have you found him?"

"I'm afraid not. I sense the Heartstone, but I can't pinpoint Yohshin."

Concussions buffeted Seraph's thick armor plating. Regan ignored them for the moment. If she couldn't find the prince, then the Riders couldn't either. She continued to scan the area when her eyes fell on a circular pool.

"There!" she cried, tensing.

Seraph expanded the view. "Are you certain?" it asked. "The Riders are moving in a different direction."

Another view opened beside the first, larger this time. A phalanx of mah-kai headed away from the water, flying high enough to use a wide scanning, low enough to capture the prince before he escaped. The Riders' armored suits averaged seventy-five feet in height, but as deadly as they were, the sight of them, so small in the distance, reminded Regan of toy soldiers.

Her eyes flicked to the smaller view. As she watched, the water began churning. Waves lapped at the beaches, small at first but growing quickly.

"We go to the pool, Seraph." She sat up and opened an immersive view. The cockpit vanished, and the alien world burst to life around her. Mountains reared up from the flat ground, row upon row of misshapen peaks, green-sided and accented with gray wherever limestone showed through. In the west, two distinct mah-kai squadrons canvassed a wide section – one scouring the lands for the prince, the other providing cover. "Activate synchronization."

The mech's sluggish response said it disagreed, but after a momentary pause, the familiar chill of Seraph's link touched her mind.

"Synchronization complete," Seraph reported. "All systems operating at peak performance."

Regan grunted her understanding. Seraph hurtled downward. Green and blue merged, the azure sky giving way to the slate gray of stone and the rich browns of soil. Explosions sounded behind her, a warning of incoming fire. A strong discharge rocked the cockpit, and she turned. Seraph twisted, its arms stretching out instead of in, silver light blooming around powerful wrist cannons.

The leader of the closest squad – an armored representation of a corsair with flared plates at the hip and an enormous cutlass – disappeared in a flash of light. A mechanical arm emerged from the smoke and rocketed past her, dark liquid spraying from severed joints. Regan caught the gleam of sun reflecting off white metal, of a red and orange sunburst tattooed on an upper arm. The wreckage grazed a mountain, careening off cliffs before slamming into the soft earth with a sickening thud.

Two more Riders raced through the falling wreckage, long and lean on the right, powerfully blocky on the left. Regan recognized them; their pilots once attended Kaidan at court and later, after he'd left, had since sworn allegiance to him at Haven. Odd he trusted them; once a turncoat, always a turncoat. Then again, Kaidan relegated these men to the infantry. High mortality rate there. Coincidence? Regan didn't think so. A short burst from Seraph's helm cannons blew both to pieces. Two less Riders here meant two less to fight later. Kaidan didn't have an infinite supply. Replacing the ones who died here would take time.

"Massive power surge," Seraph reported. "It's coming from the cenote. A secondary surge just started in the tents a mile to the southwest."

Regan cursed. The Nan-jii said this would happen. "Focus on the pool. That's where the prince is." Throwing Seraph into a steep climb, she readied her weapons.

"We're abandoning the Heartstone?" Seraph asked.

Regan smiled at the question. The mah-kai's AI was so lifelike. Instead of flat tones and robotic answers, its designers gave Seraph – and every other mech – the ability to think for itself, to ask questions and give guidance.

Letting the thought go, Regan looked down.

The enemy rushed the flatlands, ten mah-kai doubling back with a prison transport, the rest – twenty-five in all – heading for the large circular lake below. Mountains spread out beneath her, cumulus clouds dotting the blue expanse above. The Riders dropped through the ceiling, most heading for her, a handful streaking toward the Heartstone.

"What if you're wrong?" Seraph interjected, reading her thoughts. "You're taking an enormous risk. You could lose both the prince *and* the Heartstone."

She wasn't wrong. "I've made my decision," she said, bringing Seraph about. "Ready the cannons."

"I strongly urge you to reconsider. Yohshin is unpredictable. If the mah-zhin attacks, it won't matter who is friend and who isn't. We will all die."

A swarm of mah-kai appeared above her. She recognized a few of them – from Baron Kraysa's turtle-shaped mech to Lord Beshel's elegant winged victory. Each carried its own particular weapon – laser lances here, cannons there, combined with the occasional missile launcher. She grinned. An impressive array; Kaidan would feel their loss. Despite Seraph's concerns, it fought without comment. A thought drove the armor forward. Energy crackled around its fists, building and shooting into enemy Riders, bringing them down two at a time.

"Armor holding," Seraph reported.

Regan grunted and rolled away. She pulled a gleaming spear from Seraph's left shoulder and was about to hurl it at Beshel when a column of silver light overwhelmed the Baron's mah-kai. "What?" she cried, smoke and fire flaring in front of her. Seraph said something into her head, a warning perhaps, though it sounded more like a triumphant cry. Her eyes snapped to the edge of the roiling pond.

A lone figure knelt on a soft, grassy beach, his arms wrapped around his head. The pool's surface boiled before him, waves crashed against the shore, beams of silver light bursting through.

"Baiyren." Regan's voice was a mix of relief and uncertainty. She sat back, hoping she'd made the right choice.

4
THE IMPOSSIBLE TRUTH

Juno raced from her makeshift quarters as soon as she heard the explosions. Men and women ran about in a panic, some grabbing laptops and computers, other snagging keys from a pegboard and running for any transport they could find. Juno stared through the haze.

"Baiyren?" she screamed, running to where she'd left him. "Baiyren? Answer me!" A few keys remained on the board. Grasping the spare for Baiyren's jeep, she sprinted toward the vehicle and leaped in. To her surprise, Keiko jumped into the passenger seat beside her.

"What?" Keiko said. "You think you're the only one who saw that?" Juno's eyes narrowed suspiciously. "Oh *please*," Keiko grunted. "It's not what you think." She made a shooing motion with her hands. "Come on. We have to go."

Teeth grinding, Juno slammed the accelerator and willed the jeep forward. "Do you have any idea what's going on?" Juno shouted. "Baiyren said something about the Chinese."

"It's not the Chinese, not unless they're *way* more

advanced than we think they are."

"What are you talking about?" Juno's patience with Keiko was running out. Why couldn't she answer a simple question?

"I'm talking about that." Keiko pointed to the sky.

"What the hell?" Eyes wide, Juno took her foot off the pedal as she looked up. Smoky metallic plating covered a body she thought ran between seventy-five and one hundred feet tall. Wide epaulettes guarded the shoulders, spreading out and up like a cresting wave. Between, a slender, almost feminine neck ended below a helmeted head. Two tourmaline crystals blazed in its face, its eyes carved in the shape of narrow, elongated diamonds. No other features were visible save for a pair of high, angular cheekbones – partially covered by curved metal protectors that looked decidedly like daggers – and a proud, ovular chin.

Juno stared at the figure. Awe mixed with fear. "Oh my god. What is it?"

A narrow shield tapered up the left arm from the wrist, where a sliver of metal held it in place. It held a thin rifle against its right arm, the handgrip resting lightly between elegant forefinger and thumb.

Keiko cleared her throat delicately. "I think we're slowing down."

"Shit." Juno hammered her foot on the accelerator and took off down the road. The southern sky was clear and cloudless, but big cumulus clouds formed in the west, rising black plumes and red-orange flame marring their white outlines. In the north, a small mountain disappeared in a flash of light. Another flash followed, and then another, each noticeably closer than the last, until finally, the road ahead erupted in a firestorm of heat, light, and soot.

Juno cranked the wheel and braked hard enough to send the jeep skidding wildly. A gaping hole opened in front of her, and for a second she thought momentum would carry her into it. Frantically, she spun the wheel in the opposite direction and stomped her foot down. For one long second, nothing happened, but then – slowly at first – she felt the tires bite. She came to a small rise, and before she could slow, she lost control again and careened madly into a sea of thick grass. Easing off the gas, she spotted the road a few yards to her right. The tires slipped ominously as she changed direction, but the road wasn't far. After a few precious minutes, she was back on it, scooting forward.

More armored figures appeared through a rip in the blue sky. Unlike the others, these surrounded what looked like a flying galleon. Gun turrets sprang from the main deck in place of masts, and instead of a figurehead, a long gangway stretched several yards from the bow. The sinister bunker at the end dispelled the illusion of a grand sailing ship. A pair of barrels thrust from the top of the tip's enclosed bulb like devil horns. Below the muzzle, a ring of angry prongs guarded the ship, each swiveling back and forth ominously.

"Raker," Keiko said. "That's a prison ship. You must be pretty important."

"Me?" Juno gaped. "But I don't have anything to do with... with... with anything."

Keiko cocked an eyebrow. "Really?" She reached over, slid her index finger under the gold chain and pulled. The hidden pendant appeared from below Juno's collar.

"Care to tell me about *this*?"

Juno took her right hand from the wheel and clasped the stone protectively. The gem itself was unique and magnificent – perfectly round and only slightly larger than an American quarter. Rich silver and gold filaments threaded through an amber-colored surface highlighted with blue and aquamarine splashes. Occasional patches of hunter and forest green abutted sandlike patterns, the green giving way to orderly swathes of yellow and brown. Had it not been for the additional color, the piece might have reminded her of Ganymede, Jupiter's largest moon.

"Baiyren gave it to me when we stopped in Japan," Juno said, her tone sounding more defensive than she intended. "He called it a Heartstone." She frowned angrily. "What's it to you?"

"Japanese myth calls it *Kokoro*, which roughly translates as heart. Or so they tell me. My Japanese isn't very good. Anyway, your pendant is what's drawing those fighters."

Juno's stomach turned. "No," she protested. "You're wrong. Baiyren wouldn't do that to me."

"Of course he wouldn't. He had no idea the stone would attract this kind of attention."

"And you did?" Juno looked up. The ship was closer now. The road ahead branched in two different directions. Juno took the path leading to the cenote at full speed. "How do you know all this? Who the hell are you?"

Keiko tipped her head as if listening to someone. "Really?" she said incredulously. She sighed. "If you say so." Their eyes met. "Baiyren's from another world,

Juno; I'm with the Nan-jii, the intelligence service that's supposed to protect him."

The car bucked into or over the rutted and bump-ridden road. Free of Juno's grip, the stone dangling from the gold chain was suddenly hot to the touch. Juno flinched whenever it connected with her skin. She shot a quick glance into the rearview mirror to look for burn marks. "Either you think I'm stupid," she snapped. "Or you're just plain crazy."

She turned left, hit the brake and let the car swerve before leaping ahead. The big airship loomed large against the blue sky. Several giant shapes peeled away from the main host in a triangular formation and made for the cenote while the raker and an escort of maybe ten huge robots maintained both course and speed.

"Do those look like something made on Earth?" Keiko said pointedly.

The lead figure had a lean steel-gray frame. Twin spears of some unknown red-tinted alloy were strapped to each shoulder. A second set dropped straight down before arching up and merging into the lower back. Windswept triangular sails filled the space between, flowing behind a body that ended not in a pair of legs, but in a singular spike. Twin horns burst from either side of a helm whose visor slashed forward like the beak of a great bird. A crimson cross was painted across its chest, the lower bar of which was left unfinished, giving it the appearance of running blood.

"No," Juno conceded as additional suits – each differing from the rest – formed up behind the leader. The variety reminded her of the steel-encased mannequins you'd expect to see in a museum. She shifted the car into a different gear and picked up speed. A glance over her shoulder showed the strange ship closing rapidly while its entourage swept north and then west in a wide arc. In seconds, the attackers reached the wide fields and skimmed over the grass.

An open field without shelter, or protection, or hope of assistance spread out on either side. Juno fought down panic. She swung the jeep first left, then right, and back again, knowing the rhythm was too predictable. She'd never been much of an evasive driver, not that it would do her any good now. Already, beams of blue-white light traced her flight. Her necklace throbbed against her skin as if in warning; she braked and pulled at the wheel, accelerated, and then braked again.

Too late. A beam caught her, and she felt her body fly upwards. She tried to keep her eyes on the receding valley – green and beautiful in the morning light – to avoid the sickening plunge in her stomach. The throb of engines shook her, but she refused to look up.

Her eyes stayed on the large pool in the distance. As she watched, a pillar of silver light pierced the once serene beach. When it faded, Baiyren appeared where the light had been. He was on his knees by the near shore, his hands wrapped around his head, his body tense and trembling. Juno called to him, but the wind snatched her words away seconds before everything went dark.

5
SCHOOL DAYS

A year ago
Providence, Rhode Island, USA

Juno stared up at Brown University's Joukowsky Institute for Archaeology & the Ancient World. Located at the south end of the main quad, the white two-story building reminded her of an ancient Grecian temple. Inhaling the late summer air, she hefted her backpack and climbed the steps. Her class was on the second floor, but she was early. She looked around for a while, enjoying the relaxed feel of the place. Unlike the tension that charged her father's Senate offices, the Joukowsky Institute seemed to laugh at today's problems.

Juno liked that.

She located the closest stairs and headed up. Her class was in a room at the end of a hall. She found it easily and went in. Desks were arranged in a semicircle facing a whiteboard that doubled as a screen. The room's lectern stood to one side, looking forgotten and unused. Two black carts were parked closer to the desks, a laptop open and humming on the one to the right, notebooks and loose papers strewn about the one on the left. A figure lounged in the first row's desk, his sneakered feet up, a pen in his mouth and a map in his hands.

"Hey," Juno said, navigating the desks. "I'm Juno Montressen. Are you in this class too?"

"Yeah," the guy said. "I guess I am. What about you? Is this an elective or part of your core?"

He climbed out of his seat. He was of medium height, five-eleven to six feet, and rangy. Dark hair framed a chiseled face. His skin was a hue Juno had never seen before, a cross between wet sand and fallen oak leaves. But it was his shimmering silver eyes that held her attention. Superficially, they were bright and confident, but deeper down she saw sadness and tragedy. She realized she was staring and spoke quickly. "Core," she said. "I just switched majors."

The guy smiled. It was a nice smile. *Really?* he drawled. "And what, may I ask, was your former major?"

"International Programs." Juno shrugged. "It just wasn't me."

"Parents?" the man asked.

Juno rolled her eyes. "You have no idea. What about you? Major or elective?"

"Neither. I'm Professor Tallaenaq." He held out his hand. "I teach the class."

Heat burned Juno's cheeks. This wasn't happening. She hid half her face behind the palm of her right hand. "I am *so* sorry," she sputtered, lowering her hand to shake his.

"Don't worry about it. I'm a little young for a professor. Kind of ironic, though, considering the field." A few other students started drifting in. "I hope that won't be a problem."

Juno's blush deepened. "No," she lied. "No of course not."

As it turned out, Baiyren was such a good teacher that a few weeks into the course, Juno stopped thinking about how cute he was, how different. The melancholy she first sensed in him surfaced now and again, mostly when he discussed ancient monarchies and the tragedies surrounding them. She wanted to know what triggered it. Her heart twisted, and then her head. She wanted to take his pain away knowing she couldn't. It wasn't appropriate. Sighing, she pushed the idea aside and dove into her studies. For a while everything was fine, and she managed to keep her emotions in check for the rest of the term. That all fell apart the day after finals when Baiyren called her to his office.

The meeting began promptly at two, and like the first time they'd met, Juno was early. His office door was open. She knocked, poked her head in, and saw him sitting in a leatherbacked chair. "Professor?" she asked.

"Juno!" he said, standing. "Come in. Please."

She did as requested, dropping her backpack beside a chair before sitting. "You wanted to see me?" Her heart pounded. This wasn't about grades; hers had been nearly perfect. What then? What did he want? It certainly wasn't to ask her out. Since the first day, she maintained an air of professionalism. He had as well. Then again why wouldn't he? She doubted he even noticed the attraction she tried so hard to hide. He sat. She noted he left the door open.

"Juno," he said, fingers steepled. "You are a fantastic

student. You're smart, inquisitive, and – more importantly – you have great instincts. It's hard to believe you ever considered a different major."

She grinned. "I do my best."

"And then some. Look, Juno, I won't mince words. I'm a bit of a maverick when it comes to archeology. My finds are controversial, most of them remain secret."

"Why?" Juno frowned. Come to think of it, no one had heard of Baiyren Tallaenaq. She'd asked around, checked the net. Nothing. That might have bothered her in another setting. Not here. Brown had a reputation. They hired the best.

"Because they'd upset too many people." Baiyren stared at her, measuring her resolve. "The point is: I'm leading another school-sanctioned expedition this summer. We're going to Peru to check out a local legend; we'll have ten researchers, seven interns, and five students. I'd like you to be one of those students."

Juno's mouth fell open. "Me? You want me? But I just changed majors."

"Which means you're not prejudiced. You'll have a fresh perspective." He lifted a printed sheaf from his desk. Her final exam. "Like I said, you have great instincts. You will get full credit and a chance to work in the field. Most students don't get that until their junior year." He dropped the exam onto his desk. "You don't have to give me an answer now, but since we're going the first week in July, we have to start planning early next semester."

"Of course I'll go," Juno blurted. What an opportunity. She gathered her bag, stood and held out her embarrassingly sweaty hand.

Smiling, Baiyren rose and took it. "I appreciate your

enthusiasm. I'll mark you as a tentative yes. You'll need your parents' permission first; get that and we'll go from there."

"Parents," Juno sighed. "That could be a problem."

"It won't," Baiyren promised. "I've asked the school's president to call your father personally. He'll tell them I take care of my students and that I won't let anything happen to you. I'll give them my word."

"And if that doesn't work?"

"We'll find another way. We've done this before, don't worry."

6
AGAINST HER WILL

The Present

Juno woke in a utilitarian cell, the remnants of her dream fading. She sat up and, finding a pair of doors, rammed her shoulder into them. They didn't move. Undeterred, she hit them again, and again they held firm. The third try brought the same result. As did the fourth. With the fifth, the beginnings of a dull ache stiffened her shoulder. She abandoned her attempts to jar the doors open and lashed out with her fists.

"Let me out!" she cried. "Let me the hell out. You can't hold me; I have rights."

"Not here you don't." Keiko's voice came from somewhere over Juno's shoulder. She spun and found Keiko seated on a low bench, a look of utter disregard blanketing her pixie face. "No matter how hard you fight, no matter how much noise you make, they're not coming until they're ready. They don't have to."

Beaten but still defiant, Juno moved from the door. "Are you telling me to give up, because if you are–"

"Careful," Keiko cut in. She pointed to several spots around the room where metallic domes bulged from wall and ceiling. "This isn't America. The rooms here aren't private."

Juno grunted and fell silent. She stormed to a second bench bolted to the opposite wall. Sitting, she drew her knees to her chin. Dim light filtered from the horizontal lamps framing the floor. The movement pushed the Heartstone against her skin, and she flinched in surprise at its heat. Power radiated outward.

Keiko unfolded her legs, left her bench and headed over. She peered at the stone and shook her head. "As weird as this sounds, I think it's trying to tell you something."

Juno laughed. "You're right; that does sound weird." She lifted the chain to her eye. "Is she right?" she said mockingly "Are you trying to tell me something?"

The glow inside the stone grew stronger, brighter. Juno blinked in disbelief.

Mesmerized, she watched the light break through the pendant's surface in a concentrated beam, fly across the room, and strike the far wall, where it spread like spilled water. Projected images splashed over the smooth surface in kaleidoscopic colors, white-speckled azure above, emerald-covered gray below. A wide burgundy ring surrounded both. After a moment, the Li River Valley materialized.

"How high are we?" Juno asked, her head spinning.

"Guilin's tallest mountain is only three thousand feet, and we're a lot higher than that." Keiko's eyes narrowed. "You didn't really think we could escape, did you?"

Juno shrugged sullenly. "Maybe," she said warily. "I

mean... at least I liked to think we could." She slumped against the wall, the Heartstone still in her hand.

Outside, the beautiful armored suits continued their rampage. Several rocketed through billowing black clouds and wisps of rising steam. Others clawed their way out of a deep ravine bordered on all sides by severe karst peaks. To the south, huge flames danced inside a shifting whirlpool of flaming debris.

"Do you still think I'm crazy?" Keiko teased. "Oh, and for the record, the stone's blocking the cameras. I imagine the people who took us will send someone down to check it out."

Did Juno think Keiko was crazy? Maybe, but she was starting to doubt her own sanity. Was any of this possible? Her heart tightened. Baiyren had lied to her about who he was; he lied about everything. The rational part of her mind surfaced, asking what she'd do in his place. What would she have done if he told her? She sighed, ruefully, knowing the answer.

The projected image readjusted, zoomed, and sharpened to show an elegant giant cutting through the haze. Taller than the others and gracefully lithe, the stunning armor left Juno breathless. Eyes like rubies shone in an alabaster faceplate whose delicately carved features gave it the look of an angel come to Earth. A shield lay strapped to its arm and a trio of lances sprouted from its back. Even the coloring, white blending into purples and blues along the torso, suggested purity's loss.

"Who would make something like that for war?"

Keiko smiled sadly. "You're refreshingly naive, you know that?" She let out a heavy sigh. "People who wield weapons tend to objectify them. On Higo, they've just gone to an extreme. Earth's armorers did the same back the Middle Ages. They're called mah-kai, by the way."

"I hate war," Juno said bitterly. "When I was a freshman at Brown, I heard some vague rumors about a huge conflict in Japan, one the press and the US government tried to suppress. Natural disaster, they called it. Or nuclear accident. My father's a US senator; I thought I could get him to tell me."

"No luck?" Keiko said it lightly, but Juno sensed a great weight behind the words.

"No luck," Juno repeated, wondering if she and Keiko had that in common.

"And your mother?"

"A TV anchor. Network out of DC. You can imagine what dinner was like growing up. No one could say anything about work – confidentiality and all that."

"Which left you."

Juno sighed. "Right. Always about me." She moved a stray lock of red hair over her ear. "Since *I* was the only thing we ever talked about, they had my whole life mapped out by the time I was thirteen. Probably before that."

"Not surprising," Keiko added.

Juno tilted her head. "Sounds like experience talking."

"Let's just say I feel your pain. What did your father do? In the Senate, I mean."

"Nice change of topic." Juno sighed and grew somber. "He's chairman of the Senate Arms Services Committee – the guy who sends kids off to die in some stupid war. I hated him for that."

Keiko's eyebrows lifted. "So you defied him." She sounded impressed. "How'd he take it?"

"How do you think? It wasn't bad at first. I joined the peace movement at Brown and demonstrated as much as I could. The last straw, at least for my parents, came when I was arrested during a violent anti-war protest in Washington. *Senator* Montressen appeared on TV the next day, professing his love for me and my Constitutional right to free speech. He didn't mean it, because apart from paying my tuition – can't have a Montressen not graduate from Brown – I haven't heard from him since. My mother either." Letting out a deep breath, she stared across the room to where the Heartstone projected images of the battle below.

Again, she saw a beautiful armored giant speeding through the air. The machine looked in her direction and came to a shuddering halt. Juno sat up and watched the thing's head turn toward her. Its ruby eyes caught hers, and she felt a connection despite the very real wall between them. The Heartstone flashed in the darkness, a blinding light that left her dazed and blinking.

When her vision cleared, the image took her beyond the armor's pastel-colored breastplate and into what Juno took for a cockpit. "Keiko?" She bicycled her legs until her back hit the wall. "Keiko, what's happening?"

An exotically beautiful woman in a high-backed chair manipulated a control panel, her long, elegant fingers moving over various crystalline semiglobes. Black hair fell to her shoulders in waves of loose curls that looked like wild vines. The woman's skin was a deep olive, her eyes like dusty roses. Impossibly, her head came around, and her gaze fell on the Heartstone. Time stopped. Sound diminished to a low hum.

Juno reached for the pendant and grasped the

necklace. She scurried deeper into the cot, deeper into herself. Her world – everything she knew, everything she denied or thought possible – turned upside down. The woman continued to stare like a chef at a chicken coop.

"What do you want from me?"

The other woman didn't speak; she just shook her head sadly. *You can't possibly understand*, her expression said. *This is beyond you.* She drew in a deep breath, then – as if making a decision – pointed to the valley floor.

Juno looked down.

Twelve thousand feet or more below, a stray mech crisscrossed the area's only pool. White spray glistened over ebon plates like stars. A pair of guns perched between its epaulettes, their barrels trained on a large whirlpool half a mile ahead. Juno went cold. Where was Baiyren? The near shore was empty, the far one too. Fighting down panic, she swallowed and tried to remember everything that had happened. It began at their camp. She bit her lip and turned her attention to the cluster of huts and tents a mile west of the water.

Most of the structures had escaped the fighting, but the researchers weren't taking any chances. They raced about the camp, disconnecting computers and carrying them to shelter. Farther away, waves pounded the shore, some churning from the immense whirlpool, others from the downdrafts blasting it.

Tears burned Juno's eyes, but she refused to let them fall. Groping for the wall, she drew herself up, steadied her breathing, and dared the Heartstone to show her the worst. A hint of blood from the lip she'd bitten touched her tongue. She licked the welt to stem the flow and resolutely stared into the spinning maw beneath.

The black armor slowed its approach. Had it found something? Adrenaline flooded Juno's veins. Her heart assaulted her chest, and the breath she fought so hard to keep even, shallowed.

Golden flashes lit the depths, bright and fast and rising. The mech she watched swerved, its shoulder cannons firing once and then again. Water flumed high into the air, but the object in the water didn't slow. It came on, breaching the surface in one swift motion. What Juno took for gold pillars resolved into the fingers of a gargantuan hand that seized the other armored figure's ankle with lightning speed, pulled back, and hurled the helpless mah-kai into a nearby mountain. Distance muted the physical impact, but Juno thought the psychological one would stay with her. The raw power, the speed, the lack of mercy. What had been a functioning piece of machinery became twisted, smoke-enshrouded wreckage.

Juno had rarely seen anything this savage. She wanted to believe man was better than this, but statistics were against her. Angrily, she tried to rip the chain from her neck and hurl it away – anything to keep it from showing her more. But the necklace held firm, its links iron, the Heartstone an anchor. The projection flickered on, shifting from the smoldering mountain to the whirlpool, where a helm of sparkling gold broke through the cresting waves. Semicircular plates descended in overlapping layers to form a neck guard. The figure whirled about to reveal a face half hidden behind a smooth plate. Onyx eyes scanned the surrounding area as a great armored body emerged from the dying vortex.

The giant hovered over the water, taller than any of the other suits in the basin and radiating significantly more power. Light cascaded over jointed metal the color of solid sunshine.

In one fluid motion, it reached for the massive ebon mace at its hip, drew the weapon, and pointed the head at the nearest karst peak. A low rumbling crossed the valley. Tremors built. The nearest limestone mountain pulled free from the earth, splintered apart, and exploded toward a line of incoming armor. Friction and velocity transformed boulders into shooting stars, flaming bits of weaponized rock that breached hulls and pulverized armor plate.

"*Mah-zhin,*" said a stunned voice from Juno's left.

She turned to find a tall man in dun-colored robes staring at the projection in wide-eyed disbelief. Juno followed his gaze. The man jabbed an overly long hammer and said something in a language she didn't recognize. When she didn't answer, he paused, scowled, and repeated himself, this time speaking slowly.

The Heartstone flared, and a part of Juno's mind opened. She started to understand the man's speech, a word here, a phrase there, until finally, everything became clear.

"Who are you?" he demanded. Then, lifting his head, he spoke to someone she couldn't see. "We have been tricked, your grace. Prince Baiyren gave the Heartstone to someone – a woman. Another woman is with her." The man swallowed, wringing his hands nervously as he stared at Juno. "We don't have him; he's in the mah-zhin."

Juno's throat tightened, her stomach falling. Baiyren

a prince? She couldn't believe it. She wouldn't. She tried to look away, but the battle held her attention. A halo of silver light enveloped the huge armor's free hand. Fingers splayed, palm thrust forward, it shot bolts of sizzling energy at the incoming troops.

One went down, a big, bulky monstrosity with multiple gun turrets. An elegant suit – a mah-kai Keiko called them – that reminded Juno of a monarch butterfly disappeared in a haze of fire. Another exploded, then a third, and before long the main force broke ranks and raced away.

Juno buried her face in her hands. Was he really in that thing?

Keiko crossed the room in a flash and put her arm around Juno's shoulders. "It's not what you think," she said gently.

A new voice sounded over an intercom, another man. "Do we have the Heartstone?" he asked.

"Yes, your grace. We captured it by mistake, along with the women."

"Very good, Brother Shogo. Bring them to the bridge. I imagine they have questions for us."

"You're damn right, we do!" Juno shouted, shrugging off Keiko's arm and standing. "You can start by telling us who you are, and what the hell you're doing here."

But the intercom had clicked off, leaving Juno and Keiko alone with Brother Shogo, who bowed simply and swept an arm toward the door. Juno considered staying where she was, but quickly changed her mind when Keiko motioned her to move. "This isn't the time for confrontation," she whispered. "Not until we have some leverage. Maybe the pendant will give us some. These people want it. Badly."

After a short nod, Juno lifted her chin and strode past Brother Shogo without a glance. "Better get this over with," she muttered, leading Keiko out of the cell and into a wide metal hall.

7
CONFLICT OF INTEREST

Earth: Peru
A few months ago

Baiyren followed a steep incline through a dense jungle. Deep green fronds heavy from the previous night's downpours created a canopy thick enough to hide the sky, while at his feet, fragile plants fought one another for slivers of sunlight. Without the wooden spikes and yellow police tape his team used to create this path through the forest, he could easily get lost. Relying on a GPS was all well and good, but he preferred following a trail to the machine's odd, inhuman voice.

The sound of generators cut through the heavy air, and Baiyren let the sound guide him to his dig. A natural clearing appeared as if by magic: tents, huts, generators, and equipment neatly and carefully surrounding an enormous stone on which large etchings cut from one side to the other.

"Were we right, Greg?" he said to the short man mopping his forehead with a towel.

"It's hard to say for sure. We won't have any information to date the piece for a while yet, and because nothing grew over it, we can't use soil analysis or ground depth as a guide."

"Best guess?"

Greg O'Neil, Baiyren's lead scientist, removed his glasses and cleaned them. "Based on surrounding data, we believe this part of the jungle has been undisturbed for millions of years. The native Peruvians never came here. Even if they did, they wouldn't have had the tools to create the symbols."

"We haven't found them in any regional language either," Juno Montressen said. She knelt beside the stone, taking pictures she then uploaded to their computers before sending them back to the Joukowsky Institute via satellite uplink.

Baiyren looked at the stone. A huge catlike figure dominated the pictogram. Smaller animals that resembled the largest saber-toothed tigers he'd ever seen surrounded it. Behind them was the distinct outline of an open Portal. "Any sign of the big guy?" he asked, pointing at the main animal.

Greg shook his head. "Afraid not. But we did find the pride. Show him, Juno."

Juno stood, pulled the hems of her khaki shorts down, dusted her knees, and walked over. Baiyren noted her confident stride, her athletic grace, and the slight sway of her hips. "We found the first one at the far edge." She lifted her camera and adjusted the screen. A grassy area popped up. Baiyren recognized it as a spot they looked at before the others. Juno pressed a button and scrolled to the next picture. She'd uploaded this one to her camera from an SD card. This close she smelled of apples and cinnamon. "Our researchers say the fossil measures fifty to sixty feet long; no one's ever seen a specimen this big. And it's not even the biggest we uncovered. That one," she pushed the button again and a similar fossil appeared, "is about seventy-five feet from head to tail."

Greg bounced on his toes. He looked both pleased and baffled. "The size isn't the only thing we found." He pulled a pencil-sized pointer from his shirt pocket and circled the head. "From what I can tell these cats were smart. *Really* smart."

"Professor!" a researcher seated at a command station called. He was older than Baiyren, maybe in his late twenties with sandy hair and blue eyes. Odd how they all deferred to him, despite the age difference. "We have a front coming through. Looks like a bad one."

Baiyren waved back. He turned to Greg. "Secure everything as fast as you can and get everyone back to base camp. We'll start again when the storms pass." Greg bobbed his head and departed.

Juno stayed where she was. "How do you do it?" she asked, her hands sliding up her legs and coming to rest on her slender hips. "How do you find these things?"

Fighting a blush, Baiyren stepped back. He cleared his throat. "You just need to know what you're looking for. Most scientists dismiss local myths and legends, especially the ones with monsters. I simply research those myths and look for evidence to support them."

"Evidence to show they might have existed."

"Exactly. My colleagues don't see things the way I do."

Juno tilted her head, her ponytail swaying in the building wind. "Why do you think that is?" Baiyren started to answer, but she stopped him. "Why don't we discuss it later?" Her smile was confident but her eyes were nervous. "Over lunch. My treat." She turned and walked away before he could accept or refuse.

He watched her go, wondering what he'd gotten himself into. Wondering about the butterflies assaulting his stomach.

An hour or so later, they sat inside a restaurant in the middle of a nearby village. Heavy rain thundered on the roof and wind shook the wooden shutters outside. They'd managed to reach the building before the downpours began and were now seated at a small table in the back, a candle fighting the occasional gusts.

"Do you think the site's okay?" Juno asked, glancing at the ceiling. She'd changed into a pair of white capris and a shirt of deep indigo.

Baiyren had changed too, donning cargo shorts and an aquamarine golf shirt. "Our equipment is pretty tough, and the crew knows how to secure it. As for the find itself…" he fanned his hands. "It's lasted this long, one more storm won't make a difference."

A waiter appeared, took their order, and headed back to the kitchen.

"I want to thank you for letting me come." Juno smiled. "I've never done anything like this before."

Baiyren wondered if she meant the excavation, asking her professor out, or a combination of the two.

"You're a natural," he said. "I have to say, I'm impressed with how easily you've adapted. Most people don't do well with foreign cultures."

Juno chuckled softly, her tone light and musical. "You don't have to worry about that with me. I've traveled a lot with my father. His staff always made sure we studied foreign cultures before we left. Can't make an international incident out of asking for the bathroom." The waiter arrived with a bottle of wine. Juno uncorked it and poured a glass for each of them. "Or serving wine to someone underage." She swirled the red liquid before sipping. "Not a problem for us here."

"No," Baiyren agreed, lifting his own glass. "Being a senator's daughter, I imagine you've seen a lot of places."

"Capitals mostly, but nothing like this. My father didn't like getting his hands dirty. Does it bother you? Who my father is?"

Baiyren nearly choked on his wine. He wished he could tell her who *he* really was. "It won't make a difference to the school, I assure you." He hoped he sounded professional. Juno was smart, outgoing, self-confident, and beautiful. She was also his student. Or had been, he corrected himself. He taught one class, and she'd finished it. He smiled inwardly and took another sip of wine. She wasn't his student now.

"I hope you're right. The daughter of one of the most powerful conservatives isn't always a plus with professors. Lucky for you, my father and I had a falling out, something I told the dean when I switched majors."

"I gave my word I'd look after you. That still holds." A falling out. Baiyren hoped it wasn't as bad as his had been. He sat back and used their food's arrival to study her. He wanted to tell her everything, about Higo, about why he left and how he'd rebuilt his life. It wasn't the time.

Their conversation flowed naturally from the school and the dig. Neither wanted to talk much about their pasts, though a few personal memories came out, ones tied to happiness and personality instead of situation. Juno didn't need to know Baiyren's came from another world. Not yet. Not ever.

Before long, Greg walked into the restaurant. "The storms have gone, professor. We're heading back up the mountains."

"We'll be right behind you," Baiyren said.

Juno smiled pleasantly and stood. "Time to get back into my work clothes." Her gaze found Baiyren, her hazel eyes holding his silver ones. "We should do this again," she said.

8
THE NIGHTMARE RETURNS

Earth: Guilin City, China
The Present

Light and sound pounded the inside of Baiyren's head, the odd sensation of his body merging with some greater power filling his consciousness. The strength was still there, taunting him, tempting him.

Prince of Higo, Yohshin said into his thoughts. *The enemy is here.*

Baiyren's head cleared. He remembered the Riders' appearance, how they chased Juno, how she disappeared while the mah-zhin pulled him away from her. She wasn't part of this; she never had been. Saving her was his responsibility now. He promised her; he promised himself.

His mind drifted to the power swirling around him. He reached for it, then turned away. Giving in meant giving up a part of himself: the part where his conscience lived and spoke and kept his aggressive nature at bay. He'd save Juno without fighting. He'd have to. She stood a better chance that way. Whenever he used Yohshin's power, the people he cared about died. He thought of Juno's happy smile, of the smell of apples and flowers. She wasn't supposed to get hurt. The Riders had her because of him, because he was sure they couldn't follow. He pictured her inside the raker, imagined her under interrogation. All because of him. His thoughts floated to the power flickering just beyond his consciousness.

Just this once, he told himself. *Just to save her.* After that, he'd never use it again. Not ever. Tentatively he reached for it, let it flow into him, felt himself merging with Yohshin's spirit. He marveled at the mah-zhin's incredible power, at how alive it felt, conscious, intelligent and aware. The two were one and yet separate, each a piece of the same invincible whole. Neither controlled the other; to function they worked together as conscious and subconscious, switching the role depending upon the situation. Baiyren sighed as energy surged into him, making him alert, firing his synapses. A part of him loved the sensation, the feeling of invulnerability. Another part loathed it for turning him into a killer.

One last time, he thought. *And that'll be it.*

A thought lowered his defenses. Energy rushed into his mind. He luxuriated in the feeling. He was a predator, the alpha in a universe of weaker beings. Their destruction would energize him, bringing the peace that eluded him when not merged with Yohshin.

Breathing deeply, he let Earth's air fill Yohshin's lungs. He looked west. Several mah-kai closed ranks around a larger object – a five hundred-foot long raker with the unmistakable fore cannons and capture plank.

The mah-zhin measured distance and trajectory,

while he adjusted for wind and weather. Tensing, he waited for Yohshin to fire. An eternity passed, but the shot never came. Instead, a rare moment of indecision rippled through the great armor. Its gaze left the fleeing ship and swept through the river valley.

Black craters marred the once verdant fields. Clumps of metal jutted from the earth like spent arrows. The back end of a jeep poked out of a roadside gully, tires spinning wildly. Yohshin zoomed in, and the sight grew larger, filling the field in front of him, detail upon detail until Baiyren recognized his jeep. Juno. She must have followed him.

Life signs? he asked, knowing the answer.

No organic life detected, and no traces present.

The bands around Baiyren's lungs eased. *Juno has to be on the raker,* he said. *The Riders sensed the Heartstone and took her thinking she was me.*

I warned you about this. The stone ties us to God. Possessing it legitimizes the church's claim over our people and undercuts your family's position.

They weren't supposed to find me.

You should have planned for the eventuality. A squadron of mah-kai wheeled about and headed back to protect the raker's flank. Yohshin glanced from the jeep to the prison barge. A Portal opened ahead of the fleeing ship, a silvery disc hundreds of yards in diameter. *We have very little time.*

The rumble of fusing matter filled the air, and when the sound died away a dozen diamond spears rotated around Yohshin's outstretched arm. A thought loosed them into a squadron of fleeing mah-kai. Two went down – the first, a blood-red skeleton-like mech, the second a wingless demon. A third, one Baiyren couldn't see, disintegrated a moment later.

He didn't have time to identify the armored suits before they blew apart, and he was happy for that. Murder from a distance was easy. No faces to see, no friends to recognize. The shame he might have felt wouldn't come. His mind drifted, his consciousness drowning under Yohshin's greater spirit, merging with it, enjoying the chaos the armor created.

The mah-zhin found a new target and tracked it through the debris. Another target, another victim, another toy to break. He saw this one clearly – a scythe-wielding nightmare of black and white armor, its skull-like face leering at him as it charged. Smoke curled around its arms like snakes, the light of a hand cannon leading the way. It aimed and fired, and the blast slammed ineffectively into Yohshin's chest.

Baiyren smiled, flexed his hand, and shot a bolt from Yohshin's palm. Energy drilled into the splintering ground, shards of earth shooting into the sky like missiles. A thin projectile collided with the mah-kai and knocked it away. Baiyren watched it go, spinning end over end as Yohshin fired again. This strike sliced through the mah-kai's neck, severing the head and sending it cartwheeling to the ground in a blazing fireball.

Under the best of circumstances, a battalion of mah-kai could hold off the mah-zhin for a minute or two. Here, less than half raced toward the western mountains while a dwindling few remained behind to hold Yohshin. Green fields gave way to black craters. Metal barbs jutted from the earth like spent arrows as more debris rained down to join them. A smoldering body flew by; red

helm, thickly armored body flaring shoulder and hip
guards. Count Dormott, Baiyren thought absently. He
and the count had been close once, back before Kaidan
corrupted the court. The memory should have angered
him, but all he felt was a strange detachment. Part of
that he attributed to Yohshin's control, the rest because
he'd put Higo so far behind him. Only the fleeing ship in
the distance sparked his interest.

Don't worry, Juno, he thought. *No one can stand against
me. You'll be home sooner than you think.*

Yohshin halved the distance to Dormott. The armor
blew through mountains and shredded clouds. At two
thousand feet from the mah-kai, Baiyren targeted; at
a thousand, he swerved left and spun away from an
unexpected bolt of white light. Pulling up, the mah-zhin
slowed and scanned the sky. A figure of shining white
stared back through a haze of ash and burning metal. A
phosphorescent lance pulsed in its long-fingered hand,
caution flashing in its ruby eyes.

Regan lowered Seraph's lance. "My prince," she said.
Her hands flew over the controls and Seraph bowed its
head respectfully. "I apologize for the intrusion."

Baiyren didn't answer, and Regan licked her lips
nervously. Fighting beside Yohshin was one thing,
turning herself into a target was something else. Her
greater skill wouldn't mean much against Yohshin's
unknowable power. *Lamb to the slaughter.* She knew
Baiyren wouldn't attack, but Yohshin? The thing was
unpredictable at the best of times.

"I have a message from the king," she said, her voice
steady beneath the mah-zhin's withering stare. "He sent

me to find you; it's important, Baiyren."

"So you're captain of the King's Guard now," he said. "At least my father did that right." He started forward, but Regan didn't move. Yohshin lifted its hand and pointed at Seraph's chest. An ominous glow erupted around Yohshin's open palm. "Get out of my way, Regan! If you don't, I swear I'll do it for you."

Rolling her hands over crystal globes to her right and left, Regan brought Seraph's weapons back online. "You're losing time," she said.

"My father and I have nothing to say to each other."

"He's dying, Baiyren. The royal physicians say it's only a matter of time."

Yohshin paused. Its arm dipped. "I don't believe you! We're Lord Roarke's descendants; we're immune to disease, we live for centuries."

"If the king dies and you remain exiled, your brother takes the throne. Legitimately. Is that what you want?"

"I *want* you to get out of the way. This is your last chance, Regan!"

"You know I can't." Regan slid her hands over the controls. Power went to guidance and propulsion – she'd need both against the mah-zhin – the rest fueled her weapons. Her body calmed, and cool determination replaced fear.

One way or another, Baiyren would go back to Higo.

A dazzling light came from the battlefield, stopping Yohshin a few hundred yards from her. The mah-zhin's helm twisted toward it.

Regan shifted her view westward. She followed Yohshin's gaze over a wall of broken peaks, past smoking pits and the remains of wrecked mah-kai. In the distance, the raker zigzagged toward a newly opened Portal. Strands of silver and golden light leaped from the center, looping around the fleeing barge as if docking. Swiftly, inexorably, the barge plunged into the shining disc and disappeared.

"*Juno!*" Baiyren cried. Yohshin sprang forward, sweeping its mace in a wide arc that caught Seraph's chest. The blow wasn't hard enough to do any real damage, just enough to swat Regan away. Light bloomed in the air like exploding stars. Sparks burst and coalesced, and when they quieted a Portal and the church's forces had disappeared.

9
VOICES IN HER HEAD

Juno ignored the guard and rounded on Keiko as the elevator doors closed. Giant machines appearing from nowhere, people who looked human but spoke a language she'd never heard before, and a stone that not only rewired her brain to understand and talk to them, but talked to her too? How had a beautiful morning turned into this?

"What the hell is happening?" she seethed. Despite what the stone had done to her, she realized stress turned her words to English. "Who are you really, Keiko? And before you give me any more bullshit about being a spy, I'd like you to tell me how your English is so good." She breathed in to calm herself. So far she'd kept her voice to a hissing whisper, but like a geyser, she could explode at any moment. "We've known each other for weeks, and you know too much about Earth to not come from there. Don't even get me started about the way you talk. Your accent is a combination of California and New York, which makes me think you grew up in one state then moved to the other when you were older."

The guard shifted uncomfortably. Juno had been with her father when he welcomed foreign delegations to the US. She knew how it felt when you didn't understand what the people around you said, especially in something as cramped as an elevator.

Instead of the chagrined expression Juno expected, a wide smile lit Keiko's face. Her eyes sparkled and she looked more proud than cornered. "I always thought you were smart. The real question is whether you're... open-minded enough to accept what I'm about to tell you."

Juno's eyes narrowed. "What do you mean?"

"Maybe it'll be better if I show you."

"Show me? Show me how? In case you didn't notice, we're prisoners here."

Keiko gave her a wide grin. "You better hold on; you're in for a heck of a ride."

Burgundy light flashed, and Juno felt the odd sensation of her thoughts leaving her body. Time ground to a halt. She saw herself standing in the elevator with the guard in front. Neither moved, and Keiko had vanished. Then, just as quickly, Keiko was beside her disembodied mind.

"Cool, right," Keiko said. "Now watch this..." The room dimmed; flashing images replaced it. Keiko's face appeared through the swirling pictures like a surfacing seal. "Just relax, okay? What you're about to see will break your heart. You'll need to be as strong as I know you can be."

Keiko disappeared and a great plain opened before her. Fires consumed a swath of forest to her left, and as they moved toward a low clearing, immense grief filled Juno's heart. A woman lay in a ring of burning trees. Juno couldn't tell if the woman was dead or alive, but her pose was the same as one she saw at Baiyren's dig. Her thoughts shifted westward. There, a hundred and seventy-five foot tall figure in the shape of a man sprawled on the ground. Flames consumed a body that reminded Juno of a large tree as much as it did a human form.

The ground around the battlefield shook, and more fires roared up to cover the sky. A red and golden dragon stalked the edges of the burning wood as a beautiful woman with golden hair fell from a mountaintop and raced to save her friend. Beyond the trees, at the edge of Juno's sight, creatures she couldn't believe, thousands of them, stood beside glowing figures of men and women.

The scene leaped forward through time. Mount Fuji's elegant shape lifted before her. The surrounding area lay in ruins, smoldering pits, and leveled forests. A pillar of fire shot into the air from the volcano's summit, climbed into the outer atmosphere, and disappeared. As Juno watched, the burning column dissipated, and two figures fell to earth.

The golden-haired woman was easily the most beautiful Juno had ever seen, and the man she cradled in her arms looked like a sleeping angel. The pictures blurred and refocused. This time, Keiko was talking to a man in crimson robes, a young Japanese woman beside her. Keiko hugged the woman and stepped into a Portal. Momentary happiness spilled from the vision, lasting only until the scene shifted to a mountain summit, where a massive, muscular man sat in the palm of the great stone giant. Snow swirled around them, building and growing. A white curtain descended over Juno and, when it cleared, she gazed down at an alien world before the visions faded and her mind returned to her body. Exhaling, she looked questioningly at Keiko.

"If you're wondering if that was me," Keiko said. "It was. The guard has no idea. What felt like a few minutes to us was less than a second to him."

"But–"

Keiko held up her hand. "I'll tell you as much as I can when I can. As far as these men are concerned, I'm Keiko Yamanaka; I was part of Baiyren's dig, and I got caught with you. The Heartstone already knows I'm here, and that's a good thing. Promise." Keiko put her hand over Juno's. *And Roarke*, she went on. *We haven't forgotten you. We're here to help.* Keiko's words echoed in Juno's head. Juno's eyes widened but, before she could speak, Keiko turned to the guard. "Where are you taking us?" she said meekly. She quirked an eyebrow at Juno, who assumed Keiko was testing Juno's ability to understand.

Juno nodded discreetly. "There's been some mistake," she said, following Keiko's lead. "We're scientists."

The guard smiled kindly. "We're going to see the bishop. He'll sort all of this out. I apologize for the cells. We never wanted to use them, but we thought it best to take precautions."

Bishop, Juno thought. A religious order? She wasn't exactly an expert in religions of any kind, having intentionally distanced herself from them. Her father used the church for political purposes and vice versa. She'd come to look on churches as just another interest group. She sighed, knowing she needed to let her bitterness go. If she could do it on a dig, she could do it here.

Shifting her weight from one leg to the other, she studied the elevator's dull gray doors, thinking, pondering. She considered starting a new conversation, but a subtle headshake from Keiko stopped her. Staring at her shoes, she let the uncomfortable silence grow until the elevator slowed to a halt and its doors opened. The guard stepped to the side and motioned them forward.

A wide but utilitarian control room spread out before them. Workstations lined the walls on either side – six in all, while four more surrounded the central command chair. Those in the middle faced a large covered window between which the bridge's command chair sat bolted to the floor. The chair swiveled as she approached, and an ordinary looking man with short saltandpepper hair, a plain face, dark eyes, and a nose that might have been broken, studied her for a moment before rising. Dun-colored robes fell to sandaled feet, and a decorative hammer dangled off his left hip. To Juno's surprise, he smiled warmly and came forward.

"So these are our guests," he said in gravely tones. "Civilians from another world. Welcome, Miss–?"

"Montressen," Juno said. "Juno Montressen." Despite their predicament, the man put her at ease. Her confidence returned, and she greeted him with an air of professionalism. Emboldened, she returned his smile and extended a hand only to watch him stare quizzically at her opened palm. "It's how we greet each other," she explained. Touching his wrist, she guided his hand to hers and shook.

A strange, contemplative expression crossed the man's face. Letting go, he stepped back. "Curious. On Higo, we simply bow." He demonstrated a stiff bob of his head. Turning his attention to Keiko, he extended a hand as Juno had shown him. "I am Bishop Isshi. Do me the honor of introducing yourself as well."

Keiko giggled girlishly. "Aren't you the gentleman? I'm Keiko Yamanaka. It's nice to meet you." She took Isshi's hand and shook.

"Let me welcome you to the Nottori," Isshi continued. "I apologize for taking you. Our mission was to bring a certain man back with us. I assumed we'd found him. Apparently, I was mistaken."

Juno moved to answer, but Keiko beat her to it. "It's all right," she said with a shrug. "Things happen."

Not like this they didn't, Juno thought. An alien warship. Giant armor. These things didn't happen. Not to her. Not to anyone. How could two entirely different civilizations have so many similarities? The people looked, spoke, and thought alike. Science said coincidences this large shouldn't happen, but here it was.

All worlds are linked, Juno, Keiko said, her face smooth, expressionless. *Earth, Higo, and an infinite number of others. The kami are what connect them. The universe is their creation, world to world, creature to creature.*

Fighting for composure, Juno ran her hands up her hips. A nervous habit; a habit men found provocative. She bit her lip, realizing she and Keiko were the only women in the room. Still, with dirt caking her face, dusty clothes, and rat's nest hair, she was about as attractive as a dog with mange.

She forced a smile and shoved her hands into her pockets. "You'll let us go then? Since we're not who you came for."

"I'm afraid not," the bishop apologized. "Lord Kaidan

will want to speak with you. And the high priestess as well."

"But we don't have anything to do with this," Juno protested.

"And yet you wear the Heartstone." The bishop stabbed a finger at her pendant.

Keiko wrapped her fingers around Juno's arm in warning, but Juno ignored her.

"It was a gift." She clasped the gem defiantly and took a few steps back.

"A most generous one. Do you have any idea how important it is to our people?"

"How could we. We're not really from around here."

Isshi smiled. "And yet you speak our language fluently. You understood Baiyren's speech as well, didn't you? Why do you think that was?"

"A girl needs her secrets," Keiko said airily. "And we'll keep ours until we meet your superiors. I assume that's where you're taking us?"

"You assume correctly. For now, I won't press you."

"Isn't that nice." Keiko's voice was as smooth as honey, but her eyes were predatory. "You're keeping us from perfecting our story. Very wise of you."

Isshi bowed ironically. "We try, Keiko Yamanaka." He shifted to Juno. "As to your question: our god, Roarke Zar Ranok, came from your world. He created us not in his image but in yours. He also presented the Heartstone to Higo's first king. The jewel is a more important symbol than the crown."

Juno's eyes widened. "Why did Baiyren give it to me, then?" Her back connected with a workstation, stopping the retreat she didn't know she'd started. "I'm nobody."

"I can't answer that. According to doctrine, the wearer can't remove the chain unless the stone wants him to. The reverse is also true." Isshi scratched his chin thoughtfully. "This has never happened before, Juno Montressen. Not once in our history. The Heartstone is a gift from God."

"As far as we know, it's just a stone," Keiko said. Her sincere tone astonished Juno. Keiko knew more about the stone than Isshi. She'd spoken to it and still acted as if Isshi declared the sky red.

Sometimes the sky is red, a voice said into her thoughts. *At dawn and at dusk. Red like fire.*

Blood drained from Juno's face. She swayed and only the workstation kept her upright.

"Are you all right?" Though Keiko sounded concerned, a curiously thoughtful frown creased her face.

"Of course I'm not all right. You wouldn't be either if your view of the universe was just blown to pieces." Juno wiped her forehead. "It's been a long day."

"For all of us," Isshi replied pointedly.

Juno bit back a retort. The deaths of Isshi's men – and she was sure that's what he alluded to – were on him. She didn't doubt his sincerity or his pain. She just couldn't sympathize.

The man seated in front of and to the right of Isshi's chair turned. "Excuse me, your grace," he said. "We're approaching Higo's Portal." He was short and skinny and looked like an early adolescent. Even his voice was too big for him. Juno thought he should be in school or playing with friends. Anything but piloting a warship. What kind of church turned children into soldiers?

"Very good, Brother Arana. Open the view. There's

nothing wrong with sight verification."

"Understood, sir." Arana's fingers flew over the controls, and the low hum of machinery filled the air.

The floors vibrated, and a sliver of light appeared at the far end of the room as a row of jointed metal plates rolled back to reveal a panoramic window. Outside, darkness blanketed everything, while in the far distance, a growing light raced toward them.

"I've located the Portal, your grace," Arana announced. "We'll be through in three… two… one."

Juno's pulse quickened. She turned her attention to the window and the light streaming through. Twinkling stars peppered the velvet blackness above, the deeper glow of reflected sun shining below. The graceful arc of a planet spread out before the Nottori. The ship descended, and the details became clearer. Golden mountains ran from west to east over a large continent with fewer rivers, forests and plains than she was used to. A large desert met the range's western tip, encircling what had to be a lush jungle filled with pools, a grand city, and two huge towers. Unlike the Earth's vast oceans, smaller seas dotted this world, many connecting through narrow straits or wide rivers. The surface looked less developed than what she'd seen from satellite shots of Earth. A smaller population perhaps? Certainly not a lack of technology. This ship and the armored soldiers flying behind proved that all too well.

This was Baiyren's home. What made him leave? She needed to know. Determination hardened her heart. She promised to find him, and when she did, she'd help him deal with whatever pushed him away.

She just had to escape first. The good bishop could

deny it all he wanted, but she *was* a prisoner. They didn't fool her; their kindness and deference had more to do with the Heartstone than with her.

"Sometimes the sky is red," she murmured, fingering her necklace. The pendant felt unusually heavy and warm in her palm. Closing her eyes, she massaged the sides of her head.

At dawn, the Heartstone repeated. *And sometimes at dusk.*

10
FREE FALL

Yohshin exploded from the Pathways and into the sky over Higo. The sun sat low in the eastern sky like a watchful eye, unblinking and judgmental. "What are you looking at?" Baiyren grumbled, staring at the round orb as if daring it to comment on his return. Grudgingly, he turned his attention to the planet below.

Higo was the last place he wanted to be. He cursed the fate that wouldn't bring him peace. *We have to scan the area for a Portal. The Riders might be close.*

Yohshin gazed at a squad of mah-kai approaching in a tight formation, hugging the Rake's massive peaks. *Haven's forces are two thousand feet below and seventy miles east*, it said.

Why aren't they trying to hide? Baiyren frowned, Yohshin mimicking the movement behind the faceplate. *This feels like a trap. We must have missed something.* Eyes closing, he thought back to the Portal.

He saw the eastern sun but nothing else. Widening his search, he scanned Daidara, Higo's largest and most populous continent, home to both Castle Tallaenaq and

Lord Zar Ranok's church at Haven. Yohshin's thoughts overlapped his and together they pushed farther west, passing high peaks and desert sands. Finally their twined consciousness reached Kaidan's fortress of Tsurmak. The massive tower of reinforced iron and steel turned his stomach. What church needed so much firepower and why?

The caverns below hold a far more dangerous weapon, Yohshin warned, probing the depths.

Do you think it's awake?

Yohshin shook its head, its oddly human gestures always surprising. *I would know if my twin was awake.* The mah-zhin's search reached a high-ceilinged cavern where a presence much like Yohshin lay entombed. *Zuishin remains dormant.*

Baiyren frowned, hating himself for getting sucked back into Higo's troubles. *And the Riders?* he asked.

Retreating to Tsurmak.

He mulled that over. *They have what they want,* he thought bitterly. *Can we get to them before they reach the fortress?*

Unlikely.

Baiyren seethed at that, but he was out of options. *Let's go,* he said.

"Incoming communications from the Nan-jii," Seraph called.

What did the royal spy network want now? Regan punched a control. "I'm a little busy."

"Yohshin and the prince plan to attack Tsurmak. You need to set up a blockade and stop them."

"You're sure?"

The Nan-jii grunted. "He's afraid Kaidan will do whatever he can to take the Heartstone, even if that means harming the Earth woman."

Regan considered that. "Kaidan has royal blood," she said. "He might be able to seize and use it."

"Royal blood isn't enough. The stone has to *let* him possess it. Unless it does, the pendant will protect the wearer as well as it can."

"How do you know?"

"I am Nan-jii, Regan."

"Maybe we should let Baiyren attack; he can deal with the problem once and for all."

"We can't do that. The people would never allow it. Right now the division between the royal family and the church at Haven is little more than disagreement. If we let Baiyren do as you say, the people will think he's the aggressor. He will lose what support he has and hand the high priestess the moral authority she needs."

"So it's either let Yohshin stop the war and lose the planet or stop Yohshin and lose the advantage."

"Advantage comes and goes. Legitimacy does not. You face two bad choices. One is clearly right, the other undeniably wrong."

"Understood." Regan cut the connection and opened a new one to her troops. "Change in plans, Gunnar," she said to her second in command. "This is no longer a welcoming operation. Move all mah-kai into a blockading formation west of Yohshin's current position. Power your weapons, but don't attack. We want to stop Baiyren, not provoke him."

"Yes, ma'am. May I ask why?"

"The Nan-jii believe Yohshin is heading for Tsurmak.

I need you to delay it until I get there. I shouldn't be long."

"You know we won't stand a chance if it decides to fight?"

"Let's hope it doesn't come to that," Regan said.

Yohshin flew west over the Rake. *Mah-kai ahead*, it reported.

Baiyren peered into the distance. A line of mah-kai approached cautiously. He recognized the silvery figure leading the phalanx. Leaf-shaped plates overlapped its arms and legs, a wide collar and matching shoulders protecting its upper torso. The head within the armored ring resembled a cylindrical spearhead.

"Gunnar," he whispered. *Stand down, Yohshin. Those are the Royal Guard. Let's hear what they have to say.*

They've trained their weapons. Until they power down, they're a threat.

They're not a threat to you. Give them a chance to explain.

Ignoring him, Yohshin drew its mace.

Stop, Yohshin; you have to listen to me! Don't you remember what happened the last time?

Ice met Baiyren's words. *You believe your friends are here to greet you. What if they're Riders? The only way to know for sure is to disable and capture the pilots. Alive if possible.*

Overhead, a Portal opened in a blur of blended color. A solitary mah-kai dropped between Yohshin and the Royal Guard.

Baiyren glowered at it. "Get out of my way, Regan," he called. "And tell the guardsmen to lower their weapons."

"We prefer to stay armed." Seraph's head shook, the golden circlet glittering in the morning sun. "I know what you're planning to do," Regan said. "Higo's changed; your brother's increased his power, and not just militarily. He has the church on his side, and with the king sick, the people are turning to him. They're praying for a miracle."

"I don't care about anyone else. I promised to keep Juno safe. She's all that matters. She's the last chance I have to do something right." Higo needed someone better than he was. Someone like Regan.

Seraph stiffened. "Your friend is safe," Regan said. "The Heartstone won't let anything happen to her. Come back to the capital. You can see your father. He doesn't have much time."

Baiyren's mouth went dry. He didn't want to go. Guilt was easier to live with when he didn't face it; he could ignore the feeling, pretend the past didn't exist. Earth made that easy. There, he had no history, only freedom and a fresh start. Returning to Higo took that from him.

"He's asking for you," Regan said softly. "He sent me to find you."

"I'll only disappoint him. I can't be the man he wants me to be. I'm not a leader."

"Your father doesn't want to see the prince. He wants to see his son."

"He has *two* sons."

Seraph moved closer. "We sent a royal envoy to Kaidan four weeks ago with news of your father's illness. We haven't heard from them since."

Baiyren went cold. "Accidents happen on the road to Haven." The defense sounded weak, even to him. A royal envoy could leave Sahqui-Mittama, the capital city, and reach Hidari, Higo's great white sand desert, in a few hours. From there, they'd have to land and use the east-west road to approach the Yadokai. The immense but fragile forest in the desert wasn't far enough away to take four weeks, especially if they flew. Haven lay at Yadokai's exact center, a sprawling compound dominated by the church's massive basilica and Kaidan's more recent fortress. Reaching it from the jungle's outskirts took a matter of hours. The envoy was gone, either killed or imprisoned.

Yohshin rubbed a hand over its eyes. "All right, Regan. We'll do it your way."

Nudging Yohshin to the end of the line, Baiyren waited for the rest of the guard to pass before joining. Higo flashed by beneath him, and before long he spotted a thirty-mile gap in the Rake. A large, circular lake spread out between a break in the towering mountains, ringing the Ridderroque, Higo's tallest peak, like an enormous moat. From above, the slender spire seemed to pierce the heart-shaped foundation like an arrow.

Yohshin gazed at the towering rock, and Baiyren detected a slight stiffening in its body. Before he realized what had happened, Yohshin peeled away and dove for the Ridderroque's feet.

What are you doing? he gasped, bracing himself against the fall. *Yohshin? Answer me!*

But Yohshin didn't reply; it simply plowed on to the Ridderroque like a wayward comet.

Cursing, Regan punched her communications array and opened a channel to Gunnar.

"I see it," he said. "What are your orders?"

"Same as before. Return to the city and secure

the castle while I deal with the prince." Cutting the connection, she sent Seraph into a steep dive. The wind howled around her; her stomach threatened her ribcage. Only a determined effort kept its contents from rising along with it. Klaxons sounded in the cockpit, harsh, loud, and insistent. The noise alone should have kept her awake, but the punishing drop, the abrupt change in gravity from Earth to Higo, and the fatigue of a prolonged battle conspired against her.

Through the view, Higo looked like a fresh painting left out in the rain. Colors bled, and shapes lost their edges. Seraph called to her. Gunnar too. They sounded alarmed. That should have worried her, but her mind was foggy. She drifted in and out of consciousness, and though her mind knew she was falling, time seemed to stop.

She looked past the Ridderroque and into the pristine moat at its base. Her first memories, though hazy, were from here, from the time she wandered over the peak's lowest shoulders. That was when a pair of monks found her and brought her back to Haven. She didn't remember much of that time and nothing of the time before. The only solid memory she had of this place was when she brought Baiyren here all those years ago.

11
WHEN EVERYTHING CHANGED

Higo: The Ridderroque
Eight Years Ago

Regan sat behind the controls of a small submarine with Baiyren in the navigator's seat beside her. She'd donned a guardsman's gray and black uniform, while he wore a nondescript sandcolored shirt and black pants.

"You'd better be right about this," she grumbled, easing back on the controls and letting the sub drift with the current. Water dominated the view, dark and murky and filled with colorful fish. "If your father finds out, he'll have our heads."

"It'll be worth it," Baiyren said with a grin. He placed an ancient book on his lap and started leafing through it. The sound of turning pages broke the cabin's stillness. "I don't think it's a coincidence pilgrims found you on the Ridderroque."

"Why not? Monks come here once a year. Whoever left me made sure someone would find me." A faint smell of aged paper tickled Regan's nose, and she drew it in. The scent reminded her of the library in Haven. "I can't believe I let you talk me into this," she muttered. "Your father was just starting to like me."

"My father adores you," Baiyren said, without a hint of jealousy. "You're the daughter he never had."

"He only wanted a daughter because his sons were such a disappointment."

"Maybe," Baiyren countered. "He thought he'd have more success with a girl."

Regan snorted. "Not if he finds out about this." She stabbed a finger at the thick tome. "I don't care if you are the crown prince, that book isn't supposed to leave the Sanctuary."

Baiyren shrugged. "We have two, one for the king and one for the church. The one in Haven was written first, which makes this a copy." He lifted the tome; its spine cracked ominously. "How is a copy any different from a million reprints?"

"Because everyone believes it is. The Zhoku is our holiest book. The scribes who recorded Ojin Muhabat's visions created a second one as soon as they could. The first stayed with the church; the second went to the king. Bringing it here is both sacrilegious and irresponsible."

Baiyren raised an eyebrow. "So you *do* believe," he teased. "I guess the high priest didn't waste everything he invested in you."

"I didn't say I *believed*," Regan answered. Exasperated, she threw her hands in the air. "If word gets out, we'll both be in trouble."

Baiyren lowered the book back to his lap and turned a few more pages. "You worry too much."

"And you're too impulsive. You shouldn't just run

off on a whim. Your people depend on you." Baiyren opened his mouth, but she waved him off. "You still haven't told me what we're looking for."

"This," he said, tapping the page. A triumphant gleam set his dark silver eyes on fire. On the left, a firm, flowing script moved in horizontal lines away from the binding, while on the right, a picture of a huge, muscular man filled the entire space. The man knelt before a starry field, hefting a sphere onto his burly shoulders. Oceans covered most of the globe, bigger and more abundant than the ones on Higo. The seven continents floating in the seas looked as if some great calamity had torn them from a once gargantuan whole.

Enthralled, Regan looked closer. "What does it mean?" she whispered. Something about the drawing left her breathless.

Baiyren shook his head. "I'm not sure. The writing's ancient. It talks about a keystone." He tapped a line along the top. "This gives a general location; the rest's either vague or hard to translate, I'm not sure which. We're in the right spot, though." He pointed to a hand-drawn compass on the page, below which symbols dropped toward the bottom of the book. "We should find a copy of the glyph somewhere along this wall."

Regan scanned the sheer cliffs. A large sea reptile, its body colored to match the rock, sprang from its hiding place, snapped its jaws around a large dolphin, and swam away. "This won't be easy," she said. "A rock slide could have buried it a long time ago or it could have eroded over time. That book is older than almost anything else on Higo. What are the chances a carving survived?"

She swept the rock with the sub's external camera and

found nothing. A second pass yielded the same result, as did the third. Shortly into the fourth, she caught a line of bubbles seeping out of the seemingly solid rock and zoomed in.

"There it is." Her voice was a quiet breath. "Just like the book says." A tap of the controls widened both light and image. Regan's body thrummed with excitement. She saw the lines carved into the rock and traced them over a large expanse of smooth stone. An exact replica of what Baiyren found in the Zhoku, but larger. A hundred times larger. Tall and proud and undamaged by time: the man, their god, holding a great globe on his burly shoulders. Her eyes met Baiyren's. "Do you know how to get inside?"

"No, at least not yet."

Regan bit back a reply. He'd brought them all the way here without that key piece of information? She should be furious with him, but, oddly, she wasn't. Baiyren didn't plan for anything; he never had. Events swirled around him, and when they settled, they always seemed to land in his favor. It wouldn't always be that way. Life had a way of evening the odds. Sooner or later, she needed to teach him how to plan while remaining flexible. Battles favored those who did both.

"Wait a minute." He stopped skimming the pages, reached into his shirt, and pulled out the Heartstone. "I want to try something." Concentration lined his face, and a minute later sweat coated his brow. He muttered something she couldn't hear, and a halo of golden light erupted from the stone, approached the large, glass window, and passed through as easily as sunlight in a forest. The beam crossed the space between the ship and the rocks and hit the wall.

Regan reached for Baiyren's hand. She squeezed but didn't look at him, couldn't tear her eyes from the bright image before her. Four lines had appeared in the rock. Two pairs: one horizontal, one vertical. They flew around the perimeter in a wash of bubbles; when they connected, a large rectangular block fell back to reveal an entrance.

"I knew it!" Baiyren said triumphantly.

"Really?" Regan crossed her arms and tried to mask her discomfort. "You expected the Heartstone to do that? You're holding out on me, Baiyren."

Baiyren seemed genuinely surprised. "No not really," he admitted. "The stone's never done anything. Not once. I don't know how many kings we've had but you'd think you'd find a record of something like that happening. And we don't. No one in my family's ever believed what the Zhoku said about the pendant either."

"But you did?"

"It felt right," Baiyren said sheepishly.

Regan stared into the darkness. "I don't know about this."

"I do. We've had the Heartstone for millions of years. My ancestors trusted it. And I do too."

Regan didn't; she hated what she couldn't explain. Baiyren thought the Ridderroque held the key to her past. He'd spent hours studying anything he could find about the mountain, digging through histories, diaries, and relics. When he uncovered references to a sealed hall beneath the mountain, she began to believe too. It's why she'd come.

"You could have made it an order, you know," she

said, easing the sub forward. "You're the crown prince."

"I'd rather have you go because you wanted to. You'll make better decisions if you're invested."

"Better decisions or amenable ones? A person's less inclined to disagree if she's *invested*."

Baiyren shrugged. At least he had the good grace to look sheepish. She believed he'd make a good king someday – a man the people would love.

They crawled ahead, Regan checking and rechecking the instruments, Baiyren paging through the Zhoku. One mile in. Two. At three, a cavern opened overhead; at four, columned light lanced through the roof, and she angled upward.

They surfaced in a cave large enough to swallow half the capital city. Glowing gemstones gave off a startling amount of light, just not enough to chase the shadows from the infinite space overhead. She spun her chair to face Baiyren.

"We stay together," she said. "And we don't touch anything. Just because the Heartstone brought us here doesn't mean it's safe; we have no idea what's out there."

Baiyren bristled, but didn't argue. Regan watched him for a moment, then, rising, she shouldered her prepared bag and led him to the pressure-sealed doors. A stone-lined quay greeted them outside, old and dusty and running several hundred yards from the water to an oblong hole in the floor. Smooth steps disappeared into the darkness. Regan drew a light from her belt, unholstered a small pistol, and headed down. She left the steps after an easy climb and followed a wide hallway to a set of towering doors. Unlocked and open, the doors fed an enormous chamber. Stone columns climbed from the floor in parallel rows before curving toward one another. These met on either side of an even larger pillar, fifty feet wide and glowing with an inner light. Breathtaking colors swirled inside, gold and silver, black and amber.

Regan stopped and pointed. "What am I looking at, Baiyren?"

The prince joined her in the middle of a tiled floor. "A shrine, maybe?" He stepped forward, his eyes scanning, his face intent. "Is that…? Yes! Look, Regan. Something's in there." He jabbed a finger at the column, moved it up then down as if drawing. "Do you see it?"

Regan squinted, and a vague outline took shape in her head. It was massive, easily two hundred feet tall, and disturbingly humanoid. Thick, armored plates covered the body – arms and hands, torso, legs and feet. A golden helm sat low over the face, leaving only a pair of ebon eyes visible. Below them, a smooth guard hid everything to the chin and neck, the plate molded from a single metal piece.

"Armor," Regan said, noting the wide, flaring rings welded to the back of the helm, the gauntlets, the covered joints and seams.

"No armor's that big." Baiyren said it gently, but his tone carried a hint of scholarly condescension. "We need to see what we're dealing with."

Regan moved in front of him. "*You* don't do anything until I clear it. I'm responsible for your safety." She flicked her head at the entrance. "You were lucky with the doors. This could be different."

"How are you supposed to protect me when you don't know what to look for?"

"And you do?" Regan crossed her arms. The golden statue troubled her. An aura of power surrounded it, an undeniable air of battle, of wars fought and won against great odds. She didn't want him to go anywhere near the thing.

"I know enough to avoid any major traps. And I think," he added, drawing the Heartstone from his shirt, "this will keep me safe." His voice was steady, but he didn't look like he believed what he said. More likely, he found an excuse she couldn't refute – not after the stone seemed to open the cavern entrance.

Melancholy nipped Regan like a frost-touched flower. What happened to the earnest boy she met when she'd first come to Higo? Her eyes drifted to the trapped armor. Maybe the answers she sought were here after all. "All right, Baiyren," she said, nodding deferentially. "But you have to tell me if you sense *anything*. Agreed?"

"Safety in numbers." Baiyren grinned. They prowled across the floor together. At the halfway point, Baiyren held up a hand.

"What is it?" The tingling on Regan's skin returned, a kind of electric current, a sign. A warning.

Baiyren looked down. "I didn't notice at first, but the tiles have runes inside."

Regan's pulse quickened. "Can you read them?"

"It's too dark. I'll need more light."

Regan reached for the small torch in her belt, but the Heartstone flared before her hand touched it. A brilliant and dazzling glow illuminated the chamber. Baiyren didn't blink or shield his eyes, and while she stared at the stone, half in wonder, half in fear, his attention remained on the floor.

Ancient lettering burned inside each square, filaments of shining silver, copper and diamond-accented gold. Baiyren's gaze swept from one tile to the next, studying each intently before moving on. His eyes widened. "Mah-zhin," he said, pointing at the golden giant. "That's a mah-zhin!"

Regan fought for breath. Mah-zhin, one of two legendary protectors sworn to God. "You're sure?" she asked. A feeling of unease grew in the pit of her stomach. "Baiyren. You need to back away." Nothing good would come from this. "Now, Baiyren."

Baiyren didn't seem to hear. He stumbled forward, the finger he'd jabbed at the armor tracing in the air. His lips moved but no words came out. Slowly, he lifted his chin and stared into the armor's black eyes.

"Yohshin," he said. "Is that your name?" The mah-zhin didn't answer, which only irritated Baiyren. Face reddening, he lifted the Heartstone and thrust it forward. "I carry the Heartstone, mah-zhin. I am a prince of Higo, heir to the throne and son of Lord Roarke's steward. I command you to answer!"

A great tremor shook the chamber. Rock splintered and burst, and the pillar surrounding the armor shattered. Regan lunged for Baiyren, but an invisible wall came down between them. She pounded against the solidified air but couldn't break through.

Baiyren stood motionless before the ruined column. Across the floor, an enormous foot emerged from smoke and dust and landed on the tile with a sharp crack. A golden body followed, and as it came forward, the armor bent down to study the boy. Wisdom shone in those ebon pools, and infinity and emptiness.

"Is it really you?" the giant asked in a great booming voice. "He said you would come. He promised." The mah-zhin brought its head closer. "Something feels different in you, but you do carry the Heartstone." It pulled back. "The synchronization will tell me more."

Synchronization? The word thundered in Regan's head. She glanced at Baiyren. He looked oblivious, bewitched even. Maybe he *really* believed the Heartstone protected him. Regan couldn't afford to take the chance. Already, his body had taken on a filmy quality, shimmering and dissipating like a swarm of startled fireflies.

Regan brought her pistol up and leveled the muzzle in one fluid motion. "What have you done with him?" she said to the armored figure.

"It's all right, Regan." Baiyren's voice echoed throughout the chamber as if amplified. "I'm fine. I'm inside the mah-zhin."

Inside... Relief and new concerns collided in Regan's head.

"It's incredible," Baiyren continued. "I can control the armor with a simple thought."

Control it? That didn't seem right. A thirteen year-old boy controlling a god warrior?

"You don't know anything about it," Regan warned. "Who made it, why they made it. We should leave it alone until we can get our researchers out here to examine it. Come on, Baiyren. You've been in there long enough; you need to get out."

"Give me a minute." Time ticked by, the seconds crawling. "The mah-zhin's not like a ship; I'm not sure what it is."

"It's all right," Regan told him. "We can do an in-depth search back home. I'm sure the royal scientists will know what to do." She stared at the magnificent armor. So huge, so powerful. The chill she felt earlier returned, the foreboding. Again, she rubbed her arms. Something nagged at her. A thought, a recent conversation. And then it came to her. Mouth dry, she flicked her tongue over her lips. "Baiyren," she said, hoarsely. "The Zhoku says Lord Zar Ranok had two protectors. Where's the other one?"

An uncomfortable silence stretched between them. When Baiyren finally spoke, he sounded troubled. "The other mah-zhin is buried beneath Tsurmak. Kaidan just started building a fortress there. He's digging right for it."

12
IN THE LION'S DEN

Orbiting Higo
The Present

"Well, I still haven't found the new kami," Keiko said, pacing about a wide space that reminded her of Gaiyern's star-infused body. "Which means you have." She raised an eyebrow at Takeshi as she walked past. "But you knew that already, didn't you?" A bright yellow star flitted past, a tropical world of dense rainforests caught in its orbit.

Takeshi nodded. "I did." He was back in his comfortable crimson kimono and matching pants. "You're not ready to draw this kami's spirit out and teach her what she needs to know."

"And..." Keiko gestured, expecting the sound of another dropping shoe.

"Looking out for Juno suits you better than telling a kami about herself. Juno grew up on Earth and, like you, she will have a difficult time adjusting to this new reality."

"She's doing better than you'd think."

"Thanks to you, no doubt."

Keiko nodded as she walked. "I used some of my guardian power to calm her. Not enough to dull her mind, but enough to help her accept things."

"You haven't used spirit on anyone else have you?"

Keiko shook her head. "As much as it pains me, no, I haven't."

"Good. Roarke is Higo's kami. We are not to interfere any more than is necessary."

Keiko stopped pacing and faced Takeshi. "You realize how weird this is, right? Last time we wanted to keep Vissyus in the Boundary; this time we want to get Roarke out. Kind of funny, don't you think?"

"People have died, Keiko. I don't find either situation the least bit funny."

Keiko sniffed to regain the superiority she knew she'd just lost. "No. I guess you wouldn't." She sighed dramatically. "So what do you want me to do next?"

"Go back to your body and continue to help Juno. Learn as much as you can; let her get comfortable with the people at Haven. When you think she understands, help her escape to the capital. You go back to Tsurmak and watch the mah-zhin there."

"I don't–"

"You will," Takeshi said firmly. "You're learning to use your power faster than I expected, but you've always been better than most at reading another's intentions."

Keiko blushed at the compliment. "It's not all that hard," she said modestly. "You just need to let someone talk long enough. My father always said, 'If you give a man enough rope…'"

"I am familiar with the saying, Keiko. Though your father never used it when he was with me."

Keiko grinned widely as her soul headed back to her body. "I'll bet he thought it though."

"If he's anything like you, Keiko," Takeshi said with a heavy sigh. "He probably did."

Juno followed Isshi through a warren of crisscrossing corridors, pausing a little way in to wait for Keiko to catch up. "Are you all right?" she asked. Keiko had looked dazed for several minutes now.

Keiko jolted back to life, looked around quizzically, then hurried over. "Sorry," she mumbled. "My mind wandered a little. I do that from time to time."

Juno nodded, and together they trailed Isshi out of the warship, across a wide strip of tarmac, and into a vehicle that whisked them into the fortress she'd seen from the air. The transport only had room for two, so Isshi followed in a similar car.

From thirty thousand feet the structure before them looked like a small mountain; from the ground, like a city carved from one.

Juno had to hand it to these people; they respected their world's beauty. Nothing she saw was as out of place or as unnatural as the towers of glass back home. The buildings here blended naturally into their surroundings.

Thinking of home brought a momentary pang. Her friends would be worried about her. Her family? That was anyone's guess. Her thoughts flitted to Isshi. He said she wasn't a prisoner, and while she believed him, she also knew they had no need to jail her. She was wholly dependent on these people; she couldn't eat unless they fed her, couldn't explore without getting lost. What she knew of this world came in the last few hours, and none of that told her how to survive. At least she had Keiko. But could she trust her? What if Keiko was acting like a friend to get Juno to talk?

She cleared her throat. "About what you said earlier – back on the ship?"

"Which part?" Keiko asked.

"About the kami and connected worlds. It goes against everything I've learned."

"I suppose it would." Keiko stared out the window. "I guess I've gotten too close to the kami to understand how you see things." She smiled wistfully. "I left Earth after the kamis' war, what would have been a few years ago for you. Since then I've been to more worlds than I can count." She held up her hand. "Time," she said to Juno's unasked question. "It's what I do. I can manipulate how spirits move through time. Anyway, most places were pretty much like Earth, depending on the kami who ruled it. There were a few differences, planets with nothing but oceans, some with no humans at all. Those were few though."

Juno frowned, still not understanding. She was calmer now, as if wrapped in a warm blanket. The sensation came and went, strongest when her nerves frayed, weaker when she needed to think. "But why the similarity? It goes against science."

"They're gods, Juno. I can't put it any other way. They do what they do."

Juno rubbed her arms. Science had been her anchor, the one thing in her life that made sense. That was gone now, at least according to Keiko. The transport slowed to a stop, and she and Keiko got out. She picked up her pace until she walked beside Isshi.

"You still haven't told me where we're going," she said, looking up at the looming fortress.

"Lord Kaidan wants to see you right away. I apologize for not giving you time to clean up first. I'm sure you'll understand; an order is an order."

Juno's face flared. "Why? Unless he can justify kidnapping, I have nothing to say to him."

Isshi stopped and fixed her with a serious look. "We had no intention of taking you. As I said before, my orders were to recover the prince and bring him to Haven. You were the last person to see him, and you have the Heartstone. Lord Kaidan will still want to question the two of you about that."

"But I don't know anything. I met Baiyren when I was a student. As far as I knew, he was just another professor." The truth stung, more because Baiyren hadn't trusted her enough to tell her the truth.

The bishop's expression grew grave. "The time is Kaidan's to waste. If he thinks speaking with you will prevent war, who are we to say otherwise?"

Keiko's voice sounded in Juno's head. *I respect your standing up for yourself; I really do. But you need to think about what you're doing.*

Though Juno was getting used to Keiko intruding into her thoughts, the action still creeped her out. Dipping her chin slightly for Keiko's benefit, she softened her tone. "I don't know if I'll be much help," she said. "But I'll do what I can."

Bishop Isshi bowed his head. "Thank you, Ms Montressen, Ms Yamanaka." He led them into the massive tower. The entrance flowed into a high-ceilinged lobby. Simple granite tiles lined the expanse instead of the marble she expected, and she didn't see decorative items or art of any kind. This was a fortress, a place to keep weapons and train men. Juno had seen enough of them to know the difference between luxury and utility. She considered the tower's size. All this. All built for offense, not defense. How could a church sanction it?

They walked on in silence and eventually came to a bank of elevators. Isshi ushered them into the first that arrived. Another few seconds passed before the elevator opened at a pair of imposing, gilt-handled doors. The tall man in subdued robes belted with the ever-present hammer, standing to the right, opened them as they approached.

"I have to give my report to Lord Kaidan," Isshi said to the man. "He's expecting me."

The guard bowed without speaking and allowed them to pass.

The carpeted walkway, the first Juno had seen in the building, continued up a short flight of steps and through an open threshold. Beyond, the floors fell into a seemingly bottomless pit. A bridge, perhaps wide enough for five men to walk side by side, spanned the emptiness. An enormous stone giant towered overhead. Rust-colored eyes stared down from a great height, thick charcoal-colored lips pressed thoughtfully together.

Juno hurried to the edge for a better look at the magnificent piece. An iron jerkin tied at the waist with a chain of thick links covered the body. The empty loop at the giant's hip puzzled her until her eyes found a massive mace clutched in the statue's right hand. The tool on Isshi's belt differed. It was close but not identical.

At first, she assumed the giant represented their god, but after seeing its weapon she wasn't so sure. Everyone she'd come across so far wore identical hammers about his or her waist. The giant's mace was different. Religious orders didn't make mistakes like that. She frowned; if this wasn't Higo's god, what was it?

Keiko walked on, a bored expression on her face. The young kami – did Juno really accept Keiko as one? – knew something, something that brought angry blotches to her cheeks. *Do you see what they've done?* she said furiously, her thoughts directed not at Juno, but at the Heartstone. *If they weren't so pious, I'd say they were mocking you.*

The Heartstone didn't answer, drawing a disgusted *tsk* from Keiko.

Isshi stopped after a few more feet and bowed. "Lord Kaidan," he said. "I've come to give my report. I brought the women with me."

"Thank you, Isshi," a flat voice said from the shadows. "We can speak later. I'd like to hear what these two have to tell me." Isshi bowed again and excused himself. His footsteps dwindled, their echoes died, and the room grew disconcertingly quiet.

Juno peered into the gloom. The shadows beneath the statue were deeper than anywhere else in the hall. She couldn't see, not even after her eyes had adjusted. She blinked and looked deeper. Two gleaming dots stared back. She focused on them and finally realized the cold circles were eyes in the darkness. She took a step back, wondering how she'd missed them.

Once, on a safari her father had taken in India, they'd

made camp in the jungle. She woke the next morning to find a cobra staring at her through the open tent flap. These eyes were uncomfortably similar.

Forcing a smile, she pushed ahead before Keiko could stop her. "Hello?" she called. "I know you can see us." She placed a hand on her chest. "I'm Juno Montressen and this," she said gesturing at Keiko, "is Keiko Yamanaka. Brother Isshi said Lord Kaidan wanted to see us?"

"Lord Kaidan wants to see his half-brother," the voice said. Though soothing and richly timbered, Juno detected a slight edge to it. "They tell me you were the last to speak with him. Is this true?"

Half-brother? Baiyren never said anything about a half-brother. He hadn't said much about a lot of things.

"If you mean Baiyren, then yes," Juno said. "At least, I think so." The words came reluctantly, as though drawn from a deep well. She didn't want to lie, but she wasn't entirely sure of the truth any more. "I didn't see what happened to him after your ship took me."

A heavy sigh greeted the statement, another rustle of fabric following. Juno peered deeper into the gloom only to watch it pull back like a drawn curtain. Light from recessed alcoves far overhead swiveled on unseen hinges, illuminating the broad marble walkway to reveal the statue's other hand, the right. A large throne carved in the shape of a multipeaked mountain rested atop the open palm. A man sat in the great chair, elbows on his knees, his body pitched forward. He studied Juno for a moment, stood, and came forward. Taller than Baiyren and leaner, he strode across the bridge with the grace and resolve of a hunting cheetah. His brown robe covered a shirt the color of oak leaves in November. Like the men on the Nottori, he'd clipped a long hammer to the belt of black chain looped through equally dark pants. He stopped a few paces from Juno and lowered his head, his eyes flitting to the Heartstone.

"I'm sorry to hear that, Ms Montressen," he said, looking up. "I need to speak with him."

"I didn't see him either," Keiko said around Juno's back. "If anyone cares."

Kaidan's eyes never left Juno. They were the same silver-black as Baiyren's, and while his features hinted at a kinship, the rest of his face, from the lighter hair and skin to his chiseled chin, differed markedly. Baiyren could be aloof and distant at times, especially when teaching ancient monarchies and religious power structures. He never looked menacing or dangerous, though. Not like this man did.

Juno held her ground. "Why?" she demanded. "What's important enough for you to send a whole fleet to kidnap him? What does he have that you don't?"

Kaidan grinned at her with a smug, knowing expression. "The mah-zhin," he said. "Our god placed two on Higo. He has one. I have the other. I need my half-brother to show me how to wake mine."

Blood drained from Juno's face. Her stomach felt as if she'd leapt over the elegant safety rail beside her. That power she'd seen on Earth was perfect and unstoppable. What would two do to a world?

"You're wasting your time," she said, lifting her chin. "He won't help you. Not with a weapon." She recalled the look on Baiyren's face moments before the machine took him. The terror, the sadness. The shame. He knew what the thing could do; he knew and he hated it.

"A weapon?" Kaidan's eyes widened in disbelief. "Is that what you think?"

"How should I know?" Juno said, angry now. "Baiyren never told me about it. He never told me about any of this." Not that she blamed him. After Peru he had something to lose. Telling her risked pushing her away. He knew she'd question his sanity, just like she did with Keiko.

Kaidan ran a hand over his mouth, thinking. Agitated. "My father committed an unforgivable sin against God. He isn't fit to rule in the Lord's name, and neither is Baiyren." Kaidan's face grew hard, and it occurred to Juno she might have insulted him.

This close, he towered over her, but instead of fear, she felt an odd sympathy. He was imposing, but something about his long, lean frame reminded her of a broken street lamp – tall, somber, and dark.

Keiko cleared her throat and stepped around Juno. "I'm sorry if we said something to upset you," she offered. "We're new here. We don't know your history. Maybe you can tell us a little about these mah-zhin and why they're so important."

Kaidan smiled sadly, and some of the tension left his face. "Our god left the mah-zhin on Higo, one at the Ridderroque and one here at Haven, as I said. The church's leading theologians have pored over every ancient text in existence since Baiyren unearthed Yohshin, but their findings brought more questions than answers. We don't know what they are, and we don't know what God wants us to do with them."

"And don't you think it's strange that the king and the church each have one. Call me crazy, but I think your god's trying to balance the scales."

"They're not balanced now," Kaidan said angrily.

Keiko cocked her head. "And what would you do if they were? From where I'm standing, I'd say you'd be at a stalemate. Having an invincible weapon on either side kind of negates the purpose, don't you think?"

Kaidan's head snapped up. Pain contorted his face, the same pain Baiyren tried so hard to hide. "Don't you dare lecture me," he snarled. "You know nothing about us."

"No," Juno admitted. "But we'd like to."

Kaidan chuckled mirthlessly. "What if I told you my father and the church conspired against God? When the queen couldn't produce an heir, they both went into the city to find a suitable breeder. The king needed a son, and Haven was only too happy to help."

Juno gasped. "You're not serious. And the church agreed?" It was unconscionable. No church would do something so... wrong, so immoral.

Are you sure you're from Earth? Keiko smirked. *Even I'm not that naïve.*

Juno coughed discreetly to hide her startled expression. *You're reading my thoughts? You didn't tell me you could do that.*

I didn't think I needed to. I'm in your head, and you're in mine. It's part of the link.

"Love and fidelity are the most important tenets of our faith," Kaidan was saying. "Our leaders, the high priest included, sanctioned something God would hate." He took a deep breath and blew it out, but the tension in his body remained. His hands were still curled into fists, the muscles on his neck corded and swollen.

Juno moved closer.

Juno, Keiko warned. *I don't think this is the time.*

"What happened to your mother?" Juno asked, ignoring Keiko.

"What do you *think* happened? She was young and innocent. To her, being asked to the castle had to feel like something from a storybook. The queen hated the arrangement, of course. Called it a public humiliation. Two weeks after I was born, she convinced the king to send my mother back into the slums. I never saw or heard from her. I didn't even know she existed until I started my studies here. A few months into my religious training, we heard the high priest was dying. One of his attendants said he wanted to see me. I didn't understand why; I thought he wanted to send me back to Sahqui-Mittama as a messenger."

"But that wasn't it."

Kaidan went rigid. "He called me to tell me the truth. He wanted it off his conscience. My father and the church left her in the slums where they'd found her. He said she died, alone and penniless."

Juno bowed her head. "I'm sorry. That's horrible." She placed her hand on his and was about to say more when a woman's voice cut through the room.

"Kaidan?" the woman called. "What's all this?"

Juno traced the sound back to a figure silhouetted against the open door. The speaker was slim but curvaceous, and while she was of medium height, her regal bearing made her seem taller. Her clothing was impeccable, from the pristine white dress to the slender gold chain around her waist. Waves of auburn hair brushed the colorless fabric like embers on snow, penetrating charcoal eyes regarding Juno with a mixture of curiosity and interest. She came forward in a swish of skirts and seductive strides.

"Juno Montressen?" Kaidan said. "May I present her grace, Miko Ama-Nozako, high priestess of Haven?"

The high priestess, Juno thought. *And so young.* She resisted the urge to offer her hand and instead lowered her head in what she hoped was a respectful bow.

"I'm surprised to see you, Miko," Kaidan said. "I told you I'd bring our guests when I was ready."

"My apologies, Kaidan. I was… curious. It's not every day we meet people from another world." The high priestess tilted her head to gaze first at Juno then at Keiko. She might have been looking at animals in the zoo. "I imagine you're both tired and hungry. Why don't you take some time to clean up? We can continue this over dinner."

Said the lion to the lamb. Keiko sighed. *Watch out for this one, Juno. She has fangs.*

Juno smiled to hide her discomfort. Miko's invitation wasn't a suggestion, and even without Keiko's warning, she knew better than to treat it as one.

13
THE LAST PLACE

Regan went rigid, and a loud roaring filled her head. The world around her grew hazy. She closed her eyes, but her anxiety increased, as did the sensation of falling from a great height. Screams sounded in her ears, her screams. Her eyes snapped open, and the darkness gave way to dazzling light.

Panting, she glanced left, then right, then straight ahead. Control crystals gleamed below her hands; she recognized them. Seraph. Yes, she was still in her mah-kai, and judging by the alarms, she was in the middle of a free fall.

Gravity tugged at her, making the movement difficult. Even in Seraph's cockpit, she felt the extreme descent. The mah-kai's environmental stabilizers had failed, and she needed to get them back online before she pulled out of her dive. If she didn't, the abrupt course changes would be too much for her.

She half expected Seraph to level out on its own, but her last instructions were specific – follow Yohshin and, if possible, capture it. She tried to let her breath out slowly, but pressure forced it from her in a rush. She didn't have much time before velocity and distance to impact made her course irreversible.

The control crystals were so close, an inch to the left of one hand, two to the right of the other. Close and yet, given the increasing gravity, impossibly far. She lay pinned to her seat, her mind alert but imprisoned. The ground raced up to meet her. Forms and features became clear. A spark of gold hurtled through white clouds and below that, the Ridderroque's tall spire reached for heaven.

How soon to impact? Five minutes? Two? She needed to regain control. Forcing her mind to relax, she opened her thoughts to Seraph and found... nothing. That couldn't be right. She tried again and this time located a sliver of the mah-kai's operating system. So small. Barely a flicker. Her third touch found more power, if not much. It was almost as if Seraph had shut down and was just coming back online.

Regan muttered an oath. Too long. She didn't have time. The auxiliary batteries powering life support might be enough to blast the hatches and launch the escape pod, but she couldn't divert power without either the sync or the ability to man the controls. Already, the Ridderroque dominated her view. How close was she? Seraph's sensors were off, which meant its positioning, navigation, and guidance remained unresponsive.

Best not to think about that. She had other worries, chief among them how to coax enough energy from Seraph to save it. Manual control, she thought. That would have to do. She willed her hands to move, watched them inch toward the controls. Her muscles ached from the strain; sweat ran into her eyes. She worked her breath, inhaling and then using the exhalation to force her fingers onward. Her tears distorted light into a soft nimbus around her hands. She blinked and saw the Ridderroque, huge and ominous. This would be close.

Seraph passed through a stray cloud, hit a pocket of rising thermal air, and bucked wildly. Regan's sweat-slicked palm flew away from the controls. An anguished cry rose from her chest, but she refused to release it. Not until hope was lost, not until life left her. She began again, glancing at the snow-capped summit below. Sunlight glinted from the peak in rays that burst upward, the thickest, brightest streaking past Seraph's view.

A rush accompanied the sight, a roar like the howling air around her. The sensation shuddered through Seraph's body, and continued up until it hovered above the mah-kai's head. Another sound came, the hiss of something ripping through the air. The shriek of metal against metal filled the cockpit. Regan jolted upward. Her stomach dropped to her toes. Fighting for breath she glanced into her view. A pair of deep onyx eyes stared down at her over a golden faceplate.

"Yohshin," she gasped, suddenly alert. Her body trembled, and she did her best to hide it. "Let me go." Her power wasn't fully restored, but Yohshin didn't need to know that. "I am to escort Baiyren to the capital as quickly as possible," she said, making sure her tone was commanding. "The king is expecting him."

The mah-zhin cocked its head to the side as if weighing her words. The gesture looked disturbingly human, but less like Baiyren than she remembered. If anything, the movement reminded her of Kaidan. Baiyren said the thing had a mind of its own, that piloting it was like swimming against a strong current or riding a wild horse. She never understood what he meant. Not fully. Not until now.

A long silence stretched between them until finally the mech inclined its head and moved aside without speaking.

Regan frowned. "Baiyren?" she asked. "Are you all right?"

Baiyren didn't answer.

"You know I can't allow unauthorized flights into or out of the capital unless I clear the pilot." Light pulsed inside Seraph's cockpit, first on the command console, then on the arms of Regan's chair. A touch on one activated thrusters, a shift to another pushed Seraph back. Yohshin saved her by grabbing Seraph's ankle, which it now released. She righted her mah-kai and gazed at the beautiful machine. It certainly was magnificent: so powerful, so beautifully wrought. Not for the first time, she wondered who had made it and why.

The light came again, a faint flickering around her hands and up her arms. She blinked it away, attributing the glow to afterimages from the console. A third aura surrounded Yohshin, this one winked once and then again. As the light faded, the view shifted to Sahqui-Mittama.

Odd; she hadn't done that. She peered at Yohshin, thinking, wondering. Her view moved again, and this time she knew the mah-zhin was behind the change. A lone hangar in the military compound appeared, Yohshin's hangar, the only place safe enough to house a mah-zhin.

She shook her head. "You're not going anywhere until I hear Baiyren's voice." She kept her eyes on her instruments. Yohshin's weapons were still down, which meant it – or Baiyren – was trying to convince not threaten.

Seraph's sensors buzzed quietly, and Regan regained control of her view. The Royal Guard appeared in the lower corner. When they were within three thousand yards, they fell into a blockading formation and held position.

Regan opened a channel to Gunnar, and a short, stocky man with rich dark skin and stunning blue eyes filled the screen. The war had taken its toll on him, but he could still muster a smile every once in a while. This was not one of those times. His frown deepened when she explained what she wanted to do.

"It's risky," he said. "If Yohshin decides to alter its course, we're not strong enough to stop it."

"No," Regan admitted. "We aren't. Which pretty much nullifies any argument against this. The mah-zhin will do what it wants regardless. Right now, it's allowing us to escort it to the hangar bay. Let's not lose the opportunity. And Gunnar? Weapons down. Don't give it a reason to attack."

Gunnar weighed her words before nodding. "Form up," he said to his men. "I want eighteen mah-kai on Yohshin's right and the rest on the left. I will hold point while Seraph protects our flank." Gunnar's mech gave Regan a smart salute before leading them east.

The ground rolled by in a blur of gray colored rock, slow moving rivers, and patchy forests that eventually gave way to the orderly fields and beautifully carved buildings marking the outskirts of the capitol. Castle Tallaenaq climbed from the easternmost part of the city and ended at sheer cliffs that dropped ten thousand feet into the sea. Apart from a few wharves for loading and unloading inbound and outbound cargo, the area was under full military control.

Gunnar led the Royal Guard fifty to seventy-five miles to the south, headed out to sea, and started down. Regan monitored Yohshin closely for some sign from Baiyren.

She didn't get one.

Instead, an explosion sounded to Regan's right. Another followed, this one to her left.

Cursing, she threw Seraph into a wide corkscrew. "Evasive maneuvers," she called. A third blast ripped the arm off the mah-kai to her right. "I need wide scans. We have an enemy out there."

Behind Seraph, inside the burning debris, Yohshin's black eyes glittered in anticipation. Slowly, as if relishing the moment, it drew the mace from its hip.

14
NOTHING TO WEAR

A group of monks, ten in all, led Keiko and Juno from the massive throne room, down several ornate corridors, and into the fortress's austere living quarters. The monk in front motioned the two women forward, while another opened a door to her right and stepped back. Juno held her ground, arms crossing. "Where's Brother Isshi?" she demanded.

Keiko coughed discreetly. *We're not in much of a position to bully anyone,* she said blithely. *And while I'm all for being forthright, we can't afford to antagonize these people.*

They're monks, Keiko, Juno thought back.

Yeah, yeah, I know. Patient, kind, and all that. She shrugged, the movement odd-looking if you couldn't hear her. *But watching what you say will go a long way. Just saying.*

Juno forced a smile. "I'm sorry," she said to the apparent leader, a young man with a happy face, kind light brown eyes, and full lips. "I didn't mean that the way it sounded. It's just that he said he'd look after us personally."

"I'm sure he did," the man smiled. "But the bishop is an important man. He has other duties that need his attention."

"Too important to babysit us, you mean," Keiko said archly. *Okay, I know what you're thinking, but you were making demands, I'm being sarcastic.*

I don't see much of a difference, Juno said primly. *Though I appreciate the support.* She hadn't realized how nice it was to have someone with authority nearby. Isshi could make decisions where these men couldn't.

"So what are we supposed to do?" Juno's hands moved to her hips, but her tone was lighter, less antagonistic. "You all say we're not prisoners, but since we arrived we haven't had any freedom or privacy."

"Your rooms are very private." The monk's smile widened.

Keiko grinned back at him. "You're funny. Do you have a name?"

"Brother Taisho." Though the monk's bow was formal and correct, Juno thought the gesture held a touch of irony. "My apologies, ladies. I should have introduced myself sooner."

"Oh, I don't know, the priestess summoned you. Introductions were her responsibility."

A furtive look crossed Taisho's face, and he lowered his voice. "The high priestess has even more responsibility than Bishop Isshi. It was an oversight. Nothing more."

"Right," Keiko said skeptically. "And I forget to put my pants on in the morning. I understand how easy it is to do stuff like that." Her face grew serious. "Thank you for your honesty, Taisho. And the warning."

Warning? Juno hadn't heard a warning? She was

a politician's daughter; she wouldn't have missed one. But the conspiratorial look passing between her companions said otherwise. Damn it. She needed to pay more attention. Keiko's words said a lot without saying anything, Taisho's too. Her father did this all the time, she should be able to as well. Except she'd never been that good at watching her tongue.

"So," she said, nodding at the still-open threshold. Might as well start with something innocent. "You say the rooms are private, right? I guess that means we're free to lock them." Keiko gave Juno an approving look.

The monk's eyes twinkled. He understood the game they were playing. "Why would you need to? We are the most honest people on Higo. Our very souls are open to God."

"But we're not part of your religious order. And aside from the high priestess, all I've seen are a bunch of men. Forgive a girl her modesty, but I'd feel a whole lot more comfortable if I at least had the ability to lock my door. Or have the ability to reopen it if – say – someone, I don't know, locked it accidentally from the outside."

Brother Taisho slipped a hand into his robes and produced two brass key rings; matching sets dangled from a small, metal circle on his belt. The handle end was machined to resemble the hammers that all the monks wore off the chains around their waists; the other end was comfortingly serrated.

Juno took one of the rings as offered. Keiko took the other. "I don't suppose this is the only set."

Brother Taisho's smile turned ironic. "Will it make you feel better if I said they were?"

Juno had to think about that for a minute. "Who

has the others?" She crossed her arms again and leaned against the wall, determined to know how safe she was.

"You, certainly," Taisho said with a shrug. "Other than that..." He drummed his fingers thoughtfully against his cheek. "The caretakers, security of course, then maybe two others."

Juno and Keiko each lifted an eyebrow, Juno the left, Keiko the right. "It would be helpful, if you were a little more precise."

"It's hard to be precise, my lady," Taisho said earnestly. "Sometimes, Kaidan keeps the keys here in the fortress."

"And those other times," Juno asked. She already knew the answer.

"The high priestess." Taisho seemed genuinely apologetic.

Juno sighed and tried to tell herself that it wasn't that much different than a hotel. Over time she might actually believe it. She cast a suspicious eye at Taisho. "When I go in there and lock the door behind me, will I be able to reopen it once I'm inside?"

"Of course. Why wouldn't you?" Another non-answer. "I'd advise against it, though. You aren't familiar with Tsurmak. If you wandered off and got lost, you might be late for tonight's dinner. I trust you wouldn't want that."

Juno grimaced, both at the thought and the dinner reminder. While relieved to know where her next meal would come from, the idea of a formal dinner was slightly intimidating. "I hope my appearance will be acceptable," she said. "I didn't exactly pack for a state dinner." She swept her arms down the length of her body, over her dirty shirt, past her hips, highlighting the mud caked on her shorts, and finally flicked her fingers at her travel-worn boots. Keiko's garb was even less appropriate: running shorts and loose T-shirt. Not exactly what they should wear to dinner, especially not one that involved world leaders. At least, not on her world.

"It's not a diplomatic affair," the brother said. "Lord Kaidan thought you'd be more comfortable if he kept the meal casual. I understand he and the high priestess exchanged words over the planning." An amused twinkle lit his eyes. "She wanted something befitting a traveler from another world, but as I said, Lord Kaidan disagreed." Taisho studied both women, not in a suggestive way but in a measuring one. "You do look as if you've been through a great deal, though, and not just because you've been uprooted from everything you've known."

Keiko rolled her eyes. "That's an understatement."

Juno nodded her agreement. Dinner or no dinner, cleaning up would be nice.

"You'll find some clothes already in your rooms," he said. "Bishop Isshi described you fairly accurately, under the circumstances." The monk again tapped his cheek. "You may have to roll up the sleeves of the robes and possibly the pants as well. But then again maybe not. I'm heading back into the city from here, and I can have a tailor come by." He grinned again. "I'll have her bring some dresses."

"Dresses?" Juno certainly didn't have anything against formal wear – she knew how good she looked in a cocktail dress – but she was far more comfortable in clothes that gave her free range of motion. Like what she now wore: shirts, shorts, or pants, anything made for the outdoors.

"She'll come with a wide assortment." Taisho grinned again. "However, no one says it has to be a dress. The women here aren't beholden to them." He cocked his head thoughtfully. "They're really not that different from you."

Juno's eyes found Keiko. "So I've heard," she said.

15
ONE LONG STEP

Regan drove Seraph forward as hard as she could. A mile to the south, Yohshin came to an abrupt halt and floated over the ocean, cool, composed, and deadly. Head down, it scanned the area below.

What are you looking for? And why there? Regan stared into the sea. Here it ran dark and deep, the cool blue green giving way to black. Her eyes widened, and she cursed her shortsightedness.

"Weapons, Seraph! As fast as you can!" How could she have been so careless? Captain of the Royal Guard, leader, tactician. The Riders knew who she was and where she'd take Yohshin; they knew and they'd readied an ambush. Slamming her fists against her chair, she sent Seraph to the water.

Seraph's voice bloomed in the cockpit, cool and even. "Weapons online and synchronized to your thoughts."

"Scan the depths for heat and energy signatures. You're looking for mah-kai, a whole squad. Send word to the others. Tell them the Riders are in the water, not the sky." She stared down.

The ocean remained calm, its waves rippling gently under soft breezes as if mocking her. Her eyes flicked to Yohshin. The mah-zhin jolted, then moved back as a missile parted the sea and rocketed upward. Regan rolled right and threw mental commands into Seraph. Small doors opened on the mah-kai's shoulders, light building inside hidden muzzles. Her pulse throbbed as she readied her counterattack. The Riders' missiles altered course, reacquired Seraph, and sped toward her. More came, bursting into the air. Explosions sounded behind her. She wanted to look but couldn't, not while the barrage continued.

Several warheads slammed into Yohshin, doing no damage. The mah-zhin ignored the smoke and flaming refuse and calmly surveyed the bubbling waves, its mace pointing down. A hint of golden light rippled around the head, building into a ball of intense light a few feet from the tip.

Yohshin stared imperiously at a spot half a mile offshore where canyons cut across the seafloor. When it found what it wanted, it fired. The orb hit with the force of a small meteor. Water flumed hundreds of feet into the air, steam boiling upward in great billowing clouds. The ocean churned and cresting waves ripped from the calming epicenter. Black liquid – oil or some other fluid – stained the blue expanse. Debris dotted the waves, and smoke drifted upward like lonely black ribbons.

So much power, Regan thought. And so easily wielded. How many Riders were down there? That much metal – that much fluid – made for three at least. Possibly more. A second shot would finish the rest. But Yohshin decided to hold its fire.

What was it waiting for?

"Heat signatures located," Seraph called. "Ten mah-kai pulling away from the walls. Formation indicates a tactical retreat." Seraph shifted the view to show white streaks against the blue sea. The mechs were running at high speed, no longer concerned about stealth, no longer concerned about anything but survival. They'd covered a significant distance and opened a good lead. It wouldn't be enough.

Leaping ahead, Regan powered Seraph's weapons. The hand cannons were the most accurate, but they didn't have the range she needed. The blasters mounted beneath the shoulder armor had similar limitations. A glance behind showed Yohshin holding position as it searched for additional mah-kai. The fleeing Riders could be a diversion. She opened communications.

"Gunnar, keep an eye on Yohshin and let me know if it moves. Let me know if it does anything. I'm going after the Riders; we can't let them report to Haven."

"Understood." Gunnar's gravelly voice filled the cabin, Seraph's audio systems amplifying his words. "We're at the rear gate. I called for reinforcements, they'll be here shortly."

Regan grunted her acknowledgment and cut the connection. Gunnar would watch her, and she didn't need to worry about him antagonizing Yohshin. He knew better. She put him out of her mind and rocketed after the fleeing Riders. Bubbles unraveled in their wake, but as she closed, the white lines grew more distinct. She measured the distance.

"Energy spikes detected. The mah-kai have fired." Seraph shifted the view to where several lances punched through the surface. Streaks of sizzling amber energy arched over the waves and flew at her like glowing javelins. She saw the weapons, predicted their flight. They were close, but instead of engaging them, she accelerated and wove through.

The foaming wake was directly below. A thought powered down Seraph's systems, a second released a decoy ahead of the Riders' armored suits. Designed to match Seraph's signature, it drew their attacks as it crashed into the waves. She didn't have long before her mech's momentum faded and she joined the decoy in the ocean. Seconds at most.

It was enough.

Seraph's silence pushed the incoming strike to the decoy. Regan grinned as they plowed into the sea, detonating in a spray of seawater. Secondary explosions sounded one after another as depth and pressure finished what direct hits didn't. Once an advantage for the Riders, the ocean became a liability. Outnumbered and outgunned, Regan won the fight. It took more effort than Yohshin's single blast, but it was just as effective.

She ordered a simple, if unnecessary, sweep to confirm the Riders' fate, then turned and headed back to the castle's rear wall. Yohshin still hadn't moved, its head down, its hands balled into fists.

"Yohshin?" Regan called. Silence met her signal. She tried again, and again the mah-zhin remained silent. A stream of bubbles traced across the ocean, coming up swiftly and moving from left to right. The ornately decorated head of a Rider's mah-kai bobbed to the surface. Eyes dim. Dead. "Yohshin! Do you hear me?"

"Why did you finish them without me? I can't believe

you didn't leave any. I wanted them. I could have finished them all by myself."

Regan stiffened. She hadn't expected that voice, not yet, and certainly not saying what it did. "Baiyren? Baiyren, is that you?"

Baiyren paused. "I warned you; I told you this would happen. You should have listened to me."

Baiyren glared at the head bobbing up and down on the ocean surface. It taunted him, the face gazing up with accusing eyes, his mother's eyes, the eyes of everyone he'd murdered. He lifted an arm and blasted the helm away. Regan had tried to speak with him, but he'd ignored her. An overpowering need to destroy had taken over; adrenaline mixed with the joy of using his power. Maybe he and Yohshin weren't that different. Maybe he just liked killing.

Turning away, he headed inland. Wharves and jetties crisscrossed the foundations, where water met stone, and heavy gates barred the city entrance. The wall loomed before him. A row of armored suits slowed to a halt and turned. Armor became targets; he pointed his mace at the leader and summoned his power.

"*Stop, my lord! Please.*"

The voice was familiar. "Gunnar?" He and Gunnar had been close once, back before the last battle, before Baiyren left Higo and everyone he knew behind. He exhaled. "It's good to hear your voice."

"Good to hear yours as well, my lord."

The targets ahead morphed back into Royal Guardsmen. Gunnar's mech, Saizhen, hovered at the exact center. Sunlight sparkled over its silver plating. Its elegant helm reminded Baiyren of the ancient Roman armor he'd seen on Earth.

An uncomfortable silence stretched between them. "I'm here to see my father," Baiyren said, at length.

Regan's voice cut across them. "And now that I know you don't plan to level the castle, I'll allow you to enter. Given the circumstances, I'm sure you'll understand why you'll stay under full guard."

Startled, Baiyren glanced over his shoulder. Seraph hovered over the wreckage-strewn ocean. He lowered his head and shook it. "I can't believe I let you talk me into this." He moved Yohshin over the burning sea and pointed. "This is what the mah-zhin do. Bringing it into the city's a mistake."

"Your father's *dying*," Regan said. "You have to see him."

Baiyren hesitated. He'd been too lost in his own misery to consider the point. "It won't help. Yohshin lives to destroy."

"Only when you let it. You stopped it from attacking Gunnar; that's a start. If you can do it once, you can do it again. We'll need that against Zuishin if and when it wakes up."

Baiyren conceded the point. In his brother's hands Zuishin could go anywhere, destroy anything. He needed to find a way to slow it. "All right, Regan," he said. "Have the crews prepare Yohshin's hangar. Same procedures as always. I don't want anyone inside when I land. No one goes near Yohshin."

He stared at Castle Tallaenaq's graceful spires, his heart pounding, his stomach churning. Seraph flew toward him, but he soared away without looking and leaped over Sahqui-Mittama's protective walls.

The grounds inside looked the same as ever. He sighed sadly, thinking of a time when Higo didn't need weapons or hangars or mah-zhin. He'd been young, on the eve of his eighth birthday. Kaidan was back in the capital after his mandatory studies at Haven. Baiyren had been looking forward to seeing his brother. His hero.

16
GROWN TOO SOON

Fourteen Years Ago
Higo, the Royal Palace

Prince Baiyren dashed through the hidden passages above the throne room. He'd removed his shoes and placed them at an entrance just behind one of the upper floors' covering tapestries. Hard-soled shoes made noise, a truth he'd learned the previous year to his great disappointment. This time would be different; this time he'd be careful. His brother would never find him, not until the game was done.

At seven, Baiyren was almost too old for games like this, which made winning on what could easily be his last try that much more important. Kaidan's required lessons at Haven kept him away from the castle for most of the year, and when he finally came home, it was only for festivals, ceremonies, and royal birthdays. The next celebration wouldn't be for six months. So many things could happen before then. Too many. Better for Baiyren to win now than wait for a chance that might never come.

Slowing to a walk, he came to a wide fork. A darkened corridor peeled off to the right, another to the left, a marble wall dividing the two. Baiyren looked first one way and then the other. The glint of gold caught his eye. He stepped over and examined the stone, finding the rough outline of a large man hefting a globe onto his wide shoulders and framed with gold leaf etched into the marble. He chuckled quietly. Kaidan wouldn't find him this time; the carvings he followed were too well hidden.

He lifted a hand and placed it on the cool stone. As always, the Heartstone grew warm against his chest. A faint click far behind told him the hidden door had locked into place. He shook himself and moved into the waiting gloom. Choosing a passage at random, he hurried forward. He'd spent most of his free time studying and preparing and setting false trails throughout the castle.

He was going to win.

As he rounded the third of four corners, he came to a narrow walkway. Stained glass lined both sides, the pictograms identical representations of ancient gods encased in glowing orbs, enormous beasts at their sides. With a start he realized he was in a notch overlooking the throne room. He'd inspected the passage, but that was at night; no one was in the hall then. No one saw him here, and none of Kaidan's spies could rush back with news. It was almost noon now, and the room would certainly be in use. He swore at how his obsession with victory had blinded him.

Peering down, he cursed again. Glass climbed from floor to ceiling, and under different circumstances he might have admired the artistry. Now, with a royal audience beginning below, he was more concerned with the people standing about the room. One wrong move, one step too far, and his shadow would spill across the floor and give him away as surely as if he'd jumped and waved his arms.

Frustrated but not defeated, he wiped his sweaty palms on his pants and sat with his back to the wall to think. Voices drifted up to him. He ignored them until the tones changed. His ears caught a familiar voice. Kaidan? It couldn't be; he was supposed to be looking for Baiyren; this was their day together. Baiyren bit his lip, knowing he couldn't move without them seeing him. He waited as long as he could before curiosity overcame him. He edged forward, careful to avoid sudden moves until he reached a clear section of glass and peered down.

Kaidan was down there all right; Baiyren recognized his brother's athletic frame standing a few yards from the throne. Instead of his royal clothes, he wore the church's simple rust-colored robes. The customary chain of black steel circled his waist, the ornamental hammer worn on his left hip. Despite Kaidan's dress, Baiyren noted minute errors – the hammer sat too far back on a belt that was far too loose. Kaidan had the look of someone who'd thrown his clothes together as best he could. He also looked liked he wanted to be somewhere else – anywhere else.

The woman standing to Kaidan's left was a different story. She looked to be about fifteen, the same age as Kaidan. Her clothes were impeccable, her bearing nearly as regal as the king's. Auburn hair framed a delicate face whose eyes betrayed her serene expression. Ambition filled those yellow pools, something Baiyren found odd in a priestess of Haven.

The woman to Kaidan's right was entirely different. She was tall, the tallest woman Baiyren had ever seen. Her raven-dark hair fell to bare olive-colored shoulders like twisting ivy. Her eyes were the same hue as desert roses, her face heartshaped, and her full lips parted in a confident smile.

"It's out of the question, Miko," the king said, rising. "I won't let you take him – not under any circumstances. He belongs with his people."

Miko lifted an eyebrow. "And what of his lineage? You can't keep it a secret forever. Your kingdom's future is at stake, majesty. Kaidan's popular, many would welcome him as king, an honor you know he can't have. I'm offering you a way out."

Baiyren's breathing grew rapid, the glass in front of his face fogging. What did she mean? He glared at her through the window, willing answers from her, receiving none.

"You expect me to trade one spy for another?" the king said, incredulous.

The second woman bristled. "I'm not a spy." Her rich voice roared across the room like a gale through giant trees. "I don't care if you are the king; *no one* insults me to my face!"

"I see I'm just in time," a new voice said. "I will vouch for the woman, your majesty." In the corner, close to the throne itself, the air rippled and coalesced. A Nanjii in crimson robes appeared below and to the right of the dais. He was tall and bald, and though his face was young, his brown eyes reflected ancient wisdom.

A stunned silence fell over the room. Both Kaidan and Miko looked shocked to see him. Baiyren clamped a hand over his mouth to silence a gasp. No one but the king saw a Nan-jii in person. Not ever.

Miko regained her composure before the others and placed her body between Kaidan and the king. "You must excuse Regan, majesty," she said, bowing. "She's unfamiliar with social graces."

The king didn't seem to hear. "Who are you, Regan?" he asked kindly. "I've never seen anyone like you."

The tall woman hesitated, and the Nan-jii used the silence to answer. "Two pilgrims found her wandering about the Ridderroque. They didn't know where she came from, and she seems to have no memory of her life before that time. According to the church's ways, Haven took her in and did its best to care for her."

"But they couldn't control me," Regan interrupted. "I threaten them. The church put me through some test and didn't like the results."

Baiyren inched further into the hallway to hear more.

"Her blood crystallized on the altar," the Nan-jii said, folding his hands into his sleeves. "His holiness took a smaller sample than he usually does; he was careful. One drop: that's all that hit Lord Roarke's hand. Within seconds, it was solid.

Kaidan placed a hand on Miko's shoulder and motioned her back. "The blood took the shape of an arrow pointing eastward," he said. "His holiness believes it's a sign."

"His holiness was there then?" The Nan-jii's tone said more than his words. "I have it on good authority he was performing a church service at the time."

Miko flushed. "You question the high priest?"

"He is not for me to question." The Nan-jii's eyes

glinted under the light. He gazed up at the king. "This talk of an exchange was a farce from the beginning. You don't have to agree. They're testing you, probing your weaknesses. If your son stays, the succession becomes messy; if he leaves, you risk dividing your supporters."

Baiyren grimaced. The succession – always the succession. As if he cared about it. The law said the eldest son became king; it had always been that way, at least until recently. Baiyren never understood what changed, and he didn't ask, not even when his father gave *him* the Heartstone in Kaidan's absence. Sometimes it was better not to know.

"Is this what you want?" the king asked.

"He's happy with us," Miko said quickly. "No one judges him in Haven."

"I asked my *son*, priestess, not you."

Kaidan lowered his head and nodded. He was silent and still for a long moment. When he looked up his face was stone. "I'd like to say goodbye to my mother before I go. Where did you have her buried?"

The temperature in the castle went cold. No one moved. The king, Kaidan, Miko, even Regan, became icy sculptures. Only the Nan-jii seemed unaffected.

Baiyren gripped his hands into fists until his knuckles whitened. He didn't understand. Their mother wasn't dead; she was in the gardens. He'd seen her on his way to the tapestry. He crawled closer to the glass, close enough to see the intense sorrow lining his father's face.

"You don't understand," the king said. "Queen Haillen and I… We'd been married for seven years without a child." He inhaled and steadied himself. "The high priest said finding someone who could produce a child was the only way to ensure our government's stability. I needed an heir."

"And now you have one," Kaidan spat. "A legitimate one. You don't need me."

Baiyren's world tilted. *No! It's not possible! It can't be!*

"You're my son!" The king's face reddened. "You belong with your father."

"I belonged with my mother too, but you robbed me of that. How did she die, Father? Do you know? Did you even try to save her?" Kaidan shook his head bitterly; his face became granite. "How could you use her like that? Did you enjoy the time you had with her? I hope she was good enough for you to remember that much."

The king stormed down the dais. Baiyren had never seen him so angry. He reached the bottom and looked like he was about to launch himself at Kaidan when the Nan-jii slid in front of him.

"Careful, majesty," he said. "They're goading you. Imagine what would happen if word got out." He turned and fixed Miko with a contemptuous look. "The priestess has a hold over your son. She uses her beauty to chain him to her."

Miko's face went scarlet. "*Liar!*" she shouted. "Don't listen to him, my lord."

A mirthless chuckle escaped the king's lips. "A priestess and my son." He shook his head. "Young love. Does his holiness know about your budding relationship?" Kaidan and Miko looked away. "I'll take that as a no."

"I knew," Regan said. "I came across them in… in…" She blushed and fell silent.

The king's gaze shifted to Miko. "So instead of telling the high priest, you decided to remove the only person you couldn't trust to keep your secret. Did Kaidan talk you out of killing her?"

Baiyren didn't know if he was proud of his brother or ashamed. He wasn't sure of anything. His family, his life, everything crumbled around him. Not even the church was spared. The church. Thinking about it brought a rush of anger. Forced infidelity? Outrageous! Apparently, Kaidan's mother – another incomprehensible thought – had fared worse.

"I hope Miko's worth it, son. You've put me at odds with the church."

"You mean you accept?" Miko asked.

"Not for you, priestess. Kaidan's suffered enough; he's lost everything important to him. I don't like you, Miko, but if you make him happy, I won't stand in your way." He turned, then stopped. "Before you leave," he said over his shoulder, "I'll have one of my guards escort you to your mother's grave." He climbed the rest of the stairs and sat on the throne. "If it's any consolation, I cared a great deal for her. I've hated myself every day for what I put her through. The high priest assured me he'd take care of her." His face hardened. "Apparently, he was less than honest." He sighed. "You've landed in a den of liars, Regan. Are you sure this is where you want to be?"

Regan didn't hesitate. "I am." Her eyes flicked to Baiyren's hiding place, and she drew a deep breath. "Especially if it means setting things right."

Behind her, Kaidan relaxed and some of the anger left his eyes. Miko's hand found his, and she turned to embrace him. Her back was to the throne, and her face was to Baiyren, and it was easy for him to see her triumphant expression.

"The lying won't stop, Regan," the king said sadly. "And deal or no deal, things are about to get a whole lot worse."

17
OUT OF CONTROL

Higo
The Present

The Heartstone was warm and heavy around Juno's neck, but she did her best to hide any discomfort. The transport, an ornate, carriage-like vehicle that reminded her of a mastless catamaran, left Tsurmak, cut through the lush forest she'd seen from the air, and approached Haven's sprawling basilica.

Juno glanced across the seat. Keiko sat beside her with her hands folded and a wide smile stretching across her face. If Keiko had been here before, she was doing an incredible job hiding it.

"Brother Isshi told us the basilica is Higo's oldest known structure," Keiko said. "Oldest *known*… Like I'd let him get away with saying something like that."

"Of course you wouldn't." Juno wasn't really listening; she was too busy worrying what lay ahead.

"You got that right. When I asked him about the modifier he lowered his voice and said most people, even those in the church, believe the Ridderroque isn't a natural formation."

Juno perked up. "If it's not natural, then what is it?"

"No one knows," Keiko said with a shrug. "The church says God made it."

"They would," Juno said, more interested now. "But what about everyone else? What are *they* saying?"

"Pretty much the same thing." Keiko snorted. "You don't usually find that kind of agreement, even when it comes to religion. Higo's myths say God grew the mountain from the earth to remind the people of his dead wife, a kami of trees." Keiko grew sad. "Funny how a kami's thoughts can seep out of the deepest depths. He may have denied his world, but it hasn't denied him. Hopefully we can make him see that before it's too late for Higo."

"We?" Juno asked, her eyes narrowing. "You were talking to yourself, and you didn't mean me. Who's here with you?"

Keiko made a halfhearted attempt to put her finger to her lips.

"Don't give me that. What kind of all-powerful kami are you?" Though Juno's tone was firm, Keiko's transparent gesture almost made her laugh. "If you were really worried about surveillance you wouldn't have been talking out loud. You'd have kept it to yourself." Juno drummed her fingers as the transport slowed to a halt, noticing for the first time the sly triumphant look on Keiko's face.

"Not so nervous now, are you?" the other woman chirped.

Juno wanted to hit her. Keiko was clever, far more so

than she let on. Juno had to be more careful. She mulled that over and turned her attention to the world beyond the windows.

A wall of silver light blocked the road ahead as securely as a more solid one, and the car eased to a stop. Evenly spaced pillars of some crystalline material lined the road on either side. Juno counted a handful before she lost sight of them, noting how they pulsed in time to the barrier. The power source, perhaps? The two closest to the road flared, and the glow between dissolved long enough for the transport to slide through. Beyond, the trees ended abruptly at Haven's great basilica.

Nearly twice as large as Kaidan's fortress at Tsurmak, the building reared out of the earth like a range of small mountains. The main peak reminded Juno of a western mesa surrounded on all sides by wide buttes and wind-carved arches. She gaped openly. In all her travels, she'd never come across a sanctuary that wasn't grossly ostentatious. Haven was nothing like that – more tribute to the power of rock and stone than an altar to God.

A stocky monk with the familiar rust-colored robes waited by a gate. He stood patiently off to the side until the car slowed to a stop. The doors opened, and Juno stepped into warm, dry air. Though the monk looked young, the skin on his large hands and long face was deeply tanned and weathered.

"Welcome to Haven, Ms Yamanaka, Ms Montressen," he said in a soft voice. "I am Brother Gou. Her holiness sends you her greetings. If you will follow me, I will take you to the antechamber. Dinner will begin shortly. My lady regrets not meeting you herself, but she is leading the evening prayer."

Juno smiled at the taller man. "Please call me Juno. And for the record, you don't need to apologize. I'm just happy to have someone to show me the way."

Gou dipped his chin respectfully and escorted them through a pair of huge stone doors and up the wide marble staircase inside. A solid, perfectly smooth wall met them at the top. Juno was happy for the flats Taisho had provided. They went well with the light blue sundress she selected, something nice enough to meet state dignitaries, but not formal enough for an official dinner. To her surprise, Keiko had chosen a long white dress accented with green and gold. Her garb was close to Juno's on the formality scale, but she needed Juno's help shaping her short hair. Juno had pinned her own red tresses behind and to the left and let them cascade over her shoulder.

Ahead, yellow-red sparks illuminated the hall, the effect reminding Juno of a welder cutting into a vault. Huge arched buttresses supported a ceiling some thousand feet above her head.

"It's like being inside a gigantic cave," she said aloud. How could anyone build something like this? The rich brown walls were so smooth, the arches molded against the stone as if part of it.

The monk beside her smiled proudly. "Supposedly, Higo has bigger caves in the Rake," he said. "That's the large mountain range several hundred miles to the east. No one's been able to verify that, though." The Heartstone warmed against Juno's skin, but thankfully didn't pulse. "Our holy book describes a much larger cavern inside the Ridderroque, an unverified claim, I'm afraid."

Juno's heart lurched. "Your holy book? This book... Is it open to the public? Can I see it?"

"Not the original. Only the high priestess has access to that. Copies are available everywhere, though, but the most accurate ones are in our library. I'll see about getting access for you. It's a simple matter, really, but since you are an outsider I'll need to clear it."

Juno feigned disinterest. "No rush. I wouldn't want to trouble you."

"No trouble at all. It's simply a matter of waiting for Bishop Isshi's return. The library is his responsibility, one of them. I'll speak to him about it personally. Shouldn't be more than a few days."

How lucky is that, Keiko piped. *And you were worried.*

Juno made a note to guard her thoughts more carefully, earning her an irritating chuckle from Keiko. Instead of letting that get to her, she focused on the hall, marveling at its grandeur. The basilica was as beautiful as it was vast. Red stone gave way to other colors, threads of gold filtering in and out, iridescent against black, and then gray and every other color imaginable. The decor was equally impressive: ornate tables, and desks, tapestries, and paintings. Juno thought about her need to visit the library and tried to see as much in the pictures as she could. Historians claimed art said as much about a civilization as its books, especially religious ones.

"This is as far as I go," Gou said, gesturing at a bank of elevators. Translucent silver globes slid through glass-like tubes and disappeared into floor or ceiling. "The lifts will take you to a small antechamber. The guard is expecting you and will announce your arrival." He pressed his palms together and bowed. "It was an honor to meet you, Juno and Keiko from another world."

Juno did her best to copy the bow. "And you as well. And thank you for your offer about the library. I look forward to hearing from Isshi."

A pair of shining brass doors opened to signal the elevator's arrival. Juno headed between them, turned, and nodded to the monk as Keiko fell in beside her. The doors slid shut and silver light pulsed around the two women before solidifying into a clear orb. Juno barely felt the sphere shoot from the floor and rocket upward. Overhead, the arched ceiling approached at high speed, and Juno flinched as they flew into it. Walls and people-filled corridors flashed past Occasionally, a wall would open to large windows, through which she spied the jungle beyond Haven. She counted three more floors and two more windows before her spherical cabin slowed to a halt behind a sliding gray marble door that opened into a grand waiting room.

A guard stood in front of yet another door. His thick body relaxed when they left the elevator, though his dark eyes remained alert. Without a word, he twisted the diamond handles, pushed, and stepped aside.

Juno remained where she was until Keiko nodded for her to go in. Candles flickered invitingly on the other side of the threshold, but did little to break her growing anxiety. She'd been to state dinners with her father; she knew what they were like, knew what to expect. That should have made her feel better. It didn't. No one's life depended on what was said or done like hers did now.

Dabbing her lips with the tip of her tongue, she slowed her breathing, drew herself up, and strode into the unknown. For Baiyren.

18
THE GHOST

Three years ago
Higo, Sahqui-Mittama

Baiyren ran through the castle's smoldering courtyard. Explosions erupted all around him and he kept his head down to avoid shrapnel and falling debris. The mah-kai's hangar was close, closer than any other building, tall and wide, with its doors thrown open. Hurtling over falling stone, he stumbled inside, found his footing, and sprinted across the ground, weaving through a thick crowd of men determined to reach their mechs and get them airborne. He spotted a dark-haired and dark-eyed man in a loose fitting tunic of crimson and gold. Beside him, another lord strapped himself into his mah-kai and closed the cockpit.

A small group of pilots gathered by the far wall. He ran over. Regan stood with the guard, her dark hair and pale pink eyes unmistakable in the light. Noting his approach, she nodded and promptly dismissed her pilots. As one, they broke apart, some heading to waiting mah-kai, others to small fighters, command posts, and maintenance sheds.

Regan was already striding over before the first pilot reached his craft. She stopped a few inches away and slipped her arm through his. "Your brother attacked from the west, my lord," she said in low tones. "Several sections of the city are on fire."

Baiyren nodded his understanding. "Do you know what he's after?"

"We do." Regan pulled him behind a stone column and gripped his shoulders. "He came for your mother, Baiyren. Less than ten minutes ago, a raker was seen leaving her bunker. Mah-kai broke through the defenses. We still don't know if they had help from the inside, but we think so."

The news sent Baiyren to his knees. He didn't remember falling, didn't remember much of anything before Regan's eyes found his. Her hands were on his arm, helping him up, her body shielding him from his men. Leaning against the cool stone, he closed his eyes until his breath evened. "I need as much information as you can give me. Full battlefield conditions, possible escape routes, and the location of every safe house between here and Haven. They couldn't have gone far." He stared past the hangar doors, through smoke and fire and on to the edge of his sight. There, imagination detailed what he couldn't see. Castle walls aflame, a gash in their fortifications, as real and as black as a hole in the universe. "Send word to my father. Tell him I'll rescue the queen."

"As you say, my prince." Regan bowed deeply. "Our forces are airborne and scanning for the fleeing raker."

She placed a hand on his wrist. "They won't get away."

"As long as they haven't brought Zuishin we have the advantage."

"The Nan-jii say the other mah-zhin is still dormant."

Baiyren nodded thoughtfully. In waking Yohshin he had an accomplishment Kaidan couldn't match. "Get Seraph in the air," he ordered, turning from Regan and sprinting for the hangar doors. "I'll catch up as soon as I can."

"I'm sure you will," Regan said wryly. They both knew how fast Yohshin could fly.

New explosions shook the ground. The world around him blurred, then came back into focus as he skidded to a stop in a wide launching area. *Yohshin!* he called. *It's time to go.*

An answering rumble rolled across the pitted yard. Light flared in Yohshin's battlement. His world became a blinding silver curtain and he felt his body dissolve like sugar in water. In seconds, he looked down at the burning palace through Yohshin's eyes.

He saw a little girl in a white dress with flowers in her hair steal kisses from a boy preparing to defend the castle. A few blocks away, a mah-kai burned inside a wide factory while the company's owners sank to their knees, at once thankful and aggrieved. Priests in the city's churches sent the soldiers protecting the buildings off to save as many as they could. Flames painted Sahqui-Mittama's buildings with an oily orange glow, soot staining the remainder black. He tried not to think about the people who lived there or those who died in their homes.

They'll pay for this, he vowed. *Once my mother's safe, we'll break every Rider we can find.*

He searched the skies for targets and found a raker fleeing the castle grounds. A distinctly feminine mah-kai with wide shoulders and an assortment of weapons led them. Its helm tapered into a conical peak that ended ten feet over a bronze faceplate forged in the likeness of a young woman with tilted eyes and cruel lips.

"*Mindori?*" Regan's voice hissed through Baiyren's thoughts like leaking steam.

Mindori had been one of his teachers – early on when he first arrived at the military academy. Like many other nobles, Mindori vanished sometime during his second semester only to resurface at Haven with a full pardon.

Baiyren raised Yohshin's arm to block Seraph's advance. "We knew this could happen. Kaidan doesn't have a weapon strong enough to counter Yohshin, so he's using Mindori to outthink us. She's the best tactician he has."

"She taught most of the men in the Royal Guard. She knows our weaknesses. This won't be easy."

She also taught psychological warfare and was ruthlessly good at it. Baiyren remembered how much Regan hated those classes. Dishonorable, she called them, an affront to God, king, and man. Regan vowed to abolish the practice if she ever became the captain of the Royal Guard. Kaidan had no such reservations.

Yohshin scanned the surrounding area for anything out of the ordinary: a glint of metal in the stone buildings, a gun barrel disguised as a pipe, a carefully laid ambush. Finding nothing, the great armor exploded after the Riders, outpacing Regan, who did her best to keep up. A much slower Gunnar trailed with his squad in a tight formation.

Ahead, Mindori led eight heavily armored mah-kai away from the castle. An old but sturdy prison transport trundled inside the Rider's blockading formation. Its turrets – two in front and two aft – came about and prepared to fire.

Hunter. Baiyren recognized the ship, one he thought destroyed several years ago. Its former owners included pirates, renegades, and criminals, most of whom a former king caught, convicted and executed. The barge itself was sparse, plain, and cruelly built. Its captives spent most of their time in cells too small to accommodate them; light and food became luxuries, the guards who brought them, heroes.

The resurrected vessel now held Higo's queen in its cells. *Hold on Mother; I'm coming for you.* Yohshin dropped onto the main deck. Metal clanged, and plate shivered but held.

This is too easy. Baiyren smirked. Kneeling, he, drove a fist into the barge's hull. Silver light bloomed around Yohshin's golden hand. He struck again, harder this time, luxuriating in the mah-zhin's strength. The ship groaned; the hull, though reinforced, split. Armor plating opened, layer after layer, until a gaping hole appeared in the metal. Smoke wafted into the air, staining the beautiful blue sky.

Regan's voice screamed at him, shouting something about caution and deceit. Baiyren knew he should listen, but he was too angry, too close to rescuing his mother. He saw her in his head, watched her suffer in horrific conditions. Probing the breached hull and finding no resistance he was about to dive into the ship when a blast erupted behind him. Another came, and then more.

Yohshin rolled to keep the incoming fire from Hunter and his mother. A squad of Riders approached from the north, fifteen in the lead, another group trailing. Mindori took point, and though Baiyren knew her to be a skilled pilot, she flew erratically. One moment she came on straight as an arrow only to fall several hundred feet, turn, readjust, climb, and accelerate.

Baiyren stood and drew his mace. Power flooded into the mah-zhin. Mindori raised a hand in answer, but the movement was stiff and awkward. A crystal-powered lance blazed in her right hand, lifted, dipped, and lifted one last time before firing.

The shot grazed Baiyren's armor and skittered away. A second stray bolt careened wildly past, another slamming into the barge at his feet. Flames roared upward, sparks showering the sky. He aimed his hammer at Midori but didn't fire. Something was wrong. Mindori wouldn't miss this badly; the greenest cadet could do better.

He waited, waited for the mah-kai to slow or swerve or retreat. Only it didn't. It flew on, if struggling, in an overt attempt to ram him. Baiyren smiled. Mindori was another chance to use his power, another enemy to bring down. His first shot severed the mah-kai's hand. The next blew off the head. When the third pierced the chest, Yohshin went cold. Dread filled the armor, clawing its way into Baiyren's soul.

Against his will, Baiyren gazed into Hunter, shooting past its torn and shredded decks, past smoking corridors and empty cells. Wide girders had fallen atop a body, blood pooling beneath, dark hair splayed to hide the face.

Panic rolled through him. He held his breath and

asked Yohshin to keep back and not show him whose crushed form lay beneath the pile. Yohshin ignored him. Baiyren fought, but the harder he fought, the more Yohshin probed. He saw her at last, glimpsed Mindori's high cheekbones, upturned eyes – now closed – and long aquiline nose. The sight released a held breath. He relaxed, but only for a moment. Why was Mindori here? She was supposed to be inside her mah-kai. What happened?

And then he knew.

Shooting down, he followed the trail Mindori's wrecked mah-kai left in the air. The vapor was easy to track, the burning and melted metal leaving a clear path. He passed the head, then an arm. He reached the torso last, the ruined armor tumbling from the sky like a wingless bird.

He knew what he'd find inside the cockpit, knew enough to keep from scanning its smoking remains. He wished he could block Yohshin's thoughts from his, knowing what the link would show him. A quick scan of the debris identified traces of the queen's genetic makeup. His armor located a transmitter that allowed Mindori to pilot her mah-kai remotely. Last of all, the Yohshin showed him his mother's broken and bloody body.

Baiyren's world crumbled. He threw Yohshin into a catastrophic dive. Behind, the air's moisture sizzled and condensed into streaming trailers, while ahead Higo spread out before him like a warm and comforting blanket. Ready to wrap him in oblivion and end his suffering in a blaze of explosive light. Regan screamed at him, Gunnar too. He ignored everything but the rising earth. Bitterly, he wondered why God put a spirit so unfit to rule into a prince's body.

He closed his eyes, and a part of his mind noticed Yohshin's decreasing momentum. Another part drifted – lost, tormented, and rudderless. Time passed. At first he didn't know if he was dead or alive. Seconds seemed like years, the moments becoming an infinite storm that blinded him to the outside world. He thought it lasted forever, but when it finally cleared, his eyes opened, and he stared at a statue of his god inside the Ridderroque. Did Yohshin bring him, or did his subconscious somehow find its way here? Head shaking, he lifted his eyes to the statue, seeing it differently than he had all those years ago.

Tall, stern, and imposing, it stood watch over Lord Roarke. The god's face remained impassive, distant even. Baiyren didn't expect anything different, not from carved stone. Still, after what Baiyren just did, what Mindori forced him to do, the indifference in his god's stone image riled him. He wanted accusation and disappointment – anything but apathy.

"How could you do this to me?" he cried. "You could have made me anything... anything but this."

Something glittered on the wall behind the majestic figure, a silver outline inside which ancient runes stretched from left to right. The words blurred then focused and, incredibly, he understood them.

"The Pathways," he said aloud. The priests rarely spoke of a little understood passage in the Zhoku that mentioned routes to other worlds, perhaps the same route Lord Roarke traveled to Higo.

Baiyren walked toward the shining letters. Yohshin's

hand came up, its fingers splayed, reaching for the tablet
behind the statue.

"Baiyren!"

He turned its head.

Seraph stood several yards away, knee deep in the
water, droplets glistening over its pastelhued armor like
stars.

"Go home, Regan," Baiyren said.

"Not without you. What happened today was a
tragedy. You shouldn't be alone. Come with me. We can
sort this out; we can grieve together as a family."

Yohshin turned away. "I destroy everything important
to me."

Regan shouted something, but he no longer listened.
His mind closed, and he put Higo behind him. His hand
reached for the etched stone, felt light explode from the
wall. A corridor ran from the opening toward infinity.
Resolutely, he stepped into the glowing hall without
looking back.

19
ANYTHING BUT THIS

Higo, the Present

Baiyren's eyes fluttered open, and the vision faded. Instead of the cold stone he expected, his head rested on something equal parts soft, firm, and warm. He looked up at the vague shape leaning over him. A halo surrounded it – amber striated with green and gold.

"Welcome back." Regan's voice filled his ears with a softness he hadn't heard in a very long time. Rich ebon hair fell around her ageless face like thick, forest lichen, concern lighting her stunning irises.

Groggily, Baiyren lifted his head from her lap and sat up. He didn't remember losing consciousness, though he was vaguely aware of Yohshin screaming at him to pull his memories back. "How long was I out?"

"You weren't, at least not in a literal sense." Regan sat back and studied him. "You remained in control of Yohshin right through landing." She wore the king's uniform well, simple black shirt and pants, gray flight jacket. It suited her better than Haven's rust-colored robes.

"You're sure?"

Regan nodded. "You were standing in the middle of the hangar when I arrived. Your eyes were empty, and your body was rigid. You looked like you were in some kind of trance. It didn't last long, and when it passed, you collapsed to the floor but remained conscious. That was maybe five minutes ago." She left it there, which surprised him.

"How many did we lose?"

"None, thanks to you." Regan's answer made him feel better. He'd made a difference. Too bad it was one-sided. Their victory meant he'd killed.

"Have you heard from my father?" he asked. "I can't believe he hasn't sent someone to bring me in."

Regan smiled gently. "He sent me." She stood, dusted her knees, and offered a hand. "I have an air car waiting. It will take us straight to the castle."

Baiyren tried to stand on his own, but his legs were still weak, and he only managed after grasping Regan's outstretched hand. Once he was on his feet, he waved her off. "Let's get this over with." The sooner he faced his father, the sooner he could go after Juno.

He was still in his grubby, dirt-stained clothes, and didn't feel much like cleaning up. By the time they reached the doors, he'd nearly recovered physically. Outside, Regan's transport gleamed under Higo's brilliant sun. Bright, long, and silver, the vehicle made him think of a fishing lure, the opened door a wolf's maw.

Regan waited for him to climb in before following. "The Royal Palace," she said. "Main entrance, the king's court." She gave Baiyren an encouraging smile, and put her hand on his knee. The gesture was more familial than inviting, a show of support for a friend in his time of need. "I am sorry about this. I can't imagine how hard it is for you." At least she didn't pretend to understand, not that he expected her to. That wasn't her way; Regan was honest to a fault with everyone, including herself.

Baiyren placed his hand over hers and squeezed. He tightened his grip as the transport lifted silently from the ground and sped through the military compound. Castle Tallaenaq loomed at the far end of the grounds, tall and imposing, with brownstone walls and green, plant-covered domes. The structure seemed more barricade than destination. His path, his life, lay beyond. Unless he found a way past this new wall, he'd spend the rest of his life in purgatory.

"I'm not sure I can do this," he said, staring up at the wall, measuring it, knowing what lay inside.

Regan held his gaze. "I'm supposed to take you to the king's chambers. Once you're inside, I can't let you out again until the king commands it. Those are my orders. What happens inside is up to you." She leaned in closer, her pink eyes bright. "I didn't know my parents, so I never had the chance to say goodbye. Make amends, Baiyren. You'll never forgive yourself if you don't."

Baiyren nodded numbly and turned back to the castle. Guilt knotted his stomach, years of it. His father would speak words of forgiveness, but would he mean them? How could he? Baiyren had taken his wife from him. *I told him I didn't want to be king,* he thought bitterly. *He should have listened.*

The car slowed to a stop before the residence's wide steps. Baiyren stayed where he was. He sat motionless as the moments ticked by. He drew one last breath to steady himself and left the transport. The simple movement, one he managed endlessly without thinking, took all of his strength. Next, he pulled his body from the seat and stood. The sun that gleamed so beautifully off Regan's raven-dark hair held neither light nor warmth. Turning his back, he stalked up the steps, his thoughts shifting to the reunion he never wanted.

20
INTERROGATION BY CANDLELIGHT

Juno waited for a white-robed attendant to draw back a chair for her at the surprisingly small square table before sitting. Miko and Kaidan waited until she and Keiko were seated before joining them.

The room itself was elegant if simple. White marble shot through the black of its walls until breaking free to dominate the ceiling. Religious statues, all men, lined one wall, while on the other the now familiar figure of Higo's god stared down at them from the palm of his giant protector. Conspicuously absent were a woman's finishing touches. Either the high priestess had recently acquired her position, or she wasn't sure enough to make the room her own.

Someone's a little insecure. Though Keiko's face remained impassive, her tone held enough sarcasm to fill the room.

A young woman in church robes took an order from Miko before scurrying away. The ubiquitous hammer and chain were inexplicably absent. The girl returned a moment later with a cart filled with four large plates, each covered with a silver dome. The exotic smell of some unknown meat filled the air. Juno's stomach growled loudly enough to bring a heated blush to her cheeks. Keiko grinned sympathetically.

"I want to thank you both for joining us," the high priestess said with a surprisingly warm smile. "I think I speak for all of Higo when I say your arrival qualifies as one of the most significant events in our history. Even so, I'd rather not make this a formal dinner. I'm sure you're tired and disoriented, and I don't want you to think this is anything more than our way of welcoming you."

A welcome that began with kidnapping, Juno thought. She forced a smile and inclined her head without looking at Keiko. "Thank you," she said, not entirely sure how to address the woman. "That's very kind. This moment is as big for me... for us... as it is for you. We always wanted to believe we weren't alone in the universe; until now we had no proof."

How do you want to play this? she asked Keiko.

You're the one with the senator dad, which makes you more familiar with these kinds of situations.

Juno nearly choked on her water. She raised a pure white napkin to her lips to hide her discomfort.

"We never doubted," Miko said confidently. "As a matter of fact, your existence confirms what our holy book tells us about Lord Zar Ranok."

Juno frowned, but before she could speak, Kaidan's deep voice rumbled across the table. "We didn't know until recently what the Pathways were or what they meant to Higo."

Miko nodded as she lifted the silver dome from her plate and cut into her meal. "According to the Holy

Book, King Tallen woke on the slopes of the Ridderroque with the Heartstone in his hand. Lord Zar Ranok spoke to him through the stone, telling him of his journey and his past, and the sorrow he left behind."

Juno leaned forward; she couldn't help herself. Miko's voice had an almost hypnotic lilt that suited the tale. She thought back to stories of dragons and giants her mother read to her when she was young. The beasts became dinosaurs as she grew. She wanted to know how they died out, promising herself she'd learn everything she could until she found the answer.

"What happened to your god before he came here?" Juno picked up a napkin and placed it on her lap. Following the high priestess's lead, she removed the silver cover from her plate, sliced a bit of meat, and placed it into her mouth. The flavor was unlike anything she'd tasted: sweet and robust, with a touch of spice and even a hint of cinnamon. It was delicious, maybe the best she'd ever had. She slipped another piece into her mouth and returned her attention to the priestess.

"A great tragedy," Miko said, her tone somber. "There was a war, a terrible war. Our Lord's wife was among the first to die at the hands of a dear friend. Other gods died by the thousands, their guardian demigods along with them."

Juno struggled to keep her eyes on Miko. She didn't think shifting her gaze to Keiko would make the high priestess suspicious, but she didn't want to chance it.

Miko spoke of Higo's holy book – its bible – and the incredible claim that Higo's god abandoned his ancient home: a world of gods, a world beyond the Pathways. Her world. Earth.

Juno willed her face smooth. She shifted uncomfortably in her chair as Miko's voice reached a crescendo.

"The royal family is destroying this planet. Only the church has the moral authority to rule now."

Kaidan put his hands on Miko's. Something passed between them, a unity of purpose, a bond Juno didn't understand. "No one wants war," he said. "Least of all the church. Unfortunately, my father doesn't understand that. He hasn't even asked Higo for forgiveness."

Juno fought the urge to rub her temples. Fatigue clouded her thoughts. Her mind was fuzzy; she couldn't focus. "What does this have to do with us?" she asked.

"Everything. At least, I hope it does." Releasing his grip on Miko, Kaidan knitted his fingers together and placed his hands on the table. "My father is dying, and Baiyren is his only heir. You've met my brother. He isn't a leader, and he doesn't want to be one. You should talk to him; convince him to return to your world so we can resolve this peacefully. Without an heir, the church becomes the only viable government. We can restore the faith my father destroyed and move on."

An outraged expression crossed Miko's face. "The king abused his power, and everyone knows it. Higo's people question his authority, and they expect us to bring him to justice. Kaidan's right. No one wants war, but the fighting will continue unless or until we restore the people's trust. As long as Baiyren's here, those loyal to the crown will rally around him. If he goes, they lose their standard bearer. Their cause will die and this war with it."

"Why did you come to Earth then? If you left him alone, you would have had what you wanted."

Kaidan leaned forward. "My father sent his guard to bring Baiyren back. He wanted to see his son. Our forces followed to keep that from happening."

Juno studied the two figures across the table. She wanted to believe them but she couldn't be sure. Their words made sense, especially Kaidan's assessment of Baiyren. The man she knew hated tyranny as much as she did, but he simply wasn't a leader. He was a researcher and a scientist. Kaidan was right. Baiyren wasn't fit to govern. He did fine with his expeditions, but ruling an entire planet? She didn't think he'd want that. Her eyes moved from Kaidan to Miko, thinking, measuring.

"I'll need to know what you have in mind first," she said. "A lot of people died on Earth. You have to promise that won't happen again."

"We're trying to stop a very old war," Miko said forcefully. If we're successful, the deaths will end."

Kaidan steepled his fingers and sat back. "You have our word."

21
FATHER AND SON

Baiyren took a last look at Regan before making his way to the far end of the castle's grand foyer. Eventually, he reached a bank of elevators and stopped at a solitary door. A guard sat at a desk to the left. He dipped his head at Baiyren, pressed a button on the polished console, and kept his eyes on the hallway as the door before him opened. Baiyren gave the guard a curt smile and, one halting step at a time, walked into the elevator.

A low chime told him he'd reached his father's floor. He waited for the elevator to open and walked out, his legs heavy, his stomach a lead weight in his body. The arched ceiling above leaned over him like a reaper's shadow. Lost in thought, he stalked down the corridor until he came to a second guard who snapped to attention as he approached. Baiyren barely saw him. His eyes remained on the door that swung into the room beyond. He had so many good memories of those chambers: playing hide-and-seek with his parents, celebrating birthdays and holidays and feasts. Those days were gone now, forever lost to the tragedy of growing up.

Sighing again, he cleared his head and went in. High-domed and as wide as most houses, the king's apartment took up the entire floor. Windows climbed from hidden casements in the sienna marble walls and ended near the ceiling in arches that made them look like blunt spears. A stone desk stood in the middle of the room, chairs opposite. To the right, tall bookcases ran from one end of the room to the other, sofas, chaises, and an ornate rug accenting them. The king's bed, four-posted and canopied, occupied a space to his right, where, as far as he remembered, other furniture once stood.

Baiyren drew a deep but ineffective breath and walked to where his father's emaciated figure lay beneath a thick cover of blankets. King Toscan Tallaenaq had always been a great bear of a man, and still was when Baiyren last saw him. Now, he looked like a pile of bones someone wired together and papered with ancient parchment. The once-muscular frame had all but dissolved. Wisps of white hair clung to his head the way sparse mountain grass desperately sought purchase. His cheeks were gaunt and hollow, and only his silvery eyes still held life. Bright and sharp, they misted when they fell on Baiyren.

"Baiyren!" The king beamed at him, his voice too strong for his frail body. "You came home."

As if Baiyren had a choice. He didn't recall Regan offering one, and even if she had, Kaidan's forces negated it. The taking of both Juno and Keiko decided things for him; he couldn't leave them with Kaidan.

Grabbing one of the chairs near the desk, he dragged it to the bed and sat. "Father? What's happened to you?"

"Mortality," the king snorted. "Or so the doctors tell me."

"Are you in pain? What can I do?"

A wistful smile played at the king's pale lips. He lifted his hand and cradled the back of Baiyren's head. "You're here. That's enough."

His grip was still strong, his palm warm and firm. If Baiyren closed his eyes, he could almost deny the sickness. He wanted to, and not just to have his father whole and well. A strong, healthy king absolved Baiyren's royal responsibilities. Higo wouldn't need a successor. Not for many years. The king's grave condition changed that.

Baiyren almost felt Higo reaching out to shackle him. "Do they know the cause?" he asked. "Your doctors, I mean."

"Of course not. No one gets sick on Higo. They've never seen anything like it." He stroked Baiyren's hair one last time and lowered his hand. "Kaidan said God would punish me for what I did. Maybe he's right."

Baiyren let that pass. "I trust the doctors weren't the only ones looking into your illness," he said, changing the subject.

The king nodded. "Regan and the Nan-jii both looked into it. They vetted every cook and servant in the castle and tested the food and the water; they even sampled the air. They were very thorough."

"The answer's here somewhere," Baiyren insisted. "Miko benefits more than anyone else. She's been working toward this since she first met Kaidan."

"None of that matters now," his father said. "I'm dying, and no one can stop it. I need to focus on what's really important."

"Nothing's more important than getting you well again. You need to focus on that. The rest can wait."

"It's waited long enough!" Color flooded the king's cheeks. "I knew you'd blame yourself for what happened, and I wanted to tell you, as a father – as a man – that it wasn't your fault. Stop punishing yourself. Your mother wouldn't want you to live like this."

"She shouldn't have died then!" Baiyren cringed at his childishness. He lowered his gaze. "I'm sorry. I didn't mean to say that."

"Of course you did, and you're right. Unfortunately, being right doesn't change anything."

The sharp rap of knuckles on a side door interrupted them; three taps, a pause, and then two more. A hidden panel slid back, and a rippling distortion in the air stalked toward them.

Nan-jii, Baiyren thought. Only the king's intelligence network was allowed to use that entrance. He sat back and waited for the shape to cross the floor. The rippling bowed but the man didn't remove his reflective clothing.

"Word from Haven, your majesty," a voice said, deep, confident, and richly timbered. "The Riders landed in Tsurmak yesterday. They brought two women with them." The shape shifted, and Baiyren felt its gaze land on him. "One wears the Heartstone."

Baiyren's heart lurched. *Juno.* "Are they all right?"

"Both are fine, my prince." The Nan-jii bowed again, this time at Baiyren. "They dined with the high priestess and Kaidan last night. Apparently, Haven granted them diplomatic status. The women are living in the ambassador's suite."

"That won't last. They'll use Juno against me, just like they used Mother." Baiyren looked at his father. "I have to go."

The old man stiffened. His hand whipped out, grasped the front of Baiyren's shirt, and dragged him down. "You know what Miko's trying to do."

"I don't have time for this," Baiyren said, trying to free himself. "Those women are my responsibility; I need to free them before it's too late."

"Too late? It's already too late. Why do you think Miko targets the people we love most?"

Baiyren frowned. "I don't know. To hurt us, I guess. She'll do whatever she can to seize power."

"I thought so too, but it's more than that." The king released Baiyren's arm and shook his head. "According to the Zhoku our Lord came to Higo to escape the war that killed his wife. Miko's reenacting that war and using our loved ones against us. The closer the person is, the greater the pain. It started with Kaidan, then your mother, and now the woman you care about. Don't look so surprised. I may be sick, but I'm still the king." He reached for a glass of water beside the bed, sipped, and continued. "Higo was supposed to be God's refuge, his place to heal. The high priestess is taking that away from him. She thinks it will force him to end his exile."

"To deal with his misguided children." A chill swept through Baiyren. Was his father right? It didn't seem possible. He bent to take his father's glass when a slight warming bloomed on his chest.

Dazed, he tugged at the lanyard, and a strip of luminescent plastic tumbled out of his shirt. He looked at it in amazement, then in anger. "Have you changed your routine? The cooks, the staff? Have you gotten any gifts? Think, Father; this is important." The meter registered a small amount of radioactive material. Not enough to harm without direct skin contact.

The king frowned, affronted. "Of course I haven't! The Nan-jii check everything."

A distortion in the air by the desk drew close. "What about the Royal Stone?" the intelligence officer asked. "The one the priests gave you to replace the Heartstone?"

The king's frown deepened. "What's this about, Baiyren?"

Baiyren held up the card. "This is a radiation detector; it changes color, if you've been exposed. Right now, it's showing low-level radiation."

Hands shaking, the king pulled a dark stone from his shirt. He looked at the space where the Nan-jii stood. "I sent this to the royal jewelers late last year," he said slowly. "The clasp needed repair; it wouldn't stay closed, and I didn't want to lose it."

The hiss of sharp breath came from the Nan-jii. "I need to report this to our leader," he said.

The king stared at Baiyren. "How did you know?"

"Because I know Miko." Baiyren's body tightened. "You didn't come down with an illness; this was deliberate. The church has poisoned you."

22
A SNAKE IN THE PARLOR

The next day, Regan woke early, threw on the Guard's black and silver uniform, and headed for the hangars. The city's businesses opened shortly after morning meals, and she boarded Seraph just before those began. Nodding to herself, she guided her mah-kai from the military compound and leaped into the sky. Heat and ice warred inside her, burning anger, frozen vengeance. She barely saw the castle's armory fade away, barely noted the mah-kai's acceleration or the force pushing her into her seat. Nothing but the cluster of gem-encrusted towers a few miles distant mattered to her.

Without thinking, she pounded her fists against her chair. *Radiation poisoning! So simple.* Kaidan had been careful not to use too much. He knew their tests focused on food, drink, and aerated toxins. They didn't test for radiation. They barely knew how. Radioactive material was hard to come by and lethal if handled. Unless you had the proper tools – tools only an artisan or metalworker used.

Angling down, she burst through a stray cloud and

headed for a large brownstone building at the edge of a wide boulevard, its back abutting Sahqui-Mittama's tall fortifications beyond which jagged cliffs fell into the small sea.

She smiled grimly. No one would escape that way, which left the front entrance and the loading docks on the side, both of which she monitored. "I want mahkai watching every corner of that building," she ordered, broadcasting instructions to the elite squadron. "No one moves in until Prince Baiyren arrives."

"We should go now," Gunnar protested. "We can't let the suspect slip away – or worse, dig in."

Regan scowled into her view. "I'm sure he's already gone."

"We don't know that."

"What are the chances the assassin's still here? If you poisoned the king, would you stay?"

"Why are we here then?" Gunnar asked.

"To find out as much as we can. I don't like the idea of an assassin sneaking into Sahqui-Mittama without anyone knowing." She shifted her attention to an emerald-green mech with wide epaulets set upon bulky shoulders. Its head resembled a giant mollusk, its body a monstrous crustacean. The pilot, a noble Regan seldom saw when off duty, owned a small island chain just off the coast. "Ceffas," she called. "Take Gunnar's spot at the rear guard. Gunnar? You're with me."

Gunnar grunted what sounded like agreement as Regan landed before the royal artisan's main building. She punched a control crystal, and Seraph's breastplate opened, the hiss of escaping air filling the cockpit. The mech lowered to its knees, and Regan leaped into its opened palm before jumping onto the street.

Gunnar joined her as she strode up to the imposing structure. He was a good head shorter and had darker skin. Gold streaked his dark brown hair, his gray eyes surveying the compound as they walked. Like Regan, he kept his weapons holstered. When he finally looked her way, she gave him a sharp nod and marched toward the entrance.

Silence greeted them, both at the ornately carved stone door and inside where a small reception area stood empty. They moved deeper. Eventually, Regan heard the ring of hammers on metal and the quiet hum of machinery. Voices rose and fell in normal, happy conversation. If the workers inside were concerned, they didn't sound it.

Regan cleared her head and scanned the crowd on the other side of the door. How many were involved in the plot? Just one? More? She needed to know, had to think. Certainly, one man could do what needed to be done. More risked detection. One man then, two at the most. Jewelry crafters were tight, but not close enough to hear about treason and fail to report it, not unless they were related.

Following the sounds to a spacious workroom at the rear of the building, she came to a single door, some twenty feet wide and likely thirty feet tall, that opened onto a factory floor filled with smelters, work tables, tool cabinets, and various jewelry making machines. Her eyes landed on a vault near the back, and as she started toward it, a worker in a tan apron noticed her. His light gray eyes widened into saucers, and he dropped a large metal hammer onto the cement floor with a loud clang.

A long silence followed before a big man with a barrel chest, thick arms, and a ruddy complexion hurried over. Sweat glistened in his silver hair and matching mustache. He stopped before Regan and bowed, his hands clasped over a smooth stomach. He didn't look worried or suspicious. Quite the opposite. His expression said he was pleased to see her, no doubt anticipating a hefty royal order.

"Lady Regan!" he beamed. "This is an unexpected honor. Please. What can we do for you?"

"Your name, master," Regan said, smiling pleasantly. This wasn't the man she wanted. Better to keep him calm; better for him, better for the soldiers outside.

"Master Jeweler Carenkyo, my lady." The man made another deep bow.

Gunnar sauntered past Regan, his casual gait masking a deliberate move to block the door.

"We'd like to commission a major work to commemorate Prince Baiyren's return." Regan's smile widened. "We'll probably need all of your men for a project this big."

Master Carenkyo beamed at her. "Of course, my lady. My entire staff is at your disposal. What sort of piece would you like and when do you need it?"

"A statue of the king and his son for the castle gardens, suitably grand and cut from the finest stone." Regan stepped back to address the men who had started to gather. She scanned them, looking into their faces as she moved from one craftsman to another. "The crown prince would also like an official replica of the Royal Stone to hang around his father's image. I understand the man who created the original is no longer with you.

Is there anyone here familiar enough with the piece to recreate it?" A low hum coursed through the craftsmen. Regan could almost feel their excitement. A royal order of this magnitude was worth a year's pay at least.

Carenkyo gave an enthusiastic nod. "I know just the man. He's only an apprentice, but he has incredible skill, considering he's been with us for less than a year."

Regan's heart faltered. "Who'd he replace?"

Carenkyo glanced from the apprentice and back to Regan. "What's this about, my lady?"

"Your missing craftsman added a piece of highly radioactive metal to the king's pendant before plating it," a voice said from the door. As one, the men in the shop turned to the speaker. Gasps rippled through the crowd. One man lowered himself to his knees. A second followed, and then a third.

Eyes ablaze, Baiyren stormed into the building. Regan had never seen him so angry. He raged through the factory, stopped in the middle of the work floor, and looked about. Guards were everywhere now, some entering just after Baiyren, others moving into place behind him. Shifting distortions along the walls meant the Nan-jii had come as well.

Baiyren moved forward. "Where did he go?" he demanded, his shadow looming over the craftsmen.

"We don't know," the guild leader stammered. "He left right after he finished the piece, said he had to return to Haven as soon as possible, that his family was ill."

"Did anyone else work with him? Did anyone go at the same time?"

"He worked alone. Wouldn't let the other craftsmen near him. By the end, he started to look haggard, so

I offered him an apprentice. He refused." Carenkyo sighed. "And now we know why."

"He thought you might see what he was doing." Baiyren cursed under his breath and glared at the guardsmen and the Nan-jii. Chagrin, hurt, and anger fought openly across his face.

Regan placed a hand on his shoulder. She remembered when he was smaller, less tense. "Let's go, Baiyren," she said. "We have what we came for."

"But we can't prove it. Witnesses who depend on the king's patronage won't convince anyone. No one will believe them, not over the church. The priests talk to the people in ways the crown can't. Personally, intimately even. We'll never compete with that. Not without more than witnesses financially tied to my family." Baiyren's shoulders stiffened, and his expression clouded. After a moment, he set his jaw and headed out.

Regan hurried after him. Outside, she grabbed his arm and spun him to face her. "Where are you going?" she asked.

"Away from here. I'm tired, Regan. Tired of the intrigue, tired of the memories and the petty fighting. The church can't fight without an opponent. I'll get Juno as fast as I can and leave. It's the best way to ensure peace."

"It's the best way to ensure slavery. You can't leave your people to leaders who would do *this*!"

"No one else will die because of me." Baiyren shrugged out of Regan's grip and headed for the car. A few feet shy of the door, a wild keening split the air. White-hot anger filled the sound, scalding Regan's ears, searing her soul.

She staggered, caught herself, and noticed Baiyren's

motionless form at the door. An odd, silvery light ran from his chest like an ethereal chain. A leash he accepted but didn't want. Regan blinked her eyes to clear them. She squeezed her lids shut once and then again. The first blink brushed away the moisture; the second unlocked something inside her, a doorway into her spirit, a promise and an answer. She reached for the sensation, but as she did, Baiyren turned.

Pain contorted his face. He closed his eyes and bowed his head. "Yohshin registered a newly opened Portal. The mah-zhin believes Kaidan is heading back to Earth. I found something there, something Yohshin says is important." He inhaled again. "Kaidan wants to bring it home. He thinks it will please God. He thinks it will wake Zuishin."

23
A LAND OF PAIN

Juno twisted her fingers together nervously. She was on the bridge of a ship Kaidan called the *Go-Rheeyo*, a big battle cruiser with tiered gun turrets fore and aft, wide, missile-laden wings, and a sleek conning tower.

"Don't you think a battle cruiser's a little excessive?" she said under her breath. The crew largely ignored her, watching monitors and fiddling with control panels instead of eavesdropping.

"You mean like bringing a bazooka to a boxing match?" Keiko's lips curled ironically. "Yeah I guess you could say that. It's not exactly discreet either, is it? Still, I guess I can understand it, given what they're up against."

"Self-defense is the oldest excuse in the book. But I know what you mean." Juno had seen what Higo's weaponry could do, and it both scared and disgusted her. Knowing an alien world possessed the same fascination with military power as hers did was depressing.

She'd changed into more comfortable clothes, choosing a soft light green shirt and black pants while Keiko was content with a simple white shirt and black capris. Both stood out starkly on a bridge whose entire crew wore Haven's light brown robes. Keiko didn't seem to mind either way, but Juno wished she'd chosen something less conspicuous.

She was still thinking about her limited wardrobe, when the door to the bridge opened, and Bishop Isshi entered. Baiyren's half-brother followed. Juno knew he was coming, but seeing him made her uneasy. He said he wanted to secure the peace and prevent future bloodshed, and at the time – late into their dinner and after several glasses of fine wine – Juno believed him. She understood what he hoped to achieve, and she agreed with it. Now, in the bright morning light, on the bridge of a massive battle cruiser, foreboding settled over her like an old, coarse blanket.

The disappointment leaching from Keiko's dark expression added to the feeling. Everything around her looked dimmer. The bridge became a tomb, and not even Bishop Isshi's encouraging smile dispelled the shadows. As if sensing her discomfort, he strode across the floor to stand beside her.

"Are you sure about this?" she asked. "It feels wrong." A shiver threatened her poise; she fought it down.

"I don't see how." Isshi placed a comforting hand on her shoulder. "The high priestess and Lord Kaidan speak for God. They gave the order because they believe it's important for the church."

"But why a warship?" Keiko asked. "Archeologists don't need military support."

"They do when a mah-zhin is trying to stop them."

Keiko scowled but didn't argue. Juno didn't either. She'd seen what Baiyren's armor could do. Her gaze drifted upward. The bridge's giant viewing screen loomed over her, and she watched Higo dwindle into a distant ball of browns with splashes of green and blue. The Pathways were ahead, Earth just beyond.

Would Baiyren really try to stop them? Juno wondered. If he did, her presence complicated things. She didn't want to believe she was here as a hostage, but she couldn't ignore the possibility. Kaidan's determination to avoid bloodshed seemed sincere, and yet... She glanced at the command chair. Kaidan was so like Baiyren, yet so different. Both had experienced tragedy, and each wore it differently. Baiyren's sadness festered like a never healing wound. She'd noticed it when she first met him in Providence, and then again as she got to know him. Kaidan was different; an icy fog surrounded him, and layer by layer the moisture thickened and hardened and became impenetrable.

Could she trust him? He was as much soldier as acolyte. Baiyren was too, and she trusted him with her heart. A slow blush burned her cheeks. Had she really thought that? Despite what she'd seen him do, despite the carnage, the deaths. The image of him kneeling on the ground and not wanting to fight haunted her. He cursed the armor that took him, begged it to leave him alone. No one faked anguish like that – not successfully. She closed her eyes and held onto the thought. Her hand found the Heartstone, and she closed her fist around it. It still felt cold, almost empty. The tiny spark at its center still flickered, though, if barely.

A baby-faced monk to Juno's right touched a finger to the command console, and the fulllength panel at the front of the bridge came to life. "Displaying the

Pathways," he said.

The view shifted to reveal a tunnel stretching toward infinity. Darkness covered the top like an obsidian roof. A matching slash below made up the floor while colored light swirled between. The sight made Juno dizzy, but she stared into the depths all the same. The more she looked, the more she was sure she saw a speck, a pinprick, at the very heart of the light and darkness. She imagined the spark had come to swallow her, and she backed away. Seconds later, the ship burst from the Pathways and flew into a pristine sky. Blue rippled below, white feathering the space between.

Waves! Juno thought. *Those are waves.* Something was wrong. She spun and pointed. "We shouldn't be here. The dig wasn't anywhere near the coast. We're way off course."

Keiko stayed quiet, but a knowing look crossed her face. Juno glanced at her, hoping not to call attention to the other woman. Then again what would she say? What could she?

Kaidan shifted in his seat. "Do you recognize this place, Isshi?"

The bishop shook his head nervously. "No, my lord. We should be over a range of broken mountains."

A short, thickset monk at the navigation station moved his hands over the controls, and the view shifted then drew back. A blinking dot appeared in the middle of the screen to show their location. A crescent of land arched above them to the north like an upside-down horseshoe. Islands dotted the space between, hundreds of them.

"Navigational scans put us twelve hundred miles to the southwest of our target," he said. Sweat coated his face, his movements as skittish as a frightened rabbit.

Kaidan's eyes returned to the map. "Are you sure you plotted the course correctly?"

"We reloaded the coordinates from Bishop Isshi's ship. Unless the file's corrupted, I don't see how we could've made a mistake."

"An issue with the Pathways then. We don't know enough about them." Kaidan inhaled and stood. "Reset course and increase speed. I need all eyes open. We're flying over an unknown world. Be alert to any incoming threats."

"I'd value your opinion, Ms Montressen," Isshi said. "These are your people. Do you think they'll attack us?"

I don't suppose you feel like answering him? Juno said to Keiko.

Nope. Keiko examined a fingernail. *I'm sure you'll do just fine.*

Keiko's faith, even if glibly given, should have made Juno feel more confident. It didn't.

Grimacing, she faced Kaidan. "It's hard to say. International law requires governments to contact unidentified craft in their airspace and at least try to warn them off. They need to visually confirm you're not just a commercial jet that's gone off course before they take action." Juno shook her head. "That's the way it's *supposed* to be. Things might have changed. That little battle you started the last time you were here probably has governments on edge."

"I'm not worried about the Earth's forces," Kaidan said. A troubled expression tightened his face. He drummed his fingers nervously against his command chair before meeting her gaze. "Do you remember what the high priestess told you about God?"

Juno frowned. "She said something about his past – about him coming to Higo through the Pathways–"

"From a world of gods," Kaidan finished. "The fossil you found is far more important than you realize. The church believes, as I do, that they are the remains of God's wife. What if the remaining gods still guard it?"

A deafening silence punctuated Kaidan's words. Only the whirring of the instruments, the thrum of engines, and the rasp of nervous feet on metal broke the stillness.

Keiko stopped playing with her nails. *He's smarter than he looks*, she said, impressed. *A kami really is watching over the planet. For now, she's just watching. For now. We better hope that prince of yours shows up soon. Yui promised to stay out of this fight, but if it spreads, I'm sure she'll step in.*

And we don't want that?

No, Juno. We don't.

Juno gulped down air. She licked her lips and looked at Kaidan. "We've never seen any gods. They're nothing but myths." Juno kept her voice calm despite her throbbing pulse. She tried not to think of the reports coming out of Japan a few years earlier. Tokyo on fire, news of a cataclysmic event. She tried even harder to put Keiko's visions of gods at war out of her head, of the land burning, flooded, and destroyed. She couldn't. That was when Baiyren first showed up on the university circuit. Coincidence? Juno didn't think so.

A feverish light filled Kaidan's eyes. "So you say."

I take back what I said, Keiko warned. *He's careful, not smart. Add in fervor and confidence and you've got something dangerous sloshing around in his head. You need to work him carefully.*

Why me? Juno asked. She pretended to watch the large screen above to hide her expression.

Keiko sighed in disappointment. *And there it is, the first question everyone asks. I asked it too, by the way. Why? Because you know more about the fossils Baiyren found than anyone else. Just be careful with what you say and never let them know you're manipulating them.*

Keiko's answer tilted Juno's world as everything became clear. *You did this,* Juno thought. *You opened the Pathway here instead of in China.*

Keiko looked like she wanted to bow but was careful to keep her face from Kaidan. *I've done a little more; I've also put us in a time pocket to help Baiyren reach us.* She dropped her chin to hide a smug smile. *Here he is now.*

On cue, energy waves slammed into the *Go-Rheeyo*, hammering the ship from inside and out. Sparks flew from command stations throughout the bridge, arcing from one crystal to the next. The ship's hull vibrated ominously, and alarms blared in warning.

Bishop Isshi staggered to a station as the *Go-Rheeyo* listed. "Our energy crystals overloaded and knocked the main engines offline. We won't get them back until they cool. That leaves us on auxiliary thrusters only. Those are enough to take us to Ms Montressen's dig, but it'll lengthen the flight time."

A second alarm sounded, and a thin monk with a wide nose swiveled in the seat beside Isshi. Sweat beaded his forehead, and fear shone in his dark eyes. "A Portal just opened eighteen hundred miles to the northeast. I checked the coordinates – it's where we were supposed to leave the Pathways."

"Mah-kai?" Kaidan asked, his voice steady.

The monk swallowed nervously. "Sixteen members of the Royal Guard, including Lady Regan. The mah-zhin leads them."

"Right on time," Keiko murmured. "Let's hope they hold up their end of the bargain and win the battle before Yui decides she's had enough."

"What does that mean?" Juno said, the bridge noise muffling her words. "If this is her world, why would she wait?"

"Because Roarke is her friend. Here, let me share what he's going through."

Emotional torment seared Juno's body with enough force to immobilize her – the endless sorrow, the limitless heartache. She couldn't move, couldn't breathe. She trembled, teetering like a boulder on the edge of a deep chasm. Briefly, her vision shifted to the northeast. Juno heard the rustle of trees, smelled a thousand flowers. She drew in their floral scents and the pain returned, lasting for both seconds and for eons. When it fled, she was on her knees sobbing uncontrollably.

24
TO BECOME THE MONSTER

Baiyren raced over the lush green fields and jagged karst mountains of southern China. He'd left the Pathways exactly where he entered when leaving Earth, at the edge of a now ruined basin. How long ago was that? Not more than a few days, surely. Now that he was back, his time on Higo felt like a dream, or would have if not for the sight of his dying father. The palpable divisions between church and crown were now in the open. Two powers at odds, striking and counterstriking with no thought of the people caught between them.

Now Kaidan brought that to Earth.

A quick scan of the area showed nothing but smoldering pits, broken mountains, and the remnants of fallen armor. A few figures in white suits moved amid the wreckage, checking, cataloging. They wouldn't find much. A few charred bones perhaps, but nothing they could analyze. Nothing they could reconstruct. Yohshin didn't just crush its opposition; the mah-zhin pulverized it.

Banking away, he prayed he could end this peacefully.

He glanced back. Seraph flew a few hundred yards behind and to the left, Saizhen, Gunnar's mech, to the right. On Higo he had tried to keep them from following, argued their absence left Sahqui-Mittama undefended.

Regan countered, berating him for doing the same. "The king is dying," she'd said. "If anything happens to you, the capital falls, guards or no guards."

She was right, of course. In staying close to Baiyren, she ensured his return. Yohshin made the Royal Guard unnecessary, foolish even. Nothing bested the mah-zhin. But she'd brought them anyway. Interesting.

A nagging pull at the back of his head said Regan was trying to contact him. He ignored her and closed his eyes. Darkness came and with it peace and solitude. He drew a deep breath and fought against a torrent of larger sensations. Of howling wind and acceleration and a distant target whose presence enraged him.

As always, Yohshin's consciousness reached for him, tugging at his spirit like a violent whirlpool. He fought the feeling, but the pull was strong and seductive, a promise of godlike power, a hint of immortality.

The image of a thundering avalanche filled his head. Unstoppable, it rolled down a craggy mountainside, devouring whatever lay ahead. The scene shifted to the last time Yohshin took him. The valley spread out before him, green and unblemished. A loud rumbling shook the air, smoke and thrown earth billowing up from below. He recalled the devastation, remembered how helpless he felt. He was a scull in a stormy sea, a rider whose mount had bolted. From the beginning, he blamed Yohshin when something went wrong. Unpredictable, he called it. Possessing a life of its own, one stubbornly resistant to his commands. The more he considered the idea, the more he wondered. Maybe it was the other way around. Maybe he was more at fault than he realized.

He thrust the thought aside. The past wouldn't change, no matter how much he wanted it to; he needed to concentrate on the present.

Where is she, Yohshin? he asked. *Why can't we find her?*

Irritation rippled through the mah-zhin. *The Go-Rheeyo is not in the immediate area.* Yohshin's tone was the same blend of patience and impatience adults used with small children. *I've found neither energy signatures nor evidence of an opened Portal.* The mah-zhin shook its head, and Baiyren had the odd sensation of doing the same. This time he didn't fight it.

Energy built in their shared consciousness, held steady, then flew away in short bursts. Worlds opened, visions beyond sight, beyond hearing. He identified what belonged to Earth and what didn't. Haven's forces flew over a crystal-clear sea hundreds of miles away. Inside their formation, he sensed another force, a life within a life, the presence belonging to the Heartstone.

A momentary pang knifed him. What if he'd known about this ability earlier? What if he identified his mother's position before he fired on her? Would that have saved her? Emotion and guilt said yes. Reason said no. As powerful as this searching was, it didn't isolate people. Instead, the power homed in on stone and metal and other building materials.

Baiyren turned for a better look, but Yohshin resisted. The mah-zhin kept its eyes locked on Kaidan and his Riders. *The Go-Rheeyo flies over a wide bay*, it said. *The area is heavily populated, but only on the coast; the islands remain uninhabited. Intercepting the flagship over water means fewer casualties.*

The vision of a glittering sea opened for him. Limestone pillars climbed from the waves, breathtaking formations of gray stone and green vegetation. A crescent of land embraced everything, while a smattering of large and small islands haphazardly interrupted pristine blue water. Baiyren glimpsed cityscapes along the shores and hotels, beaches, and marinas around the bay.

The *Go-Rheeyo* hovered far to the south and east of a long, dagger-shaped peninsula. There, the land pulled back and opened into a wide ocean. The closest port was a hundred miles away or more, the nearest island about half that. Baiyren stared at the scene and went cold.

The ship remained over a relatively deserted stretch of sea. Most people were too far away to feel the effects of the upcoming battle. He wished he could say the same for Juno. What he was about to do put her life in grave danger. He hesitated. Should he turn back? Not attacking ensured her survival.

But for how long? Kaidan was determined to take everything Baiyren cared about. Sooner or later, he'd take Juno too. This was her only chance; her fate was in the hands of a cursed man. Desperation burned inside him before exploding in a tortured howl. Louder than the wind, it assaulted the air. The ground trembled, and ripples spread across the cenote. His forces pulled up and assumed a defensive position, all but Seraph powering weapons.

Regan's mech eased over. The buzzing he felt earlier intensified, and this time he opened his mind to it, to Regan. Her voice bloomed in his thoughts, clear and strong, and less distorted than when his ears filtered it. "Baiyren? Are you all right?"

The mah-kai floated a thousand feet over the ground, its blended coloring looking like a sunset against the valley's rich green grass. The blazing light he'd seen around Seraph faded to a dull glow, barely visible under the bright sun. Baiyren lifted his hand to rub his eyes and stopped. Looking down, he saw a golden arm suspended before a golden torso, Yohshin's torso. Chagrinned, he forced it down and willed his body to relax. Or was it Yohshin's body. He couldn't tell anymore.

"We're fine." The words sounded strange in his ears. "I've located the *Go-Rheeyo* eighteen hundred miles to the southwest." A thought connected his mind to Yohshin's, and he sent the image of Kaidan's flagship to Seraph. Regan would work the mah-kai's controls and bring them up on its view, something Baiyren no longer needed to do.

Her face filled his head. It was like looking into a view and yet not. She seemed more real, more solid. "That's way off course. Is it damaged?"

"I don't know, and we have about a minute before Kaidan realizes we're between his ship and the relic. When he does, he'll head straight for a large city. He'll dig in and force us to engage. I need to stop him before that happens. Form up the Guard and tell them to follow me."

Regan lifted her chin. Pride filled her beautiful face, her eyes shining with an inner light. "They've waited a long time for that order," she said. "I have too."

"Don't get used to it. This is a rescue mission, nothing more. I'm not starting a war on Earth, and I'm not ending

Higo's either. I'm saving Juno and Keiko and that's all."

Closing his mind, he spun away and opened a Portal to the *Go-Rheeyo*. Excitement thrummed through Yohshin, and despite his best efforts, he felt it too.

25
MORE THAN THIS

Yohshin pulled away, and an odd feeling of loss filled Regan. For a moment, she thought she'd connected with the golden giant and felt an indescribable bond. She could have imagined it, but after Yohshin spoke to her she was more aware of her surroundings, more linked to everything and everyone. She heard the Earth's rumbling and noted the great plates shifting below the crust. Lava beat through vein-like fissures like superheated blood whose pulse felt like a living, growing creature. Flying from the mantle, her mind lifted from the soil and climbed into the forests, where she swayed in time to the breeze. The scent of a million flowers filled her. Woodsy smells joined those and with them came a damp and musty scent.

No wonder Baiyren wanted to stay here. Did he feel the same connection she did? She inhaled deeply, held the breath, and then let it out. So many questions, one after another, each associated with her arrival, with Kaidan's arrival.

The thought reminded her of Tsurmak's great battle

cruiser. She saw it in her view, saw the titanium skin reflected against a deep cerulean sky. Regan's heightened senses would have found the ship regardless. As long as the Heartstone was aboard she'd know exactly where it was. She wondered at that, noting her ability to sense the gem came from her heart and not from Seraph's instruments or scanners. Baiyren said Yohshin had similar abilities, but couldn't describe them in any detail. He just felt them.

His vague answer always irritated her. Now, for whatever reason, she understood. The stone never called her like it did now, and the power intoxicated and disoriented her. A consciousness guided her on. She sensed a chasm of heartache that ghosted toward her like thick mist. What was it? Where did it come from? She had to find out.

Opening communications, she called to her forces. "Prince Baiyren's found the *GoRheeyo*," she said. "We'll follow him on high alert. Be ready to move when I give the order."

Regan's words burned through the Royal Guard like sparks through dry tinder. Gunnar moved Saizhen into position and drew a sizzling lance from a scabbard on his back. More mah-kai followed. Captain Nibari, a grizzled veteran with salt-and-pepper hair, pulled his black armor behind Gunnar. Lieutenant Taro came next, his mah-kai a nightmare of bronze plate, shoulder spikes, and a horned helm. The rest fell into line quickly, a menagerie of painted and sculpted metal, each one wielding weapons unique to its form.

Regan couldn't see them, but she knew they were there. Seraph monitored their progress for her.

"Formation complete," it intoned. "Mah-kai primed for battle."

"Distance to target."

Seraph widened the view to show the planet's surface. Water covered most of it, and the sight made Regan uncomfortable. Higo's oceans were considerably smaller, its continents larger; she'd never been more than a few thousand miles from shore. Vast plains and towering mountains were easier for her to accept than these seemingly infinite seas. Unfortunately, the *Go-Rheeyo* hovered between two huge, watery expanses. Slivered land divided them, and while Seraph's readings showed large cities peppering the whole, against the endless blue waves, what rose above sea level looked uncomfortably small.

"Eighteen hundred miles." Seraph's soulless voice contrasted with Earth's vibrant life, with what she heard from Yohshin.

Yohshin.

Baiyren's armor soared through the clouds like a golden dawn. Regan knew the mah-zhin could outpace her, but Baiyren cruised as if waiting. He wouldn't attack without support. Not this time.

Regan nodded. He'd learned.

Tamping down her anxiety, she lifted Seraph's fist into the air and motioned her forces onward. The ground became a blur of green, gray, and blue. Grass and mountains opened to tranquil seas, while above, storms rolled into and past her. The Guards climbed through a spring squall and, rainbows breaking around them, closed on the golden figure ahead.

Regan saw Yohshin in her thoughts as clearly as she

did with her eyes. The mah-zhin turned and regarded her intently. She saw Baiyren behind that gaze, more of him than she had in the past. Another presence regarded her as well, one deliberately repressed. She felt a connection to that second soul. An air of loneliness swirled around it, coupling with a deep need to understand its place. Its past.

Yohshin, Regan thought. *What are we?*

Yohshin inclined its head, and for a moment she thought it might answer. Instead, the mah-zhin spun away and disappeared into a Portal. Regan and the Guard followed. The need to know more about herself was a bright flame, an aching need, a sealed door. Long ago, Baiyren said they'd find answers in the Ridderroque. Their search uncovered Yohshin but nothing else. After that, she'd been resigned to ignorance. Maybe Baiyren was right after all. Maybe they found more in the subterranean chamber than either of them suspected.

The thought sent her pulse racing. She almost forgot where she was and what she'd come to do. Almost. She brushed her palms over a globe to her right, and her view shifted to the trailing mah-kai. Their pilots needed her too; they were her responsibility. Now wasn't the time to worry about herself. Over and over she rebuked Baiyren for running away, for leaving his people. She couldn't do that. She wouldn't.

Will hardening, she opened communications. "Seraph to the Royal Guard: I want to remind you that this is a rescue mission. You are not to attack unless I give the order."

"What about the Riders?" Gunnar asked. "Lord Kaidan wouldn't come without support."

"As far as we know, they're still in the ship's hangar. Expect that to change. We don't know how many he brought with him, but he'll want the better part of his forces to defend the *GoRheeyo*. I would, if Yohshin came against me. The rest will head straight for us. Kaidan isn't afraid of throwing his prisoners into battle; I want to confirm the alien women's location before we engage."

"How will you do that? We can't see inside the Riders' mah-kai."

Regan smiled grimly. "We won't need to. The Earth woman wears the Heartstone. No one, not even the high priestess, can remove it. If they move her we'll know. Kaidan's best option is to reopen the Portal and run for home. Ours is to pin him down. The mah-zhin is stronger and better equipped than we are. It can get close without sustaining damage. The prince will have to complete the rescue while we prevent the *Go-Rheeyo* from escaping."

"The ship hasn't moved, and it's way off course. Either it's damaged, or Kaidan's laying a trap." Nibari's voice was as gruff as his face. Regan still had trouble reconciling the man's hard exterior with his golden heart. After all he'd been through, too. Arming the capital after centuries of peace, commanding the crown's forces in Higo's first battle, seeing men fall, and then having the king turn the Guard over to Regan. None of that fazed him. Not outwardly.

"Neither changes the situation," Regan said. "They still have their guns." Her view shifted to where the *Go-Rheeyo* sat in the sky. Easily a thousand feet long, the battleship was sleek and beautiful, with a cylindrical hull that tapered and flattened as it ran toward the tail. There, a pair of wings swept back from either side of the hull, large missiles hanging ominously beneath. A silver tower climbed from the stern, the bridge overlooking massive, turreted guns both fore and aft. Those would still function, as would the hangar doors. The ship wasn't moving, but it was still dangerous. "As soon as Baiyren attacks, we'll circle around and hit it from behind. I want half the Guard in a blockading formation while the rest press. Kaidan can't afford to have his hangars open, not with Yohshin approaching from the tail. He'll launch the Riders as quickly as he can then seal the ship before we're in range."

"What about the prince?" Gunnar asked, interrupting. "He'll need a few mah-kai to cover him."

Regan shook her head. "Too many things can go wrong – a stray shot, an opportunity for Kaidan to use the women as a shield. Keeping our distance gives him the best chance."

"Some of the Riders will come at us," Nibari said. "That also works in the prince's favor. The fewer mah-kai he has to fight, the better his odds."

Regan punched a crystal, and a tactical map appeared in their shared views. "I expect Baiyren to drive straight down from the northeast as fast as he can." A golden arrow moved down the map. Regan tapped another control, and a second arrow, black with Seraph's image overlaying it, swung out from behind the first. "My sensors show a thin strip of land on the bay's eastern side. It's heavily populated, which means we have to keep Kaidan away. The north and southeast have their share of cities too, but the south is open ocean. We'll split into two groups – one to cover the land, the other to keep the *Go-Rheeyo* from running for the cities." She used a flickering pointer to show how the operation would unfold. "Gunnar gets the east, Nibari the west. I'll take the south."

Gunnar and Nibari bowed. Each divided his men and formed rank. Together, they followed Seraph out of the Portal, over wide fields, past massive cities of concrete, stone, and glass, and through deep mountain passes. They met a blue ocean spreading away to the west. In the east, the land thinned into a peninsula of jagged rock and thick jungle. The *Go-Rheeyo* loomed over them, a huge and threatening shape silhouetted against a tranquil sea. Between the ship and the bay, a golden figured raced through the atmosphere like an incoming meteor.

26
THROWN BACK

A pair of strong but gentle hands found Juno's shoulders and lifted her from the floor. Her world was a haze of pain and memories. She blinked to clear the tears from her eyes, and found Bishop Isshi's face staring into hers.

"Ms Montressen? Can you hear me?" Juno nodded woodenly. Isshi let out a relieved sigh. "You gave me quite a scare. I wasn't sure what happened. One minute you were fine, the next you were on the floor, unconscious. We had a lot of debris flying through the bridge, and I thought you might have hit your head. When I didn't see any bruises, I was afraid it was something worse. You were standing over a relay during the power surge. The energy could have shot through your feet and up your legs."

Juno stared back, unable to speak. Unconscious? She didn't remember blacking out. She thought back, recalling the Heartstone's heat, her tears, the incredible loss. Had she imagined it? Curious, she started to look at the stone then stopped herself. Better they didn't know, she thought. They'd have questions she didn't think she could answer. Or want to. She was aboard a ship filled with religious acolytes. How would they respond? They'd never believe her; they might even accuse her of spying or sabotage.

Slowly, she lifted her hand. "I'm all right. How long was I out?"

"No more than a few minutes."

"A few minutes," she murmured. She didn't remember any of it and took a moment to check her bearings. Little had changed. The *Go-Rheeyo* still listed badly, its engines quiet, its alarms blaring. Tension clung to the air like mist over a valley.

The stocky weapons officer gazed unblinking at his instruments. Sweat streaked the robes of the monk next to him, a wiry young man who licked his lips and continuously pushed his floppy brown hair from his forehead. The pretty blonde woman running shipwide diagnostics was the most nervous, and for good reason: the *Go-Rheeyo* was helpless and adrift. Everyone aboard waited for her report. They wanted to hear her say the engines would be back online soon. Some cast furtive glances at the view, others at tactical; all wondered which race would end first – the engine restart or Yohshin's attack.

A surprised gasp to her right further charged the atmosphere. The willowy, dark-haired woman monitoring the mah-zhin's progress spun to face Kaidan. "I've lost Yohshin!" Fear and desperation played across her sharp features, giving her the look of a hunted animal.

Alarm flashed behind Kaidan's eyes. "Recheck your readings. Start with the mah-zhin's last known position.

Hurry. We don't have much time."

"I've rechecked everything, my lord. There's no sign of it."

"So, Kaidan; How do we fight something we can't see?" Keiko stood to the man's right, and though Juno was happy to see her, Keiko's tone had become mocking.

I hope you know what you're doing, Juno said through their shared minds.

Keiko's eyes shifted to Juno. *I'm pretty sure I do.*

Kaidan's expression hardened; he drew a deep breath and squared his shoulders. "Full alert," he ordered. "Plot Yohshin's course using the information we have. We need to know how quickly the mah-zhin can reach us. Just give me your best guess and have all weapons armed and ready to fire. Make sure we're covered on all sides. And Isshi, I want all Riders in the hangar and ready to launch."

The bishop bowed and rushed to a communication link. Juno headed for Kaidan.

Don't do it, Juno, Keiko warned.

Juno ignored her. Two guards moved in to block her path. Where had they been when Keiko slid in next to him? "You said you wanted to end the fighting," Juno cried. "Just tell Baiyren what's happened. Talk to him. He won't attack if he knows you can't defend yourself."

"My half-brother has every reason to want me dead." Kaidan's eyes gleamed under the bridge's soft lighting. Pain lingered deeply inside them, regret too. He blinked both away.

Juno's breath left her. "What did you do to him?"

Kaidan waved her off. "The crown uses and discards its people like chattel. No one hears the cries of those it throws away." Kaidan put a hand to his chest. "Not any more."

"You can't do this," Juno said pleadingly. "You share the same blood."

Kaidan stiffened. His face grew cold, glacial. He pulled the ceremonial hammer from his belt and sliced it across his forearm. Red liquid oozed from the wound, a bright streak against his tanned skin. "Tyranny has no place on Higo. Miko and I will remove it forever."

Juno faced Kaidan, matching his ice with her heat. "You lied to me; you said I was supposed to help you stop the fighting, not escalate it. What about the relic we found? Was that a lie too?"

"Those relics belong on Higo; the Zhoku confirms it." Kaidan's eyes glittered like dark marbles. "Bringing them home will solidify the support I need to take down the monarchy."

"Those remains won't help you," Keiko warned. "Disturbing them will put you in a deeper hole than you're already in." She looked at Juno. "This charade's gone on long enough. Take me to Zuishin and let me wake it. Your people aren't pawns. They deserve better than that. I'll give you a chance to fight for Higo, one mah-zhin against another." She lifted a finger. "A word of warning though. You might find your savior uncooperative. Things like Zuishin have their own agendas, ones you can't hope to know until it's too late."

"Keiko," Juno gasped.

"You lose either way." Keiko continued as if Juno wasn't there. "If you fight here, you face a superior enemy; if you go home, you wake a force you probably can't control. Your choice."

Kaidan rounded on Keiko. "Who are you again?"

"Who I am doesn't matter. You need to worry about *what* I am."

Kaidan walked over and started circling her. "I'm intrigued," he said. "You obviously want to tell me. I'm listening."

"I'm... a friend."

"A friend?" Kaidan arched an eyebrow. "Funny, I don't remember seeing you before. Miko and I remember our friends."

"I never said I was *your* friend. I'm a friend of Roarke. You know him, right? Your god?" Kaidan stopped pacing. The bridge crew shifted uncomfortably in their seats. "Yeah, I know," Keiko said with a shrug. "It sounds crazy, but it's true. I was on Earth when Roarke and his friends fought another god, what we call kami."

"So you're a god now?" Kaidan's laugh was full and deep. He was enjoying himself.

"Of course not," Keiko scoffed, crossing her arms. She looked like a cat that had already beaten its unsuspecting prey. "I'm a guardian – a kami's protector."

"Uh-huh. So tell me, *guardian*, what are you doing here? Where is your lord?"

"Wouldn't you like to know?" Keiko sighed, and her tone grew serious. "As for why I'm here... The answer is pretty straightforward: I can't let you dig up those remains."

Kaidan reddened. *"Can't let me?* You think you can stand here, on my ship, and tell me what I can and can't do?" He stopped and stared, measuring her. "That fossil must be important. Why else would you create such an incredible story?"

"Because I'd rather not watch Roarke turn Higo into a dust bowl. I've met some pretty nice people back there; I really don't want to see them, or anyone else, suffer because of you."

Kaidan laughed harshly. "You have a pretty high opinion of yourself, considering how you hide your arrogance behind an unassuming nature."

"I'm not hiding anything. I am who I am."

"A – what did you call it? – *guardian*." Kaidan shook his head in disbelief. He spun on his heels, stalked back to his chair and sat. "Prepare the *Go-Rheeyo* for battle," he said, watching Keiko for the reaction she didn't give. "Launch the Riders. And get those engines back online. The prince is on his way. Unless you'd like to prove what you say is true," he said to Keiko.

"I hoped that wouldn't be necessary, but I sort of figured you'd want some proof. People like you always do." A nimbus of bright burgundy light surrounded Keiko's body. She looked up and made a wide circular motion with her finger. A section of the metal wall aged and rusted. A hole just large enough for her orb opened, revealing clear sky. Keiko lifted from the floor, flew through, and turned. Chestnut eyes burned brightly beyond the bridge's muted light. "I'm sorry, but you don't get a say in this." She made another circular motion with her hand, and the hull repaired itself, the hole disappearing as if it had never existed.

Baiyren punched through a furious squall and into clear air. Water sluiced off his armor. The wind barely touched him. Nothing existed but pain. He'd suffered so much, had lost so much. He tried to push it away, but the images kept coming: members of the Royal Guard who gave up their lives to protect him in battle; friends who deserted to join Kaidan's Riders; his mother; the scientists who went with him to China. Keiko. Juno.

Being with Yohshin helped him forget. Its power overrode his mind, making him feel invincible. Power intensified his sight, gave him the ability to see clearly despite the distance. Kaidan's ship sat in the sky like a titanium vulture. A pair of malignant domes with protruding cannons decorated the spine. The bridge was somewhere in the tower between the guns, probably embedded near the center where angular cuts of metal and impregnable glass bowed outward before tapering back and climbing to an arching observation deck.

Wispy strands of white vapor whipped past him, the clouds that appeared so solid dissolving the farther he flew. Below, turquoise water flashed by, dotted here and there with atolls and other green-covered islands, some large, some small. A perfect azure sky sparkled above; Yohshin's golden armor would be impossible to miss.

Escape pod, Yohshin reported.

Is it Juno? He wanted it to be her, hoped against hope she had found a way to escape.

No, Yohshin reported. *The Heartstone is still aboard the ship.*

And Juno still has it, a voice said in Baiyren's head.

Keiko? Is that you?

Yes, Keiko said. *I've escaped the* Go-Rheeyo, *but I couldn't take Juno with me. Don't worry, the Heartstone will protect her. Stay alert. Watch for Kaidan's armor. She'll be with him.*

How do you know?

Keiko didn't answer. She'd clearly said what she

needed to, taken her burgundy escape pod, and fled. Baiyren flew faster. The *Go-Rheeyo's* guns swiveled toward him. Armored double doors at the back slid open, and a swarm of mah-kai took to the air.

The flagship itself looked like a crooked painting – low aft starboard, high fore port. Apart from the guns and doors, the ship remained motionless. Damaged, perhaps? He wasn't sure. Kaidan might want him to think so. Make him lower his guard. Lure him in.

The *Go-Rheeyo* appeared powerless, the Riders' defensive stance adding to the perception. Instead of charging, they split into three squads. The first surrounded the ship in a blockading formation, the second and third set the perimeter. They kept the space between their lines to a mile or less. Fighting there would be tight, increasing the chance of a stray shot damaging the *Go-Rheeyo*. Or worse.

Baiyren needed to think but didn't have time. His mind became a ceaseless whirlpool. He couldn't focus, couldn't form a plan. Then, an idea clawed its way from the darkness, a strategy. A hope.

Lure them away, Yohshin said, bringing his thoughts to light. *Break their lines and pull them from the* Go-Rheeyo. The mah-zhin showed him where to strike, noted which attacks worked better than others.

Baiyren chose the least likely. The most audacious. He liked the plan, couldn't wait to watch it in action regardless of consequence. Grinning, he lifted his arm.

A thought fired a chain of solid energy that sliced through the atmosphere, blew past the mah-kai's lines, and wrapped around the *Go-Rheeyo's* hull. The charged rope sizzled but didn't cut, and the longer he watched the more he wanted to tighten his noose. It would be so easy. Bring the pressure. Crush the ship. Sever it in two.

He could almost see it happening, could almost hear the shearing metal and the screams of men and women tumbling out. Would Juno be one of them? He imagined her there, her hazel eyes wide with accusation and fear. He couldn't do that to her. He wouldn't. Instead, he pulled back, hauling the chain in with the speed of a released spring.

The *Go-Rheeyo* came with it.

Powerless, the ship was an anchor without weight, a lionfish at the end of a line – caught, possibly wounded, but still deadly. Reeling it in was too easy. Baiyren extinguished the rope and was about to train his weapons on the Riders' first line when the *Go-Rheeyo's* big guns came to life. A Rider, caught between Baiyren and the ship, disintegrated in a blaze of smoke and fire. Baiyren recognized the armor – a mah-kai designed to look like an eagle in flight with wide, sweeping wings and a distinctly avian head. The pilot, Yara Sanish, was a young nobleman from the north who believed – wrongly – that every woman at court desired him. He bragged his mah-kai was the most beautiful one on Higo. Now it was little more than windblown ash.

The explosion charged Baiyren's soul. He wanted to leap forward, to join the carnage and see which of them, him or his brother, would bring down the most fighters. It would be one more game between them, another chance to relive his treasured memories. He thought about their times together: Kaidan laughing as he carried Baiyren on his shoulders, their annual game of search, the emptiness Baiyren felt whenever Kaidan left for Haven.

Lifting his eyes to the wreckage, he watched the gusts blow it all away. Smoke shredded and scattered the dying embers, erasing Sanish's existence from Earth. Behind the emptiness, behind the hole in the sky, the *Go-Rheeyo* adjusted its aim and readied another volley.

Life means nothing to him, Yohshin said. *You have to stop your brother before he spreads his poison.*

The *Go-Rheeyo* fired again, but the energy that burned Sanish away simply broke around Yohshin like waves against stone. He barely felt it; it was a tickle on his skin, the kiss of a light breeze. Baiyren stared into the flashing muzzles, mocking their power, daring them to fire again.

Each Rider they bring down is one less to fight.

But he wasn't here to fight; he was here to free Juno. For that, he needed to draw the Riders from the ship. Kaidan was ruthless enough to kill his own men, what would he do if the tide turned against him? Sacrifice the *Go-Rheeyo* and take out his vengeance on Juno? Baiyren traced the ship's deflected shot as it flew from him. Smoldering stone and boiling ocean marked where it struck. The debris tugged at him. Inspired him.

We are the rock and the earth, Yohshin told him. *They are ours to control. Touch them. Use them! The enemy won't expect you to. They will never see it coming.*

A light, almost paternal amusement flickered back to him. Acquiescence followed, and then Yohshin's presence receded. New thoughts and experiences filled the void left behind. He was an amnesiac whose memory returned in one large flash, a puzzle whose pieces rearranged without help. When complete, he understood more about Yohshin's abilities than ever before.

And they terrified him.

The mah-zhin controlled and manipulated soil and minerals. It commanded a portion of the planet's layered plates from core to mantle. Yohshin tapped into that same energy in China when it uprooted mountains and hurled them at the Riders. Now it offered him that power. Accept it and become the monster he once was. Deny it and condemn Juno to Kaidan's chains.

The choice was no choice at all.

Turning away, he dropped to the ground. The rushing wind tickled him, the cold air growing warmer as he fell. A thought sent power into his arms where it erupted around his gauntleted fists like brilliant sunlight. He held heat and let it build as he selected a target. Islands both large and small thrust from the waves, each as different as one person from another.

Baiyren lifted his arms and aimed at an archipelago of small islands that looked more like forested spears than rock. He checked for signs of life but found none.

He fired.

A squat limestone island to his right disintegrated, a slender sail-shaped one to his left became pulverized dust. Rock shattered, and the green tree-covered tops became torches. Debris drifted upward to stain the perfect sky; slivers of black, like rotting fingers pointing at the devastation below.

Re-sighting, Baiyren fired again. Another island, a cylindrical, moss-covered column toppled like a felled tree. Steam joined smoke, the hiss of vaporized water adding to the crackle of flame in a symphony of destructive sound. He ignored the noise and focused instead on the broken rock. The lightest wafted along the morning breeze while the rest peppered the calm water. Baiyren seized everything – motes, dust, and rubble. He didn't know exactly how he did it, only that the broken earth responded.

He hurled commands into the heavens, packing matter together and sliding the fused whole between the *Go-Rheeyo* and the Riders. Thoughts forged the broken pieces into a wall he then wrapped around Kaidan's ship. Isolated, the mah-kai scattered like a flushed covey. The rear line tried to reform, but farther away. They couldn't afford to stay close, not if Baiyren launched a second rock wall at them. Farther out, the Riders in the middle line held while the outer moved into attack formation behind a large, black mah-kai with thick arms and legs and a helm that resembled a snarling bear.

They were coming for him now. The ship itself lay behind the stone barrier, cannonfire booming as it tried to break free. In the distance a new formation crested the horizon.

Regan's forces, the ones that would attack the *Go-Rheeyo's* back, were in place.

27
AN UNFAMILIAR SELF

Regan swatted at a large boulder with Seraph's arm-mounted shield, blasted a second with helm cannons, and rushed ahead. Instead of tumbling from the sky, the rubble rolled toward an enormous stone ring. More stones followed, forcing her to navigate through debris at high speed. Explosions sounded ahead and behind. Above and below. Some came from the ring itself, others from the Guards' attempt to clear a path through the rubble.

"What the hell happened here?" Gunnar's voice filled her cockpit; he sounded more baffled than fearful.

"Yohshin," Regan said without clarification.

"You sound like you've seen this before."

Regan nodded. "Last time I was here, the mah-zhin uprooted mountains and threw them at the Riders. I meant to ask Baiyren how he did it, but I never had the chance. Maybe he learned during his exile. He always said he needed time to study the thing."

"You also said he's different in the mah-zhin, more aggressive and less careful. Unless you've heard otherwise, we can't assume he's changed."

Regan conceded the point. A tap on a crystal to her right widened her view; a second tap shared it with Gunnar. "All we know for sure is that Baiyren has isolated the *Go-Rheeyo*. The ring itself is the primary boundary, and the wall of incoming rock is the deterrent." She highlighted the space between the Riders and the *Go-Rheeyo's* last known position. "The stones in this area are much closer together, move at a greater velocity, and eventually fuse together. As strong as they are, the mah-kai can't get too close without getting caught."

"Baiyren's trapped the Riders between his attack and our incoming forces."

Regan nodded grimly. "We need to press that advantage. The less support Kaidan has, the better the odds for Baiyren's success." Her thoughts drifted back to the *Go-Rheeyo*. She wondered how Baiyren would maneuver once he was inside the ship. Yohshin was a twohundred foot-tall behemoth. Outside of the hangar, cargo bay, and engineering, no deck was more than ten feet tall. Had he thought of that? Was he thinking about anything other than Juno Montressen?

Regan hesitated. Should she break the Riders' line and cover Yohshin's inevitable approach or support it from a distance? The latter meant light, probing attacks designed to harass the mah-kai and keep them occupied. The former demanded a more significant and prolonged strike.

This wouldn't be easy.

She closed her eyes, and the strange sensation of touching rock, earth, and soil returned. Disillusionment brought dizziness, and for a moment, she didn't know who she was or what she was doing. She pictured boulders soaring upward and then saw them in her view, huge rocks pulled from the Earth and hurtling toward the *Go-Rheeyo*, climbing into the sky, wrapping around the ship. Shielding it.

Fear seized her. She'd always been in control. Now, she didn't know what was happening – either to her or the world around her. She felt as if her consciousness entwined with another, coexisting force. Hope and determination filled one part of her soul, despair and heartache the other. Eventually, they would separate like oil in water. If they didn't, they'd destroy each other. Nausea filled Regan's stomach. Her hands slipped from Seraph's controls and she felt the mah-kai dip.

"Regan!" Gunnar's urgent call hit her like a hard slap.

Her eyes flew open, and she cursed. Somehow, she'd let Seraph drift into the debris field. Broken earth stormed up from below like inverted rain. Several Riders, caught between the new barrage and Baiyren's wall wilted beneath the onslaught, crushed and pummeled into amorphous lumps. One, a squat mech designed to withstand extreme ocean pressure, crumpled as easily as a tin can. The elegant falcon-inspired armor to her left backed away, only to have shrapnel pierce the ordinance on its back and explode. The two Riders had broken away from the main force and stalked toward Regan and her Gaurdsmen. How close were they when the wave hit? Fifteen hundred feet? Less? They were close enough for Regan to see the first cracks in their armor, the leaking fluid, the thin, bloody streams. Rock, dust, and earth swallowed them. She should have been dead too.

Only she wasn't.

The clouds and rubble that crushed the mah-kai blew past. Again, she felt commands hurled into the ground. Unlike before, she recognized the source. This time she knew the orders didn't come from Yohshin; this time, they came from her. Her thoughts and reflexes merged, her subconscious manipulating the Earth, parting it until a wall similar to the one surrounding the *Go-Rheeyo* cradled Seraph, protecting it. Protecting her.

"Regan? Are you all right?" Gunnar sounded desperate.

"I'm fine." Regan lifted her hands and turned them over, examining them. A faint silvery light shimmered from her wrist to her fingers before winking out. In her view, Seraph mimicked her movements. Lowering her arms, she turned to face Gunnar. "Just lucky." Drawing herself up, she pointed to the wall surrounding the *Go-Rheeyo*. The rocks holding it together had thinned until only a fine powder swirled between them. "Ready the Guard. That wall will make the Riders nervous. They can't cover the flagship as long as it's up. Hurry, Gunnar; we don't have much time."

Fifty miles to the northeast, Yohshin cut across the horizon like a golden comet. Friction boiled the humid air around the outer armor into a tail of vivid steam. The mech pulled out of its dive moments before hitting the ocean surface and continued to skim the turquoise seas. Displaced water flumed into the air before returning to earth in a fine, showery mist.

The mah-zhin's passing carved a wide trough in the bay. The ripples grew into dangerous swells that pounded sandy beaches and island cliffs, eroding the former while cutting the latter's foundations. One island, little more than a slender spire of gray rock dotted with spindly trees, cracked at the base and toppled with a large splash.

Yohshin continued on in a fury of rainbows and seawater. The armor plate behind one shoulder opened as it approached a tower of rock. With one swift motion, Yohshin drew a massive chain mace from a hidden sheath. A single swing sheared the island in two. The peak teetered but didn't fall. Gravity reached for the top, grasped at it, and missed. Instead, the cloven limestone shot toward the Riders, swept through their ranks, and headed for the *Go-Rheeyo* like a missile. More islands exploded and more chaos filled the air, filtering light, hiding Yohshin.

"That's it!" Regan cried. "That's his cover. We have to move. *Now*!"

"But that doesn't make any sense," Gunnar protested. "Deep scans can still see him." He paused abruptly. When he spoke again, confusion and disbelief filled his tone. "He's gone. I don't understand; he was just there. We saw him; our instruments identified him."

"He's found a way to make the armor look like any other metal. It's why he's throwing so much into the air. The more we trace him, the harder he is to spot."

Regan grimaced at the thought. She didn't know where it came from, or why, but a window to her soul had opened. Information and understanding flowed into her. Baiyren kept saying how much he hated using Yohshin's power. Finally, she understood what he meant. Could she do what Yohshin did? It seemed impossible, and yet, a part of her thought she could.

You already have.

Again she saw the debris deflected from Seraph. She

shook her head, wrestling with the idea, denying it. Burying it. Her thoughts turned to the forces arrayed before her. Caught between Baiyren's rock wall and Regan's Guard, the Riders swarmed aimlessly around the shielded ship like homeless insects. They couldn't protect the *Go-Rheeyo*, and their enemy eluded them. She had to hit them before they regrouped.

"Yohshin isn't gone, Gunnar," she said. "It's camouflaged. Baiyren's fooling their scans, but they can still identify him visually. We can't let that happen. Ready the Guard. We're charging the Riders on my mark."

"Charging?" Gunnar was incredulous. "You're asking the Guard to fly into *that?*" Saizhen stabbed a needle-like finger at the flying rock. "Those boulders will pulverize us. We should hit them from here. Our weapons have the range."

"A frontal assault will only push them back. We want them as far from the *Go-Rheeyo* as possible."

Gunnar wasn't convinced. "The wall's behind them. The Riders can't go anywhere."

"That doesn't mean they won't try. They're duty-bound to protect Kaidan. The worse their situation, the harder they'll fight." Gunnar grunted his concession, and Regan widened her communication's channel to the rest of the Guard. "Form up! I'm leading you through the debris field; I want all Guardsmen in a single line with no more than ten yards between each of you. Once we're beyond the rocks, fan out and engage the Riders. We need to pull them as far from the *Go-Rheeyo* as possible. Is that clear?"

No one responded; they simply saluted and moved into position behind Seraph without comment. Regan wet her lips. Her men trusted her judgment more than she did herself. What they were about to do was crazy. Battles were unpredictable enough. Minimizing that unpredictability was what won or lost them. The best and longest surviving soldiers were both audacious *and* cautious, planning yet accounting for as much as they could. *This* didn't feel like planning; it felt like desperation.

Reckless, she thought. *Irresponsible*. Reason screamed at her, told her to stop. She ignored her doubts and focused on the path ahead. Dust clouds swirled, and broken monoliths roared past to block her way. She swallowed, uncharacteristically nervous.

Regan's sweat-slick palm connected with Seraph's control crystal, and Seraph inched forward. Staring into a storm of rock and dirt before her, Regan searched for a gap and found none. Adrenaline heightened her senses. Her mind opened. Again, she sensed the world below and the uprooted fragments between the Guard, the Riders, and the *Go-Rheeyo*. Yohshin's thoughts rippled through both, Baiyren's consciousness coating the mahzhin's mind like temporary varnish. The armor's ability and control took her breath away. It wielded elemental solids as if they were part of its body.

Sensing Yohshin's power, she watched Baiyren control the airborne debris, learned what he did, and how. An image formed in her head – one of clearing sky and shielded paths. Regan fixed the picture in her mind and looked on as the flying wreckage parted. A tunnel appeared. Faint, silvery light bathed the inner lining while, beyond that, Yohshin's detritus launched into the air unabated. Regan drove Seraph into the flying maelstrom, her Guard following, their line perfect. Her forces broke apart as soon as they hit the eye and fanned out.

Regan's thoughts drifted to Baiyren. How much time did he need? They didn't have any cover, and they couldn't retreat. The Riders outnumbered them three to one. She thought about the flying stone behind. Could she wield it like Yohshin? Was it worth it? She might succeed in throwing it at the Riders only to watch it ricochet into the Guard. Or worse, plow right over them.

This was the helplessness Baiyren had told her about. The confusion. He knew Yohshin possessed incredible power, but he couldn't predict what would happen when he used it. Too often, his plans spun out of control.

Regan couldn't afford that. The Guard couldn't afford that. And neither could Higo. Better to use what she knew and let her training take over. She'd studied the Riders, both during her time at Tsurmak's military school and since leaving Haven's city limits. She knew them. Their tactics hadn't changed, and she expected them to come at her in a wedge formation, fake battering her line, and then whip the edges past to surround her. She watched them from a distance, her view zooming in to catch their movements.

Downdrafts buffeted the calm seas below. Whitecaps formed, and the water churned ominously. Twelve objects flew in from east and west, and Regan shifted the view. Between them, the lead mech – a sleek metal suit, fashioned in the shape of an elegant dagger – drifted ahead. A gilded crossbar cut across its chest to form a hilt. The lower three quarters of the armored ship tapered to a fine point, their titanium sides as sharp as any blade.

Brother Shimono.

Regan had trained with him; he was a gentle man, pious and quiet and easy to like, especially after he brought her into the magnificent garden he'd spent his life tending. Facing him in battle sickened her. He had a large family, children and grandchildren. How many times had she fought the Riders, and of those, how many had she faced him?

None that she remembered. Regan was still a trainee when she left for Sahqui-Mittama. Her former classmates, if they made it into the Riders at all, would still be lower-level soldiers. Her stomach twisted.

Slowly, regretfully, she ignited Seraph's lance and lifted it high into the air. Silver light shimmered around the cold blade, pale green suffusing the glow. The blazing aura didn't faze Shimono. His mah-kai hefted its great iron sword over its head and, completing his salute, lowered it respectfully.

Regan nodded and, returning her hands to Seraph's controls, ordered the charge.

28
THE LION OR THE GUN

Kaidan rounded on Juno, seizing her wrist and dragging her close. "What was that? Who is she?" His face was feverish, manic even. "Tell me what you know!"

Juno twisted out of his grip. "I don't know anything. I only met her a couple of weeks ago. She said a few things," Juno admitted, hoping it was enough. "But I just thought she was crazy. I mean, who believes stuff like that?"

Kaidan looked like he was about to hit her. Instead he swirled to face the crew. "No one says a word about what happened here. Do you understand?" Everyone answered in the affirmative, but Kaidan wasn't satisfied. He stared at the crew, his face pale, his hands shaking. The silence was palpable, holding and lingering until loud alarms shattered it.

"Yohshin's disappeared," a woman with rust-colored hair reported from a rear station.

"The mah-kai have lost visual," another said. "Baiyren is using the debris as camouflage."

Kaidan glared at Juno, and she fought the urge to

back away. "This isn't over," he said before turning on his heels, heading back to the command chair, and taking a seat. "I need a full report. What are we looking at?"

"Fifteen Riders confirmed down, another five damaged. The mah-zhin's last known position put it outside the rock wall but on a path that would take it to the hollowed-out top – ETA five minutes or less."

Juno looked into the *Go-Rheeyo's* view with wide, tear-filled eyes. A control console stood to her right, and she reached for it, welcoming the cool sturdy metal as she fought to right her world.

Fifteen dead in seconds with more to follow. "What's happened to you, Baiyren?" she whispered. Head shaking, she watched Baiyren's homemade weapons close, spears of rock, limestone missiles. The man she knew would never do this. Never!

Something had changed, but what? She needed to think but didn't have time. How could she understand the whole without the pieces? What was she supposed to do? She clutched at her shirtfront, her thoughts whirling.

Kaidan attacked everything Baiyren treasured: first his mother, then his father, and now... Juno's eyes widened. No! It couldn't be. Realization slammed into her. Kaidan didn't bring her for her archeological expertise, and he sure as hell didn't bring her because he enjoyed her company. She was his hostage, his insurance against Baiyren and his invincible war machine. That might have worked before, but Juno didn't think it would now. Her rescue represented Baiyren's redemption, his last chance to prove his worth, not to Higo, but to himself. This time, Kaidan had miscalculated. Badly. He'd given

Baiyren a reason to fight.

Angrily, she turned her back on the view and faced Kaidan. "I hope you're happy," she spat. "We're all going to die; you know that, right?"

"We don't have a mah-zhin," Kaidan said, without looking at her. He sounded less sure of himself than he did before Keiko's magnificent exit. "I need your relic in its place."

"What if you're dead? If Miko had to choose between you and some stupid fossil, what do you think she'd do? She'll be alone for the rest of her life. Just like your god. Is that what you want?"

Consternation and anger cut across Kaidan's face at the mention of Miko. "We both agreed to this. Miko understood the risks."

"Did she? Did she really? Your engines are down, and even if they weren't, you can't outrun Baiyren, not as far as I can tell. And that's not even including Keiko's revelations." She crossed her arms. "You might get what you came for, but the information will die with you."

Kaidan's gaze slid from the view to regard her with the same cold, pitying stare a snake gives its prey. "I don't need to outrun him when I can out-think him. Opening Portals takes minimal energy; it's remarkably similar to sending a command message. We use the same equipment, frequencies, and communications array. I have enough power for that, Ms Montressen."

"So what? You still can't go through."

Kaidan's eyes glittered like polished silver. "I can if the Riders push me. We'll retrieve the relic and bring it back to Higo." He nodded to the young monk seated just below the command chair. "Brother Onibi, launch the remaining Riders and have them wait for instructions."

"As you command, lord." Onibi's voice was too big for the monk's reedy frame, but even so, Juno barely heard it.

The ridiculous image of tugboats and tow trucks filled Juno's head. Necessity might be the mother of invention, but determination was its father. She should have known Kaidan wouldn't give in so easily. He wanted what his brother had too badly for that. Bitterly, she moved to confront him.

"Don't you want to know why Keiko warned you about the fossil?" she asked, fighting desperation.

She'd almost reached the base of his elevated chair when the Heartstone flared again. Lightless but hot, it burned her skin. *Botua*, it said, its tone hollow and sad. Anger followed. And regret. *This will end like it did for me: in fire.* Power flashed through the stone, seeping into the ship's hull and surging through wires and conduits. Juno felt it slam into crystals, manipulating their structures, overwhelming them.

Juno ground her teeth against the pain, against the futility. Violence. Vengeance. All of it meaningless. The stone's final words ripped at her heart. Anguish filled them, and she felt the open wounds behind the outburst. She wanted to reach out and say something soothing but couldn't. She was a mere mortal, a speck, seeking to heal something greater. She opened her mind, but the voice and the presence behind it had gone. She tried a second time and a third. A low vibration tickled her feet as she began her fourth attempt.

"We have power!" The woman at the helm, Sister Hanoka, glanced at Kaidan with shining eyes. A moment later, more alarms rang out to smother their triumph. Deep and ominous, the first klaxon sounded from Onibi's station like a tolling bell. The monk looked up, his face ashen. "Yohshin's reached the ring's western wall. Seraph is leading a squad of Royal Guard from the northeast."

Kaidan touched a crystal, and the view shifted to Yohshin flying over a beautiful sea. Calm waves, crystal clear waters. The mah-zhin climbed toward the *Go-Rheeyo*, dodging sky-bound boulders as it raced upward. Beside the image, a second scene played out. Here, the stunning armor Juno first saw in China led a large force over a mountainous shoreline. The second weapon was as breathtaking as the first; the blended pastel blues, crimsons, and purples so like a sunset, its golden circlet glinting under the sun. So beautiful. So deadly.

Juno's thoughts flew back to her senior year in high school. Her boyfriend, John McDermitt, captain of the cross-country team, was everything she thought she wanted: smart, funny, handsome, and caring. All her friends wanted him too, but she was the one who won him. They'd dated through the first semester and into the second, and when it came time to apply for colleges, she was stunned to learn he'd sent his application to West Point. West Point! That school turned people into killers.

She was so hurt. How could he do this to her? She called him a murderer-in-training, accused him of worse. Through hot tears, she demanded an explanation. Did her father put him up to it? The senator who liked sending troops to war but had never gone himself?

John placed his hands on Juno's trembling shoulders.

"Your father's got nothing to do with this," he said gently. "There are bad people out there, Juno. People who want to hurt us. Someone's got to stand up to them." Juno started to speak, but he put a finger to her lips. "If a lion's charging at you, you make a choice. It's either the lion or the gun. I'm going to West Point so you never have to choose between one or the other. I'll make sure the lion never gets that close."

The lion or the gun. Those words had stayed with her. She'd never seen a battle then, and now, staring into one, she still disagreed. Lions and men were different. A lion was an animal; you couldn't reason with one the way you could a man.

Juno's gaze slid to Baiyren's half-brother. Kaidan was on his feet, directing the bridge crew, readying them for battle. "Weapons online! I want the forward batteries trained on those incoming mah-kai. Keep the aft guns in reserve; we'll need them for Yohshin. The missiles too. And get that Portal open. We have to get through before the mah-zhin gets too close."

Juno wrapped her arms around her body to suppress a shiver. *Missiles? Jesus!* This wasn't how it was supposed to be.

Sister Hanoka's panicked voice cut through the din. "The power is still climbing. Engineering, weapons, life support. Everything. There's nothing I can do!"

Isshi rushed to Hanoka's station, placed an arm on the back of her chair, and leaned over to study her instruments. His gaze flicked from one to the next, each glance drawing more blood from his face. "The crystals are overloading." Panic laced his otherwise even tone. He stood and turned to Kaidan. "We don't have much time. Ten minutes at most before the ship blows. You need to launch the remaining mah-kai. Get as many off as you can."

"As many as you can? You mean you can't get everyone off?" Juno felt sick. The *GoRheeyo* was huge; it needed a large crew. But how large? A hundred? More? Her hand found the Heartstone. *Stop it,* she pleaded. *Please.* The stone didn't answer. After sending the power surge into the *Go-Rheeyo,* it had gone silent.

"We removed escape craft to make room for more Riders. They were our defense against the mah-zhin." The defeated slump of Isshi's shoulders said he realized what a mistake that had been.

The mah-zhin! Juno glanced at the large screen above her. Yohshin raced toward the stone ring like a golden comet; the Royal Guard closed from the opposite direction. *The lion or the gun.* One or the other. She stared at the incoming forces and saw them not as a threat, but as salvation. Her ex-boyfriend was wrong; it didn't have to end the way he thought. And she could prove it.

Spinning about, she raced to Kaidan's command chair. "Send out a distress call. Ask Baiyren for help." She stabbed a finger at the view. "Between your forces, you should be able to evacuate the whole crew. No one has to die, Kaidan."

She swallowed and stepped back, anxiously waiting for his response. She'd given him a way out; he had to see that. This is what Keiko was trying to tell her. She could stop the fighting if everyone stood down. Saving his crew and ending the tension between the Haven and the crown would make Kaidan a hero; Higo would revere him. That kind of leverage brought power – as much as any king. She looked up at him, stared into his eyes, hoping to see his understanding. Willing it.

Instead, pity drew his brows together, the same pity, the same disdain her father had for his constituents. The disdain of the ruler for the ruled. She'd seen it her whole life, hating it as much now as ever.

"Ask Baiyren for help," she repeated, hating her pleading tone.

Kaidan ignored her. He stood and studied the bridge crew. "Order the Riders to their mah-kai," he said. "Everyone else stays. Keep the *Go-Rheeyo* on alert with its weapons primed. Do whatever you can to lure Baiyren into the blast radius. The explosion will do the rest."

"*What*?" The word left Juno's lips like a last breath – low, constricted, and weak. Her hopes, once so strong, became fragile soap bubbles. Kaidan climbed from the command chair, took her wrist, and led her toward a rear elevator. She barely noticed. She couldn't think, couldn't control her body. She stared at Kaidan, at his lean frame and dark, almost feverish eyes. Anger roiled them, the promise of vengeance tightening his jaw. Her body slumped. How had she failed so badly?

She started to speak, but a swift movement from her left startled her to silence. "I respectfully surrender my mah-kai to another crew member."

Juno blinked. "Isshi?" she said, her head clearing. "What are you doing?"

Isshi ignored her. "I am a bishop of the church, and these men are my responsibility. I want to stay with them."

Kaidan leaned close to the bishop and dropped his voice. "I can't let you do that, Isshi. The church needs you; I need you."

"The crew needs me more. They're mostly children. You can't ask me to leave them now."

"Isshi–"

"Avenge us, my lord." Isshi stepped back, his finger touching a crystal on the wall. The hidden door opened silently to his right. "Give our death meaning."

The words slapped Juno from her stupor. She lunged forward, jerking to a halt as Kaidan's hand tightened around her wrist. A low humming filled the ship as the building power reached critical levels. Explosions followed. Overhead, power surged into the view; the screen flared, bright and blinding, then went dark. The few minutes Isshi gave them had run out: the *GoRheeyo* was coming apart.

Juno didn't care. Isshi had been good to her; she couldn't let him die. She struggled to free herself. "Let me go! You can't leave him behind!" Her feet scrabbled against the floor, its surface too smooth for them to grip.

"He's made his choice," Kaidan said, pulling Juno into the waiting elevator.

"I told you to let me go!" Juno tried to throw her free arm between the closing doors only to have Kaidan haul her back. "*Isshi!*" she screamed. "*Isshi! No!*"

Isshi smiled at her through the narrowing gap, his face calm, serene. "It's all right, Juno. We go to meet our Lord. He will care for us."

The doors shut with an ominous hiss, and Juno stopped struggling. Tears rolled down her cheeks. She was dimly aware of Kaidan releasing his hold. She fell, and her hands pounded against cool metal until her strength gave out.

29
NO MORE RUNNING

Baiyren pointed Yohshin's mace at a sail-shaped island to his right. A single shot sliced off the top third and sent rocks tumbling hundreds of feet into the waiting seas. A wall of water erupted high into the air, and Yohshin burst through, wove in and around a maze of flying limestone teeth, and made for the half mile-wide stone ring surrounding the *Go-Rheeyo*. He didn't need the extra stone – in truth, the more he added, the more he had to remove to reach the trapped ship.

Why did he do it then? Because he enjoyed it? Maybe, but even if he did, that wouldn't help him. He needed to think strategically – like Regan. For the first time since finding Yohshin, he was sure he could.

The stone ring he and Yohshin created loomed ahead, and he angled upward, skimming the surface until he reached the top. There, he landed close to the inner lip and looked down at the trapped and lifeless flagship.

Where are the guns? he wondered. *Where are the defenses?*

Apart from the mah-kai trapped outside the stone, all was quiet. Baiyren leaned forward for a better look.

The muscles in his neck – already tense and knotting – brought a dull ache. He reached up to massage it out, remembered the mah-zhin's armor, and promptly lowered his arm. Peering down, he searched for life but didn't find any. The *Go-Rheeyo* looked more like a berthed ship than an active one. Nothing moved, and despite Yohshin's presence the gun turrets remained silent.

Baiyren frowned. Power loss would do that, but was it accidental or intentional? Just because a target looked idle didn't mean it was. Baiyren scrubbed a hand across his faceplate. Should he strike? Should he wait? Each second was one more Kaidan had to plan.

Explosions pulled his attention away from the battleship and up the far wall. Another came, thick, billowing clouds wafting up a second later. Concussive waves came last, loud, incessant, and deep. Yohshin moved toward the chaos and crouched. Carnage filled the air, embers arcing toward the seas like dying comets. A gust shredded overcast skies to reveal Seraph's graceful form deep in the clouds. It hovered motionless, a lance of silver and green energy sizzling in its hand. Below, a decapitated mah-kai tumbled earthward. Sparks danced across its blemished plates. Those closest to the neck leached a stream of viscous liquid.

Seraph watched the wreck slam into the waves before lifting its lance in a formal salute and hurrying off to engage more incoming Riders. More sounded. A great weight formed in Baiyren's chest, another in his stomach. He shouldn't have let Yohshin distract him, shouldn't have hesitated. Now it could be too late. Sickened, he catapulted into the air.

The *Go-Rheeyo* loomed beneath him, light flickering

behind bulging hull seams, in portholes, and on the
bridge. The brightest came from the aft section, where
a ramp abruptly dropped down. A lone mah-kai shot
out – deep blue with white accents and a horned helm.
Another followed, and then another, until the initial
trickle became a steady stream. Flames licked at their
heels, while overhead, a large section of the wall burst
open. Inside, a silvery glow illuminated the darkness.
Green tinted it, growing in intensity until finally Seraph
emerged from the smoldering hole.

A massive, elephantine mah-kai with wide shoulders
and great curled tusks trailed Regan's armor. Wrist
cannons fired continuously, bright red streams that
Seraph evaded easily. Several more Riders appeared,
twenty in all, a menagerie of differing styles; some
resembled animals, others mythological creatures, the rest
either a combination of the two or some warped human
mutation. Baiyren couldn't count them all, and he didn't
need to. His gaze remained on the lead mah-kai, a big
black suit with curled horns on its head, anger contorting
its face, and bright yellow eyes burning like twin furnaces.
Righteous, Kaidan named it, Haven's finest armor and
premier defender. Until they woke Zuishin.

Zuishin.

Powerful emotions flared in Yohshin's consciousness.
Rage. Resentment. Jealousy. The mah-zhin's lock on
Seraph wavered, and it turned its attention to the ever-
growing Portal. The rearguard stopped just beyond the
entrance, pivoted, and fired a beam of golden light into
the opening. Rock groaned; stone melted. The tunnel
Seraph drilled through the rock vanished as if it never
existed.

Another battle raged on three thousand feet above him, the *Go-Rheeyo* coming apart half that distance beneath. He leapt forward as Yohshin's thoughts stirred. The *Go-Rheeyo*'s image shifted in his head, and he felt the Heartstone moving along with Righteous.

Juno. Hope and relief washed over him. He started moving toward Kaidan's mah-kai, but Yohshin brushed him aside and headed for another part of the battle. His eyes darted up, locking on Seraph, tracking the mah-kai's fight intently.

A part of him hoped Yohshin would rush to Regan's aid, block him from fighting, and free Juno's fate from his calamitous hands. Doing nothing meant letting her live. But for how long? Kaidan wanted Baiyren to suffer, and as soon as Juno outlived her usefulness, Kaidan would kill her.

Two battles in two different directions. Deep down, he knew which one they'd join. Yohshin's will overpowered his whenever it mattered. What was he as far as it was concerned? An afterthought? Something to tolerate because… *Because it needed him!*

Baiyren smiled. Finally, he had leverage, something he could use to get his way.

Eyes closing, he calmed his mind and pictured his body leaving the mah-zhin. Light suffused him, his skin tingled, and the slow build of wind, loud and keening, filled his ears. He saw the stone ring above and pictured the rippling ocean far below. In seconds he would be there, unprotected, falling to Earth. Was it worth it? Would Juno understand what he did for her? The wind grew into a neverending crescendo. He embraced the sound, the feel of it. He was ready to join with the gales when Yohshin's voice filled the silence.

Stop, Prince of Higo! You'll destroy us both.

Baiyren doubted that. Nothing harmed Yohshin. Nothing could. *Not unless you do as I say. Regan can take care of herself. We need to help Juno.*

The Heartstone protects her. She is safe.

Baiyren didn't think so. If Yohshin could exaggerate its vulnerability, it could also overstate the Heartstone's protection. *She won't be safe until she's away from Kaidan, Haven, and everything else poisoning Higo. I'm going after her, even if I have to eject to do it.*

Yohshin hesitated. Did it believe him? Probably. It wouldn't have spoken to him if it didn't. Silence stretched between them, broken time and again by the huge explosions rocking the *GoRheeyo*. The once sleek airship yawed to one side, pitched downward, and fell from the sky like a wounded bird. Smoke poured from the cuts in its hull, and flames leaked out of its sleek silvery skin, the trail lengthening as the wreckage picked up speed.

What's it going to be, Yohshin? We're running out of time. A curtain of pure energy appeared near the far wall, a large and growing Portal that reached for the dying ship. The *GoRheeyo* gleamed before it, a spark of silver and orange flame fleeing its light. How long before the curtain consumed it?

Baiyren held his breath. He'd always run from a fight. Not this time. This time he urged Yohshin to join one. His heart railed against the decision, but his instincts said to stand firm. He turned his thoughts to Yohshin. *Juno is my responsibility,* he said. *You won't interfere. Do you understand?*

Grudging acceptance rippled through the bond he shared with Yohshin. The mah-zhin knew what he'd do if it fought too hard. That comforted him. A small victory, but an important one. He was tired of running. His smile grew; he was at peace. The time had come to take a stand – for Juno, for Higo.

For himself.

30
INTO THE PORTAL

Juno huddled in the mah-kai's gigantic hand. She shivered against the cold she never planned for, gulping at the thin air, fighting for breath. She didn't dare look down, was afraid to see how high they were. Above was even worse. Silver flashed there, then orange and yellow. Heat followed, the acrid tang of smoke accompanying it. Within the howling wind, she heard a muffled shrieking, and it took her a moment to recognize the voice as her own.

She tried to burrow deeper, knowing it was useless. Consciously, she understood the black metal wouldn't give, but that didn't stop her from trying. Reflex and survival instincts overrode reason as her arms came up to cover her head. Not that it mattered. What was her body compared to the *Go-Rheeyo's* flaming wreckage? Pieces screamed past, one after another, some close, others less so. Over and over she flinched, refusing to look, afraid of seeing Isshi's broken body tumbling away from her. She recalled his kind face, easy smile, bright gray eyes, and gentle nature. Tears spilled over her cheeks. Isshi stayed behind to comfort the men and women Kaidan abandoned. How many would a ship as big as the *Go-Rheeyo* need? Isshi said only the Riders with mah-kai would leave, which meant the rest were dead or dying.

The fleeing Riders didn't even try to save them, soldiers who were supposedly men of God. *Men of God*, Juno snorted. They carried themselves like warriors. She'd met some in the hangar, a solemn group – men and women alike – calmly making their way to the waiting mah-kai while loud booms rocked the ship. Neither affected the Riders, who boarded and launched without fear.

Without fear. The thought brought a bitter laugh. Knowing you had a mah-kai standing by did a lot to calm your nerves. She remembered rushing through the hangar, fifty armored suits on either side. The mechs were a blur of crystal and strong metal, and though different in design, they blended together in Juno's head until a suit of shining blue plate caught her eye. Tall and elegant, with a crested helm and a long, lean body, it opened its chest-hatch slowly, almost reluctantly, for the figure kneeling before it.

Brother Onibi didn't look up, but Juno recognized him all the same. Youth's blush had left him, anguish and sorrow morphing him into a figure with rigid shoulders and a haunted expression. A ceremonial hammer dangled from his hands, its chain wrapped around his wrists like cuffs. It wasn't his. Monks of lower rank wore steel hammers. This was black onyx; only the high clergy had those.

Isshi. The *Go-Rheeyo*'s oldest crewman sacrificed his life for the youngest. Juno's throat tightened. The tears she thought spent threatened again. They needed more men like Isshi. Hopefully, Onibi would remember what the bishop did and follow that example. She shook her head, knowing the only way wars really ended was when the next generation tired of them.

Which is exactly what she'd tried to do. She spent a life railing against the conflicts her father supported. Necessary, he called them. Patriotic. In the country's national interest. She never believed him. He used his influence as senator to send men and women to die because doing so kept getting him elected. Juno hated him for that. She wanted to make a difference but couldn't. She didn't have power or money or influence.

Now she did.

The wind still screamed through the mah-kai's fingers, a mournful, keening sound that carried the cries of the dying. The noise clawed at Juno as if begging for justice, pushing at her, threatening to buffet her away. She ignored the sound and pushed herself unsteadily to her feet. Despite the danger, despite the mah-kai's smooth and slippery surface, she turned to face the giant armor. An air of brutality swirled around the machine – in its yellowed eyes and angular face. Malevolent spikes thrust from iron epaulets, three per shoulder; another set, though smaller, sprang from each knuckle. This was a thing of nightmares, part monster, part demon.

Shoulders back, she hurled her voice at the helmeted head. "You said no one would get hurt!" She expected the wind to snatch her words away, but they rang out like clear bells. A sphere of living fire burned at her chest, embracing her voice, magnifying it. Giving her power. "How many have to die, Kaidan? How much blood is enough?"

The mah-kai's head tilted toward her, draping her body in shadow. "A plague ravages Higo, and we are its cleansing fever. Just as a body's defenses fight infection, so too do we sacrifice to preserve the whole. Higo's rulers lost their way a long time ago. How else do you explain what the king and his advisors did to my mother? She was nothing to them. They took her life, took her child, her love, and her youth and cast them away as soon as they had what they wanted. Debauchery like that has consequences. God won't stand for it; He lost his wife to violence. When He realizes what the king's done He'll destroy us. I have to bring those responsible to justice. It's the only way to save our world."

"You're using *that* to justify all this? Jesus, Kaidan." Juno threw her hands into the air. Wind whipped her sleeves and pushed at her body, threatening to force her from the mah-kai's hand. "Do you even know what you're saying? What happened to your mother sucks; I get that. But because of you, some other kid's lost his mother or father or both. And it's not just kids; this war is stealing husbands from wives and wives from husbands. You're doing exactly what your father did but a whole lot bigger. How do you think your god feels about that?" The mah-kai's fingers flinched, but Juno held her ground. "Go ahead. Add me to the list. What's one more?"

A dull glow burned in the armor's yellow eyes, but the fingers pulled back. "You're an outsider; you wouldn't understand. You don't know our ways; you never saw how righteous our people used to be. But that was before my father sanctioned hedonism and immorality. Now we're nothing but an embarrassment.

We're selfish people who turned our backs on God and debased ourselves." His voice faded, and when it came back it took on the musing quality of one speaking to himself. "Bringing Higo back won't be easy. We'll have to mandate church attendance and create severe penalties for absences. Everyone goes, no excuses. It's the only way to restore lost morality. After that, we can enforce the laws against prostitution and create new ones to fight infidelity and illegitimacy."

The words cut through Juno like the frigid wind. She wanted to clamp her hands over her ears or wrap her arms about her head, anything to keep from hearing more.

"Once we've seen to the major cities, we'll turn our attention to the nomads on the plains. They're decadent heathens. Punishment is not enough for them; we've tried it before, and it's never worked. This time, we'll just have to wipe them out. It's the only way."

The longer Kaidan spoke, the more Juno recoiled. Her body went numb and she wanted to scream at him, to tell him he was exchanging one form of tyranny for another. But her mouth was frozen, her lungs empty. Grief and rage had wormed their way into Kaidan's soul and twisted what was once a normal man. John McDermitt tried to warn her about what happened to a madman with an army at his command and a church to support atrocity. She didn't want to believe it; even now, a part of her resisted, believing she could convince Kaidan to… To what? Ignore a lifetime of pain and humiliation? She might as well talk to a hurricane.

Sobs built in her chest, rolling upward and threatening to wash over her. Everything she thought was right now seemed wrong. She'd been so naïve. Kaidan was Juno's charging lion, Higo his prey. Nothing she said could stop him. War stalked him, Yohshin ambushed him, and somehow he escaped every time. Already, she watched Kaidan's mech lift its free arm, thrust its hand forward, and fire a beam of light into the sky. Energy twisted into a sizzling, power-infused rope that raced for the wall ahead only to slam into an invisible barrier well short of it. There, power rippled outward, spreading and widening until a Portal took shape.

How far was it? Juno glanced up and caught a glimmer of gold far overhead, too far, she thought, to reach Kaidan before he escaped. The mah-zhin was fast, faster than anything she'd ever seen. It just wasn't fast enough, not with the Portal so close.

The first mah-kai filed in: a gray figure shot through with amber veins, a jade green giant whose armored body resembled a runner's lean frame. The last – a crimson suit with a sickle moon on its helm – dropped from above and looked over its shoulder. Juno didn't remember seeing it in the hangar, but with all the chaos, she could have missed it. The mech paused in front of the Portal. Juno's breath caught. Was it looking at her? It seemed to. Either at her or the gem around her neck. She peered at it, trying to follow its piercing gaze; but it turned away before she could decide which.

The Heartstone? She'd almost forgotten it. Would it help her now? Lifting her hand, she clasped the pendant. Her thoughts flew into it, frantic and pleading. *Help me! Can't you see what he's doing? Why won't you do something?*

Heat coursed through her body like liquid metal, reaching for her while racing for the Portal. It slammed into the white light, power against power, one commanding, another yielding. Gasping, Juno crumpled to the mahkai's palm. Vaguely, she was aware of a change in the gate. It looked bigger, more menacing. Sparks flew from the edges, increasing its size. In seconds, the opening filled the sky. A sharp burning seared her palm, and the acrid smell of charred skin assaulted her nose. She shook her head to clear the frantic buzzing that filled her ears. The sound came again, more insistent, and Juno realized Kaidan was speaking to her.

"What have you done?" he screamed.

Juno opened her mouth to speak. She wanted to deny any involvement but couldn't. Unable to meet his gaze, she turned her head away and watched the Portal swallow her world. Explosions sounded, but they were far away. If not for the flames she might not have noticed. These came in flickering light that tinted the Portal's white walls with wild and angry color. As Juno's mind drifted, the words that first erupted from the Heartstone filled her head.

"Sometimes, the sky is red," she recited, drowsily.

At dawn, the stone answered. *And at dusk.*

Juno nodded, her thoughts fading. "The color of fire," she murmured.

And blood.

31
BOY AND MAN

Juno's subconscious wandered aimlessly through a dark, forbidding plain. Tall, sere grass surrounded her, the ground below dry and dusty. Overhead, roiling clouds ran from horizon to horizon, while to her left and right, golden eyes gleamed in the darkness. Juno looked fearfully to one side, glanced to the other. She knew she was dreaming, but her heart pounded nonetheless. The surrounding world was so real, so terrifying. She heard each rustle of grass, each menacing growl. A musky animal odor mixed with the scent of dry leaves and arid dirt. They were closing in on her, surrounding her.

The first shadow crept from the reeds behind. Another followed. And a third. Juno didn't need the dim light to know what they were; her thoughts had summoned them, conjured them from fear and guilt. The first lion lifted its head, its roar shattering the silence like a bugler's trumpet. Was it a signal or a warning? Juno didn't know, and as her mind wrestled with the question, the pride separated to form a path. A huge, glowing shape strode through the gap between them, tall, magnificent, and rare. White fur covered its feline body, from its great flowing mane to the end of its tufted tail. Wise eyes the color of Bermuda sand regarded her without fear.

She scrabbled back, knowing it was useless. Where would she go? Where could she hide? Hunger burned in the lion's imperious eyes; it would have her. She swallowed, retreated a few paces. The lion came forward, more measuring than attacking. Waiting for the inevitable. It didn't wait long. Unable to contain her fear, Juno turned and ran blindly into the grass. She felt the big cat bound after her, imagined its breath on her neck, its claws raking her back. Sobs warred with panting, each inhalation growing shorter. More painful.

Swerving right, she veered onto a dirt road. Deep ruts cut through it, but she didn't slow. If she hit one and twisted her ankle, the end would just come sooner. Sooner than what? Her legs already burned. She couldn't go much farther. Maybe she could reach the hilltop ahead. How far was it? How tall? Frantically, she traced a line from the base to the summit, climbing over downtrodden grass and beaten earth. There, standing tall and comforting at the summit, she saw a familiar figure staring down at her.

He looked exactly as he had the last time she'd seen him. Short dark hair perfectly cut and brushed back from his boyish face, square jaw, dark eyes, and broad shoulders. His varsity jacket rippled in the air before shifting into army fatigues. His face, John McDermitt's happy face, grew serious. He lifted his arm, offered it to her. His fist held a long-barreled rifle, cool and glinting in the moonlight. Adrenaline surged through her. She raced forward, hope building. The distance lessened, then grew. She reached for the gun, then fell back toward the darkness. For each inch she gained, she seemed to lose three. Then, incredibly, she was close. Her hand came up, grasping and flexing like a beggar's. Fingers spread, she reached for it, reached for sanctuary and damnation, only to have a blinding light tear it away.

She squinted and blinked. Her eyes fluttered open. She saw steep cliffs dropping into a stormy sea. Above them, walls climbed into ramparts beyond which a city seemingly carved from stone climbed out of the earth.

Higo. She was back on Higo. Groaning, she pushed herself into a sitting position and looked up. Oily clouds smeared the shining cobalt sky in a dying arc that began at the closing Portal and stretched toward her like a grasping hand. Juno followed the path from its origin, down the billowing trail, and on to the fiery head directly above her. The disintegrating *Go-Rheeyo* sputtered like a dying comet, the hull breaking apart halfway between the tapered nose and the towering bridge. Flames sprouted from either end, trailing smoke and showering the sea with burning debris.

The shape grew in the sky, huge and ominous and heading straight for her. The starboard wing and the bottom third of the bridge tower disappeared as new explosions ripped through both. Juno flinched at the shrapnel sizzling toward her. A large section of hull smashed into the smaller pieces, igniting the fragments and blowing them away like discarded petals.

Juno was exposed, vulnerable. She tried to hide in the mah-kai's sheltering hand, but she knew the fingers towering over her offered minimal protection. Kaidan screamed something at her – a question. An accusation.

She strained to hear him, but the *Go-Rheeyo*'s death throes were too loud.

He probably blamed her for this, just as he had before they entered the Portal. *Do I really care what he's saying?* This wasn't her fault; it was his. He was the aggressor; he started the war. And for what? Personal justice? That wasn't a reason to sacrifice so many lives. She glanced up at the wreckage. A part of her hoped it would slam into Kaidan's armor and take Haven's leader and his war with it. That turned out to be wishful thinking; the mah-kai banked away long before Juno felt the heat from the first flaming pieces. Not that the change increased *her* survival chances.

The once-flat palm tilted sickeningly, and she began an ominous slide toward one edge. Digging her rubber shoes into the metal barely slowed her skid. She slammed her hands down, felt them burn. Wide blue skies opened before her, drawing closer. How far was it? Juno swallowed and redoubled her efforts. Her first foot hit open sky just as Kaidan rolled again. This time, the mah-kai's free hand came up to cover the one holding her.

Juno was grateful for the protection, but it didn't stop her from tumbling back across the palm and slamming into one of the cupped fingers. Pain radiated from her left shoulder and again at her elbows. It was better than the alternative. Not that she had to worry about it. The mech had already leveled out. The air quieted, and the hand sheltering her withdrew.

Warm air assaulted her body. Smoke threaded through it, blistering heat intermittently spiking then falling. Juno knew both came from the *Go-Rheeyo*, even if she couldn't still see it. Nothing else moved in the sky, not bird, or mah-kai, or cloud. The flagship was the only object she'd seen, and the black trail before her marked its descent better than any beacon. She wondered about that, wondered where the Riders had gone. They entered the Pathways before Kaidan but were nowhere to be seen. The *Go-Rheeyo* had been directly above and falling toward them. That it followed the mah-kai into the Portal wasn't a surprise; the Riders' absence however...

She held onto the mah-kai's finger, hauled herself to her feet, and scanned the skies. Nothing above, ahead, or behind... Which only left down. She swallowed uncomfortably. The *Go-Rheeyo* was down there, and she didn't want to see it, didn't want to know what happened to the crew. *If I don't, who will? Kaidan?* She couldn't trust him to tell the story without alteration. The dead deserved better than that, their families too. Without her, they'd have no witnesses. Fear shackled her, and she fought it. *Come on, Juno,* she thought. *You can do this.* Her head dipped, her chin lowered. She looked to the horizon to steady her nerves and slowly inched her unwilling gaze toward the sea.

Red flickered inside the blackness like embers in charcoal, but the clouds were too thick for her to see more than the occasional flashes of metal. She heard them, though, heard every deathly rattle. Her voice joined the symphony in a long and piercing wail, a desperate aria, a eulogy. She cried for the future the crew would never have. The unfulfilled wishes and dashed dreams. At first, she couldn't bring herself to look, and now she couldn't look away – not when the *Go-Rheeyo* smashed into the seas, not when it broke apart.

To its left, a gigantic wall climbed out of the waves, and beyond that a large city sprawled inland, its graceful spires bright in the morning sunshine. A large crowd had gathered around the parapets. Men, women, and children stared out with ashen faces and tortured expressions. A few turned in her direction and pointed. More followed. Panic rippled through them, and before long, they backed away, slowly at first but gaining speed as they retreated like the tide below.

Kaidan ignored the scene, rolled away, and aimed for the sprawling cluster of buildings and towers at the rear wall. There, a giant keep dominated a large citadel. Brown stone climbed upward in the series of subtle ledges, hidden parapets, and discreet windows. Flying arches that might have been carved by the wind joined the towers to other turrets. The roof was cut at irregular angles that reminded Juno of the American southwest.

Like Haven, the city's organic beauty took her breath away. She thought of Baiyren running from his home and going to hers. Did he feel the same wonder about Earth? She didn't think so. For him, it was a sanctuary, a place to forget the past and start over. She couldn't blame him for that. Higo's war revolved around him, not because of anything he did, but because he existed. Would she have done the same in his place? She gnawed on her lip, uncertain. She'd never been in a position where people lived or died because of her decisions. The thought sobered her, explained the sadness she saw behind his eyes.

He'd been getting better too, but that was before Higo's war caught up with him. Looking up, she stared at Kaidan's mah-kai, and her anger died. Baiyren's brother grieved too, he just dealt with it differently. When she first met Kaidan, she assumed he was emotionally stronger, but she didn't think so now. He was the charging lion from her dream, a deeply wounded one. Had anyone tried to heal him?

She doubted it.

Sycophants and enablers surrounded rulers, something she'd experienced firsthand with her father. People who wanted or needed something, people afraid to confront or contradict. Miko could stand up to Kaidan, but the high priestess obviously chose not to. His rage fueled her revolution; she'd never defuse it.

Which left... Who? Who could reason with him? Who could make him pull back? Miko wouldn't and Isshi hadn't been able to. Kaidan shrugged off Juno's attempts, both on the *GoRheeyo* and after. He didn't listen to her then, and she doubted he would now. Her faith in diplomacy died with Isshi, her naivety along with it. Unfortunately for the people in the city, she was all they had.

Releasing the mah-kai's finger, she drew a deep breath and was about to speak when Kaidan hurled the mech's free hand into the tower wall. Stone cracked and a large section opened behind it. A young man, no more than a boy, in a light brown robe fell from the tower. Terror played across his youthful face as he lost his balance and toppled over. An older woman with iron-gray hair pulled severely into a bun raced over, barely stopping before she reached the hole. She wore a charcoal dress that hung loosely on her pudgy frame. Her hands covered her mouth, her eyes tearing. Carefully, she slid forward one inch at a time. She was careful enough, or would have been if the floor above hadn't come crashing down upon her.

Red spray joined the flying dust, sickening Juno. Her stomach heaved. She tried to scream, but shock paralyzed everything but her eyes and her mind. Those tortured her, revealing her helplessness.

"I know you're in there!" Kaidan bellowed. He cocked the mah-kai's arm and launched another strike at the keep. The stone beneath cracked and tore free. Large chunks slammed into a low building at the tower's base; dust flumed, and dark liquid oozed from the rubble. "Show yourself! Come out and face me!" The mah-kai drew its arm back a third time, but instead of launching its fist into the turret, the armor paused.

Juno wrenched her eyes from the pooling liquid and stared into the darkened keep. Something moved inside, something important enough to earn a reprieve. Gradually, a gaunt, shambling man in white robes emerged from the shadows. His proud, regal face and sharp eyes seemed at odds with his shrunken frame, but when he spoke, his voice was surprisingly strong.

"*That* was unnecessary, Kaidan." The man gestured, first at the ruined siding, then at the bloodstained rubble far below. "I can't move quickly, thanks to the *gift* the church's craftsman prepared for me." He shook his head sadly. "I'll admit… I'm surprised to see you. I didn't think you wanted to do this yourself."

The mah-kai's arm whipped past Juno and slammed harmlessly into the wall to the man's right. Startled, she lost her footing and would have fallen if not for the tight hold she had on the metal finger to her left.

"How dare you lecture me about morality? You took an innocent girl from the city and turned her into a prostitute. Everyone knows it." Kaidan opened the armored breastplate and thrust his body forward. The restraints dug into his robes, pulling him back. "Were you relieved to hear she died, your *majesty?* Was it good to be rid of that particular problem?"

"We've all done things we're ashamed of. Or should be." Smiling sadly, the king hooked his fingers through the slender golden chain around his neck and pulled. A pendant similar to the Heartstone appeared from his robes. "You are better than this, my son."

Kaidan's expression darkened. "You can't trace any of that to me," he said defensively. "All you have is the word of a mercenary."

"I have more than that." King Tallaenaq lowered his head and shook it. Grief lined his thin face. He inhaled deeply, a raspy sound, more like a death rattle than a breath. "Fifty years ago, while working a mine in the Rake, a group of researchers from the church unearthed a vein of glowing metal. They'd never seen anything like it and were curious about its properties. Their leader took a small sample back to their labs for study." The king's head came up, his eyes bright, though pained. "The entire team died within a week, and the technicians working on the material followed days later. The high priest immediately ordered the researchers to return the metal, seal the mine, and destroy anything associated with it. No one was to know it existed. Not ever. Only one record remained. The one I keep in my library."

Kaidan paled. Juno knew guilt when she saw it, and despite his best efforts, Kaidan looked like a boy who had hit a ball through his neighbor's window. "How did you find out?"

The king pushed closer to the edge of the tower. A dizzy drop lay beneath him. "As fate would have it, Baiyren had a device that detected radiation. He knew as soon as he came to see me. I didn't believe him; I didn't *want* to believe him." He let go of the torn brick, his eyes misting. "I knew what you were doing at Haven; I knew about your army and how you co-opted the Riders. Regan urged me to stop you, and against my better judgment, I left you alone. I know what it's like to have blood on your hands; I didn't want that for you. It's why I let you get this close. I won't let you kill me, Kaidan. I won't let you live with that guilt."

Juno's chest seized. She cursed. Why didn't she see it? A part of her wondered where the city's defenders had been. And now she knew. Helplessly, she watched the king spread his arms and lean forward. He smiled through tears and nodded.

"I'm sorry, my son. Sorry for so many things. I'll always regret what I did to your mother, what we all did. Understand, though, that I had you because of it, and I wouldn't change that – not for anything. You're my boy, my little Kaidan. I hope one day you'll remember how much I loved you."

It was over in seconds. One moment, the king floated in the air, the wind keeping his slight body aloft like an autumn leaf. Then, after what felt like an eternity, he dropped from sight and disappeared into the ruin below.

32
A FALLEN HERO

A deep and suffocating silence blanketed the castle grounds, crushing Juno's spirit like a can in the deep. She gulped for air, her chest burned, and her eyes were raw. Death was everywhere, swirling around her in tightening circles. First Isshi and the *Go-Rheeyo*, then the keep's two servants. The king was Kaidan's latest victim and likely not his last. So many dead in such a short time. One moment they were there, their lives burning brightly through time, then, like wind-stolen flames, they were gone.

She desperately missed Keiko, missed having someone to talk to, to lean on and turn to for guidance. She hadn't realized how much she'd relied on the other woman until now. Keiko never took the lead, and apart from her dramatic exit, she let Juno handle most situations. Juno thought she understood why. Keiko knew far more than Juno ever could; she was comfortable in this strange and often unbelievable situation. In allowing Juno to step forward, Keiko was building her confidence.

Unfortunately, that confidence only lasted as long as

Keiko was with her. Kaidan's recent carnage had numbed her. After Isshi, the king's death hit Juno the hardest. He was Baiyren's father. She'd deny romanticizing getting to know him, of him getting to know her, of her winning his approval.

That would never happen now. She thought of Baiyren, and her stomach twisted. How would she tell him? What would she say? Deep down, she knew he was strong; she believed that with all her heart. But tragedy had buried that strength beneath a thick yet brittle layer. Something like this could shatter him. Could she do that to him? His happiness was everything to her. She loved how she made him laugh, loved the light in his eyes when he looked at her. Dimming that would shatter her too.

Too quickly, she uncoiled her bent body. Blood rushed from her head. She staggered, and the firm metal beneath her feet became emptiness as she pitched forward. Her screams sounded distant, as if the wind had stolen them. Tears formed in her eyes, and she watched with curious detachment as momentum pulled them from her face. The tiny spheres hurtled into the sky. Light hit them and refracted to form rainbows. They were so beautiful, multi-hued and suffused with golden rays.

Darkness tried to overtake them, but the light forced it back. Deep shadows grew into black columns, the light into an ebon pillar with sun fire at its base. Slowly, as Juno's eyes adjusted, she saw a huge mace obliterate a wrist of black iron. Sparks flew in bright, burning showers, shrapnel tumbled from above, and fiery liquid poured out like lava.

Juno wondered which would kill her first, the falling

wreckage or the ground below. She thought of calling
the Heartstone for help, but dismissed the idea. Why
should she ask it to save her when it turned its back on
so many others? It wasn't right, and she couldn't bring
herself to do it. A part of her stoutly believed a rescue
would come, which was how she remained calm despite
her circumstances. Kaidan still needed her; she was too
important to him, both as the key to the relic they left on
Earth and as a hostage.

His voice came to her through the carnage, soft at
first but strengthening. She frowned, listening to the
cadence. It sounded like Kaidan and yet not. Her eyes
widened, and a wild hope took root in her heart. Could
it be? She looked up, afraid she was wrong, afraid her
frantic mind conjured a dream.

But it wasn't a dream.

Above and closing, a massive figure sped toward
her like an avenging angel. Clouds shredded before it,
the nightmare receded, and showering sparks skittered
harmlessly over its metal plate. Eyes like black opals
stared intently from a face of yellow gold, while above,
a graceful helmet surrounded the head, its semicircular
plates descending wavelike to form a neck guard.

Yohshin's gaze found hers, and Baiyren's voice hit her
ears like a sweet symphony. "It's all right, Juno. You're
safe now." Below, the mah-zhin lifted its hands, careful
to keep pace with her fall, until she landed easily in its
cupped palms.

Juno let out a shuddering breath and hugged herself.
"What took you so long?" She tossed her head, all too
aware of her limply hanging hair. She tried combing
her hands through it but stopped when she realized

how foolish it was. Her eyes found the keep, and she swallowed. "I'm sorry, Baiyren."

Yohshin shook its head. "I'm the one who's sorry. You're only here because of me."

"I can pretty much say the same thing to you."

Yohshin shrugged. The movement was eerie and wrong somehow, a too-perfect imitation of Baiyren. Juno peered into the mah-zhin's metal face, searching for... What? She didn't know. She hadn't seen Yohshin up close before. And yet, the wrongness persisted.

"Baiyren? Is everything all right?" It was a stupid question. His father just died; of course he wasn't all right. Still, Juno didn't regret asking. Something *was* wrong. Something unrelated to the king or Kaidan or Baiyren's return. She looked into Yohshin's eyes and the feeling intensified. Emotion burned inside them, and despite their color – despite the fact they didn't belong to him – she swore she gazed into Baiyren's silver irises. A chill ran through her. Every time she saw the mah-zhin, it seemed more alive, almost as if it stole Baiyren's soul one piece at a time.

Juno swallowed her fear. She was tired and emotionally drained. Fatigue had finally caught up to her and made her see things. Her subconscious was fighting through psychological trauma. These machines killed people she cared about; distrusting them was only natural. She sighed and pushed the doubt from her head, happy she hadn't shared it with Baiyren. He had enough to worry about, and he disliked Yohshin too much as it was.

Thankfully, he waved her concern away. "I'm fine, Juno," he said. "Better than I've been in a long time."

Juno caught the meaning behind the words. She

blushed and was about to tell him she felt the same when a violent light flashed behind Yohshin's shoulder. A loud clang followed. Slowly, as if irritated, Yohshin turned.

Kaidan's black armor floated in the air a thousand feet away. One arm dangled uselessly at its side, the hand missing. The other pointed at Yohshin's chest. A hellish light swirled around the open palm, two more at hidden shoulder cannons.

He won't do it, Juno thought. *He loves Baiyren.* But he'd fired once already. Just because she didn't see it, just because Yohshin repelled the attack easily, didn't make it any less true. Anxiously, she peered into the mech's face, willing her thoughts through. Her body tensed in readiness, and while she felt safe and protected in Yohshin's hands, an assault would bring more than physical damage. It would change everything she wanted to believe. She put a hand to her chest and pressed it against her pounding heart.

The Heartstone was there, cold and oddly empty considering what was about to happen. Didn't it care? Her gaze drifted up to Yohshin. *Tell him,* she thought. *Knowing his father forgave Kaidan might help. Maybe they'd stop fighting and find a way...* To what? Chase a fantasy? She shook her head at how crazy the idea sounded.

Baiyren shifted Juno to Yohshin's left hand and drew her down to the armored left hip. He then rotated the mah-zhin's body until its right side faced his brother. Juno appreciated the gesture. He had shielded her from any incoming fire, but he'd also obstructed her view. How was she supposed to help if she couldn't see? Edging her way forward, she crawled toward a gap in the fingers where light streamed through. There, she grabbed on and pulled her body up to peer between the knuckles. The space was wide enough to afford a clear view across Yohshin's body, but at perhaps a foot, she wasn't in any danger of falling. Not for the moment at any rate. She shoved the thought aside and searched Higo's bright blue sky for Kaidan.

She didn't think he'd move, and she found the black mech exactly where she'd last seen it, distance unchanged, weapons still primed. Losing its hand made it look more threatening somehow, like a wounded animal with nowhere to run. Yohshin's aggressive stance – mace raised and pointing at Kaidan's armor, a ball of energy building around the head – only made it worse.

And then there was the bloody scene below. Soon the whole city would know what had happened. What would that do to Kaidan's self-proclaimed moral authority? He may not have killed the king himself, but that wouldn't matter. He was responsible. Anyone close enough to hear would know. Kaidan's dream of theocratic rule suffered a major blow. No one would follow a church that assassinated the king. Kaidan had to know how much damage he'd done. Would that stop him? Juno doubted it, and if she did, Baiyren probably did too.

"It's over, Kaidan," Baiyren said, echoing her thoughts. "You did what you came to do. Go back to Haven, and when you see the high priestess, send our regrets. We won't expect her for Father's funeral. The king's priest will handle the ceremony in her absence. Given the circumstances, I'm sure she'll understand."

Juno's head snapped up. "No, Baiyren! You can't! He killed your father. He's nothing but a murderer. You have to arrest him. If you let him go, more people will die."

"He won't come quietly. Higo's shed enough blood over this. Kaidan has what he wants. The king's dead, and if we hold him, Haven will retaliate. I want this to end."

A thin sensation bloomed inside the Heartstone. Juno felt as if it wanted to say something, thought better of it, and fell silent.

Across the gap, Righteous tensed. A malevolent light shone in its grotesque face. "That's how it's always been, isn't it, brother?" Kaidan said to Baiyren. "This is about you and what you want. I exist because you didn't. Once you were born, I became irrelevant. What I wanted didn't matter. *I* didn't matter."

"*You mattered to me!*" Baiyren's tone was raw and anguished. "I looked up to you. You were my hero."

"*I was your spare!* Until you, my mother gave Higo what the queen couldn't. Your birth made her disposable too. This is your fault. Everything that's happened was because of you!" Whatever else Kaidan said, if anything, fell beneath the sound of cannon fire. A whoosh followed, and the sizzle of light-based weaponry. Juno moved back into the safety of Yohshin's palm, hoping with every shuddering heartbeat that the mah-zhin remained invincible.

Yohshin held its ground in the face of the incoming fire. Unconcerned, it flicked a wrist, and a glowing orb appeared before its body. The globe grew with lightning speed, outpacing Kaidan's impending strike, dazzling silver light flowing outward like an enormous bubble to encase the mah-zhin's golden body.

The first missile slammed into a section close to

Yohshin's head; the next pounded into the space in front of its chest plate. More came, too many to track, the impacts spattering against the shield like evil rain. Incessant, deafening, and relentless.

Juno didn't know how long she cowered in Yohshin's palm. The explosions were so loud, her fear too great. She expected Kaidan's attack to breach the strange dome at any moment. Light didn't seem like much of a defense, and Yohshin didn't return fire. Instead, the mah-zhin floated motionless over the damaged castle, absorbing everything Kaidan threw at it until finally, imperceptibly at first, the barrage lessened. A moment later, it stopped altogether.

Juno waited through several long seconds, certain more attacks would come. When they didn't, she removed her hands from her ears and looked about. A wall of smoke curled around the lighted shield. Fire flickered inside and at the edges, strong winds peeled it apart. To her surprise, Kaidan had disappeared, and an array of armored giants hovered in his place. The elegant mah-kai she'd first seen on Earth floated before the rest, tall and imposing. She recognized the alabaster faceplate, the large golden halo above its head. The unique colors – ethereal purples blending to blue, then white – mesmerized her as much now as they had when she first saw them. An aura of power still swirled about it, stronger now but less tangible than before. Like sunlight or the turning from winter to spring.

Juno's skin prickled, and she couldn't help feeling as if the entire planet held its breath as the beautiful mah-kai made its way to the tower's foundations. It advanced haltingly, stopping every few yards before crawling forward. Yohshin reached for it, then drew back, afraid to interrupt.

A hush fell over the city, a respectful silence, a recognition of mourning. Eventually, Baiyren pulled up next to the mah-kai. "I'm sorry, Regan," he said. "He was as much a father to you as he was to me."

A flawless face flashed through Juno's mind, black hair falling about it in waves of loose, vinelike curls, a pair of dusty rose-colored eyes, full lips, and olive skin. The last time Juno saw this woman, she wore an expression of confident determination. Not so now. Anguish contorted her beautiful features. Her eyes were raw and tearing, her high cheeks tight. The depth of her pain surprised Juno. Baiyren hurt – she heard it in his voice – but his feelings paled beside hers.

Needing answers, Juno lifted the chain and stared at the Heartstone. *What's happening?* She shook the chain, but apart from a strong and steady pulse, the Heartstone remained silent.

33
WHAT DESPERATION WROUGHT

Kaidan limped toward Haven in his ruined mah-kai, the once imposing machine wheezing and clanking like a dying steam engine. He flew over the Tatanbo Plains without seeing them, lost altitude near the three thousand-foot waterfalls known as Siren's Tears, and staggered through a gap in the Rake. Seething, he ran his hands over a control crystal and jettisoned the mah-kai's heavy armor. He didn't need it, and its added weight drained too much of his dwindling power. With any luck, he should reach Tsurmak before his reserves ran out. Not that luck had been on his side lately. His expedition ended in disaster. Not only did he suffer two devastating military defeats within hours of each other, he'd lost the *Go-Rheeyo* and too many Riders. Worst of all, he'd lost his faith. Everything he believed in – his cause, his sense of morality, of right and wrong – was as blown apart as his flagship.

He swore under his breath and slammed his fist into the armrest. Angrily, he jabbed a finger at the command console and opened a channel to the basilica. That would cost some of the power he needed to stay airborne, but he didn't care.

A sister's face appeared on his view. Young and pretty with bright eyes and deep russet hair. "My lord? How may I help you?"

"I need to speak with the high priestess privately. It's urgent."

The sister bowed her head. "Yes, lord. She's leading a service, but said to interrupt if you called. I will bring her to you." The woman stood and disappeared. She was back a moment later, pink staining her smooth cheeks. "The high priestess will be here momentarily." Though she lowered her head, her gaze darted about nervously. "By your leave." A final nod, and she was gone.

Seconds ticked by. How long would it take Miko to walk from the Sanctuary to her office? She wouldn't hurry, couldn't afford to. Not with the entire church watching. Three minutes, then. At most. How much would that cost Kaidan? The cockpit lights dimmed, and the view flickered. If she didn't hurry, he'd lose the connection whether he wanted to or not. Soon, the mah-kai would shut down superfluous systems to conserve what little energy it had left.

Just a little longer, Righteous. I need to see her. The wavering screen calmed like stilled water, and when it stabilized, Miko stared back at him from behind a desk of pink marble. Bookcases lined the wall behind her, while a large fireplace sat cold adjacent, her official portrait dominating the space above. The strikingly clear image gave him pause; she'd see his damaged cockpit as easily as he did her study.

Her perfect brow creased in worry, her yellow eyes

wide and anxious. "What is it? What's happened?"

Bitterness burned Kaidan's throat like hot liquor. He nodded without speaking, the gesture giving him a chance to compose himself. "Yohshin," he said.

Miko nodded her understanding, and he appreciated it. The two of them shared a special bond. Both believed the planet conspired against them, purposefully skewing their fates and throwing obstacles in their way. Miko said it tested them, made them better. Kaidan disagreed but didn't argue. He thought they were cursed, that Higo punished them – him for his father's sins, Miko because a young initiate raped and impregnated her mother. Kaidan was the only one Miko had told. That was a long time ago, back when their relationship was just beginning.

Now, he told her everything, beginning with the *Go-Rheeyo's* inexplicable course change and ending with his father's suicide and the mah-zhin's appearance. Relaying the news about his father sent a wellspring of emotions flooding through him. Relief and euphoria. Guilt and grief. Memories he kept locked in the back of his mind surged forward. His father's embrace, the children's stories he'd read; his laugh, his smile.

Abruptly, Kaidan was back before the keep. His father spoke to him, the words as sweet as honey, as bitter as lye. *You're my boy, my little Kaidan. I'll always love you.* Kaidan closed his burning eyes. He tried to swallow, but his tongue was too thick and heavy. Around him, Righteous's systems sputtered like dying candles, light failed, and the enveloping darkness deepened his already black mood. He'd killed a man who'd shown him nothing but love. Shame tightened his throat. This was his punishment. He deserved it; he deserved worse.

"*Kaidan!*" Miko's voice startled him out of his reverie. "Are you all right?"

He blinked at her, expecting anger, finding concern. *Are you all right?* Four simple words with such a complex answer, one he couldn't give. One he didn't want to. "One of our guests escaped. She... She said things."

Miko moved closer to the screen. "What things?"

"It was just before she got away." Kaidan gulped bile. "She said she and Lord Roarke were friends, that they knew each other."

"And you believed her?"

"I didn't at first; who would? I was sure she was stalling for time, but then she talked about the war in the Zhoku. She knew things only the church would know. And then..." Kaidan ran a hand through his hair. "She encased herself in light, just like the Zhoku said the gods did. With a wave of her hand she opened a hole in the *Go-Rheeyo*'s hull. I don't know what she did, but the metal looked like it rusted before turning to dust. After that, she flew through the breach and resealed it." He took a deep breath. "The last thing she said was that she was returning to Tsurmak to watch over Zuishin. I don't know what she is, or even if she's telling the truth. This could be one big play by the Nan-jii. Either way, you need to be ready. We're about to have a spy roaming Tsurmak's halls."

Miko paled. She looked as shaken as he'd been. She was about to speak when the cockpit lights fluttered again. Miko noticed, and the worry in her eyes deepened. "You should go. You've used enough power talking to me. We'll finish this when you're back. Are you close?"

"Not far," he lied. "I can see the Yadokai beyond the mountains." He was barely into the Rake, and given his mech's condition, Haven might as well have been on the other side of the world. His view showed the Rake's snow-covered peaks, tall, jagged and forbidding. The range's peaks were smaller this far south, small enough for him to see the Ridderroque in the distance.

That lonely silhouette, with its sheer cliffs, forbidding bluffs, and conical spire, dominated the Rake's eastern side. No mountain came close to its breathtaking size, and none rivaled its beauty. The Zhoku named it the holiest place in the world, a site of peace and serenity. Despite his faith, Kaidan had always seen it differently. To him, the Ridderroque looked like a dagger thrust through the planet's heart.

Miko lifted her chin and flashed a weak smile. "Be safe. And don't worry. I'll double the guard around Zuishin. When you're back, we'll look into her story." Her voice was a soft and breathy whisper. "I'll wait for you at the hangar. I'll be there. No matter how long it takes."

Kaidan wanted nothing more than to wrap his arms around her, to hold her and let the world roll on without them. But they didn't have time for that. Not now. He didn't know how their father's death would affect Baiyren. Until the keep, he assumed his fragile half-brother would withdraw. Now, he knew he wouldn't.

Eyes closing, he opened himself to his failures. "You need to set up a defensive perimeter around the city and move everyone into shelters before Baiyren brings Yohshin against you." Miko gasped at him. "Yohshin is more powerful than we imagined." The admission shamed him; it sat heavy on his shoulders and coated his tongue like tar. "Something's happening, Miko. I can feel it."

Kaidan didn't tell her about Juno and the Heartstone. The last time he saw her, she was sitting in Yohshin's hand, talking to it. Once, on the *Go-Rheeyo*, he spied her clutching it, a look of fierce concentration on her face. First Keiko, then Yohshin, and then the Heartstone.

Doubt lingered in Miko's eyes, but she nodded all the same. Kaidan returned the gesture, cut the connection, and redirected what little power he used in communications back to Righteous's core. It wasn't enough. Slowly, inexorably, the mah-kai's flight systems shut down, and it diverted its remaining energy to life support.

Kaidan closed his eyes, afterimages of the Ridderroque staining his eyelids. He lowered his head. Miko would have a long wait in the hangar. Righteous was going down.

34
UNTIL THE FIRST SCREAM

Keiko slid into a frozen gap among the seconds and strolled into Tsurmak's cavernous laboratory. Rust-colored walls reached toward matching arches. Between them, a huge pod that reminded her of a giant acorn stood among the derricks. "Well that's new," she said, cupping her chin with a hand and thinking. She shrugged and sent her thoughts eastward. *Found it. And right where you said it'd be.*

And that surprised you? Takeshi replied blandly.

Keiko snorted. *Nothing involving you surprises me. I might need a minute or two to process what I find, but no, I've gotten used to how you operate.*

And yet you wonder about the guardian's form.

Who wouldn't? Apart from you, of course. Akuan was the last new guardian I saw. From what you showed me, Vissyus created a dragon with his will alone, and even then he used his guardian to clone it. Akuan took shape in seconds; Vissyus didn't need some kind of pod to hold it.

Keiko remembered how Vissyus, the great Kami of Fire, copied Fiyorok, his own guardian, and cloned

Fiyorok's body to create a vessel in which to place Akuan's spirit. The process shattered Vissyus's mind, turning the once noble kami into a rampaging force.

If you recall, Yohshin was in a pod too, a crystal one. Crystal versus wood. Inorganic versus organic. Unlike what you saw with Akuan, these two guardians created their bodies long ago, back when their kami first called to them. They remained in stasis for a very long time. The only reason Yohshin woke was because its kami was close enough to call it. At least subconsciously.

And I'm here to make sure everything goes smoothly this time? Keiko asked. She knew the answer, but she wanted to hear Takeshi say it. Leaving Juno behind still hurt. Keiko had grown fond of the Earth woman. She smiled wistfully, understanding at last how Yui felt about her, warts and all.

On the contrary, you're there to make sure this goes as planned. There is a difference.

Keiko winced at that. *You realize she won't give in easily.* She tossed her hands into the air. *Why do I bother asking? Of course you do.*

I am sorry, Keiko, but this is necessary. We don't want another Vissyus on our hands.

I know, Keiko said, slumping. *I just wish we had another way.*

Wishing rarely makes something happen.

And you have our kami ready?

Takeshi paused. *Not just yet. I've seen glimmers, some I've pushed along, others came naturally. Still, I think its time for me to… intervene. Our kami will be disoriented, but we expected that. It's part of the journey.*

Takeshi cut the connection before Keiko could ask

any more. Not that she would have. Takeshi Akiko still kept his secrets, and she knew when not to press him.

This was one of those times.

Sighing, she left the hall and headed for Tsurmak's living quarters. She climbed a flight of utilitarian steps, rounded a corner, and made her way into the apartments. She knew who she was looking for; she just didn't know which room belonged to her quarry. After several failed attempts, she finally came to the right room. The door was as plain as any other, but the inside was wide and comfortable. A quaint space greeted her, a door to her right leading to a kitchen, the one right in front of her opening to the bedroom.

An elderly woman lay on her side in the bed, her right arm shoved straight out, her left keeping her body from rolling. Her mouth was open, and if Keiko wasn't still walking between seconds, she probably would have heard the woman's snores – loud ones by the look of things.

Keiko studied the woman, taking in every detail. She then formed a translucent shield around herself, pulled it tight against her body like a second shield, and reconfigured the outer layer until she looked exactly like the woman in the bed. A check in the mirror showed how well she'd crafted her camouflage. She smiled happily before heading to the woman's closet and donning the lab clothes hanging inside. Satisfied, she then shifted places with the woman, putting Haven's chief scientist between the seconds and leaving Keiko free to head back to the lab.

She arrived a few moments before the high priestess, carefully entering through a side door and greeting the workers whose shift was barely half over. A few gave her odd looks when she spoke, and she silently cursed herself for not hearing the woman's voice before completing her disguise. She bowed her head respectfully, careful not to speak until spoken to. With any luck she wouldn't need to. Lucky for her but not for Miko. Takeshi Akiko taught hard lessons. Miko would learn hers, but not without a price: a painful one.

Half a world away, Regan stared at Sahqui-Mittama's ruined keep in disbelief; her mind was blank, her body numb. Where were the Guardsmen? Where were the city's defenses? Sahqui-Mittama was more secure than any other spot on Higo, Haven included. Her thoughts flew back to her battle with Shimono. The Rider put up a good fight, lasting longer than she'd expected. She was proud of him; she'd trained him, had sparred with him, made him into the threat he was. She also cursed him for being such a good student, for standing in her way and delaying her return. It was a wonder she'd spared him.

A sob threatened to break from her chest, but she held it back. She would *not* cry. Higo needed to see her in control. Baiyren did too. Her view shifted to the mah-zhin, tall and imperious, and hanging in the sky like a great statue. It didn't move, just hovered as if frozen. Regan expected Baiyren to race after Kaidan, to hunt him down. He hadn't, and that both confused and infuriated her. What was the matter with him? Didn't he want justice?

The king was like the father she never knew, as much hers as Baiyren's. He had loved her, had taken her in when everyone else, including the church, saw her as an oddity. Losing him like this left her hollow. She knew it would happen – his illness made that inevitable – but she still wasn't ready. It was too soon.

Dizzy, nauseous, she gave in to the grief-born knot twisting inside her. Her breath pulled inward like a whirlpool, sucking her life into darkness. She curled in on herself until her head touched her knees. Then – when the knot couldn't shrink any more – her soul exploded outward. A piece of her spirit died in that blast, everything she was shattering. Another piece, one locked behind walls she never knew existed, lifted from the wreckage like a lighted curtain.

Power suffused her body, heightening her senses. She saw Higo as never before, felt its rocky foundations and caressed its layered stratum. The sensation came once before, but only in slivered fragments. She saw the whole now and felt her overwhelming power, her ability to touch and manipulate Higo's physical properties. She felt both liberated and terrified. How much could she do? Who was she?

What was sh*e?*

You are a kami, a voice said in her head.

Regan's eyes widened. Nan-jii. She shook her head to clear it.

That won't work, Regan. I am here with you, and no, you are not imagining me. I am a kami too.

"I don't..."

With your thoughts. Think the words and we can speak easier.

Regan took several deep breaths to calm her racing heart. *I don't understand? What are kami?*

You would call us gods, but that is an oversimplification. And you can call me Takeshi. I am the Kami of Spirit. My guardian, what your Zhoku calls a mah-zhin, has been helping me.

Regan shook her head again. *How long?* she panted, barely able to speak the words. *How long have you been here?*

I've come off and on since Higo formed, but I came more often after I found you wandering the Ridderroque. Your body had just formed, and I needed to find a place for you to grow. I've guided your steps and watched over you ever since.

That's not true! Monks found me during a pilgrimage; they're the ones who brought me to Haven.

Takeshi chuckled lightly. *I can look like a monk when I want, Regan; I spent my existence on Earth as one. My guardian was the other. She wasn't exactly thrilled with the masquerade, but she dressed the part nonetheless.*

Energy burned through Regan's body. Images came, of the Ridderroque and the two travelers who found her. One, a tall man in crimson robes, stood over her. His face was hidden but as she concentrated, her thoughts cleared and she saw the Nan-jii staring down at her. Beside him, a shorter woman with cropped dark hair and a pixie face looked on.

You! Regan cried.

Me, Takeshi said in return. *You are my responsibility. You are also the only one who can bring Roarke peace. The Kami of Stone and I are friends. I am here to help him end his grieving. I'm here to show him happiness in its purest form.*

What about me? What about what I want? I've spent my whole life wondering who I am; you say I'm a kami, but that doesn't mean anything to me.

It will, Takeshi promised. *I ask you to wait a little longer before you learn the truth.*

Hearing Roarke's name woke something inside her, a warmth, a comforting sensation she'd never known. She let her guard down. *How?* she blurted.

Open your mind.

Slowly, Regan sat up in her chair and looked at her world, not through tear-ravaged eyes, but with her thoughts. She sent her mind flying into the skies. She saw to the far corners of Higo, saw its shifting plates and shaking ground. Sahqui-Mittama's retaining wall had fallen into the sea. Farther out, titanic waves born from undersea quakes rolled toward the continent. Regan shivered. Yohshin commanded rock and soil, metal and mineral. Her abilities went farther, coursing through Higo's crust to the plants that drank them in. Their thirst was a strong and insatiable yearning. They'd waited for this touch the way they waited for the spring thaw.

Regan let the feeling carry her through the planet's roots, leaping across forest and plain, touching flora, nourishing it. A million stems called to her, and her power flowed to each one. She reached Sahqui-Mittama, roared through trees and grassland, and shot into the Rake like a loosed arrow.

A sleeping presence lay buried beneath Tsurmak's fortified walls. It stirred as she approached, and drew her in. The familiarity tugged at her memory. She knew it but couldn't say how. Everything else faded, her grief dulling, her curiosity replacing emotion. She turned her thoughts to the presence and opened her mind.

Takeshi's voice returned. *Trust your instincts, Regan. A kami listens, but we also command.*

Dazed, Regan touched her hand to the side of her head

to anchor her senses. The image of a cavernous space with rust-colored walls and arching ceilings formed in her mind. Derricks and scaffolding surrounded a huge pod that towered over the people scurrying about it. An older woman in a sister's white robes leaned over a series of monitors and frowned. To her left, a monk with a clipboard ran to the door in the middle of the hall and gestured wildly to someone Regan couldn't see.

Regan stared at the space, unable to look away. She held her breath. Something was coming, she knew it instinctively – a change in the pod's woodlike appearance, a change in the world.

A change in her.

Yohshin called out in warning, but Regan didn't answer. She had so much to learn in what she felt was a very short time. Leaning forward, she focused on the distant chamber and the giant casing. She had a lifetime of questions, more than just who she was or where she'd come from. She didn't know how or why she knew, only that her spirit screamed answers into her head. The loudest, the most urgent, told her this was both the beginning and the end.

Miko didn't walk into the lab, she glided, her auburn hair flaring over her shoulders and down her back like an avalanche of gravel, her ceremonial rust-colored dress motionless despite her stride. Her coterie was armed, and unlike the high priestess's dress, their eyes never stopped moving.

Keiko hurried over, carefully maintaining the movements of someone as old as she looked. When she reached Miko, she bowed and coughed discreetly.

"My apologies, priestess," she said. "Shouting at the technicians has made my throat hoarse."

Miko lifted an eyebrow. "Shouting? Has something happened?"

"You didn't know? I'm sorry, your holiness. I assumed that's why you're here." Keiko cleared her throat again. "Less than ten minutes ago the pod started shuddering. There," she pointed. "It's doing it again."

A stunned look crossed Miko's face. She hurried forward. "What does this mean?" she asked in a rush.

"It means a lot," Keiko said, dropping her disguised tone. "Zuishin is waking up."

Before them, the pod shuddered again. Light streamed into the chamber, enough for Keiko to see fingers reach through the opening. They curled around the lacquered edges, long, slender, and powerful. A single shove threw back the casing to reveal a gigantic armored figure, larger than the mah-kai, maybe as large as Yohshin.

Reddish-brown armor covered a lean and supple body. Unlike Yohshin's smooth plating, these looked organic, fibrous. Ruts covered each piece, reminding Keiko of a dried delta, or cracked leather, or the bark of some ancient tree. The helm was long and tapered, like an arrowhead but of the same dull reddish brown material as the body. A pair of horns curved up from either side. About the waist, a dark green rope held a sinister flail. The weapon looked different from the ceremonial hammer the priests wore, and yet its location – resting easily on the left hip – bore a striking resemblance.

The monks and sisters gathered about its feet drew back.

Miko noticed neither the change in Keiko's voice

nor the workers. Her attention remained solely on the giant figure before her. "Greetings, Zuishin!" Miko's bow, though respectful, was not subservient. An air of authority swirled about her. She would bow to the mahzhin as custom demanded, but she wouldn't let it usurp her authority. "As Lord Roarke Zar Ranok's servant on Higo, I ask you to stop this world from crumbling. His kings have fallen. The most recent ignored our Lord's grace and debased himself. It is up to you to erase this stain from our world. I offer you Haven and all that makes it holy. Take it. Use what you must to save us from ourselves."

Zuishin's lids opened, saffron eyes flaring to life. It tipped its helm and regarded the slender figure standing before it. The sisters behind Miko flinched beneath its unearthly gaze. One – a short, plump, woman with long braided black hair – stumbled and almost fell. The others continued to back away. Keiko waited for them to reach a safe distance before forming a time pocket around them.

The great armored figure radiated confusion and anger. Craning its thick neck, the giant scanned the ceiling with shining eyes. Intelligence sparkled behind them, and emptiness. The great head swept left, then right. It looked up, tilted to one side, as if listening or searching.

Head back, chin lifted, Miko had never looked so happy.

Keiko hated what she was about to do. She cleared her throat. "I'm sorry, Miko," she said. "This won't exactly go as you expected."

This time the high priestess noticed the change. She

spun and stared at Keiko. "*You!* You're the spy Kaidan warned me about!"

Keiko spread her hands. "Yeah," she said, her disguise melting away. "You got me."

The sudden change took Miko by surprise. The priestess backed away, fear widening her eyes. "Guards!" she cried. "Seize the intruder."

Keiko sighed. "About that... We're the only ones here at the moment." She swept her hand. "I'm kind of holding their spirits out of their bodies." She shrugged in embarrassment. "That's my power."

"What do you want?" Miko demanded, every piece of her imperial bearing gone.

"I want to fix Higo. It's the only reason I'm here. I said the same thing to Kaidan. Your Roarke and I are friends. I didn't know him all that long before the kami's war ended, but I saw his pain. I'm a guardian, Miko. We're supposed to protect the kami. I may not be Roarke's guardian, but he's my friend. I think you understand what I'm saying, about guardians, I mean. Your heart is telling you to serve God. It's always been telling you that."

Miko recoiled. "You're crazy. You don't know anything." Miko lifted her hands as if to block Keiko.

"Yes I do," Keiko said. She frowned and shook her head. "I want you to know I'm sorry for what's about to happen. You'll fight it at first – you'll shout and you'll thrash, but then you'll realize you left a part of yourself behind a long time ago. Eventually, you'll wonder how you survived so long without your other half." Calling her shield, she sent her thoughts to Takeshi. *We're ready*, she said.

Instantly, a pillar of light erupted from Zuishin, flaring and lancing out to Miko. The light enveloped the high priestess, held steady, and then dissipated.

Keiko lowered her head and waited for the screaming to start.

35
NO TIME TO MOURN

Higo said goodbye to its king two days after Baiyren's return to Sahqui-Mittama. Exhausted and emotionally numb, he rode behind the procession in an air-car of shining silver and gold. He'd left the planning to others, people better prepared to organize royal ceremonies of this magnitude. He had no intention of helping; Higo's kings never did. Affairs of state required the monarch's full attention, especially in wartime. Besides, he did what he returned to do. He didn't have a reason to stay. No roots to keep him, no family left. Not any more. He wondered how his father would feel about that. The thought made him uncomfortable. Duty, honor, responsibility – they weren't just words to King Toscan Tallaenaq.

He gazed through the car's safety glass at the crowds along the streets. Men and women dressed for mourning lined the city's broad, central avenue, their faces grave, their heads bowed. Girls in simple yet elegant dresses of pristine white fabric threw flowers at the cortège as it passed. They were young, no more than five or six, but they cried as the king's casket passed them.

A tall, lean man wearing a billowing crimson shirt over black pants caught Baiyren's eyes. He nodded solemnly, then knelt to say something to a girl in front of him. She turned her pixie face and regarded him with sad and knowing eyes.

He'd seen that look before, but never from one so young. Wars did that to people – aged them – especially children. This war had aged him too, changed him.

The girl edged closer to the road. She smiled at him, earnest and hopeful. Her expression tore his heart to pieces. War was coming; its probing fingers had already reached into Sahqui-Mittama and brought tragedy. He looked past the girl and scanned the crowd, seeing so many innocent faces, noting and counting them. A boy, head down, gripped his father's hand. A pair of dark-haired girls in matching white dresses argued while their parents tried to hush them. Another girl, blonde with ruddy cheeks and a gap-toothed smile looked on as if she didn't know what was happening. How many were there? Thousands? Tens of thousands? In a week's time, their eyes might have the same world-weary look as the pixie-faced girl. Those who weren't killed.

Baiyren had to do something, but what? Maybe if he reached out to Kaidan, publicly renounced the throne, and handed Higo's government to Haven. Life would change – freedoms lost, lives given over to zealots, morality dictated. Still, a chaste life was better than no life at all. The people would realize that. In time.

Regan wouldn't, though. She'd never accept it. She loved Higo too much, distrusted Miko too much. Just like his father had. Baiyren wasn't like that – saving lives was what mattered, not some disagreement between the crown and the church. His father was dead; the bad blood should die with him. And it would, no matter what Regan thought; Baiyren would see to that. They'd been friends for a long time, but he needed to put that aside for the sake of his people.

Resolved, he returned his attention to the crowded sidewalks and again spotted the young girl and her tall companion. They'd moved a few yards ahead and to the right of his car. Unlike the other children who lofted their white flowers into the procession, this girl hurled hers at him as if disgusted. The golden blossom streaked through the air like a multi-petaled starburst.

Baiyren followed the flower's flight up the hood and over the glass shield until it disappeared behind the roof and emerged a second later. The wind carried it past the rear bumper where gravity caught it twirling in the car's wake and pulled it to the road. The plant stayed there, a splash of living color against sunbaked stone, more beautiful for its transience.

Baiyren turned away and cursed himself. He thought he was beyond the running, beyond avoidance. He'd rescued Juno but hadn't put his ghosts to rest. He hadn't rescued Keiko, though, and according to the Nan-jii he didn't need to. He considered that, thought about what she'd said to Kaidan. Could it be true? And if so, what did that mean for him? Until now, Juno had been the lone spark in his increasingly bleak life. He fought for her and this time he'd won. Shouldn't that count for something?

The girl with the flower flitted uninvited into his thoughts. The rest followed. Higo's people deserved better than what Haven would offer them, and he knew it. Kaidan. Miko. Their rule would banish freedom. Baiyren's will hardened.

Looks like Higo isn't finished with you, he thought wryly.

Regan always said life wasn't a well-mapped road or some hidden journey. Day to day, hour to hour, no one knew what was coming. Situations changed, events differed. That was her creed, the warrior's way.

Plan, but be flexible, she'd told him. *Adapt. Survive.*

Baiyren had learned more from her than from any of his teachers, and now, for the first time, he wondered what her life was like: not knowing who you were or where you came from. Lifting his gaze to the Royal Crypt, he saw Seraph standing guard beyond the gates. If not for the slow sweep of its head, the mah-kai looked like an angel on guard: tall, beautiful and strong. An aura of power suffused the armor, a force that reminded him of Yohshin.

Regan had returned to Higo like a falling meteor. Shockwaves shook the planet, the air vibrated, and the clouds about the keep had lifted. She'd been different since their attack on the *Go-Rheeyo*, quieter, introspective. At first, he assumed she was mourning the king's death, but instead of paying respects as tradition demanded, she went from the hangar to the Nan-jii's quarters and, finding the leader gone, locked herself in her chambers for the next several hours. The only message she sent was an order for the Royal Guard to bring Juno to her offices for debriefing. That was the last Baiyren had seen of either one of them until he spotted Seraph standing guard over the crypt.

Chills ran through him. *Where's Juno, Regan?* he

wondered. *What have you done with her?* Baiyren knew
Regan well enough not to think the worst. He shouldn't
worry, not when protocol said ministers and officials
were the only ones allowed inside the burial grounds.
Just because he didn't see Juno didn't mean Regan held
her against her will. Not without talking to him first.

A hush fell over the crowd as he left the car and made
his way to his seat. Pennants snapped smartly in the
breeze, mixing with the distant roar of surf and the more
immediate rustle of robes. A simple marble casket stood
on carved pillars, a flag with the king's crest draped over
it and secured with black ties. Guardsmen surrounded
the coffin, Gunnar in solemn black at the head. Behind,
the king's priest climbed to the makeshift podium and
bowed his head. A moment of silent prayer followed,
then he took a book from under his arm, set it down on
a glass lectern, and opened the tome to a marked page.

The bishop was one of the king's oldest and closest friends
and the only religious leader Regan trusted enough to give
the eulogy. Short, white-haired, and stocky, the normally
happy-faced man choked back emotion as he delivered a
short benediction. His sermons were notoriously brief, and
given recent events everyone thought it best to minimize
the church's participation. When he finished, he blessed
the casket, stepped aside, and let Gunnar and his Guards
escort the king into the mausoleum.

The men reappeared a moment later and the doors
swung shut, closing with the finality only a funeral
can conjure. Baiyren stood, turned, and strode down
the aisle of dignitaries. Thankfully, no one tried to stop
him or offer condolences. Those had been frequent and
sincere in the days following the king's death. Men and

women came and went, family friends Baiyren hadn't seen since he was young. They were all here, standing respectfully back while he passed, their heads bowed.

His car waited for him at the end of the polished tile walkway. Juno leaned against it, stunning in a black, silken dress. A suitably solemn expression darkened her delicate features, but her hazel eyes sparkled when she saw him.

Her presence melted his heart, and he fought the urge to quicken his pace. Seeing her safe loosened the knots around his heart, and the need to throw his arms around her filled him; he might not be king, he might never be king, but out of respect for his father, he didn't. This wasn't the time for affection or happiness. It was a time to mourn. Somehow, he kept his pace steady, which only made the distance between them feel greater. Finally, after what felt like ages, he stopped in front of her.

He couldn't believe how much she'd been through because of him. Kidnapped, thrown into battle, and brought to another world. Somehow, she'd coped with all of it. He knew she was strong, but he never expected her to accept her new reality as easily as she did. He wanted to tell her he was sorry, to apologize for throwing her into danger, but the words were a jumble in his head. He couldn't speak and remained on the pavement, awkward and uncomfortable.

I'm so sorry, Baiyren," she said, slipping her hand into his. Her lips found his cheek, and his knees weakened.

He managed a quick thank you and gestured to the open door. Juno let him go, smoothed her dress under her as she went inside, and slid across the seat to make room for him.

"Are you okay?" she asked, once they were settled.

A low hum filled the cabin as the car lifted and moved into the street. Baiyren stared off into the distance. Though a horde of mah-kai had begun their repairs, the keep retained most of its battle scars. Baiyren barely recognized it.

He ran a hand through his hair. Not looking at her helped him find his voice. "I can't believe this is happening," he said. "I shouldn't even be here." Responsibility beat on him like the desert sun, a new weight on his shoulders, another shackle around his legs. He glanced at Juno, then looked away. "I'm sorry too. About everything." His shoulders slumped. "I wish you had never met me; you'd have been better off."

Juno's hands found his. She pulled them toward her. "Don't say that. Don't ever say that."

"It's the truth."

"No," Juno said firmly. "I don't think it is."

"After what I've put you through." He shook his head.

"Bad things happen. We bleed, we heal, and we're stronger for it. You will be too once you put this all behind you."

"I've *tried*," Baiyren insisted. Frustration and bitterness seethed through him. No matter what he did, no matter where he went, he couldn't escape. He was a seed in a hurricane, a breakwater of sand. Running was useless and standing meant being swept away.

"Starting over isn't the same as moving on." Juno's tone was soft, gentle. She squeezed his hands to show she understood, that she didn't judge him. He appreciated that. "It's easier emotionally because you turn your back on what's hurt you. You're safe, but you're stuck too."

She moved closer and lifted her face to him. "That's no way to live. Sometimes you have to face what scares you. No matter what happens next, no matter what you say, I want you to know I'll be here for you. I'm not going anywhere. Do you understand?"

Baiyren swallowed. "People died because of me, Juno. Their families blame me; I saw it in their faces. I had to get away – from them. From everyone." He didn't want to tell her about Yohshin, about how the mah-zhin made him feel. How he enjoyed the power.

"You can't run from yourself, Baiyren." Juno held his gaze. "You need to deal with this. It will haunt you for the rest of your life if you don't."

Baiyren lowered his head. She was right, and he knew it. Believing he saved more lives than he'd lost was the best place to start. He could live with that, and maybe Yohshin could too. The walls around his heart toppled and light seemed to warm his soul.

"There's something else you should know." Juno moved her hands from his and twisted the hem of her dress in her fingers. "Keiko said not to worry, that she'd be fine. She said she had to go back to Haven to finish her mission." Juno lowered her head, unable to meet his eyes. "She didn't say what that was, and I didn't ask. I've told all this to Regan, which is why I was with her so long…"

Her voice trailed off, and she didn't look up. She was holding something back, something she didn't want to tell him, or couldn't. Juno had never been a good liar, and he saw how much she hated keeping the truth from him now. He didn't want to push, decided against mentioning that an escape pod left the *Go-Rheeyo* a long time before Kaidan's mah-kai did.

He smiled soothingly. "I don't know what happened to you, and I don't know what Regan told you to say; the important thing is that you're safe. That's all I care about."

He desperately wanted to ask about Kaidan, wanted to know if his brother was as cold and cruel as he seemed. Over and over, Baiyren convinced himself Miko had changed the man he knew into the monster who killed their father. Instead, he reached for Juno and was about to pull her close when the car swerved violently. Juno's body slammed into his. His arms were around her, shielding her. Despite the danger, he lost himself in the feel of her, soft and supple, hard and strong.

The moment was over as soon as it began. Holding onto her with one arm, he freed the other and groped across the seat for the command console. His fingers found lacquered wood and then crystal. He searched for the largest, cupped his palm over it, synched it to his thoughts, and ordered the car to power down. Momentum carried it a few yards farther before it stopped in front of a large stone building. Baiyren swallowed. Another couple of feet and...

Loosening his grip on Juno, he leaned over and searched her face. "Are you all right?" he asked.

Juno nodded. "Yeah. I think so." She sounded dazed, almost groggy. Catching her breath, she looked up, her tone strengthening. "What was that?"

"I don't know." Baiyren kept himself between Juno and the windshield as he inched forward.

"What are you doing?"

Baiyren gestured for her to stay down. "I have to see

what's out there. We might need help." Carefully, he peered out.

Seraph stood in the middle of the street, a lance of blazing green and gold in its hand. The twelve Riders she'd brought back from Earth hovered in the air behind her, weapons drawn. Baiyren stiffened. So many mah-kai arrayed against him.

The control crystals glowed under his fingers. He shifted to the left and opened the car's communications. "Regan! What's the matter with you? You could have killed us."

A new fear twisted his stomach. Regan understood him as well as anyone. With his father dead, the crown fell to him. She knew he didn't want it, and he hadn't exactly shown he was up to the job. Is that why she was here? Was a coup a real possibility? With Regan in charge, finishing Haven's war was a foregone conclusion.

"I received a report from the Yadokai," Regan said flatly. "Tsurmak's in ruins. Our Nan-jii say a huge mech destroyed the entire fortress before flying into the Rake."

Baiyren gaped at her, his insecurity forgotten. "*What?* You're sure?"

Seraph nodded slowly. "I'm afraid so, your majesty." She lifted from the ground, Seraph's eyes glinting at him, her words hanging in the air like a challenge. Again he started to speak, and again she cut him off. "You need to get to the bunker; you're safer there than anywhere else."

"I'm safer with Yohshin." Baiyren regretted the words as soon as he said them, hated watching the blood drain from Juno's face, hated himself for wanting Yohshin's power.

"Maybe you are, and maybe you're not. You are the king, and we can't risk you before we have more information. You are to stay safe until I tell you. I'm still in command of the guard."

"But–"

"No, majesty. I can't it allow it. This time it's different. This time, Zuishin's awake."

36
TO THE SLAUGHTER

Regan blew through the Rake like a gale, scarring the land, triggering avalanches. Valleys and mountains disappeared, and her passing left an unnatural line gouged into the earth. She ignored the damage and flew on. Inside the cockpit, light bloomed around her, white and green mixing with amber, some from the mah-kai's controls, the rest from the nimbus surrounding her body. Both seeped into the armor, adding and magnifying its ambient power.

She thought back to the times she noticed certain oddities – an aura around her hands, a whisper of energy coursing through her. The changes came when she was in danger, or when instinct took command of her body. While she could argue she'd been under duress each time, the Nan-jii's words – Takeshi Akiko's words – proved it was more than that. The change was real; her power was real. She could touch it, wield it even. Higo called to her through rock and tree, mountain, and forest. Countless souls blazed across the planet's surface.

Two burned brighter than the rest. One was behind

her, the other ahead. Yohshin's consciousness snapped open while its body remained docked. Regan let it go and turned her attention to Zuishin.

Pain and confusion tortured its spirit. It lashed out like a cornered and injured animal, first blasting Tsurmak to pieces, then hurling sand against Haven's towering walls.

It shouldn't be able to do that. It can't command inorganic material. The thought startled Regan. How did she know? The same way she knew Yohshin was the opposite. She shook her head, chuckling lightly. Information without experience. That was new. A soldier relied on training to stay alive, and she'd trained harder than most. Her instincts had changed, and she didn't know how or why or what she was supposed to do. Fight a mah-zhin? How? She'd never win with Seraph, not even on her best day. She sighed, wishing Takeshi had told her how to use her power. She was a warrior armed with a missile launcher and no activation key.

Had she ever sent a recruit into a fight unprepared? Not that she remembered. That only happened in training, when she wanted the junior officers to make mistakes and learn from them. Suddenly, she understood. Instead of telling her how to wake her power, Takeshi let her do it on her own.

She sent her thoughts back into the Yadokai. Tsurmak was still dark, the damage greater than she imagined. Toppled spires lay across the city, unrecognizable structures slid into newly opened fissures, and green fuzz appeared on every surface. Regan concentrated, and the view zoomed closer. From here, the sand looked more like fine golden powder. The damage she attributed to wind-thrown grit came instead from inside the buildings' stone facings. Dark lines suffused them. They grew and twisted, splitting both the buildings and their foundations. Delicate blossoms of varying shapes and colors appeared along the tendrils. They darkened and lengthened as she watched, filling out into thick green leaves and multi-hued vegetation.

Not sand, Regan realized. Pollen. Her inner gaze shifted to Tsurmak's ruined base. There, great yellow clouds vented from the fallen tower. They spread into the Yadokai, carrying seeds and spores into the desert. Before long, seedlings painted the soil, while water rushed up from below to nourish them.

Water? Here? Apart from the Yadokai's rain forests, this part of Higo had always been desert. A thought sent her mind into the planet, past Tsurmak's foundation, and into a newly formed tunnel. The trail continued through soil and rock and into a vast cavern where it plunged into a subterranean sea. From there, it resurfaced in a far cavern before disappearing into a high ceiling.

Regan hit the Rake's East-West Passage – a wide but winding valley through the towering mountains – and accelerated. Haven's transports followed the route on their way to the capital while travelers from Sahqui-Mittama reversed the path to reach Haven. This time, Zuishin raced in from the west, while Regan pushed Seraph from the east. The Rake made the passage difficult.

Four thousand miles long and fifteen hundred wide, the range cut across the continent like spikes on a dragon. Tens of thousands of peaks and just as many valleys. Inside, steep gorges zigzagged through a forbidding landscape of avalanche-prone cliffs and the

Ridderroque's solitary peak.

A fitting place to end this, Regan thought. *On Higo's holiest soil.* Too bad she wouldn't be there. She jammed the controls forward. A burst of speed halved the distance to Zuishin, another put her within striking distance. Ahead, earth exploded upward. Valleys collapsed, their walls filling in the space behind, closing off pursuit. A haze of pollen and dirt built along the horizon, and the area where a small mountain once stood became a pile of rubble and strewn rocks.

Regan felt the mah-zhin's pain grow as the distance diminished. She put a hand to her head, but that only made it worse.

Help me! The words were soft but anguished, and Regan was shocked to hear them in her head.

Zuishin? she called into the Rake. *Is that you?*

The voice, Zuishin replied. *It soothes. Do you hear it, Miko?*

Yes, Miko said dreamily. *I hear her. Do you think she can help?*

Two voices answered, two minds. Miko was the dominant, Zuishin the submissive. *We are two parts of a whole separated long ago,* they said. *We want to be one again. We are incomplete, part shell, part spirit. You are our kami; make us whole so we can serve you.*

"Serve you." The words threw open a door in Regan's mind. She looked at her hands, saw the silver aura streaked with the green and gold. Two colors. Two powers – one for her mother and one for her father. Her breath quickened. Two powers – two mah-zhin. She swallowed. *Are you my… guardian?*

Guardian. Yes. That is what we are. The voices came together as they spoke. *We… I am your guardian. You summoned me and I have come. I, Miko, guardian of flora. One of my kami's guardians.*

Regan's head spun. Miko. A guardian, and not just any guardian, but *her* guardian. One of them anyway. Two mah-zhin, two guardians. Inhaling, she brought Seraph in from the southeast, through a cross canyon that bisected the main ravine before it broke from the Rake. Shadows darkened the far side, sunlight painting the near. She slowed to a stop between the two and held her position as the world around her trembled. Getting used to this wouldn't be easy. Not easy, her heart told her, but right.

I'm sorry Miko, Regan said softly. *I need you to do something you won't want to do. I think it's the only way to bring both of my guardians home. First, you will continue to use the name Zuishin until I formally summon you.*

I will do as you say, my lady. What else do you need?

The rest was more complicated, but to Regan's surprise, Miko didn't argue. She sent the instructions a second time to make sure Miko understood, and received the same reply. Satisfied, she turned her attention to her mah-kai. "Seraph," she said, her voice tight, if controlled. "Open a channel to Sahqui-Mittama. Baiyren needs to see what's about to happen. And Seraph... I'm sorry."

37
CHOOSING THE GUN

Baiyren paced across the War Room's polished floors. How long had Regan been gone? An hour probably and still no word. *Damn you, Regan! You don't honor your king's memory by rushing off to battle.* That was selfish. Higo needed a leader, and – like it or not – she was the best it had. Without her, the decisions fell to him, the worst of Higo's poor choices. That kind of responsibility would have weighed him down. No more running. No more freedom.

No more Juno.

He felt her by his side, reaching for him, twining her fingers through his. She wasn't going anywhere, the gesture seemed to say. He wasn't alone. Not everyone left him. Not everyone would.

"Anything?" he asked.

A young woman with charcoal eyes and a pretty face the color of dark lava spun in her chair. She shook her head, her sandy plait swinging like a pendulum. Baiyren tried to pull her name forward and failed. Unlike his father, he'd always been bad with names.

"No, lord. Seraph went silent as soon as it reached the Rake. We haven't heard a word since despite repeated hails." Her voice was deep, musical, and unfamiliar. Maybe Baiyren hadn't met her before. She was young, and he'd been away a long time.

"Show me the feed from Haven, Lieutenant...?"

"Asahi," the woman finished, dipping her head respectfully and working the crystals on her console.

The view's dark surface lightened to a gauzy gray. As it sharpened, a smoldering landscape took shape where Haven should be. Smoke plumed over ruined towers, walls lay toppled and strewn about the grounds. An odd green tint covered everything, light in places, dark in others. Apart from the crack of stone and a hiss of venting steam, an eerie silence hovered about the city.

"You can do this," Juno said into his ear. "It's just like running a dig. Tell your people what you need, and they'll do the rest. Trust them, Baiyren. Trust yourself." She smiled encouragingly and backed away.

Baiyren watched her go, wishing she'd stay, knowing she couldn't. No crutches, no support. He had to do this on his own. Squaring his shoulders, he turned to the lieutenant. "Show me the church," he said.

Asahi nodded crisply, and the view dissolved again. When it came back, Haven's grand basilica reared defiantly into the sky, as untouched as the oasis surrounding it. Farther out, where desert sands should have shifted, the beginnings of a forest sprang from the ground, and a new river glistened under the sun.

Baiyren squinted, and drew back as if bitten. "Follow that," he said, pointing. The screen zoomed in and panned across the oasis until it found Tsurmak. Kaidan's stronghold looked more like an active volcano than a fortress. Asahi took him deep inside, zipping past broken floors and bloody bodies. Baiyren tried not to look, but his mind recorded them nonetheless. A young monk with unblinking blue eyes, a woman with dark hair and olive skin. He saw them all, young and old, male and female. None moved, and no help came.

He let out a relieved sigh when Asahi dove into a cluster of hangars and laboratories inside Tsurmak's walls. Fewer bodies lay scattered about here, and most of those wore the sisterhood's white robes. The largest group had fallen at the edge of a gaping hole, along with several other people in what looked like white lab coats. A column of turgid water jetted through the opening and climbed to a second hole in the hangar's once-armored roof. From there, it ran down the sides of the building to the foundations, where it became the wide river meandering through Haven and into Yadokai.

Asahi glanced over her shoulder. "I'm sorry, your majesty. That's as much as we have. The Nan-jii's sensors can't reach any farther."

Baiyren nodded and turned. Gunnar stood by the doors, and Baiyren motioned him forward. "How long will it take to equip a team of elite Guards and get them to the Yadokai?"

"Fifteen minutes to mobilize, another few hours to reach Haven at top speed. We'll have to use the Rake's southern passes. It doesn't look like the mah-zhin went that way."

"Get them moving. Use as many as you think you'll need but leave enough to defend Sahqui-Mittama. That includes you, Gunnar. Without Regan, we don't have anyone to lead the Guard. That's your job now. And Gunnar, this is a rescue mission. Impress that point on your men. I'll have the Nan-jii inform the king's priest right before you head out. He's inviting us – at least that's what his message to Haven will say. Do you understand?"

An odd change came over Gunnar's face. His eyes brightened, and the hint of a smile curled his lips. "As you say, my prince." He bowed formally, pausing as he turned to go. "Do you want me to send a squad after Regan?"

As if summoned, Regan's face materialized in the view. Determination set her jaw, her expression somehow bright and melancholy. If she was surprised to find Baiyren in command, she didn't show it. Quite the opposite. She dipped her head respectfully and delivered her report.

Baiyren opened his mouth, but she held up a hand to stop him. "Please, majesty; I don't have much time." Explosions sounded beyond the cockpit; the view grew fuzzy. "By now, you've seen what happened to Haven. This war is no longer about the church and the crown. Other forces move across Higo, both above and below. You will stand for the people while I bring the mah-zhin together." A sad smile curled Regan's lips, undistorted despite the interference. "I'm sorry, Baiyren, but that means using Yohshin one last time. I wish I could say more, and I would if I understood everything about to happen."

A deep silence fell over the room. Men and women shifted in their seats. Their gazes shot to him. They worried about their future, their fate in the hands of a man who ran from responsibility. No one would say it, not openly, but that didn't mean they didn't think it. And they were right to doubt him. What had he done to earn their trust?

Lost in a nightmare, he didn't see Regan's hand slip to her controls, didn't process her final goodbye. One minute she was there, her rose-colored eyes drilling into him. He returned her steely gaze, caught the nod that conveyed a confidence he never felt.

And then she was gone.

Mind numb, Baiyren looked around the room until he found Juno standing against the far wall. Radiant in her black mourning dress, light red curls touching her shoulders. Knowing him nearly killed her, but unlike so many others, she lived. He became her hero, her savior, and she became his lifeline, his only way out. Nothing else helped him through his pain; no one else righted him. She gave him the slightest nod, and slowly, deliberately, he turned back to the view.

Seraph now filled the space where Regan had been, floating between the walls of a wide canyon. Sunlight stabbed into the depths to light the large gold ring around the mah-kai's head, the filigreed gold leaf on its brow glowing brightly. The far end of the gorge rumbled, and dust carried upon the wind spilled into the canyon. The left-facing wall collapsed, the right tumbling after it. Seraph tensed, its ruby eyes shone in its alabaster faceplate like searchlights. Arms flexed, the mah-kai lifted its lance, a streak of blazing gold and green in the darkness.

Baiyren willed Seraph to move. He'd never seen Zuishin, but he understood what Regan faced better than she did, better than anyone else on Higo – incredible, godlike power, unguided and nearly unstoppable. Like Yohshin. Dread filled him. He was helpless; he had Higo's most powerful weapon, but for the second time since finding it, the mah-zhin was useless.

And then it was there, Yohshin's twin, a blur of reddish-brown armor covering a lean and supple body. Ruts covered each piece like random cracks in worn leather, or the bark of some ancient tree. The helm had the look of a long and tapered arrowhead, though instead of silver, the same dull reddish brown metal as the rest of the mah-zhin covered it. The mismatched horns reminded Baiyren of ivory branches, the slender sash around Zuishin's waist, a dark green vine. A sinister whip looped about the belt, cinched to the right hip while a mace like Yohshin's sat on its left.

One massive hand reached for the weapon, the other fired bursts of viridian light into the rock walls. Zuishin came on fierce and wild and seemingly unstoppable, a body without conscience, a god unleashed. Seraph looked small and vulnerable in comparison, like a glass bird ahead of a meteor shower.

Baiyren staggered forward. He gripped Lieutenant Asahi's chair to steady himself, to give his fingers something to latch onto while he watched Zuishin hurl its mace at Seraph. The weapon hit Seraph's breastplate with a sickening crunch, flew into the air, and arced back toward Zuishin. The mah-zhin didn't hesitate. It pulled the whip from its hip and snapped. A trio of chained thongs flew across the gap. One looped around Seraph's neck, another pinned its arms; the third bound its legs. They writhed as if alive, long and slender and made from a dull green substance Baiyren had never seen before. A squeeze severed Seraph's head. Two successive pulls ripped the arms free, two more removed the legs.

Baiyren's mouth went dry. What should he do? All eyes in the room were on him, all thoughts, all questions. He fought the turmoil, knowing he had to stand firm for the sake of his people.

"Change of plans, Gunnar. Get your mah-kai moving and ready all emergency personnel. I don't know how much time we'll have before Zuishin reaches the city." The words tasted bitter on his tongue. Preparing for the worst meant Regan had failed. Her survival was a childhood fantasy, a boy's hope, one that wouldn't save Sahqui-Mittama. Only he could do that. "And get frigates in the air too. Save the larger ones for Haven and the capital. Regan will need immediate attention, but she's only one person. Populated areas come first. Is that understood?"

Gunnar nodded but didn't speak. He didn't need to. Regan wouldn't win this fight. They all knew it. Saluting, he turned and headed for the corridor.

Back in the Rake, Zuishin held out its hand. The hammer it threw returned in a blur of shining black metal. Elongated fingers wrapped around it, lean, powerful arms cocked and ready. A deadly light flickered in its eyes, a saffron glow, rich yet cold, bright and somehow dull.

The swing came in a blur of motion. Momentum carried it, Zuishin's strength adding power. The head punched through Seraph's armored chest with enough force to cut it in half. Clear fluids sprayed from severed tubing to mix with the sparks that erupted from damaged wire and energy sources.

Baiyren felt the blow. His chest constricted, and his body went numb. Pain flared in his knees. He looked down and found himself kneeling in the middle of the command center. Something blocked him from the view, a familiar shape reaching for him. Soft hands found his face. Held it.

"My fault," he panted. "All my fault. I didn't fight. She had to show me what that cost."

"Zuishin's accelerating," Asahi said from her station. "ETA to the city gates: an hour. Maybe less."

"Unless I stop it." Baiyren tried to shake his head, but Juno's hands held him in place. His head pounded, his mouth felt like sand. "I don't want to fight," he whispered.

"I know," Juno said, her voice soft yet firm. "But you have to."

38
REBIRTH

"I can't," Baiyren said quietly. "That thing steals my soul; it makes me into someone I hate."

Juno's face was inches from his. "I know it's not what you want to hear, and I'm sorry. You saw what Zuishin did. You know what will happen when it reaches the city. More people will die." She stroked his cheek. "You heard what Regan said about Haven. You saw it for yourself." Juno's gaze held him. Conviction burned through – bright, strong, and unwavering. He wanted to pull back but couldn't.

"The Nah-jii's reports were from Keiko, weren't they?" he asked.

Juno lowered her eyes and nodded. "Unless Regan had other agents in Tsurmak."

"At least we know she's still alive." He pushed himself to his feet. The stares he expected didn't come. These were Regan's soldiers, impeccably trained, professional. They deserved better of him. "You know what you're asking me to do?"

She pushed back and searched his face. "I'm asking

you to save Higo... Just like you saved me. You're the only one who can do this."

"What if I don't come back? What if I'm... different?" Baiyren hung his head. Why did everything go wrong for him? Wherever he went, fate stalked him like a shadow. Running to Earth hadn't solved anything. Coming back to Higo was worse. Juno was all he wanted, what he'd dreamed about since their lunch in Peru.

"You *can* do this. Regan believed it, and I do too." Juno stretched up and kissed him lightly on the lips. Her eyes were bright, her lips glistening. "You still owe me a second date."

"I guess I do." He pulled back reluctantly, wishing the moment could last longer. He still felt her body pressing against him, still smelled the sweet, flowery scent of her hair, the touch of her hands against his face. He stared at her and saw determination.

He moved away.

The first step was eternal, the second less so. By the time he reached the communications station, a steady resolve hardened his will. He touched a glowing green crystal to open a channel then hit the red one beside it to record his words.

"This is your king," he began. "I am declaring a state of emergency. Please make all necessary arrangements and wait for further instructions. I leave command of Higo to Gunnar until I relieve him. No one else has the authority to do so. I say this according to the law and in front of witnesses. Kaidan murdered your king. I hereby strip him of any claim to the throne. If he returns to Sahqui-Mittama, he is subject to arrest for treason. Anyone who helps him will face similar action, by order of the throne." His hand came down on the crystals and cut both the connection and the recording. Then, without looking back, he strode from the room and into the hall.

A transport hovered a few feet from the open door. Gunnar was just climbing in when Baiyren emerged from the threshold. Baiyren paused and smiled sadly. "I'm sorry, Gunnar." He stepped up to the car. "But I need you to look after Juno. Make sure she's taken care of. Take her home if that's what she wants."

Gunnar clapped a hand on Baiyren's shoulder. "I promise, but only because I know you'll be back to tell her yourself." His eyes grew serious. "Be careful out there, Baiyren. And remember, we still don't know much about either mah-zhin. You should keep Yohshin on a very tight leash."

"Noted," Baiyren said. "And thank you." He left Gunnar and hurried down the corridor. Images filled his head as he went. He saw his mother's body inside the torn-out chest of Mindori's armored suit, his father falling from the tower, white robes billowing in the air as he dropped. Last of all, he watched Zuishin rip Seraph apart. By the time he reached the courtyard, he was ready to end the pain, was ready to fight for the happiness Higo owed him.

A squat spire stood half a mile to the southeast and on the other side of the castle's battlements. The wide dome at the top opened, revealing Yohshin's gleaming form against the mid-morning sky.

This is your world too, he said. *Help me save it.*

Yohshin dipped its head, and with a slight bend of the knee, it exploded from the platform. White vapor streaked the air, the golden armor tinting the sky like sunlight. At fifteen hundred feet, it resembled a runaway comet, at five an armored god. It slowed to a halt over the courtyard but didn't land. Instead, Yohshin's consciousness invaded his head.

Tell me what you need, it said.

Take me to Zuishin. Regan's face flashed through his mind; his stomach knotted. She couldn't be gone. She just couldn't.

Zuishin is coming this way. I see no need to go out to meet it. If, however, your goal is to save the city, I suggest we lure it somewhere secluded. We need a place Zuishin won't resist.

The Ridderroque! Baiyren said firmly. *We go to the Ridderroque.*

Agreed, young king. The time has come to go home.

Yohshin's presence touched Baiyren's thoughts. His body dissolved, only to reassemble inside the mah-zhin. *You'd better be right about this. We're leaving the capital undefended.*

What we do is the best way to defend it. We will decide Higo's fate in the one place its people are not permitted to go.

Regan fell through smoke and fire. Soot clawed at her only to slide from her body. Her eyes remained clear, the air in her lungs clean and pure. She was calm, at peace even as she fell.

Higo came alive in her head, each living creature, the rocks, mountains, rivers, and forests. She felt connected to every aspect of the planet. She saw it up close and from a distance, saw multi-hued dots streaking away from its surface. The feel of lives ascending and leaving.

Power rolled through her, a charge tied to her soul.

The amber glow she'd seen around her hands exploded to life, and her thoughts, her mind, her very essence, became something greater than she ever thought it could. Some of the gaps in her memory came back. She longed to know more. Yearned for the knowledge eluding her. The need became overpowering, obsessive. Everything else fell away. Only a mournful cry pulled her back. A tortured soul, a spirit in anguish. A second voice cried out from the east to surprise her. Yohshin. The other mah-zhin needed her. Her mah-zhin. Her guardian.

39
VINE, EARTH, AND MAN

Baiyren pulled out of a steep climb and left the Tatanbo Plains far behind. The Rake loomed before him, peaks, tens of thousands of feet tall, spreading from north to south in an unnaturally straight line. The length made the range's width seem narrow by comparison, deceptively so. The whole was a twisting warren of caverns, gorges, and mountains of every shape and size. Long ago, the crown and Haven blasted a highway through, a single passage that ran around mountains and spanned wide gorges. Travelers seldom strayed from it, not if they wanted to find their way out.

Baiyren was still over the Rake's edges, barely fifty miles from the first peaks, and two hundred south of the Ridderroque. Despite the hour and full sun, mist wafted over the deepest valleys, clinging to places the sun couldn't reach. The chasms were particularly stubborn, and blooming clouds hovered as if daring him to enter. To the west, a trail of black smoke marked where Seraph went down. Baiyren grimaced and raced toward it. The sight tightened his throat. He brought his hand to his face and felt cool metal.

Repulsed, he dropped his arm. Sensations tingled through what should have been metal. The change began slowly, like the greening of grass or the budding of trees. He noticed it first on Earth, but the feeling wasn't this strong. This fundamental. A small part of his mind screamed at him in warning. He ignored it. Merging with Yohshin was a small price to pay to save millions. Regan gave her life for Higo; he wouldn't do any less.

The planet sparkled below, and he took a moment to stare at its breathtaking beauty. Mountains, plains, and deserts ran from one horizon to the other. Yohshin reached for them, the need to protect every inch welling inside its once hollow frame.

Baiyren nodded in understanding. *Let's go, Yohshin*, he said. *It's time to end this.*

Time to fulfill a promise, Yohshin agreed. *One made long ago and a world away.*

Baiyren opened his mind. Human instinct blended with otherworldly power. A thought sent him racing toward a spot in the far distance. His expanded awareness understood everything about their position, their altitude, their course, wind speed, direction, friction and resistance. Information came to him before he asked for it and, just as quickly, commands flowed from his thoughts to Yohshin.

They flew faster.

The Rake became a blur of snow-covered summits and gray mountainsides, a dark ribbon bisecting east and west with a half mile-wide gorge that was as wide and deep as the mountains were tall. Seven hundred miles behind, the Ridderroque dwindled to a tiny spear against the azure sky.

Baiyren spared one last glance at the holy mountain and bowed his head reverently. Whether the movement came from him or from Yohshin was hard to tell. They were so connected now, the line between each becoming blurred and indistinct. The prayer he uttered under his breath was entirely his, one his mother taught him when she put him to bed. He said it without thinking, and when he lifted his head, he was pleased to note the surprise rippling through his bond with the mah-zhin.

Merged but not completely. A relieved smile split his face. He wouldn't lose himself this time. He knew how to retain a piece of himself. They could think and fight as one and break apart when this was over. Hope bloomed inside him. Yohshin couldn't hold him, not if he wasn't a match. Eventually, self-preservation would force the mah-zhin to let him go... or vice versa.

Chagrin flickered through the link, but the mech didn't speak. Baiyren used the silence to refocus his attention on Zuishin. Together they cast their shared gaze into the deep passes. Smoke from Seraph's destruction – though dissipating – still clung to the sky. A faint wind-borne whistling blew through the labyrinthine canyons, and Baiyren cocked his head to pinpoint the location.

Yohshin brought the image of rust-colored armor into his thoughts. Tall granite walls zipped past on either side, one in shadow, the other bright and sun-streaked. Rich green fuzz tinted the gray rock behind it, the blush of flora springing to life amid the desolation.

Just like the Yadokai. Baiyren remembered seeing emergent plants in the desert beyond Haven. Then, he thought the underground fount brought the dormant foliage to life; now, connected to Yohshin, he sensed

Zuishin's power spreading through the Rake like seeds through air. Anger coursed along the shared link. The mah-zhin ruled rock and earth. Having Zuishin deface its elemental providence ignited a blinding rage.

We must stop it, Yohshin hissed.

The words echoed in Baiyren's head, as loud as close thunder and filled with the emotion a mech shouldn't possess. He fought against them, but failed. Helplessly, his body responded, his adrenaline mixing with the mah-zhin's power until the two became a terrible force. Higo's structure came to him in flashing images. Rock and dirt. Minerals, precious gems, even the faults between the massive plates holding the strata together.

On Earth, he'd summoned spears from the ground itself, uprooting mountains and hurling them at Haven's Riders. That was a mere shadow of what he and Yohshin threw into Higo. Together, they found cracks between, seeping into them like rainwater. Fissures widened, and mountains broke apart. The walls on either side of Zuishin slammed shut with the force of a closing vise.

Did we do it? Baiyren breathed. The attack left him both awed and afraid.

No, my king. We've only slowed it down. Defeating it will take more than this. That's why we'll lead it to the Ridderroque.

Baiyren nodded and felt Yohshin mirror the movement. He glanced down, his heart pounding. Below, the ground continued to shake. Rocks slid down hillsides, and boulders pitted the topsoil. A dust cloud plumed high into the air and, as it cleared, Baiyren could just make out a seam where the valley's two sides came crashing together. He studied the ragged line, searching for some sign of movement. A prickling at the edges of his awareness guided his eyes several hundred yards down the ruined earth to where a thin rippling marred the smooth cliff facing.

What is it? he asked, driving Yohshin closer. They halved the distance. In seconds, they hovered above it, Baiyren edging closer, Yohshin retreating. *What's the matter with you?* He demanded. *We need to see what's happened.*

We need to move back. Yohshin seized control and started to pull up. But Zuishin was faster. Shoving at the seam with arms as strong as gnarled roots, Haven's mah-zhin pushed the earth open. Zuishin's horns climbed out of darkness, its body unfurling between its outstretched arms, tall, willowy, and strong.

Baiyren considered smashing the rock back together but quickly dismissed the idea. Doing so didn't work the first time, why would the second be any different? Instinct, whether his or Yohshin's, forced him to raise his arm. Silver light bloomed at the wrist. He let his reflexes target the widest spot on Zuishin's chest and quickly fired. Energy flowed through the gap in a trio of sizzling pillars. The first slammed into Zuishin's breastplate, the rest pushing the mah-zhin back. None damaged the strange, organic armor. No scratches appeared on the rough surface. No breaches. No burns.

Baiyren grimaced. The voice in his head felt less like him and more like Yohshin. Or was it the other way around? He didn't know any more. Thrusting the thought aside, he adjusted his flight, diving for the pit at high speed. He'd do what he always did, place his problems on the shelf and deal with them later. Later. Such a wonderfully vague word. A never-time, the far off future he wanted to avoid.

The golden plate covering his mouth muffled a disgusted snort. *A runner can't win the race if he keeps moving the finish. Fight for now, and let the others live to see your victory.*

A runner. Is that what he'd become? He fled Higo in guilt and didn't stop until he landed on Earth. Juno's face flashed before him, her shy smile, her confident eyes. She'd changed him. His confidence grew around her. Doubt disappeared. For the first time in his life, he felt alive. Not because he was away from trouble, but because she believed in him, in who he was, not *what* he was.

He curled his hands into fists, the metal cool to the touch. Sparks flared around his wrists, but instead of firing he lowered his arms and dropped like a stone. Zuishin's whip shot past him, one thong winding around a tall basalt pillar overhead, the other wrenching it free.

Baiyren banked right to avoid the avalanche. Zuishin unleashed a volley of pod-shaped bullets from its hands. The first few missed, but the rest hit home.

Explosions rocked Yohshin in a shower of red and gold sparks. Baiyren buckled beneath the onslaught. Stabbing pains erupted across his back as more pods slammed into him. Grunting, he tried to dodge, but a strafing run hit him just below the breastplate and sent him spinning into the abyss.

Dazed, head foggy, he fought to reestablish control. Everything had come so easily – for the mah-zhin and for Baiyren. His reluctance to stand against aggression was both the naïve emotion of a bitter child and the manifestation of his arrogance. Running and turning away hadn't brought peace. If anything, it extended the war and emboldened Haven.

Those days are over. You are not running now.

No. No, he wasn't. Thanks to Juno. Thinking of her, of what would happen to her if he lost, helped clear his head. He slowed his fall and leveled out. A quick scan of the darkened gorge showed Zuishin readying another strike. Rage floated through its body, touching his mind. Zuishin glared at him from above, its eyes sad and full of pity.

Baiyren returned the stare with a nod, a challenge thrown down and one returned. This time, before attacking, he lifted his arm and commanded the armor to expand. Plate after plate unfolded to form a shield as long as his body and wide enough to block Zuishin's incoming volleys. Would it be enough? The damage to the armored shoulder brought the shield into question. How vulnerable was he?

Zuishin fired again, and this time Baiyren was ready. His instincts directed power into the canyon walls on either side. Granite filled the mountains, along with marble and other hard rock. None would hold Zuishin for long. Its whip could drill through like the roots of a fast-growing redwood. He needed something else, but what?

His thoughts drifted through Higo's surface layers, past rocks and stone blocks and down to a thick vein of iron ore. Would it work? He had to try. Working swiftly, he pointed a finger at the wall and fired a thin beam. Rock peeled away to reveal the black metal. Again he fired, this time cutting and shaping and eventually prying the iron free. Then, gripping the large slab with both hands, he shoved the makeshift barricade into the debris filling the cavern.

The action required less effort than he imagined. He wasn't winded, or tired, or sore.

Don't think about it. Finish this first; you will have time to ponder what's happened when the battle's over.

He smiled inwardly and, straightening his broad golden shoulders, waited for Zuishin's counter attack. An eerie calm settled over the gorge, a silent pause amid war's ravaging thunder. Baiyren remained alert through that peaceful moment, wishing it would last, knowing it wouldn't.

An endless minute passed before the low and sinister sizzling vibrated through the iron. Acrid smoke wafted from the other side, and black liquid oozed through a growing hole in the center. Baiyren peered closer. What was it?

Acid! Don't get any in your eyes. The armor will hold and your optics will clear eventually, but you can't afford blindness, however temporary.

He couldn't afford to miss an opportunity either, and the widening hole in the iron gave him one. Dropping back to avoid potential splatter, he pointed at the melted portion of the wall. Adrenaline raced through him, and though his heart hammered behind Yohshin's breastplate, he kept his hand steady. Ahead, black metal oozed from a wound in the iron block, slowly at first but growing. Light appeared behind, a pinprick that quickly became a gash wide enough to fly a ship through. Baiyren smiled grimly and fired. Energy erupted from his wrists, vibrant gold and silver twisting and intermixing into powerful ropes. The assault flew toward the opening, reaching it, slamming through.

A distant scream sounded, but before he could celebrate, Zuishin returned fire. The strange pods it used earlier flew through the gap, longer, liquid-tipped spears following quickly behind. Baiyren lifted his shielded arm to block the attack then dropped to the bottom of the gorge. Above, Zuishin vaulted over the iron barricade and followed, launching another barrage as it dove.

The projectiles hummed as they whizzed past. Baiyren ignored them, concentrating instead on the rapidly approaching ground. At one thousand feet, he still hurtled toward it; at five, he somersaulted and landed on a low hill with a sharp jolt. Glancing up, he found Zuishin and, without pausing, drew the chain mace from his hip and hurled it at the incoming figure. The head caught the mah-zhin above the right hip, the chain wrapping about its waist. Baiyren hefted the hilt and started to reel in the chain. He stopped, deciding instead to hammer the pommel into a nearby hillock.

Zuishin thrashed, but the chain held. Slowly, head lifting, it glared at Baiyren with its cold eyes. The gaze held a familiarity he couldn't place. He'd seen it before, had been on its receiving end more than once. Who? And why from Zuishin? His inner voice remained silent, offering no hints or guidance, apart from an urgent call for wariness.

Baiyren noted the warning too late. Zuishin's struggles had freed one of its hands above the wrist, not enough to work its arm free, but enough to fire more pods. They came on, only a handful this time and aimed not at Baiyren, but at the rock around his imbedded mace. Dark veinlike marks appeared in the stone, growing and thickening as he watched. A loud crack shattered the silence. Another followed. *Crack! Crack, crack, crack!*

Zuishin's imperious stare shifted into one of victorious superiority. The mah-zhin lurched forward and the chain slackened. The once-solid rock anchoring it broke apart to reveal a network of growing vines. Green shoots thickened and browned, growing and boring through hard granite, pulverizing it, breaking the wall apart. In seconds, Zuishin was free. The lean mah-zhin cast one last triumphant look at Baiyren before exploding upward and racing not to the east and Sahqui-Mittama, but to the north where the Ridderroque speared the sky.

Baiyren swore. He wanted to lure Zuishin to the holy mountain, but once again, his opponent made him look foolish. He'd lost his advantage. Zuishin staked out its ground, and Yohshin would begin this fight at a disadvantage.

40
DESPERATE TO HELP

Juno ran through the king's residence, heart pounding, thoughts churning. She nearly missed the turn at the end of the corridor, stopping inches from the dead end ahead of her. The Heartstone pulsed to life. A strong and insistent pull to the left spun her toward a widening hallway that ended in a luxuriously carpeted flight of stairs. Juno followed them up for several yards before they leveled out. A rectangular landing spread out before her, hooked right, then climbed another few yards. Tall doors stood at the top, soft light reflecting on their bleached wood surface. Juno hurried forward. She twisted the handle and pushed her way into the space beyond.

Fresh spring air tickled her cheek, and she turned to find a gash in the wall beside her. *The tower*, she thought. *Probably a few floors below the king's rooms.*

The king's room. The image of the king bloomed in her head, of his arms widening, his body pitching, then falling. Her stomach knotted and fresh tears formed in her eyes. She scrubbed the back of her hand over her face.

"What a horrible day," a voice said from her side.

Juno whirled to see Brother Taisho studying the damaged wall, his expression both sad and grim. No longer wearing the ceremonial robes of Haven, the monk had changed into a black shirt and matching pants. His chain was still looped about his waist, the ceremonial hammer cinched to a spot on his right hip.

"I wasn't sure you'd still be here," Juno said. "I hoped you would, but…" She shrugged and fell silent.

Taisho smiled sadly. "But we're supposed to be enemies. I am from Haven, and you have feelings for the uncrowned king."

Juno lowered her head and looked away.

"Lucky for you, my oaths are to God. A monk's duty is to help those in need, and not just you or Baiyren or even the capital." Taisho cupped Juno's chin and lifted. Her eyes met his. "I may not like Miko, and I definitely don't agree with what she's done, but she's in pain, maybe more than anyone else on Higo. My oaths extend to her too."

"Even if saving her continues the war?"

Taisho smiled lightly. "One step at a time, Juno. My sources tell me Zuishin took Miko. Without her, Zuishin stops, which is what we both want. These ancient armors are keyed to their pilots somehow. The person is important. By saving Miko, we deprive Zuishin of its pilot and eliminate our greatest threat. We just need to learn how to do that."

Juno eyed the monk intently. He'd given this a good deal of thought. Good. She had too. Gesturing to the stairs, she led him to the street. "I'm sure that's easier said than done. Do you know how they pick their pilots?

The mah-zhin, I mean?" Her mind was racing. This was the key to stopping both of them.

"We know next to nothing." Taisho frowned at her, but didn't slow. "Whatever the church discovered would be in the basilica."

Juno shook her head. "What about here? Are there official libraries or something?" Juno really missed Keiko. The kami, or whatever she was, would have the answers Juno wanted. Which was probably why she stayed away. Haven and Sahqui-Mittama had to settle this on their own.

"Well, yes. Of course. But every scholar on Higo's been through them. After the mah-zhins' discovery even members of the Royal Guard combed through every book we have, both at Haven and in the Royal Archive. All anyone's found is a single passage in the Zhoku where they're mentioned, and only in passing. There's so little to go on. Two to three sentences, a paragraph at most. It's a little hard to misinterpret something so short."

"No one's looked at it the way I can," Juno said, her jaw set. Determined. "Maybe what we're looking for is not in the Zhoku. What if it's somewhere else? The answer is out there, Taisho. I *know* it is."

The Heartstone burned against her skin, then tugged to the right. Juno followed the pull without comment, leading Taisho down the stone stairs, through a covered courtyard, and into a vast building of reddish-brown stone adjacent to the castle. An empty wooden desk stood behind the opened doors, and their echoing footsteps were the only sound in the lonely space.

Taisho slowed to a stop. Confusion spread over his face like rain-rippled water. His lips moved and a slow stammer left his mouth. "I don't understand; this is the Royal Archive. Why would you ask about it if you already knew where it was?"

Juno fought a furious blush. Thankfully, the hall was dimly lit and, with her back to the door, any outside light left her hidden in shadow. "I wasn't sure until now." Juno didn't like lying to Taisho, but she didn't want to tell him about the Heartstone either. Bishop Isshi suspected a link of some kind between her and the gem. Not that she really believed their god was speaking to her. Not until recently.

Damn you, Keiko. What have you done to me?

Stopping, she pointed to a large engraving on the open door, the words *Royal Archive* clearly visible on the stone facing. "If in doubt, let a sign do your work for you." A sheepish smile completed the deception, though it did little to ease her guilt. She'd make it up to him somehow. *That might be a little hard to do without confessing,* her conscience admonished. *And you know you're not going to.* Taisho's expression softened, and she pulled him forward. "Getting here was the easy part. I don't have access to anything inside."

Taisho's shoulders drooped. "Even if you did, where would you start? I told you, people have pored over every scrap of paper and found nothing, even after years of searching. And we don't have years; we don't even have hours."

"We have faith, *Brother* Taisho." Juno gave the monk's cheek a teasing pat. Turning, she faced the cavernous space, a frown crinkling her brow. "Where *is* everyone? You said I'd need access, but I don't see any guards."

"Because it's closed," Taisho said. "Or should be.

Today's a national day of mourning. Every government official, guardsmen included, was at the funeral or along the processional route." His glance drifted from the empty desk to the open doors and back. "Someone will lose his job over this. You can't leave the archives unlocked."

"Maybe they *were* locked," Juno said, punching Taisho's shoulder. "A little faith, remember?" Stepping aside, she swept her arm in a wide arc. "After you."

Taisho muttered something under his breath and, head shaking, led her into the hall. Juno fell in beside him, his longer stride forcing her to a near jog. Halfway across the floor, he pulled the ceremonial hammer from the chain and swung it in a smooth circular motion. A dull glow surrounded a large tile set between two granite columns. They headed over, Taisho increasing his pace, Juno working to keep up. The monk stepped onto the illuminated tile without pause, and Juno held her breath as her feet broke the line.

Blinding flashes assaulted her eyes. She flinched and looked away. When she looked up again, she found herself descending through a translucent shaft. As big as a domed stadium, the chamber had enough light for her to make out filigreed balconies lining the walls like bleachers. Row upon row of shelving ran from one to the next. Before them, ornately carved pillars climbed to support an arched ceiling made from the same polished red stone as the castle.

"How are we supposed to search this?" Juno muttered, her heart sinking as much as their floating tile. "You were right; this will take forever."

"Maybe, but not for the reason you think." Taisho

pointed to what looked like a small hut a hundred or so feet from them. "The archive is completely catalogued. As I said, many have looked here for information on the mah-zhin. More have studied our history without coming across any word of them, either before or after their discovery. Searching for answers isn't the problem; finding them is."

Eventually, the strange transport touched down on a floor of matching stone. The Heartstone, which had been cold and silent, came to life with a sudden burn. Once again, Juno felt a change in its weight, a pull that guided her to the hut. Her spirits lifted.

Up close, what she'd taken for a hut look more like a freestanding cabana – open on all sides with a domed roof spreading over four slender columns of white marble. A crescent-shaped desk curved beneath the ceiling, the now familiar crystals decorating a console like a myriad of multicolored stars. Juno rolled a comfortable-looking seat of black leather away from the desk and sat. "How do I use this?" she asked without taking her eyes from the controls.

"The crystals synch to your thoughts," Taisho puffed, catching his breath. "Everything's catalogued, every book, page, or scroll. If it's in the archives, you can look at it here. The archivists thought this was the best way to preserve our records. Fewer people turning pages or walking off with things." He leaned over and pointed at a large diamond globe embedded to her right. "Just set your palm over the crystal and say what you need. That's all there is to it."

Like the Heartstone, Juno thought, putting her hand down. She took a deep breath and focused on the warmth beneath her fingertips. "I'd like to search obscure texts," she said aloud. "Anything attributed to prophets or prophecy and the mah-zhin."

A pair of books appeared in the air, projections, she guessed, of the actual volumes. "Two," she breathed. "Thank God." She inhaled to steady herself. "Cross reference with the name *Earth* and show the results."

"Earth?" Taisho started. "But–"

Juno held up her hand for silence as the book on the left dissipated. She leaned forward. "Magnify." The remaining book zipped forward until it dominated the space before her. Juno stared at the cover, and her mind went numb. She wheeled on Taisho. "How old is this book, Taisho?"

"I don't know. I've never seen it before." Juno's reaction threw him. Color bloomed on his cheeks. His hands came up, palm out placatingly. He took a deep breath and studied the image. After a moment, he gestured at the notes glowing beneath the book. "According to those, Higo's first high priest entered the volume with the first known copy of the Zhoku." Stepping back, he stared at her, concern lining his face. "What is it, Juno? What do you see? Tell me. Please. A thousand scholars have looked at it, but it's written in a language no one understands."

"I do," Juno said stonily. "That's English, Taisho. That's *modern* English."

41
AGAINST BELIEF

Juno crossed her arms and slumped into the transport's passenger seat. "Can't this thing go any faster?" She glared at the landscape below, cursing its slow roll. Worry knotted her insides, and a dull ache bloomed at her temples.

Their trip to the Royal Archives had been a revelation; one that connected everything Keiko had shown her with Higo. The giant fossils Baiyren uncovered in China and throughout her world supported some of the story. Each find was unique and impossible in nature, more like mythic creatures than any animal known to man. No ecosystem could support creatures like that, and the only record of them came from legend and folklore.

She tried to make sense of it: the Pathways, Higo itself, and an ancient book written in contemporary English. That last item still left her woozier than the rest. No wonder the people didn't know about the mah-zhin; the only book with any information was the one book they couldn't read.

Taisho's small ship reminded Juno of the wireless

mouse she used with her laptop: thin and streamlined and without windows or seam, and while Taisho assured her the craft flew faster than any other ship outside of the mah-kai, once airborne, time passed as slowly as a snowy winter.

She fidgeted. "You're *sure* we can't go faster?" she said for what felt like the hundredth time. To his credit, Taisho simply nodded. Thank God for a monk's patience; anyone else would have gagged her by now. She opened her mouth to ask again, thought better of it, and burrowed deeper into her seat, scowling with the effort it took to keep from badgering him. A glance found him watching her with an understanding if wry expression.

"Want to talk about it?" he asked.

"I was *hoping* we wouldn't have enough time. You said this transport was the fastest one on Higo."

"And so it is. Unfortunately, the mah-zhin are faster than any transport ever built. And they have a significant head start."

Juno snorted. "I hope that's not your idea of comfort, because if it is you *really* need to rethink this whole monk thing."

"Fortunately for us," Taisho continued, ignoring the comment, "the mah-zhin are in the Rake. We know where Seraph went down, and that spot's even farther from the Ridderroque than we are. Even with their superior speed, we won't be that far behind. Assuming of course, they head for the holy mountain."

"They will. From what I read, something important is supposed to happen there."

Taisho shook his head. "And this is the part where I remind you how little you've told me. Again." He returned her glare with a disarming smile. "I want to help you, Juno. I do. But you have to tell me what you know."

"You're assuming I know anything." Juno let out an exasperated sigh. She stared into the mountains ahead. "I can't believe I made him go."

"It was the right thing to do. At least I think it was. I would understand better if…" He shrugged and gave her a meaningful look.

"*If* I tell you what I know." Juno inhaled deeply and released the breath in a rush. "I'm sorry, Taisho. I don't mean to keep anything from you. I'm just worried about Baiyren; it's hard to concentrate, you know?" The monk nodded sympathetically but remained silent. "Anyway – *the book*." She mimed a pair of air quotes, ignoring Taisho's puzzled expression and gathered her thoughts.

The first few pages described what she learned from Keiko: a devastating war on some distant world, a mass exodus of powerful gods, including the newly widowed Roarke, a search for new homes and new lives. It's what followed, the missing details, the mention of gigantic guardians, that nearly stopped Juno's heart. The more she read the more she understood, and the more she understood, the more troubled she became. No wonder Baiyren distrusted Yohshin; he had good reason, even if he didn't exactly know why.

And she'd sent him right to the mah-zhin. Head shaking, she lowered her gaze and watched in detached fascination as her hands gripped the soft fabric of the dress she wished she'd changed out of. A dress. In the mountains. She forced back a shiver and tried not to think about how her heels would handle the rugged terrain. Not well, she imagined.

"You've all assumed the mah-zhin were some sort of weaponized armor, but they're not." Juno let go of her dress, ran a hand through her hair, and lifted her eyes to the Rake. "They're alive, Taisho. At least partially." The monk opened his mouth, but Juno held up her hand to stop him. "I know it sounds crazy, but if you really start to think about it, what I'm saying makes some kind of sense. Every religion talks about our souls, and how our bodies are just vessels. According to your book, the mah-zhin came to Higo incomplete. They're sort of alive and sort of not. You've been saying they need a pilot, but that's not it. The mah-zhin need a soul, and not just any soul. Didn't you wonder why it took them so long to wake up?"

Taisho frowned. "I don't know. Even if what you say is true, you're talking about stealing an existing soul and putting it into a different body. Lord Roarke wouldn't do something like that."

"I only know what I've read, which admittedly sounds really crazy when I hear myself say it. Maybe not to you – you're a monk, believing this stuff is part of your job description. It's different for me. I'm learning to be a scientist."

"Believing is just as hard for me, especially after what you found in the archives. It might help if you shared some of what you learned."

"I know." Juno sighed. "I'm still working my way through it, but as far as I can tell, Regan was with Baiyren when they found Yohshin. The armor left her alone and took him instead. It *chose* him, probably because of his royal blood. I'm sure carrying the Heartstone didn't hurt.

A holy relic like that would attract attention, especially if I'm right about what Yohshin really is."

Taisho's head came up, his eyes narrowing. "You're sure about this?"

"Of course I'm not sure. I only have one source and no way to prove it. Still… it's all we have to go on. If any of it turns out to be true, then Yohshin's even more of a threat to Baiyren than Zuishin is." Tears formed behind her eyes, but she forced them back. "Maybe the book's just one more myth, but I'm not willing to take the chance. I can't. Whoever wrote it said Yohshin would become whole as soon as it absorbs a chosen soul. Do you understand what that means? If we don't get there in time…"

"Even if we do, how are we supposed to stop a god?"

A good question, and one she couldn't answer without revealing her secret. Reflexively, she grasped for the Heartstone. The stone felt cold through the thin fabric of her dress. *It's no use hiding; I know you're there.* A faint pulse stirred within, teasing her like a warm day in deep winter. *Please. I can't help you if you don't help me.* A second pulse came, this one stronger, colder, telling her to leave it alone. *I don't know who you are, or what your problem is, but you're going to help me!*

The stone gave her one last sullen pulse and went silent.

Sighing, she located Higo's sun and stared to the north. The Ridderroque was somewhere out there, a cold and forbidding spire she'd only seen from a distance. "You're forgetting about Baiyren. He has a say in this too. I *will* remind him about that."

A troubled frown darkened Taisho's normally placid

face. "Forgive me, Juno; I mean no disrespect, but the king isn't emotionally strong. We all understand how much he's been through, but he has a reputation of running from a fight."

Sunlight glinted above the horizon. Imagined or not, Juno believed the rays hit the Ridderroque's lonely summit and blazed outward like a beacon. Head high, heart racing, she stared back defiantly.

"He'll fight for *me*," she said.

42
TO THE RIDDERROQUE

Baiyren threw himself into a tight corkscrew to avoid incoming fire. Wind howled in his ears, mixing with the shrill whine of Zuishin's missiles. The Rake's narrow passes left little room for maneuvering. He banked left, his shoulder grazing a narrow tor. The impact brought a dull throbbing to his upper arm. He gripped it with his opposite hand. Was he wounded? Did he bleed?

The pain should have worried him, but he shrugged it off and accelerated. Deep inside, a small voice screamed out. A pilot didn't feel his ship's damage, not the blast of shells against its hull or the rain on its deck. But Baiyren wasn't a pilot any more. He was rage in physical form, the one who judged, sentenced and punished. Tragedy had plagued Higo for too long. That was over now. A new day was coming, one of hope and peace and righteousness. His people would have salvation.

And he would deliver it.

He stared into the oncoming storm. Thought and reflex merged; his thoughts sped forward as if into the future, time slowing, his senses sharpening. He saw the approaching phalanx clearly, and moved to counter. Energy raced from his body in waves. Golden light arced over him, coalescing into a bright, protective orb. The first missile hit his newly constructed wall and disintegrated. The next followed its predecessor into oblivion, as did the rest.

The barrage ceased, and Baiyren used the lull to shoot forward. He accelerated through the Rake. Nothing but the receding speck in the distance mattered to him, the lean body, with its dark, bark-like armor and long, willowy limbs. He laughed grimly. This new power, this ability to shield himself, changed everything. No more wounds, no more scars. For the first time in his life, nothing could touch him. He was insulated, possibly invincible. A smile spread behind his golden faceplate. Higo didn't have to suffer like he had. He would end tragedy, stop it before it began. He'd beaten Zuishin, and the fleeing armor didn't even know it.

Unless it had a shield too.

He pondered the idea for a moment, slowing slightly as he flew. The valley ahead narrowed. He swept his arm wide, and the ridges on either side separated with a loud crack. What could Zuishin do? What weapons did it have? Defenses? What sort of power? He knew so little about it.

Until recently, he hadn't known much about his own capabilities either. *That* came earlier today, the information slowly revealing itself like the room behind a cracked but stubborn door. Something about the long ignorance troubled him. Wielding and channeling his power into Higo's rock, earth, and minerals was as natural and reflexive as breathing. Why hadn't it always been so easy?

Another burst of incoming fire broke against him like windborne seeds. It swirled around and over him, lighted flecks without substance or power. He stared into the tempest, reveling in the barrier that deflected it. A barrier. Another barrier. How many would he encounter? He had one to save his life and one to keep him from living it. The more his thoughts roamed back in time, the foggier they became. Without your past, what were you? A small voice at the back of his head told him not to worry, told him to surrender.

Let go, it urged. *Put the pain behind you. Rewrite who you are; step into the future unbound and unburdened.* The words caressed him, wafting and clinging like the smoke billowing around his shield. Giving in would be so easy. He liked the idea. His heart spoke of tragedy and pain. *Not remembering is a blessing. It's what you've wanted.*

Was it? He didn't think so. Vaguely, he remembered fleeing from something, emotionally as well as physically. A face flashed behind his flickering eyelids, sweet and angelic with hazel eyes and a pert, upturned nose. Below, a pair of rosebud lips parted, but instead of words, hope passed through them, wafting from her mouth to his, filling him, calling him back.

The explosions roared on. He saw flames, ineffective against his shield, fall to earth and ignite. Riven ground yielded to smoldering fragments then burst into raging fires. His safety meant nothing if he alone survived.

The thought struck a chord within his new self. A corner of his heart knew how it felt to outlive loved ones, to be lost and adrift in a sea of loneliness. *We won't live like that again. We can't.*

No, Baiyren agreed. And neither would Higo, not

when he had the power to prevent tragedy, the new and the ancient. He saw them both. His mother, his father, and a woman he didn't recognize but somehow knew. Yellow flowers dotted hair the color of ivy, her olive skin shining in the light of searing fires. One moment she stood, the next she was gone, leaving a rending emptiness in her place.

He stared through the curling smoke, past ravines and broken mountains. He drew in a breath, and as his gaze landed on Zuishin, his subconscious bored into Higo. Thirty thousand feet below, rock and dirt trembled and fell. Avalanches tumbled into gorges to smother the fires before they could spread into the lush plains bordering the Rake.

Necessary, his other consciousness said. *We can't let the plains burn. Zuishin can revive the crops, but it knows we don't have the ability.*

Baiyren nodded grimly and turned to the northeast. The Ridderroque speared the sky like a finger pointing to heaven. Zuishin streaked through the atmosphere before it – far, but not far enough to outrun him. He readied his weapons. Power rolled through him. Emotion boiled his blood, and his senses sharpened. Space and time opened before him, and he felt as if he could touch the very roots of Higo.

His mind flashed back to Earth with its green forests, thick vegetation, tropical rains. Woodland was scarce on Higo. The plains couldn't match what he'd seen in North America; they weren't as rich or tall. Here, they grew, certainly, but not to the extent that they should. Higo's plants seemed stunted in comparison. As if missing a key component of their molecular makeup.

A ruthless smile split his face. Zuishin might control the plants, but he held rock and soil. Without him, nothing would grow. With a thought, he shifted the ground under the Tatanbo Plains. Hard rock raced from the mountains, slivered fingers grasping for fertile soil, the following sheets threatening root and nourishing minerals.

Ahead, Zuishin looked over its shoulder. A few short miles from the Ridderroque, it pulled up sharply and doubled back.

That's right Zuishin, Baiyren thought. *Come and get me. Force me to stop!* Not that he'd really let farms die. Starve his people? Out of the question.

Fortunately, Zuishin didn't know that.

The other mah-zhin roared into the Rake with the force and speed of high winds. The loud whistling of incoming missiles filled the air. Long, evil-looking spears sprang from Zuishin's willowy form. Sunlight shone on their smooth green surfaces, giving them the appearance of needles. Or thorns. Were they strong enough to pierce Baiyren's new shield? He didn't know, but the change from the smaller seedpods concerned him.

Rolling away, he dropped through the clouds. Visibility fell to nothing. Above, the scree of multiple objects preceded the whoosh of something large rocketing past. Baiyren fought the urge to look back, but his curiosity got the best of him. He turned his head and in the moment it took to glance behind, he flew into a patch of clear sky. A pillar of sunlight punched through the clouds, hit his metallic skin, and reflected in all directions. He might as well have fired a flare. Zuishin would know exactly where he was.

Already, he could see it trailing him, shredding clouds as if drinking the moisture. The sickly yellow light of the whip emanated from its fist like bioluminescent poison. Zuishin hurled it at him. The oozing light drew closer.

Baiyren pulled the great mace from his belt and slammed it down, severing the whip before it reached his unprotected ankle. The shield; he'd forgotten about the shield. Cursing, he quickly raised the orb and reset it about his body. A strange chill washed over him. He turned to see Zuishin watching him, the fire in its eyes burning coldly. In seconds, deep green light rippled around its body. The glow shimmered tentatively, a gossamer curtain more ethereal than solid. Yellow and lilac streaks slashed through the orb, and as Baiyren watched, the filmy layer brightened and hardened.

His heart sank. A shield. And Zuishin learned about it from him. He needed to be more careful. What one could do, the other could too. Power for power. Force against force. His mind whirled, searching for a strategy. What could he do that didn't unleash devastation? Was that his weakness? His need to save as many as he could? Would Zuishin care? He didn't know, and he didn't have time to find out.

A flicker of movement pulled his attention back. He stole a glance and watched Zuishin lift its arm, lilac motes swirling around its opening palm. Energy bloomed in the air like spring flowers. Instead of sweet perfume, living bolts shot forward.

Baiyren accelerated through a narrow ravine. Conscious thought succumbed to instinct. Time slowed, and anything beyond the battle fell away. Spinning left, he swerved and came about. He raised his mace. Power vibrated from the pommel, climbing upward to the massive head. He slammed it into a nearby mountainside. The earth directly below shook. Cracks appeared, racing forward, touching the Rake's sheer cliffs. Dust and ash flumed up to replace the shredded clouds. Rocks streaked past him. A sliver of blue sky widened as he approached. He shot through the gap and into clear daylight. Beyond, the Tatanbo Plain spread out before him, wide and flat, its grasses rippling in a slight breeze.

Zuishin still led him on. Debris concealed its flight as thoroughly as his, and although he couldn't see the armor's slender silhouette, he felt its presence. It knew what he'd done to the rock, and it mimicked his land-strike with one of its own. Rose-colored light erupted in the clouds. A ray plunged down like lightning. A second followed, then a third. The ground rumbled and cracked.

Baiyren fought to regain control of the breaking earth only to find he hadn't lost it. The only changes were so subtle he almost missed them. Nutrients, like those feeding the plains, leached from the soil. Zuishin's attacks had scattered seedpods throughout the mountains. Eyes widening, he cursed his stupidity. Without the thick rocky mantle, the seeds were free to grow. For the first time in centuries, trees and plants took root in what had been a forbidding and inhospitable landscape. A layer of green sprouted through cracks in the topsoil, rapidly spreading and thickening into a deep carpet.

Baiyren stared at the new growth, unable to look away. New life, so easily and so quickly created. Life endured, despite war and hardship. The idea lightened his heart and lifted his spirits. Hope filled him and before he realized what he was seeing, the grass knitted together into a series of massive ropes. Long and dense and shining with morning dew, they whipped upward.

The first wound around Baiyren's shield, the followers reinforcing what the shield burned away. Together, they drew him down with lightning speed. His stomach lurched. Up and down switched places, and waves of dizziness threatened his consciousness. He tried to summon his weapons, but couldn't concentrate long enough. Finally, mercifully, he slammed into the ground. The spinning stopped, and the jolt cleared his head. He looked about but saw nothing but the blackening vines and a sliver of rock where his shield split the mantle.

So, Zuishin used the plants to tie him down. An interesting strategy, but ultimately useless. Working swiftly, he sent energy bursts into his shield. Golden light radiated from him in searing waves. The vines withered and burst into flame, peeling back to give him a glimpse of the world beyond. Instead of tall, imposing mountains, a pair of saffron eyes stared at him from a beautiful face. Zuishin removed its faceplate to reveal delicate features, lips like carved roses, and a pert nose that gave Zuishin the look of an angel carved into a living redwood.

You attack my plains! Zuishin said, its voice a lyric contralto. *First with fire and now with stone. With fire, Yohshin! How could you?*

How could I? How could you? You destroyed Haven; you killed thousands of people! The thought flew from Baiyren's mind before he could stop it. He regretted both the accusation and the childish tone.

Zuishin pulled back and looked away, the gesture disturbingly human. *My spirit was... troubled. I have found peace. You will too, in time.*

Spirit. Troubled. The words sent shivers through Baiyren. His subconscious reared up, but he smothered it before it took control.

You don't know, do you? Zuishin's carved features didn't change, but confusion lined its face. It moved close to Baiyren's shield, its wide eyes studying him. *What have you done?* it demanded. The mah-kai's musical voice hollowed, the dull sound reminding Baiyren of wind through reeds. *You've chosen the wrong spirit! We need to get to the Ridderroque and separate you as soon as possible.*

The Ridderroque. Isn't that where he planned to go? What was he doing here? What had changed? Baiyren cursed and shook his head. This was happening too fast. He didn't know what to do. Should he go? What would happen if he did? To him. To Higo. He hadn't trusted Zuishin before this; he shouldn't trust it now. Throwing his power downward, he sent his thoughts into the planet.

He touched the heat in Higo's molten core and ordered it to the surface. The ground shook violently, and the acrid smell of burning filled his nose. Grass and stunted trees roasted as great sections of the crust melted.

No, Yohshin. A pleading tone filled Zuishin's voice. *You've made a mistake. Think about what you're doing! We would never use lava; Lord Roarke wouldn't allow it.*

Baiyren didn't answer. Instead, he sent more power into Higo's core until the vines holding him turned to ash. *Free!* he breathed, catapulting from the ruined mountain and spinning to face Zuishin. He hovered in space, waiting for the charge that never came.

Zuishin floated two thousand feet over the Rake, its head down, its shoulders slumping.

Shame raced through Baiyren like icy fingers, his triumphant escape slipped into darkness, and the image of a beautiful woman with flowers in her hair returned. He stared at Zuishin, wanting to hate it but unable to. It wasn't the monster he always thought it would be. It almost seemed like it was trying to help him. What if Zuishin wasn't the problem? What if he was? He pressed his palms to his temples to stop the world from spinning. The urge to run bubbled up from deep inside.

No, his other voice said. *We can't. We promised.* A new face flashed before him, replacing the woman he vaguely knew. Light red hair, hazel eyes. Juno. *She wants us to end the fighting. She believes in us. We can't let her down.*

Zuishin's head snapped up, and its eyes became glowing slits. *So that's how it is,* the mah-zhin muttered. *Listen very carefully, king of Higo: Yohshin is using you. It needs your royal blood to escape its dormancy. You think you're in control, but only because it wants you to. You need to come with me to the Ridderroque.* Zuishin offered its hand. *It's the only way to free you both.*

A sea of emotions rolled through Baiyren, some his, some from his other self. He leapt at Zuishin and swatted the hand away. *Why should I believe you? You abducted someone too. How is that any different than what Yohshin did?* Yohshin, he thought vaguely. How had he forgotten the name?

Zuishin shook its head sadly. *We both lost a piece of our soul a long time ago.*

You're wrong. We work together for the greater good!

Zuishin's lips curled into a desolate smile. *That's what you call this? We've divided the world. It's up to us to put it back together – Yohshin and me. The two of us. Without you. You are yourself, free and whole and human. You know that, just as you know Yohshin won't let you go. It can't afford to. Try, and the mah-zhin will force you to obliterate everything you love.*

Baiyren stiffened. His memories swirled. He saw his father throw himself from the castle walls, his mother's broken body, his brother running from him in fear. Last of all, he saw the Heartstone lying against Juno's skin. The stone pulsed as if alive, the sensation increasing, growing stronger. Coming closer. Dread fluttered in his stomach. He hefted his mace and pointed the head at Zuishin. *I don't believe you. You're in my head. You're reading my thoughts and using them against me!*

I can no more see your thoughts than you can see mine. This is Yohshin's doing. As I said, the mah-zhin will fight us; it has no other choice, not if it wants to remain free.

Without lowering the hammer, Baiyren glanced eastward. The Heartstone still thrummed in his head, louder now and nearer than before. *Quickly,* his inner voice urged. *Finish this before she gets close.*

Silence fell. Higo stilled, and eternity stretched before Baiyren. He didn't know what to do. Who to trust. The remaining grass had blossomed. Dull leaves gave way to vibrant green, and colorful flowers covered what had been barren. Saplings sprouted from the earth, their branches reaching not toward heaven but toward Zuishin. The mech barely noticed; it floated in place, waiting for Baiyren to make up his mind.

If only he could. Fear's icy tendrils twisted, ropelike, around his psyche to bind him. He couldn't think, couldn't move. His life had been a series of bad choices and now he had to make another. People died whenever that happened, people he loved. Was this Juno's turn?

He curled his hands into fists.

No. Zuishin offered him a way out. A way without violence. So what if that meant surrendering at the Ridderroque? No one else had to be there, no one else would be at risk. They'd be alone.

Nodding to himself, he formed the words in his head and was about to accept Zuishin's proposal, when another consciousness burst from the dark corners of his mind to smother him.

Liar! Yohshin's voice sounded in the silence, each syllable loud, trembling, and discordant. *I will find no healing at the Ridderroque; it's just another prison. You can't believe I would follow you back there. You just want to cage me again.* Yohshin's thoughts flew from its body and drilled into the soil. Rock columns shot from the ground in response, as thick as castle keeps and far taller. More came, pillar after pillar, their line bending and arching until they fenced in the battlefield. *I won't let that happen. Higo is mine!*

Without warning, Yohshin seized one of the columns and launched it.

That's not for you to decide, Zuishin countered, easily dodging the incoming strike. *We're protectors, not rulers.*

We're slaves to a power that's turned its back on us. You say I've taken the wrong soul, and maybe I have. But Higo's king knows the burden of living for others; he also knows what it means to be free. No responsibilities. No cares and no pain. Why can't we have that too? Why are we any different?

Baiyren groaned inwardly. He'd been right; this *was* his fault. He should have listened to his instincts and abandoned the mah-zhin the first time it overrode his control. Now it was too late; the armor held him; he was a prisoner in his own mind. No matter where he went, conflict would follow. Zuishin was his only way out; he had to go to the Ridderroque.

How though? Yohshin had turned him into an observer. He could still think independently, and his senses still worked. He still smelled the smoke-filled air, still felt gravity's futile tugging at the mah-zhin's heels. But he was as helpless as the forces Yohshin defied. Nothing he did slowed the armored suit. His commands dissipated like mist, his control severed, his life shrinking into obscurity.

Outside, time moved without him. Yohshin hurled more pillars at Zuishin, ten to twenty at a time, each slamming into Zuishin's shield and exploding. Rocky fragments burst open like spring flowers, their fiery tails streaking the sky as they fell. In response, the plants below turned their leaves over. Wide pores opened on fronds hundreds of feet wide and nearly twice as long. A loud hiss filled the air, louder even than the rumbling earth. Water vapor rolled from them like rising clouds, thick, dense, and wet enough to douse the incoming fire. Without the flames, the showering rock fell harmlessly into the ravine, the thick vegetation slowing and cushioning the debris like mesh netting.

Zuishin zigzagged through the flying wreckage, arms outstretched, its hands splayed. Fine dust flew from its opened palms, mixing with the air and passing through Yohshin's shield. Dimly, Baiyren noted a slow burn in his lungs. Yohshin convulsed, its vision dimmed, and the world around seemed to drop and spin.

Vertigo. Baiyren had experienced it several times – the dizziness, the confusion. Usually, the feeling came when under stress: when his brother betrayed him and joined the church, after his mother's death. And Regan's. This time, the sensation didn't start with him; Zuishin's attack caused it, and for the first time since he merged with Yohshin, fear and uncertainty rippled through the mah-zhin's consciousness.

You didn't expect it to just roll over, did you? Baiyren grunted. Though he didn't utter the words, imagination put a rasp into them. *Zuishin's going to fight; I hope you're ready, because right now, I'm not all that impressed.*

Still learning, Yohshin gasped. Its body dropped a few feet. And then a few more. Little by little, the mah-zhin lost altitude. *Didn't know about the shield... until today. Will get better.*

When? Baiyren pressed. *After it defeats you? You let it poison us.*

Better than... surrender. Won't let it rule Higo. Can't. Have to stop it.

Baiyren snorted. *Stop it? You've barely slowed it, and only then because it wanted to talk. Since this battle started, Zuishin's almost beaten you, not once, but twice.* The second attack might be all Zuishin needed, especially if they didn't pull out of freefall. *You've never faced an opponent like Zuishin. If that mah-zhin can fully synchronize with its pilot, or spirit, or whatever you call it, then we're at a disadvantage.* A mile ahead, Zuishin came about for a second strafing run, arms outstretched, palms facing Yohshin. *You have to let me out so I can help you. It's our only chance.*

Their fall continued, the mountains on either side becoming amorphous gray blurs. Shadows deepened, though not enough to obscure the ground below. Baiyren noted the increasing clarity, the ruined boulders strewn about the valley floor, and the enormous trees shooting through newly emergent fissures. They grew as he watched – one hundred feet. Three. Five. At eight hundred, they exploded upward, closing in, heading for Yohshin.

All right, the mah-zhin rasped. *But don't even think of betraying me. If you surrender to Zuishin, I'll sever the link and throw you right back into the dark. Do you understand?*

Baiyren nodded. *Yes… yes, of course. We do this together… on one condition.*

Yohshin stiffened *What is it?*

If Zuishin is right, and we can't fully synchronize, then we shouldn't try. We can stay separate and still work in tandem. We'll be more effective that way, and we'll stop fighting each other.

Agreed. But don't fool yourself into believing this is permanent.

Instantly, the link between Baiyren and the mah-zhin lessened. Baiyren's senses sharpened, and he regained control. He noted Zuishin's poison in Yohshin's lungs, but the dust, so toxic to Yohshin, barely affected him. He nodded knowingly. What killed one life sometimes nourished another; he'd seen it time and again as a scientist. Drawing a deep breath, he cleansed Yohshin's body. Power returned, flowing to his wrists, swirling around the armor in alternating silver, black, and bronze. He raised his hand and fired at the incoming vines.

Light lanced down; wood shattered, their splinters bursting into flame. Some shot toward him, glancing off his armor as he wheeled around and soared out of the deep valley and toward the mountaintops. At twenty thousand feet, he slowed and scanned the landscape. The damage didn't look as bad from here and, apart from a stream of black smoke, Higo seemed calm. As he turned to the northeast, he spotted a solitary figure silhouetted against the heavens. Zuishin's eyes sparkled in that smooth and beautiful face, watching him with a mixture of curiosity and wonder. Did it know what he'd accomplished? Did it understand? He wanted to ask, knowing he couldn't, not without revealing the deception to Yohshin. All he could do was stare at the other mah-zhin and hope against hope it knew what to do.

Slowly, agonizingly, Zuishin moved. The nearly imperceptible drop of its chin could either represent a nod or a show of respect. Baiyren couldn't be sure if it was either. Frustrated but hopeful, he held his position and waited as Zuishin spun away. A small white transport had appeared on the horizon, streaking toward the Ridderroque, carrying the Heartstone.

No! Yohshin roared. *Zuishin is after the stone. We have to stop it! Don't you understand? The Heartstone is our connection to God. He's been dormant forever. He's waking now. We can't let Zuishin have it.*

Give me all the speed you can, Baiyren commanded. *We'll intercept Zuishin by the moat.* He pointed at the wide ring surrounding the Ridderroque's roots and fought a satisfied smile. That was far enough from the mountain to ease Yohshin's concerns, but close enough to lure it in once the battle started. Hope leaped in his heart only to die when his gaze fell on the distant transport. *Juno,* he thought, carefully shielding his mind. *I'm going to do it; I'm going to end this just as I promised. I'll need you to be there when this is over. Don't you die on me before then. Understand?*

The wind howled in reply, a mournful wailing that intensified as Yohshin accelerated toward the solitary mountain.

43
BREAKING THE CYCLE

Juno's head was a storm of thunder and icy rain. Sweat dampened the black fabric of the dress she clenched in her fists. She'd been a fool, projecting heroism into Baiyren because she wanted to see him standing in its brilliance. Fight for her? Of course he would; he already had. Three times by her count. He fought for her on Earth; he followed her to Higo – the last place in the universe he wanted to go, and he repeated the process one more time before rescuing her at the base of his father's castle. Fighting for her wasn't what she wanted. He had to fight for himself. Could he do that? After everything he'd been through, she wouldn't blame him if he didn't. Damn her wandering mind; she knew she shouldn't listen to it. He'd be fine. He would!

Taisho cleared his throat delicately. "Are you all right?" Concern tightened his youthful face, his dark eyes probing, his lips a thin line.

Juno stared into the horizon, thinking about what they faced. Mah-zhin. One destroyed Haven in minutes, and now there were two. Memories of the devastated church city flashed through her mind, events she barely remembered. She saw an elderly woman in a light cloak rushing past, groceries filling thin but strong arms. Beside her, a trio of monks was in the middle of a heated debate as they padded through a busy side street on their way to the basilica. They passed the elegant shop where a pretty, dark-haired girl baked sweet-smelling cakes. Did any of them survive? The thought sobered her.

"Is this thing armed?" she asked.

Taisho blinked at her. "Armed? This transport is for diplomatic envoys only. People–"

"People who need protecting." Juno's father was a diplomatic envoy, and the secret service never let him travel without placing armed agents all around him. Juno reached for Taisho and placed her hand over his, the control crystal pulsing beneath. His skin had taken an unhealthy pallor, and he shrank into himself as if she'd shattered his world. She squeezed, and his eyes met hers. "I'm not asking you to do anything. Just tell me where the weapons are and how to use them."

"Four concussion missiles, one beam-cannon in the belly, a load of anti-aircraft countermeasures, and that's it. We won't even be able to scratch them."

"I don't want to scratch them," Juno said, grinning. "I just want to piss them off."

"You want to *what?* Are you out of your mind? Those things will kill us."

Would they? She had the Heartstone; that had to count for something. Besides, Baiyren wouldn't hurt her; he'd protect her no matter what. She stared into the mountains. A figure sliced across the summits, tall and lean with a globe of forest green light glowing around it.

Zuishin flew in a tight arc, pausing at the peak to stare at Taisho's transport before diving back into the clouds. From below, a phalanx of missiles rocketed upward and slammed into the shield in bursts of flaming fragments. Yohshin sailed up from below, accelerating through the wreckage like a golden god. Obsidian eyes searched, spotting something, pivoted, and reversed course.

The movement, so precise – so methodical – bothered Juno. Something about it, something she knew. *What are you doing? What are you…?* And then it hit her. A search grid! She'd seen Baiyren use them so many times, first marking his dig on a computer, then walking the actual site as soon as he arrived. The revelation warmed her body; it meant Baiyren's consciousness still existed. Yohshin hadn't stolen him from her. Determination filled her. Like a sailor in the middle of a ferocious storm, she set her course and held to it. The mah-zhin's superior power didn't matter; its speed didn't matter. All Juno cared about was the man trapped inside. She felt the attraction when she first met him at Brown. It grew throughout the semester. Their first date in Peru confirmed it. He might not have known it was a date when it started, but he did by the end.

Sliding her hand to her chest, she clasped the Heartstone in her slick palm and concentrated. *Kaidan?* she thought. *Are you out there?* Her mind shifted. The mountains lurched, and her consciousness screamed south. Her thoughts didn't travel far, a few hundred miles at most. The Rake wasn't as forbidding here, the peaks more rounded, the valleys wider. A long gash drew Juno's attention, a wound in the landscape, a scar on Higo's surface. Righteous, Kaidan's mah-kai, lay at the end in a tangled heap, its surviving arm cradling and protecting a dented helm. Her heart both leapt and faltered. *Kaidan?* she called again. He had to be alive. Everything depended on it. *Kaidan! Your brother needs you.*

Her heart thundered through the agonizing seconds. *Be alive,* she prayed. *Please be alive.* If what she read in the Royal Library was right, Kaidan was Baiyren's only chance. Of course that would mean exchanging one brother for the other. Could she do that? Did she have any choice? She shook her head. One step at a time. She called again, and this time, after another excruciatingly long wait, a faint presence tickled the edge of her mind. Juno reached for it, drawing it out, the Heartstone's power amplifying the source, healing it.

Am I dead?

Kaidan? Oh thank God. Juno gulped in air. *You're not dead.* Her mind touched the armor and found it functional. *You need to get it airborne. You have to go to the Ridderroque.*

Don't know... what I can do, Kaidan gasped. *So weak. Dying, I think. Everything's broken. Lost. Too. Much. Blood.* He coughed, a wet gurgling sound. *I betrayed my family, and now God is punishing me.*

Juno's optimism sagged. Dying? It couldn't be; she needed him alive. *The mah-zhin steal souls, Kaidan. Zuishin took Miko, and Yohshin's trying to take Baiyren. Once Yohshin has him, it will turn on Zuishin and destroy it. You'll lose everything you love. Don't you understand? God abandoned you a long time ago.*

We follow his example. Kaidan's bitter laugh turned into another round of wet coughing. *My father did the same thing; he abandoned his wife to my mother. I wanted to think*

I was different, but I'm not. I'm the same; I walked out on my family for Miko without giving them a chance to explain. And then there's Baiyren. He ran too. He's still running.

He's not running any more. He's fighting for what's important to him. Juno pressed her hand to her heart. *That's what I'm doing. It's what you should do too. I don't know if we can still free Miko, but Baiyren still has a chance. Help him, Kaidan. End the cycle; save your brother.*

Righteous shuddered at her words. Slowly, the mah-kai started to move – a curling of spine, a shifting of weight from tattered legs to scorched feet. A silvery glow shimmered around the ruined form as Righteous staggered upright and smashed its good fist into the rocks. Chunks of wall tumbled down from above, while below the earth split. Kaidan's voice echoed through the chamber – an anguished cry, a desperate howling.

The sound tore at Juno's heart. She tried to call out, but the Heartstone severed the connection. Power coursed through it, the heat uncomfortable against her skin. She yanked it from her chest, pulled it out of her shirt, and let go, sucking on her thumb. The faint smell of burned flesh filled her nose, but she refused to look at the potential wound. What was a burn next to the loss of soul and self? Ignoring the pain, she kept her thoughts focused on Righteous. The mah-kai teetered on the edge of a great pit. Kaidan swiveled the helm in her direction, nodded, and then dropped into the abyss.

Good luck, Kaidan, she said, pulling her thoughts back to her body. She blinked, and found herself staring at Taisho. Concern twisted his features.

"Are you all right?" the monk asked again.

Juno ignored the question. She couldn't really answer

it. All right was a relative term, and she hadn't been okay since Baiyren left Sahqui-Mittama. At least now, she had help. Drawing a deep breath, she nodded to Taisho and straightened her shoulders. "We have to go. I used the Heartstone; the mah-zhin will know where we are." A glance at the western mountains showed Yohshin abandoning its search and racing through a cluster of mushrooming clouds. Light slashed within where a forest green ball flitted in and out of the shredding vapor.

Taisho studied her before nodding. His hand slipped to a control crystal, and the transport leaped ahead. "I need a heading, and it'd better be close. We can't outrun one mah-zhin let alone two." He stabbed a finger at a blinking yellow gem. "That controls all onboard weapons. When you touch it, the targeting scope and firing console will drop down." A sad, apologetic expression lined his face. "You're in the gunner's seat. The controls default to you; I never changed them. Didn't really see the need; no one's ever attacked a diplomatic ship before."

"And let's hope they still don't." Juno gauged the distance to the Ridderroque. "How far to the lagoon?" She pointed to the wide moat surrounding the mountain. "We've seen what Yohshin can do with rock. We might have more luck with water."

"A minute ago, you wanted to know what we had for weapons, and now you're saying we might not need them? Something's changed. Mind telling me what that is?"

Juno bit her lip and shook her head. "Maybe something, maybe not. We'll know in a minute." She lowered her hand to the weapon controls. "Be ready for anything."

Taisho grunted but didn't reply. Instead, he sent the transport into a steep dive and headed north. The Ridderroque speared the sky, dividing the heavens in two. Below, azure water rippled placidly in a nearly perfect ring. Its beauty stole Juno's breath. She'd never seen anything like it. If she stared long enough, if Taisho inverted their flight, she could almost picture it as a watery halo.

"We'll never make it; they're closing too fast." Taisho's voice shattered the image and pulled Juno back. She blinked and, as her vision cleared, she saw Taisho staring into the windshield, his face tight. He'd opened a rear-facing view, and kept glancing at it as he flew. Within the frame, Yohshin roared through the gorge they'd left minutes before. Silver light flashed around its body, and several huge boulders broke from the earth. Up they hurtled, flying in a slow arc, gaining momentum, closing on Zuishin like cannon fire. A nimbus of forest green erupted around Zuishin in response. Huge roots exploded from either side of the steep valley walls. Thick and sinuous, they knitted together as they moved from one side to the other to form a protective wall. Yohshin ignored the barrier, vaulting over it as boulders pummeled it from below, chasing Zuishin without gaining.

Taisho expanded the view, pulling back to show more of the landscape. "Zuishin's heading right for us." He frowned. "I don't understand. It's faster than we are. A better move would be to head straight for the Ridderroque and cut us off before we reach the gap." He pointed to a spot on the near shore. "Why isn't it doing that?"

Juno leaned in closer, taking in the geography. "How

long before it catches us?"

"Provided it doesn't start shooting – which it could easily do by now – it'll intercept us well before we reach the holy mountain." To his credit, Taisho kept his voice calm. His shoulders didn't droop, and he didn't throw any accusations at her.

Juno wasn't as calm. *So fast. How can something so huge move like that?* Her heart thundered in her ears and her stomach lurched like a runaway rail car. Again, her hands found the stone and, holding her breath, she cast her mind into it. Her world whirled, spinning sickeningly into a deep vortex before darkness overwhelmed her. She heard nothing, saw nothing but bright silvery light and a towering obsidian shadow. Peering closer, she could barely make out the outline of an enormous man lifting what looked like his arm. He pointed in Yohshin's direction.

Juno followed the gesture across the plains, dimly aware that the man had disappeared. Thought seemed to follow vision. She felt wind against her cheek. Gradually, light returned. The Ridderroque loomed in the distance, impossibly tall, and needle-thin. Its height made it seem slimmer than it was. Baiyren had said it easily measured seventy-five miles in diameter. Sheer and beautiful, it drew her eyes. She blinked and wrenched her gaze back to the Rake.

Closer, the two mah-zhin flew about each other in a wild twisting dance, their contrails knitting together. Yohshin's silver shield loomed before her, hot, sizzling, and ominously solid. Her heart thudded. She lacked physical form, but she still feared the impact. The experience felt so real, and she knew if she were soaring through the physical world, she would crash into the glowing light and know true darkness.

But she didn't crash. Incredibly, she slid through the glowing wall as easily as climbing into bathwater. Silver light flashed around her – blacks and copper blinking as if in reply. Some invisible defense seemed to lower, and Juno formed words in her head, thrust them away, and directed them into Yohshin's breastplate.

Baiyren? Are you there? It's me. Juno.

You shouldn't be here, a voice said. It wasn't Baiyren's; it was deeper, as deep as a bottomless gorge. *I know why you've come. But it's already too late. Your prince has agreed to help me defeat Zuishin.*

Juno's heart sank. *And then what?* Her voice was surprisingly strong. Anger filled it, her feelings for Baiyren surprising her, bringing courage. *Once you finish this, you'll let him go?*

A long pause followed. *I'm afraid I can't do that.*

You're making a big mistake, Yohshin. You've chosen someone with nothing to lose. I'm the only thing Baiyren cares about, and I'm telling him to fight! Juno looped her finger through the chain around her neck and lifted the Heartstone. *Ignore your servant,* she said to the pendant. *And let me speak to Baiyren.*

Yohshin came for her in a wave of psychic fury. The force should have hit her and either imprisoned her or turned her aside. Instead, she passed through like wind in the rushes. Beyond, a familiar, featherlight touch tickled her mind. *Juno?* Baiyren's voice said. *Is that you?*

Hope surged inside her. She tried to reply, but Yohshin was there to stop her words from reaching him. That shouldn't have surprised her as much as it did. The mah-zhin wouldn't simply give in. It had too much to lose. Maybe if she got close enough, he'd sense her presence. People communicated without words all the time. Why should this be any different?

Juno fought on, one inch at a time, not caring how many seconds passed or what happened in the physical world. Baiyren was all that mattered; he was her spark in the darkness, her star in the void. She clawed her way forward, fell back, and then pushed on again, never tiring, never giving up. At her back, Yohshin threatened, tall and unstoppable. She didn't dare turn, didn't dare look back to see how close it was.

Was she closing on Baiyren? She didn't know, couldn't know. This strange otherworld made no sense to her. A minute ago, Baiyren seemed close. Now much less so. If she could just reach him, talk to him. She'd give him a reason to fight. To live. Unfortunately, reaching him was out of the question. Yohshin blocked her at every turn. Baiyren might as well have been on the other side of thick glass. She needed find a way around or through, but how? Yohshin controlled this space, controlled Baiyren. She considered the Heartstone, but the presence within seemed both reluctant and distracted.

Distracted? In the physical world, her palm connected with her forehead, and she was vaguely aware of the confused look Taisho threw her way. She wanted to laugh, might have even, if the situation wasn't so dire. Instead, she repeated the words that formed her strategy: confusion, distraction. Those were what she needed. Rousing her body, she willed her hand to the blinking yellow light Taisho had pointed out a moment earlier. A console dropped from above and covered her face. She didn't need it. The Heartstone channeled her thoughts into the crystal, merging with it, commanding it.

The first missile launched in a roar of smoke and fire, the second rocketing a heartbeat behind. Taisho shouted something, but with her mind focused on Baiyren, Juno couldn't make out the words. A flash lit the skies, and turbulence rocked the transport. Taisho worked the controls to keep the little ship airborne, ultimately deciding to drop below the blast radius and race for the Ridderroque before the inevitable counterattack began. But Yohshin didn't strike back, not at first. Taisho wouldn't know why; he'd assumed they either dazed or damaged the mah-zhin. Or that his god had saved them.

Juno knew better.

Inside her head, inside the strange psychic world, she felt the barrier between her mind and Baiyren shatter. The blast didn't damage the armor, but it did what Juno needed it to do. Distracted, unable to keep its concentration, Yohshin lost control long enough for Juno to throw her thoughts into the abyss. *Baiyren!* she called, the name thundering through the emptiness, desperation adding force, emotion amplifying sound. *Baiyren, can you hear me? I've come to get you out!* The light ahead dimmed and cooled. A chill ran through Juno that had nothing to do with temperature. *Baiyren?* she called again, her voice uncertain now, brittle. *What's wrong?*

Go home, Juno. You can't help me. The mah-zhin are fighting to control Higo. I can't leave until I stop them. I haven't been much of a prince, but I can at least do this for my people. They need me, Juno. I don't have anyone else.

You have me. Juno scrubbed away what tears she could and fought down the rest.

I know; I'll always know. But as much as I want you beside me, I need you to go before you get hurt. Use the Heartstone, open a Portal to Earth and don't look back. Knowing you're safe will make this easier.

And then he was gone.

The emptiness left Juno dazed. She couldn't go. She wouldn't; she wasn't done here. Head spinning, she tried to think, tried to form some plan that would...what? Stop a god? Who was she kidding? She might as well stop the Earth from turning. She probably should open a Portal and...

Thinking of a Portal stirred a wild hope. Baiyren's idea was a good one, better than he intended. She knew what to do now, knew how to escape and buy Kaidan the time he needed. Pulse raging, she directed her thoughts into the Heartstone. Power surged from her, her eyes flew open, and she found herself staring into a flying vortex.

Taisho, pale and sweating, cursed and tried to swerve.

Juno put a hand on his shoulder to stop him. He looked at her, and she nodded ahead. "You need to trust me, Taisho. We're going in."

"That's a Portal. Did you...? *How* did you...?"

Juno held up a hand. "Straight ahead, Taisho. Everything will be fine. I promise."

"If you say so." Though the words suggested acceptance, the monk's tone held more than a little skepticism. That was fine with Juno. He'd see soon enough. Bracing herself, she waited for the transport to enter the yawning Portal. Light bent and swirled and, just as quickly, they were through. A tall white obelisk reared up to their right, a long building with a copper roof adjacent. Far down a wide rectangular stretch of grass, a familiar dome surveyed the city below. Juno stared at the cityscape, aware how little it now felt like home. "Unidentified objects closing from the northeast," Taisho said from her side. "They're hailing us, but I don't understand the language."

"Ignore them," Juno replied, turning away. Again, she closed her fist around the Heartstone, and a new Portal opened. This time, Taisho didn't hesitate. He drove through. Rippling water filled their view, a great shadow spreading across it. Before Taisho could tell Juno to brace herself, the transport slammed into the watery surface and submerged.

44
HOPE FOR THE HOPELESS

Object in the water! Yohshin cried. *Fifty-three miles north, just short of the Ridderroque's southern shore. Size and shape indicate one of Haven's transports.*

Baiyren let out a stream of curses. *Damn it, Juno! What have you done?*

Initial scans show damage to the transport's navigation. Other than that, I cannot say.

Haven's transports were armored and designed to withstand water landings, even at maximum speed. Juno should have survived easily. So, why didn't Yohshin report on her condition?

Because it didn't want him to know.

Yohshin understood him better than anyone. It saw everything, catalogued the smallest thought or emotion. Hope and fear, disappointment and grief, Yohshin experienced them as he did. Baiyren always gave too much away, always suspected Yohshin used the information against him.

He wouldn't let it, not this time.

Seizing power, he flared a shield and hurled his

thoughts into Higo. Infinite sensations rolled through him. Rock, dirt, and strata came alive in his head. He felt their textures, understood their makeup, and could command them to do what he wanted. His mind raced north, zipping through the ground below Zuishin. There, he snatched iron, fused the metal into solid granite, and launched the whole skyward in a protective wall. Behind it, Baiyren shot a globe of hollowed-out titanium from the moat floor. A thousand feet from the seabed, he cracked it open. Bubbles sizzled toward the surface, water flooding the space within. At five hundred feet, the orb met the downed transport. Baiyren let the former settle into the latter, a flawless pearl recaptured, a diamond secured. When he was sure the transport was safely ensconced, he snapped the protective domes back together and sent the now sealed sphere spinning into the Ridderroque.

Safe there, he thought. *Safe from you.*

Ahead, Zuishin slowed to a stop and turned to face him, rotating slowly, elegantly. *I have no interest in the Earth girl.* Zuishin's eyes narrowed into saffron slits. *She has nothing to fear from me.*

She has everything to fear; she's been a pawn since Haven took her prisoner.

Zuishin lifted its hands, palms facing him in supplication. *I am trying to help you. Both of you.*

Like you helped Regan? I don't need that kind of help, and neither does Higo. Again Yohshin's spirit surged from the depths, and again Baiyren fought it down. He couldn't let the mah-zhin retake control. Not now. Not yet.

Zuishin moved closer, and Baiyren again leveled Yohshin's giant mace at its heart. *That's close enough.*

He pictured his father's final sacrifice in his head, and Regan's. *I hope you're serious about wanting peace; I really do. Because you're about to get the chance to make that happen.*

Forming a shield around his inert body, he severed all of his connections to Yohshin. No more air to breathe, no more nourishment to keep him alive. Without him, Yohshin would go dormant again, this time forever. No more royals to fuel its spirit. No more human spirits to use against Higo's people. That was a gratifying thought, one he could hold on to without regret as his life ebbed away. He closed his eyes and tried to relax, tried to let go.

Outside, Zuishin exploded toward him, frantically calling out, begging him to stop. More pods flew from its opened palms, thick liquid from hidden spots along its back. The first volley mixed with the second, the two combining to shower both the Rake and the plains. By the time they hit, long, rootlike tendrils split them open and burrowed into the ground, some toppling mountains, others weaving up the slopes and using the peaks to launch themselves at Yohshin. How many were there? Twenty? Fifty?

Baiyren didn't know. The first reached him in seconds, whipping around his waist and holding him in place. The rest caught up, and Yohshin's arms disappeared under living ropes. More writhed about his legs and feet; the thickest secured his torso while avoiding his neck. Light and dark blended together. Was he losing consciousness, or had a frond lashed itself to his head? He didn't know. Maybe a little of both.

Zuishin hissed at him, reeling Yohshin in like a caught fish. *Foolish boy. We need you alive.*

And Higo needs me dead! Why aren't you helping me? One

squeeze; that's all it'll take. Crush the chest. Stop Yohshin's heart; stop the fighting. How long did they have before the gold mah-zhin recovered? Seconds if they were lucky, much less if they weren't. Already, Yohshin stirred from its stupor. Rage and fear filled it, the two knitting together into psychic chains that attacked as fast and as hard as physical ones.

Its first strike pounded against Baiyren's shield, the next made him wonder if he was strong enough to fight. *How could you do this to me!* Yohshin screamed. *We had an agreement; I trusted you!*

So did my mother and look what happened to her. Trusting brings tragedy.

Despite Yohshin's attacks, the darkness continued its inexorable crawl. Baiyren's smile widened; he was winning. After a lifetime of failure, his final action would bring the peace he craved but wouldn't live to enjoy. He took one last look at Higo, at its breathtaking mountains, sweeping plains, and single, wide sea. A vast doorway appeared behind them, its blackness calling him seductively. *Come to me*, it tempted. *Step through the doorway; find peace.*

Baiyren opened his mind. *I'm sorry, Yohshin*, he said. *This is the only way.*

Be as sorry as you like, King Baiyren. Just remember you brought this on yourself. With that, Yohshin formed a shield. Energy pushed outward, severing Zuishin's vines. The moat lay below, crystal blue and calm despite the violence above. Zuishin skimmed the ground on the near shore, sending showers into the air as it left the land behind and raced for the Ridderroque.

I'm the only one left with royal blood. Baiyren's breath

was low and shallow. *I die, you die. You'll have no one else to give you life.* Speaking was a chore. Moving impossible. His arms and legs were lead, and his head had grown fuzzy.

You've chosen your way, and I've chosen mine. You'll understand if I don't wish you luck.

Baiyren managed a nod. He was so weak, too weak to stop a determined attack on his mind. If Yohshin broke through, it was all over. The uncomfortable feeling of that happening already flittered through his addled head. Yohshin projected an air of confidence Baiyren couldn't explain. Why was that?

The answer is remarkably simple, my king, the mah-zhin said smugly. *You're not as shielded as you think. You've secured your body remarkably well, but your thoughts? Those still leach through. Every creature's subconscious fights to keeps its host alive. All I had to do was tap into that part of your mind and command it to work with me. Your body's chemicals and your spirit's will to survive add to my strength. I no longer need you to defeat Zuishin and restore order.*

Haven's mah-zhin had reached the moat's far shore in a blur of brown and green. It glanced over its shoulder, and a look of alarm crossed its serene face. Resignation followed, then determination. At the white sandy beach, Zuishin turned and backed into a patch of newly forested land, shoulders straight, head thrown back. Ready.

Baiyren remembered how barren the coast had been when he first came to the Ridderroque. Now, he marveled at the lush vegetation, so rich, thick and vibrant. In seconds Zuishin brought it to life; how sad this green space would become its grave. If only he could stop that from happening. If only he had the strength or foresight.

But he was just as he'd always been: a passenger in a runaway car, knowing how to drive but unable to.

Some defensive line he turned out to be. An old and crumbling barrier, age and weather-weakened, a breached and defeated wall to stand against the oncoming storm. *I'm sorry, Zuishin; I did everything I could. You put your trust in the wrong man.* What a way to spend his final moments, watching one last failure unfold before him.

The once eternal moments now raced by at an incredible pace. Drawing as much energy from Baiyren as it could, Yohshin roared over the moat. Water flumed into fierce waves, rainbows painting the air. The moat became sand, then grass, then trees. Vines reached for the mah-zhin, either missing or snapping instead of growing taut. Nothing Zuishin threw at Yohshin stopped it; nothing even slowed it. A barrage of acid pods came first, but the released liquid beaded on Yohshin's shield and rolled away.

Zuishin tried again, uprooting trees and launching them from the jungle. It wove nets from roots and great branches and tried to snare its enemy. The distance between them dwindled. At a thousand feet, Yohshin drew the forged chains from the earth's metals; at seven hundred it hurled them at Zuishin. A loud crack joined the sound of snapping wood and tearing plants. Half the flail curled about Zuishin's neck, the other half ensnaring russet wrists and ankles.

Adrenaline flowed into Baiyren's body and then out to the giant armor. He fought as best as he could, but the pull was so strong, and he was so weak. He wished he could let go, prayed he could close his eyes and become one with infinity. Each time he tried, his subconscious fought back. More adrenaline flooded through him and more fed Yohshin's power. Baiyren cursed his body for fighting to survive while his mind fought to die.

With Baiyren's strength, Yohshin was faster and stronger than Zuishin, strong enough to hold its enemy with one hand while swinging its mace with the other. The head smashed into Zuishin's chest with a sickening crunch. Air whooshed from Baiyren's lungs in sympathy. He grew dizzy, felt nausea building inside him.

Yohshin stole those sensations too, turning them into energy, using everything Baiyren had to give. Why did he have so much? He couldn't do anything right. Dying was too easy for too many. Not even Zuishin avoided it. Why was it so hard for him?

Because you are strong, a soft voice said to him, one that reminded him of roses. *Strong enough to give us the time we needed*. Unlike before, words accompanied the thoughts. He knew the tone, soft and lyrical and part of him since he was little. Not his mother. He frowned, reaching for recognition, needing to know the source. The harder he focused, the more the answer eluded him. Like mist it dissipated, a breath given then taken. He looked up, and the feeling faded as if it never existed.

The chaos below wiped everything from his head. A large crater marred the new forest, and smoke wafted up slowly, almost peacefully, to mock the devastation. So much beauty gone so quickly. So much new life wiped out before it had a chance to grow and breathe and become. Baiyren hated what he saw, and he hated Yohshin for making him a party to ruin. It was using him, tapping into his emotional turmoil to fuel its leap into the pit; stealing his rage to strengthen the booted foot that came down on Zuishin's breastplate. Shadows flitted across the pit as they stood before the Ridderroque: one of victory, two of defeat.

Sweeping the great mace, Yohshin lifted the weapon over its head, but the strike went wide, intentionally so. The mah-zhin released the barbed staff, stepped back, and stared at Zuishin in disbelief. A damaged mah-kai had emerged from the deepest part of the crater and thrown itself across Zuishin. Defiance shone in its dimming eyes, the power behind them flickering like dying candles.

"Don't hurt her," the mah-kai pleaded, speaking through a communication device. "Please. She's everything to me."

Baiyren started. He knew the voice. He would never, could never, forget it. Images rushed through his head. He watched his father talk to him in the throne room while a taller boy stayed at his side; he saw Sahqui-Mittama's great palace and recalled playing a game of hide-and-seek with the other boy; he remembered crying, remembered loneliness. He tried to swallow, but his throat was dry. He knew the broken form below him; he recognized the black oversized armor; he knew each severe injury, injuries he and Yohshin had inflicted.

Heart pounding, he fought through death's haze and opened communications. "Kaidan?" he rasped. "Is that you?"

45
NOT ALONE

Regan guided her shield through the Ridderroque's thick, stone walls and into the immense caverns under the mountain. She'd been here before. Once. Long ago. Even then, she'd felt a familiarity with the place, a faint echo like the memory of an old, forgotten friend. Adrenaline coursed through her body as she flew; she didn't know what to expect, and while her spirit remained confident, a slivered fear hunted around its edges. Would she like what she found? Would it change her? She didn't think so. She was who she was, and whatever lay ahead wasn't going to change that now.

The thought made her feel better – enough to realize how badly she let her attention wander. In battle, that could kill you. Here, it could… what? An image of the mah-zhin locked in combat flashed through her head – of Yohshin hurling its black mace, of Zuishin reading and defending. She had to end this before anyone else died.

A determined smile curled her lips. In that moment she was sure she was still the same old Regan. She knew what was important, what was right, and what wasn't.

Maybe she understood the difference better than she had before; maybe she saw it more clearly. Either way, she had the means to make things right, and she promised Baiyren she would. Peace would come because of what she did here today, a peace that would last as long as she lived. And if her newly gained knowledge was right, her life would be a long one. An infinitely long one.

Crossing her arms, she stared through her shield into the illuminated earth. Despite the orb's vibrant color, the world beyond appeared natural and untainted. Large caves gave way to tunnels that Regan thought looked eerily straight. Were they leading her? She could run a test, of course, but doing so would take time. Better to let instinct guide her than steal precious seconds from Baiyren.

How long have I been down here? she wondered. Hopefully no more than a quarter hour. It felt longer. Being inside a mountain, especially *this* mountain, made it impossible to tell.

Grimacing, she concentrated on the way ahead. For the first time since entering the Ridderroque, a wall blocked her way. Diamonds and iron veins reinforced the granite facing. It looked impregnable and yet, as she approached, a seam appeared down the middle. In a flash, the wall split, the two sides parting then closing and resealing as if they'd never opened.

Looks like you won't need that test after all. Grinning, she guided her shield into the vast space. Unlike the pitch-black tunnels above, phosphorescent gems scattered throughout the walls and ceiling illuminated an enormous hall. What light there was remained muted and somber, and apart from a polished marble floor that looked more like ice than rock, the great hall was empty. No pillars or buttresses soared up to support the roof, no furniture of any kind invited visitors. Only a gigantic statue at one end broke the monotony – a two hundred-foot tall stone likeness of a man with a wide chiseled brow, onyx eyes and a jerkin of iron mail worn over a muscular body. The traditional hammer sat on its right hip, looped through a belt of black metal.

An arm – its right – extended outward, palm closed into a loose fist. The left lay at its side but, as Regan looked closer, she caught a minute twitching in its fingers. She approached cautiously, landed at what she thought was a safe distance, and stared up at the figure without extinguishing the protective energy surrounding her body. The glow intensified but the color faded as if diluted. White blended with amber as another shield entered from her left. Startled, she wheeled and squinted into the newly emergent glow. Within stood a man in crimson robes that rippled despite the still air. He lifted his hand before she could ask him what he was doing here, the gesture silencing her.

Not now, Regan, Takeshi Akiko said into her head. His voice, though firm, held a soothing quality that reminded her of a stringed instrument. *You will have your answers, I promise. Just not now. Your reaction to the revelations to come must be genuine. You have been under my care for a very long time. I wish I could tell you more, but doing so would only hurt our chances.*

Regan frowned. *Chance for what? I don't understand.*

That's the point. You can't understand. Not before it's time. Regan tried to ask for more, but the man's attention had moved to the statue. *Hello, Malog,* he said in a serene yet commanding tone. *It's been a long time.*

The statue's eyes burst to life, and the giant lowered its head respectfully. "Lord Takeshi," it rumbled. "We'd begun to think you'd forgotten us."

"Easy to do, considering how long you and your master have remained hidden." Takeshi's tone carried a wisp of disapproving sarcasm.

"Exactly how long has it been? Maybe your new guardian can tell me." Malog's penetrating gaze swept from one side of the chamber to the other. "Where is she, Lord Takeshi? Why isn't she with you?"

As if summoned, a burgundy shield popped into the space beside him. The orb melted like a snowball on hot coals, revealing a pretty girl of about eighteen. Her straight, nearly black hair was cut into a short yet stylish bob that framed a pixie face. Dark brown eyes shaped like upside-down crescents sparkled with humor and mischief. She was slight, but she radiated self-confidence that made the slender form beneath the white robes seem iron hard.

Frowning, she put her hands on her hips. "Late again," she huffed. "I'm never going to get the hang of this." She glared up at the man next to her. "I think you need to work on your teaching skills, old man." Takeshi cleared his throat and gestured at the stone figure. The girl rolled her eyes; clearly, she knew it was there. "Hi, Malog. You look good. I guess your master hasn't been overworking you." Her eyes hardened again as her gaze drifted to Takeshi.

Hidden behind the two, Regan watched the exchange. None of the three paid any attention to her. She was what she'd always been: the outsider, the one who didn't belong. The man, the girl, and the living statue had a history; she couldn't help but see it. She'd stumbled upon an old argument, a rift among what seemed like family. The thought tore open wounds she believed forever healed. Loneliness filled her. The family she thought she'd made was broken and almost gone. The king was dead, and Baiyren was fighting a battle he could easily lose. If he did, she'd have no one; she'd be alone.

I was alone once too, said the girl in the burgundy shield. Regan recognized her, she'd been with the Earth girl, the one Baiyren rescued. *Trust me. Our lives aren't that different. The name's Keiko, by the way. Nice to meet you.*

Regan opened her consciousness to respond, but Keiko shot her a warning look. Rose-colored eyes met deep brown, the latter urging both silence and caution. Regan tried to let the girl know she understood, tried to nod slightly or flick her fingers. Her body didn't respond. Everything around her had stilled. Nothing moved, not sound, nor air, nor water. Time itself seemed to have paused. A smirk crossed Keiko's face before she turned back to the crimson-robed monk and bowed her head. When she lifted it again, Higo lurched forward.

The monk was closer to the statue than Regan remembered, gesturing with his arms as if in the middle of a speech. "It's time to summon your lord, Malog," Takeshi said. "Tell him I've come to fulfill my promise."

Malog sighed, the sound coming like the rush of gigantic bellows. "I'll tell him, but I doubt the news will make much difference."

"Oh, I think it will make all the difference in the world."

Deep skepticism darkened Malog's features. Strangely,

though, the statue didn't argue. Instead, it unfurled the fingers on its outstretched hand. A large silver globe hovered over the palm, inside which sat a huge, dark-skinned man. Brown robes fell from his broad shoulders, the arms beneath thick and strong. Seated, he measured at least five feet from his waist to the top of his head; how tall would he be when standing? His head, as smooth and bald as a polished stone, remained down, his massive shoulders drooping as if a great weight sat upon them. Sadness wreathed him like smog over a once pristine valley.

"What do you want, Takeshi?" the man said in a voice as deep as the Rake's canyons. His tenor might have been soothing if not for the despair lacing it.

"I said I'd be back, Roarke. I've brought someone I'd like you to meet."

The man – Roarke – looked away. "I'm not interested."

"I think you might be," Takeshi said, stepping forward.

Wariness spread through Regan, the soldier in her reawakening. *Me*, she thought. *He means me.* Was this some sort of ritual, a sacrifice maybe? She readied her new power but didn't unleash it. Never attack unless you have enough intelligence to know you'll win. Or unless you have to. And she didn't have to, at least not yet. Or did she? She thought of Baiyren and the battle raging outside. What if he needed her? How much time did he have?

Her mind flew to the world outside. She touched the mah-zhin, felt a connection to them. For the moment they'd stopped fighting and were on their way into the Ridderroque. An odd kinship with them bloomed inside her. She could use them; they would defend her. She reached for them, only to have the connection severed.

I wouldn't if I were you, Keiko warned. *You need to make a good impression here and fighting isn't exactly the best way to do it. They care about you, or will once they know the truth.* Keiko's tone was still mischievous, but this time a touch of steel lined its irreverence.

Inhaling, Regan pulled her thoughts from the mahzhin and let her power go, certain she could summon it quickly if necessary.

"I just want to be left alone," Roarke grumbled. "*You* created this world, not me. I came because you asked. Because you said you'd help me with my pain." A bitter laugh rose from his throat. "I found no healing here, only a reminder of what I lost. If I hadn't given my word, I never would've stayed."

"But you did give your word," Takeshi said pointedly. "And I expected you to live up to it. You have a responsibility to Botua and the gift she gave you."

Botua: the name sent shivers through Regan. A tiny sliver deep in her soul snapped open. Her heart beat faster, and thought exploded from her body to touch the stone surrounding her. Below, a dormant seed awakened. Branches pushed between a crack in the tiles, twisting. Growing, and thickening as they climbed upward.

Fifty feet above her, Roarke's head snapped up. Wonder painted his dark face, hope and disbelief blazing in his eyes. Hundreds of images flashed from his mind to hers. She saw a beautiful green-haired woman standing beside the man now seated in the statue's palm. They looked happy, joyous. More images came, a lifetime's worth flashing breathlessly forward. Regan tried to hold onto them, to understand and decipher their meaning.

The harder she tried, the more she missed. Eventually, she gave up and let them wash over her in a raging torrent that ended with the woman lying dead in a scorched grove.

Roarke stabbed a trembling finger at her. "What is this?" he demanded. "Who is she? What have you done?"

"She is Regan Zar Ranok," Takeshi said. "Your daughter – yours and Botua's."

The revelation sent Regan's stomach lurching. One hand pressed against it, the other going to her mouth to silence a gasp. *It can't be true.* This man was a stranger; she didn't know him, had never seen him before now. *But what if it is? What would it mean?*

That you're not alone, Keiko said, her voice more serious, more emotional than Regan had heard so far.

But that would make me…

The Lord of Stone's daughter. A kami, just like Takeshi said you were.

Kami.

Head lifting, Regan's eyes locked with Roarke. Something greater lay behind their shared pain, a bond that had nothing to do with commonality of experience. She felt the connection, and by the furrowing of his dark brows, she knew he felt it too.

"I don't believe it. Don't toy with me, Takeshi. Not about this." Like Regan, Roarke's pain wouldn't let him accept what he knew was true. He was afraid, and Regan couldn't blame him. She was scared too. Before she realized what she was doing, she moved toward him, her steps at once slow and incredibly fast.

Above, Roarke rose unsteadily, strode to the edge

of the hand holding him, and vaulted into the air. He landed a yard or more away, crashing to the tiles like a wayward meteor. He nodded at a spot on the floor. Stone tiles flew into the air and reassembled into a pyramid. A patch of bare earth lay where the stone had been. Roarke gestured at it.

Regan stared into the dark soil. He was testing her; she just didn't know what he wanted her to do. Mind racing, she stared at the open space, concentrating on the dirt. Nothing. She tried again with the same result. Frustrated, seething, she glared one last time before sighing in defeat. She shook her head. Her body relaxed.

And then she felt it.

An almost palpable affinity between her spirit and the ground tickled her thoughts. Higo called to her, and she responded. Summoning her power, she sent a part of her consciousness into the velvety soil, another into the impregnable rock. The two shot upward, fusing together into a twisting pillar of gray, brown, and green. Diamond veins sparkled beneath the surface before fading beneath a carpet of thick multi-hued vegetation. Roots and stems gave way to budding branches that exploded in a symphony of color and floral scents.

Roarke staggered back. "Stone. Vegetation. My power and Botua's." He shifted his tear-streaked gaze to Takeshi. "How did you do this?"

"I didn't do anything. Botua called to me just before she died. I was too late to help, but when I arrived I sensed Regan's infant spirit within her. So small, so young." Takeshi sighed at the memory. "Regan's spirit wasn't strong enough to take shape. She needed time. When she was finally ready I brought her here to be close to you." The enigmatic man nodded at the vast space. "Her spirit's roamed these caverns for millions of years. Eventually, she took physical form, and headed into the Rake."

"Where you found me," Regan said, her eyes wide.

Takeshi folded his hands into his robe and grinned, obviously pleased with himself. "What better place for the daughter of Higo's god to grow than in his church?"

Regan shook her head. The audacity. Every day, Higo's religious leaders went about their business, praying to their god and never once suspecting a piece of him lived beside them. She pulled her gaze from Roarke and pivoted to face Takeshi, only to find the Spirit Lord's body dissolving.

"Wait!" Regan shouted, rushing forward. "You can't go. I have so many questions."

Takeshi smiled happily. "And you have a father to answer them," he said. "I suggest you start by asking Roarke about your guardians. They are coming for you. Learn as much as you can before they arrive. Right now, they need you more than you need them. I'll have Keiko give you some time."

"It's what I do," Keiko said with a shrug. "Mess with time. More accurately, I pull spirits from the time stream and put them back in different places. Sometimes, I even hold them between seconds. I think I'll do that with you two. I'll need your permission first. My power doesn't work on a kami or a guardian without it." Regan looked at Roarke and they both nodded. "I can't keep you out for long," Keiko warned. "A week at most. I wish I could give you more, but I'm still learning, and this is my first non-test try. I held Higo for a really long time, but I had

Mr Takeshi's help for that – his and his guardian's." She waved then, disappearing the same way she'd come in: her burgundy shield flaring before bursting like a popped balloon.

Regan stared at the empty space for a long time before looking back at her father.

Father.

She tested the word, let it run through her, and decided it was the sweetest word she'd ever known. She shook her head, at a loss. "I… don't know what to say. I don't know where to start."

"Why don't we start with your guardians? If Takeshi's right, you need to know what they mean to you and how to link them to your will." He opened his thickly muscled arms, his expression guarded but hopeful.

Regan wasn't sure what to do. No one but the king had ever hugged her before. She found herself moving toward him, slowly at first but gaining speed with each step. His hands touched her shoulders before sliding around her back and drawing her to his chest. Stone was supposed to be cold, but Roarke was surprisingly warm. For the first time in her life she felt safe, at peace. She sighed and let the sensation wash over her. "Guardians," she breathed dreamily. "And then what?"

"Then," Roarke rumbled, placing his cheek on her head. "I'll tell you about your mother."

46
THE FIRST STEPS

Righteous lifted its battered face and stared at Yohshin. "So you're still free," Kaidan rasped. "She told me you would be. They both did. I didn't believe them." Sparks crackled from a hole where the mah-kai's left knee had been, the rest of the leg long since torn away.

Baiyren swallowed and averted his eyes. He'd done that, and he'd taken it as a victory. Now, after seeing the damage, after hearing Kaidan's blood-thickened voice, shame swept in to dampen the pride that had cleansed him. His chest heaved as he sucked at what little air he had left. "Who told you I'd be here?" His gaze flicked left then right. Guilt placed judges in the shadows, ready to leap at him, to condemn and punish him. "Did someone send you after me?"

"Juno," Kaidan panted. "Juno called me. I don't know how. The Heartstone maybe. Can't be sure." Kaidan's words ended in another wet cough. He was hurt. Badly hurt. Baiyren's guilt deepened. "She asked me to save you. She loves you, little brother. Just as I love Miko." Righteous shivered, its arms tightening protectively around Zuishin.

Brother. Baiyren closed his eyes and sighed. How long had it been since Kaidan called him that? Tears burned his eyes. He had to make this right. For his family as well as himself.

What about Higo?

A weak snort escaped him, expelling the odd scent of roses. Higo. A world divided since the beginning. Twin heads with separate priorities trying to manage one body. Children without guidance. Could one person, someone who never made the right choice, save a whole planet? He didn't know, and to be honest, he didn't really care.

Squaring his shoulders, he dissolved, the shield keeping Yohshin at bay. The sparkling dome unraveled in bright, silvery strands. Life returned to his body, his hands and feet tingled, and his head cleared. The shadows darkened thought, emotion fled, and though the threat of Yohshin remained, he no longer feared its power. Unlike the major decisions he'd made in his life, this one, this decision to act, came so easily. A slow breath left his lungs, and he smiled grimly. No one else would die today. He repeated the thought in his head to harden his building resolve and hurled his commands at Yohshin.

The golden giant had recovered quickly from Righteous's shocking reappearance. The long mace was back in its hand, and energy flowed into its weapons. Baiyren held his breath; for the moment, Yohshin had forgotten him.

He called out again, this time more forcefully, adding power and command to his inner voice. *No, Yohshin! You have to stop.* He redirected his thoughts to Righteous and was surprised when Yohshin stabbed a finger at the fallen mah-kai. He and Yohshin weren't as separate as he'd thought. He needed to remember that. *Royal blood! Prince Kaidan is in there. He's weak and probably dying. He's vulnerable. Do you understand? You can take him in my place, and he won't be able to stop you. He'll have the power he's always wanted, and you'll have a spirit to complete you – one who'll go to you willingly. You just have to save his life first.*

Vulnerable, Yohshin repeated. Then, *save his life.*

Yes. Hurry, Yohshin, he doesn't have much time left. Yohshin? Yohshin! What are you waiting for?

The mah-zhin had stepped back, mace lowered but weapons still powered. *What will I become?* It sounded small, afraid.

Complete, Baiyren replied, thinking of himself and the changes taking place within him. *For the first time in your life, you'll be at peace.*

And if it's too late? If I can't save him, will you promise to return and take his place?

Baiyren swallowed a gasp. He hadn't thought of that. Eyes closing, he nodded, praying it wouldn't come to that. *Yes. I promise; I swear by crown and blood. I won't abandon you, if you just do this for me.*

Very well then. Yohshin dipped its head. *For my part, I promise to do what I can to save him. Please clear your mind; I will begin the transference.*

A familiar light shimmered around Baiyren, and the odd combination of warmth and tingling filled his body. The light dimmed, dissolving and moving from the mah-zhin like a cloud through space. Darkness and light intermixed until he couldn't tell them apart. He reached the armor's inner coating. As he passed through, another presence, this one traveling in the opposite direction, ghosted by him. Time stopped, and in that moment, his life seemed to roll backward.

He was in his father's study, a boy of five, listening to the man talk about lineage and responsibility. Kaidan sat next to them, his face kind and encouraging. *I believe in you*, his expression said. *I know you'll make a great king.*

But Baiyren didn't want to be king, not then, not ever. His father might as well lock him in a prison for the rest of his life. No more fun, no more being who or what he wanted. Just a lifetime of responsibilities and false faces. That wasn't him. How could Kaidan think it could be?

The memory faded and another took its place. Kaidan leaned on one of the castle's parapets, his body rigid and his face drawn and strained. Lines ran from his eyes and over his cheeks, and though his face was dry, Baiyren was sure his brother had been crying. Kaidan straightened at Baiyren's approach. Happiness lifted a veil in his eyes and the sparkle Baiyren knew so well returned.

"You shouldn't be up here, little brother," he said. "It isn't safe." Brilliant sun shone down from above, and the only shadow lying across the land came from the Ridderroque. A long sliver stabbed westward toward Haven like a pointing finger or the hand of some enormous clock.

Baiyren fought a shiver and drew up his body, determined not to look intimidated. "If it's safe enough for you, then it's safe enough for me."

"But I'm not going to be king. You need to be more careful than I do." Kaidan's smile was equally proud and sorrowful.

Baiyren's father had told both of his sons who would succeed him. And who wouldn't. That had been months ago. Too much time had passed for that to darken Kaidan's mood. Something had happened – something bad. "Good thing I have Higo's best fighter up here with me," Baiyren said, doing his best to make his brother feel better. "That makes this the safest place in the city." Baiyren slapped his palm on the cool stone for emphasis.

"I suppose it does." Kaidan nodded, placing his hand on Baiyren's head and ruffling his hair.

The sensation morphed into the brush of stone. Baiyren was back in his hiding place over the throne room, Kaidan, Miko, and Regan below. The scene played out as he remembered with Kaidan accosting his father before leaving the castle for the final time.

And then, just as the king turned to leave, Regan lifted her gaze to the ceiling. Her piercing eyes cut through brick and stone and found him. The look chilled him. He shrank back, certain his imagination had tricked him. In his memory, Royal Guards came to escort Regan away. She hadn't looked up, and she most definitely didn't speak.

"You made the right decision, majesty." The king was the only one with her in the room, but Baiyren swore she cast words to the hidden alcove above her. "Mercy is always the right choice. Higo's forgotten that. Together, we will remind her. Higo and God both." She smiled then, her expression bright and confident. "I'll be waiting for you. *Inside*." Her smile widened even as the figure evaporated. The room followed, and then the light. Darkness returned but only for a moment. When it lifted, Baiyren found himself staring at a beach of soft white sand. A light breeze rippled otherwise still waters. A long shadow stretched over him, and he turned to see

Yohshin stagger from Zuishin and collapse to its knees.

The impact sent sand spraying high and wide. "What's happening? I... hurt," Yohshin said aloud.

Baiyren scrambled to his feet, fighting dizziness and rubbery legs. He'd come close to dying too. "It's Kaidan," he panted. "You're connected to him now. He's dying; that's what you feel. If we don't heal him soon, we're finished."

Yohshin pitched over. Only a reflexively thrown hand kept it from collapsing face-first onto the beach. "Can't move. Can barely think." Yohshin shook its head in disbelief. "Legs numb. Don't... know... what. To do."

Regan's words echoed in Baiyren's head. *I'll be waiting for you. Inside.* Inside! "The Ridderroque!" he cried, spinning to face Zuishin. "We have to get Yohshin into the Ridderroque." Baiyren glanced from the mech to the spot where he hurled Haven's shielded transport. *Juno?* he thought. *Are you there? I need you!*

A warm essence filled him, strong and familiar and radiating love. *Baiyren? Thank God. You're all right, aren't you? You sound fine but...* She sounded on the verge of tears, but her voice ran over him like a fresh spring breeze. His skin prickled and he felt refreshed.

Baiyren luxuriated in the sensation, but only for a moment. *I'm fine. I don't have time to tell you more. Just trust me, okay?* Juno's acquiescence rippled back to him; he nodded and straightened his shoulders. *I need you to talk to the Heartstone. Tell it we have to wake Zuishin right away.*

Zuishin? Are you sure?

Yes, I'm sure. That mah-zhin's been trying to help us. We just didn't see it.

It killed thousands of people, Baiyren; people I knew and

who were good to me... It killed Regan.

Please, Juno. Before it's too late. Baiyren felt the questions forming in Juno's head. They started to take shape, then, just as quickly, he felt her dismiss them. Her will hardened and her thoughts turned from him to the Heartstone.

For a long moment, nothing happened. Then, as Baiyren was about tell Juno to keep trying, Zuishin shivered. The mah-zhin rolled to its side, placed a foot on the ground, and pushed unsteadily to its feet.

Did it work? Juno's thoughts came at Baiyren in a tired rush.

Yes, Baiyren rasped. *It worked.* He stared at the magnificent giant. As tall as a redwood with its russet-hued armor, willowy frame, and lithe limbs. Large saffron eyes burned in a smooth and beautiful face. *We're heading for the mountain. Can you see where you are?*

Hold on. Baiyren felt an odd sensation of movement. *The stone shell Yohshin put us in fell apart as soon as we got here. Looks like a cavern of some sort. We're in the water, near a stone pier.*

I know it. Stay where you are. I'm on my way. With that, he turned his thoughts to Zuishin. *I did what you wanted,* he declared. *Yohshin has Kaidan, but he needs to heal.* Baiyren thrust a finger at the mountain's roots. *The mountain shrine is his only chance. Can you get us there?*

Zuishin peered at the mountain as if measuring it. *Yes, but only so far. A barrier stands between the entrance and the shrine itself.*

One step at a time. *If you get us there, I'll do the rest.* He'd been in once before; he could do it again. Zuishin nodded and lowered its palm. Baiyren didn't hesitate. He sat, and

Zuishin raised its shield. Forest green light arced from the mah-zhin's body, moving swiftly to create a large orb that included Yohshin. The light flared and, when it faded they were inside the Ridderroque. Yohshin lay on a wide beach to Baiyren's left, Zuishin standing guard over it.

The hum of an engine sounded behind him, and he glanced over his shoulder to see a twin passenger vehicle bobbing up and down on the calm water. Smooth and white and typical of the church, the transport was docked fifty or so yards away. A door opened, and as soon as Juno jumped out, it closed again, and the transport slipped silently into the lagoon.

Juno raced across the wet ground, her feet leaving deep imprints in the sandy shore. *Safe*, Baiyren thought. *She's still safe*. In seconds, her arms were around him, her body pressed against his. She buried her face in his shoulder. She made a sound that was equal parts sob and relief.

"Are you all right?" She touched his face. "I was so worried."

"I was worried about you too." Baiyren didn't want to push her away, but Kaidan still needed healing. He had to move, and he had to move fast.

"Hey," Juno said, her tone soft. Gentle. She cupped Baiyren's chin and drew his attention back to her. "What are you thinking?" Baiyren tried to look away, but her hand on his chin remained firm. "I have to know." Her words were steady and unafraid and said, Baiyren realized, not for her benefit but for his. Because he needed to let them out if he wanted to heal his wounded spirit.

He drew a breath and focused on her, blocking out the mah-zhin, seeing nothing but her bright hazel irises. "I've spent the last few years of my life running – from my past and my future, even from myself. The only time I stop is when I'm with you. Do you understand what I'm trying to say?"

A satisfied smile crossed Juno's face. "I understand what you're trying really hard not to say." She laughed then, a light, triumphant sound. "It's okay, Baiyren. We'll talk about this later. She planted her hands on her hips and looked around. "What're we supposed to do next?"

"I wish I knew."

Juno raised an eyebrow. "Maybe you just need to take off your crown for a minute and go back to being a scientist. Don't think about this place the way Higo's king would; look at it like any other site you want to excavate then tell me what you see."

Leave it to Juno to speak to him like that. Nodding curtly, he walked around the cavernous space.

A pair of large doors lay thrown open at the far end. Those led into the chamber where he had found Yohshin nearly a decade ago. Nothing else appeared disturbed. *What am I looking for?* he wondered. *What did God hide in here?*

To his left, Yohshin staggered to its feet. Its right arm slammed into a near wall for balance. The clang of metal on stone echoed for a moment before fading into the clack of falling pebbles. Golden light pulsed around its body, a strobing nimbus that never fully formed. Then Zuishin was there, supporting the other mah-zhin, adding its shield to the glow until the darkness fled.

Juno gasped, hurried to Baiyren, and pointed up.

Overhead, a large pictogram spread across the ceiling. More perfect than any sculpture, the image might have been part of the rock itself. The story, for that's what Baiyren assumed it was, started at the left and worked its way to the right. An image depicting a lush plain and huge mountains provided the background on one side, an ocean cutting off the other. A handful of men and women stood inside shining globes at various points. In the mountains, a woman with lush blonde hair shot from the peaks, an emeraldgreen nimbus encasing her perfect figure. Below, a man inside a black orb cowered before another, more powerfully built man with tawny hair and fiery eyes. The second man held his arms over his head, flames flying from his fingers. Between the two, a beautiful woman lay upon a bed of charred trees, her body burned, her face untouched.

Baiyren stared at her in wonder, taking in the woman's face – her long hair, the flowers sprinkled through tresses the color of fresh ivy. He saw ruined mountains, a majestic dragon, and a fallen giant that reminded him of Zuishin.

Juno tensed beside him. She put a hand over her mouth. "Is that…? It can't be. I don't believe it."

But it was. "The fossil we found in China," Baiyren said numbly. "The woman, the creature." He pointed a trembling hand to the far edge of the carving where the silhouette of an enormous man had fallen to his knees. Grief contorted his dark-skinned face, and diamonds ran down his cheeks to represent his tears. "And *that* is where we have to go." Baiyren lowered his finger, air-tracing a barely visible rectangle on the wall below the image.

Juno lifted her eyebrow at him. "So, you're telling me you have the key, is that it?"

"I don't," Baiyren said. "But you do. Take out the Heartstone, Juno."

Frowning, Juno pulled the pendant from the top of her dress then stared at him, uncertain. "How is this supposed to get us in?" She looked disappointed.

"The Heartstone's a little like the mah-zhin. It has a… consciousness to it."

Juno let out a relieved sigh. "You have no idea how happy I am to hear you say that. I was starting to think I'd lost my mind." She straightened, turned to the wall and, holding the stone in her palm, held out her hand. "So what now?"

"Just ask it to open the door. And what did you mean about losing your mind?"

"The thing talks to me – in my head. It also listens and does what I ask it to."

"What did you say?" Baiyren grabbed Juno's shoulders and turned her to face him. "Are you sure?"

"What's wrong with you? Of course I'm sure. I said it, didn't I?" Juno studied him, her head tilted to one side, her brows creasing. "Why's this so important?"

Baiyren removed his hands. "I'm sorry; I shouldn't have done that." He paused to gather his thoughts. "My family passed the Heartstone from one generation to the next, always saying God would talk to us through it one day." He shook his head. "Until now, it's never spoken to anyone. Not once. My father and grandfather didn't think it would. Not ever. They said no king believed the story. Why would they? No one had any proof."

"And they still don't. Not really."

Baiyren smiled gently. "They will soon enough; we all will. He gestured at the wall, moving aside and giving her what he hoped was an encouraging look. "Come on, Juno. Let's test the theory."

Juno drew a deep breath and let it out sharply. "All right," she said, lifting her hand again and thrusting the stone at the shuttered doors. "Here goes." She closed her eyes; her brows furrowed then relaxed. Her eyelids fluttered and, when they opened, wonder filled her hazel eyes. Nodding, she smiled at Baiyren, and – her fingers unfurling like a new flower – presented the stone like an offering.

Baiyren stayed very still. Watching. Waiting. His palms grew sweaty, and he rubbed his fingertips over them without thinking. He wondered why Lord Roarke spoke to Juno and never anyone else. What did that mean? That royal blood was less important to Him than it was to Higo's people? The idea both sobered and reassured him. Maybe God differentiated between being king and earning it, birthright be damned.

Baiyren had his chance now, and he vowed to prove his worth – to Lord Roarke, to his people, and to himself. Inhaling, he prepared his mind for what was to come. He swallowed. Maybe it was better not to think too much about that. Instead, he focused on the Heartstone and waited through the eternal seconds.

How many had passed? He couldn't tell if it was a few or a billion. It could have been either. Then, just as he was about to turn his attention to the door, he heard a soft, delicate chiming. The stone vibrated with the sound of tiny hammers on small brass bells. A rumbling came next. Not the door, not yet. This was the mah-zhin,

Zuishin helping a wounded Yohshin to its knees.

The chimes became a loud, insistent calling. Vibrations rippled from Juno's hand and radiated outward. A second wave followed, this one originating from the stone. The floor trembled, and a loud grinding joined the swelling chorus. Ahead, the door's outline widened. The left side rolled back and then the right. The brilliance Baiyren expected from the Heartstone burst through the opening instead.

He blinked furiously, but the light remained strong and unfading. Was that his god? He reached for Juno, supporting her as she did him. She gave him a quick squeeze, as much to let him know she was all right as to say they stood together. Her other hand remained open a moment longer. Eventually, she curled her fingers and lowered her arm.

The light before them dimmed and rounded in response and when it went out, a dazzling globe of amber light hovered several feet above the floor. Bright cyan streaks flashed over its surface like lightning. They came and faded and, with each fading, Baiyren could just make out a figure behind the energy.

Tall and slender with long hair like black ivy, a flawless olive complexion, and eyes the color of pale pink roses. Baiyren's mind rebelled against what he saw. He closed his eyes, then reopened them. The woman was still there, unmistakable in the light. She smiled back at him with a gaze he'd recognize anywhere.

"Regan," he breathed. "How?"

47
OF TERRA AND VERDURE

Regan stood just beyond the doors, robed in light. Her royal black and gray uniform transformed into tan robes slashed through with forest green vines. "Baiyren?" she said, "I didn't expect to see you. I heard the guardians were coming, but I thought you stayed on the beach." She smiled. "I'm glad you didn't; I was worried about you."

She didn't look worried; she looked majestic. He inched forward, afraid of her for the first time in his life. "I watched you die," he said.

Regan laughed lightly, a sound that reminded him of rain on pavement. "I'm not a ghost, if that's what you're worried about. It's all a bit confusing. I'm not even sure I can explain it."

"Then maybe you should let me," a voice said from the darkness. An enormous man emerged from the far room. His skin was the color of rich soil, and his wise, round eyes looked like sand-filled crystals. The robes he wore were so similar to the church priests' that for a moment Baiyren thought he was a pilgrim. "Do you know who I am, King Baiyren?"

Baiyren gaped, his eyes became wide saucers, his mouth a perfect oval. He fought for words. "You are Lord Roarke Zar Ranok, God of Higo," he said falling to his knees.

"Kami of Earth and Stone," the man said with a nod. He gestured at the two hundred-foot tall walking statue standing guard at his back "This is Malog, my guardian, what you call a mah-zhin." He smiled proudly at Regan. "You already know Regan, or Regan as she used to be. Now she is Regan Zar Ranok, Kami of Terra and Verdure. My daughter."

"Daughter? Regan?" Baiyren blinked. "Is this true?"

"From what they tell me." Regan sounded happier and more content then he'd ever heard her. She looked from Roarke to Baiyren. "I can barely believe it." A pained look flashed over her face. "This doesn't mean I've stopped grieving, Baiyren. I want you to know that."

Baiyren lowered his head and nodded.

"This war is more my fault than anyone's," Roarke apologized. "I left you alone far too long. I think it's time to correct that." Straightening, he glanced at each of them. "Making my first appearance in over a millennium will give you some privacy. Besides, as I understand it, Regan has a guardian to save. You need to be there when she does, King Baiyren. To see you're not alone after all."

"Me?" Baiyren said, puzzled. "I don't understand."

"You will." Roarke smiled. He drew the enormous hammer from his belt, lifted it, and brought it down in a smooth, sweeping strike. The walls shook, and dust stirred into the air. He made a great swirling motion with his hand, and the debris curled and twisted into a small cyclone. Velocity and momentum increased, ripping up tiles and drilling a hole in the floor. Roarke motioned again, and a silver orb surrounded his body. His guardian mimicked the movement to raise a shield of its own, this one a large globe of shining copper light. Together, they lifted from the ground and dropped into the opening.

"What did he mean about a guardian?" Baiyren demanded, once the dust settled. "And why is it so important for me to know?"

"Every kami has a guardian," Regan explained. "Like the one you saw with my father. The best way to describe them would be to say they're like demi-gods. Older, stronger kami have one guardian, like my father has Malog. As for me…" she shifted uncomfortably. "My parents both had different powers; my father controls stone and earth, my mother was a kami of plants and flora. Which is why–"

"You have two guardians," Baiyren finished. He looked at the two mah-zhin and understood. It made sense, especially after giving so much of himself to Yohshin. *That's why it needed me, that's why I lose a part of my soul whenever we merge.* He was right all along: they weren't complementary pieces, they were too much alike – the same half of a coin. What Yohshin needed was the other half. It needed Kaidan. "So what happens now?" he asked.

"First I heal Yohshin's wounds. After that… we'll see." Regan walked past him, as Juno returned to his side, slipped her arm around his waist, and drew him close.

"Don't worry, Baiyren," she said. "Everything will be okay. Regan will heal your brother. You'll see."

Baiyren nodded. He rested his cheek atop her head

and sighed. Her hair smelled of apples and honey, and he inhaled deeply, each breath relaxing him one piece at a time. As always, Juno was right; Regan would take care of everything. His smile broadened, and as he watched her walk to the mah-zhin, he spied Keiko hiding in a small alcove across the room. She winked at him, and he had the odd feeling that she planned to tie up one last loose end. One concerning his future, one he couldn't figure out. The thought brought a twinkle to her eye.

Chuckling quietly, she lifted a finger, urging silence. He nodded and, turning away, strode to the mah-zhin.

48
JUST THE BEGINNING

Regan wasn't used to fear. Being alone for so long, having no family to worry about, came with that advantage. Now, as she was about to tie Miko and Kaidan to her, her nerves danced, knotting her stomach and tensing her muscles. Her father said she needed to link the guardians to her – he even showed her how. Knowing wasn't the same as doing, though, and what was she supposed to do when she finished? That was the bigger question, the one she didn't ask.

Zuishin still cradled Kaidan in its arms as she drew closer. She stopped, and Zuishin helped a wounded Yohshin from its knees. Regan's thoughts reached for them, summoning them to stand at her side throughout eternity.

Zuishin answered first. "So you have called me," it said. "So I have come."

"And your name?" Regan prompted.

"Miko, guardian of flora."

Regan bowed and turned her gaze to Yohshin.

"So you have called me," Yohshin said. "So I have come."

"And your name?"

Yohshin hesitated.

Frowning, Regan slipped a part of her mind into Yohshin's subconscious. Another part went into Kaidan. Manipulating both, she showed them one dream after another. She designed the scenarios to elicit responses and no matter the situation, Kaidan and the mah-zhin reacted the same way – emotionally, instinctively, and intellectually. They even came to the same conclusions, made the same decisions. The two were one; they just wouldn't merge.

Miko, Regan said. *I need your help. I want you to show Yohshin what it means to be whole.*

As you say, mistress. Miko placed her hands on her head and pulled. The hiss of escaping air sounded in the hall. Auburn tresses spilled onto the mah-zhin's shoulders. Dimpled cheeks came next, then her stunning yellow eyes.

Smiling, she knelt beside Yohshin. "Look at me. I haven't changed, not inside and not outside. I'm still Zuishin, but I'm Miko too. Please, you have to complete the merge. Your body will die if you don't. If it dies, you die too." Yohshin pulled back, but Miko held fast. "I don't want you to die." She leaned in and touched her forehead to his. "You saved my life, let me save yours."

Yohshin gazed into Miko's eyes and finally nodded. With a shift of its knees, Yohshin bowed before Regan.

"So you have called me," Yohshin began. "So I have come. Kaidan, Guardian of Ore and Mineral."

Regan brightened. "Welcome, my guardian," she said. "I need you to open your mind so I can heal you."

Kaidan nodded, and Regan slipped her thoughts into his.

Pain assaulted her, but she brushed it away and moved deeper. *Your wounds are serious,* she said. *But I am in time.* She knitted Kaidan's mind and body together, and when they were one, he stared at his hands in amazement.

Regan emptied her lungs. She was tired but happy.

"Regan?" Baiyren said, coming up beside her. His face was ashen, his soul worried. Juno was with him; she stayed a step behind, far enough to give him space, close enough to support him. "He's all right, isn't he?" Kaidan was his only family now, and he was afraid of losing him.

"Yes, Baiyren, he's fine. Look."

Miko had already moved her hands to his helm and lifted. The hiss of escaping air echoed throughout the chamber for a second time, a nice counterpoint, Regan thought, to Baiyren's sharp inhalation.

Like with Miko, Kaidan's handsome face emerged from the helm. He looked about in wonder. "Miko," he whispered. Tears streaked his cheeks. Their foreheads touched, and they stayed like that for long moment. When they broke apart, Kaidan turned his eyes to Baiyren. Shame reddened his skin, but he didn't avert his gaze. "Brother," he said. "I can't tell you how sorry I am."

"You didn't know what you were doing. None of us did."

"We do now," Regan said. "And we'll start by putting Higo back together. My guardians don't have a choice, but what about you, Baiyren? What have you decided?"

Baiyren exhaled loudly. "Higo has a god now, but it doesn't have a king."

"Rebuilding what we've torn apart will take time," Regan said. "I'll give you what support I can, but I think

I'm staying in the Ridderroque for a while." She drew in a deep breath, stood tall, and called to the mah-zhin. "Come guardians; it's time to go."

Miko put her helm back on, but before Kaidan did the same he stared at Baiyren with a nostalgic expression. "If I remember right, we have a game to finish. The one from the throne room? You were hiding, but I never looked for you."

Baiyren smiled back. "I look forward to it," he said, watching Kaidan turn away and step into a globe of shining amber.

Regan was the last to enter. She lifted her arm in salute before heading deeper into the cavern. She emerged in the now empty chamber where her father had closed himself off from the world and grinned. *I should have known you'd be here.* She scanned the room. *You can come out now, Keiko.*

You realize getting your permission takes the fun out of it.

Is that all you have to say?

No, Keiko admitted, stepping out into the hall. *You were right about Baiyren and Juno. They're both stubborn. Don't worry, though, I'll make sure they know where they belong and who they belong to.* She sighed happily. *After watching so much go wrong, it'll feel good to see something go right.*

I know what you mean, Regan agreed. *Now if you'll excuse me, I'd like to talk to my father about Earth.*

I could have told you what you needed, Keiko grinned.

Regan suppressed a laugh. *This isn't for you, Keiko,* she said, reopening the hole her father made. *It's for him.* She leaped into it and let Higo embrace her. She knew he waited for her in the depths, and she didn't want him to be alone too long. They needed and completed each other. Just like Miko and Kaidan.

Juno and Baiyren were the same as well. Regan trusted Keiko would do as she promised and make them admit their feelings for each other. She smiled contentedly. For a guardian of spirit, that shouldn't be too much of a problem.

49
ANSWERED PRAYERS

Less than a week later, Higo celebrated Baiyren's coronation. The entire city of Sahqui-Mittama turned out to welcome its young king, and people from as far away as the Yadokai made the long journey to show their support. He had stopped the greatest war in the planet's history, and he'd started to heal the fractures between its religious and political leaders.

In a show of solidarity, he asked Taisho to place the crown on his head. Though the church had not officially elevated the monk to high priest, no one within the hierarchy voiced any opposition. Baiyren assumed it existed, but when he learned Lord Roarke had appeared briefly before the Council of Priests and named Taisho as his primary servant, the ordination was all but assured. Baiyren wished he'd been there to see the council's reaction. *Priceless*, Taisho had called it.

The crowd around the dais breathed a sigh of relief when Baiyren promised to restore the public's trust. The church and the crown may have been at war for years, but for the most part, Higo's citizens remained loyal to both.

Baiyren ended his remarks with strong words of friendship, emphasizing reconciliation between people from one end of the Tatanbo plains, through the Rake, to the Yadokai and beyond.

Two days later, he boarded a transport bound for Haven with members of Sahqui-Mittama's aristocracy, the castle's chief priest, and Juno. The new high priest hadn't asked Baiyren to make the trip, but he felt he needed to honor the religious city by participating in its most important ceremony.

Large and spacious, the floating ship reminded Baiyren of the fifteenth-century galleons that once cruised Earth's mighty oceans. The thought made him somber. It was a reminder of Juno, and that one last piece of unfinished business. He glanced at her and offered a heartfelt smile, only to find her studying him with a blank expression.

She'd been that way since their return to the city. Baiyren wondered about the chill that had settled over her. He'd taken to reviewing his actions toward her. Had he said or done anything to upset her? He didn't think so, but no matter how many times he relived the time between their return to Sahqui-Mittama and his coronation, he couldn't find a single reason for her to be angry with him. Whenever he asked her about it, she simply shook her head, offered a weak smile, and said she was fine.

Sighing, he joined her at a seat in the main cabin, a large room with panoramic windows, an array of tables and chairs, and a bar for refreshments. Sitting, he took her hands and searched her face.

"I imagine you're anxious to get home." The words came out reluctantly. More than anything, he wanted her to stay. But he knew he couldn't make the decision for her. "As soon as this is over, I'll make sure I get you back."

The words only widened the distance between them. Juno stiffened as if frozen, then fell into a stony silence. Without a word, she pushed back from the table and walked away.

She remained closeted in a small office for the rest of the journey and as much as Baiyren wanted to talk to her, official duties kept him closer to the transport's bridge than the office at the ship's stern. He hoped she hadn't chosen that room for that particular reason. Deep down, he knew she had. Once, while walking past, he was sure he saw a burgundy glow leaking from under the door. The sound of conspiratorial whispering came with it, one voice frustrated, the other soothing. Baiyren stopped to knock then thought better of it. He stalked away, wondering who Juno would let into her room.

The four hours between leaving Sahqui-Mittama and arriving at Haven turned out to be the longest he could remember. Still, when the ruined city appeared on the horizon, he didn't know whether to be relieved or worried. The wounds Zuishin's awakening had caused were all too visible. A huge bore opened where the Higo's sanctuary had been, the walls caved in, sand spilling down in a swirl not unlike a sink's drain. Farther out, the damage, though less severe, leveled much of Haven's commercial and residential districts. Mah-kai moved through the wreckage. Clearing either would take months, if not years.

Baiyren didn't think asking Regan to help was out of order. He stared at the devastation, wondering how to broach the subject with her.

A temporary access road ran a quarter of a mile to a makeshift speaker's platform at the ruined basilica's gates. Four mah-kai lined either side of the road and another ten guarded the platform. Within their protective ring, two hundred chairs faced the podium; the occupants turned their expectant faces as the doors opened and Baiyren stepped out with Taisho. Juno did not appear, preferring to remain locked in her cabin.

A good deal of work had gone into the event, and as he headed for the elevated platform he noted many familiar faces. Baron Nattaka, a devious man with a grandfather's face, sat on one end, a reedy, middle-aged monk next to him speaking in his ear. The shock of white hair several rows back belonged to Mamoru, one of his father's oldest friends. He'd aged considerably since Baiyren last saw him, but then so had most of the others.

Unlike his coronation in the capital, the ceremony here was not a great, unifying event. One sister in particular – a plump, little woman with short dark hair – lowered her head close to the thin birdlike woman next to her and muttered something that, by both of their expressions, must have been nasty. Baiyren wasn't naïve enough to believe he could heal the rifts Miko and Kaidan created, but at least many of Haven's guard, the Riders included, had become Regan's most devoted followers. When the newly anointed kami returned from her training, Baiyren would encourage her – along with her father – to join Taisho for a revelatory service outside the damaged Basilica. Thinking about what *that* would do to all these grudge-holding, supposedly devout brothers and sisters brought a grin to his face.

A thousand possibilities sped through his mind, but before he could sort them out, Brother Shimono strode toward him and bowed formally. "Welcome to Haven, your majesty." The man was a few years older than Baiyren's father had been, but he'd always had a chiseled face. Now, he looked careworn around the eyes and mouth, his hair more gray than dark.

Keeping Haven together after such a tragedy probably had a lot to do with it. Baiyren wondered if leadership would do the same to him. Having Juno at his side would have gone a long way to prevent it. To his surprise, he caught her standing behind the last row of seats. She had changed into a stunning gown of silver and onyx. The collar was low and rounded, the bodice fitted and tapered to a flowing skirt. Her face glowed like a sunrise, but when she realized Baiyren had seen her, the indifferent expression returned.

For what, though? He wished he knew. Trying to put her out of his head, he nodded to Shimono and gestured to the stairs. As they climbed, Baiyren felt hundreds of eyes watching him, some searching for answers, some revenge, others hope. Their uncertainty was like a weight on his shoulders. Turning, he stared into the deep pit behind the platform. Rubble littered its depths, fragments from once-familiar statues laying in pieces, stained glass shattered, walls, roofs, and pillars, all unrecognizable. How many had died here? How much had they lost?

When he reached the platform, he headed for a lectern of dark wood. Drawing himself up and wearing what he hoped was a regal expression, he squared his shoulders and gave the people seated before him an encouraging nod. Taisho stood to his right, his rust-colored robes rustling in the light breeze. Baiyren smiled at him, headed for the podium, and stopped, staring curiously into the crowd.

Below, a balding bishop with a hooked nose and wide, fleshy features leapt to his feet. He pointed a trembling finger at the skies. Faces lifted, then paled; a chorus of quivering voices shivered through the gathering. Baiyren wheeled and spotted a figure in shining white robes approached from the eastern sky. Thick black hair blew across a perfect face, her stunning eyes sweeping over the people.

A ripple ran through the city. Most people bowed their heads, but others, those who knew Regan, those who fought against her, muttered angrily. She nodded to them and opened a hand. Light flew into the sky and exploded into vibrant, spark-filled showers. The smoke cleared. Kaidan stood on the eastern end of the deep chasm, Miko on the west.

Regan looked east, and Kaidan lofted his hammer. He brought it down with an earth-shattering boom. Quakes spread, and the ground split open. Rock heaved and climbed and in seconds a new basilica climbed out of the earth. Stone peeled away, and details emerged in the facing. Flying ramparts connected to spires, continued on, and melded with a great domed roof. A new tower replaced the old, looking both familiar and profoundly different.

Satisfied, Kaidan lowered the hammer and placed his hands on the pommel.

Regan dipped her head again, and Miko dropped to her knees. The guardian's fingers bored into the soil. A second ticked by, then another. After a minute, green fronds appeared. They sprang from the earth and raced from one end of the city to the other. Trees grew and flowers bloomed. Baiyren inhaled the sweet smell of new blossoms. Vegetation had always been sparse here, but now it grew with abandon.

New beginnings, he thought. *If Haven can have one, then so can I.* Hope filled his heart. He looked about, searching the crowd for Juno.

He found her standing at the back of the crowd. Keiko Yamanaka was beside her. Keiko shook her head at him. Her burgundy shield blazed to life, startling the people around her. Inside, Juno lifted her face to him as if giving him one last chance. He stood frozen, not knowing what to do or why she was so angry with him.

He ran forward, knowing he should say something but unable to. His mouth moved, but no words came out.

Tears formed in Juno's eyes. She gestured at Keiko, who gave Baiyren a final, pitying glare before pointing at a spot in the sky.

Light exploded from her finger, and the air behind Juno transformed into a silvery curtain. At first, Baiyren didn't recognize what he saw. Then, in a moment of horrified clarity, he knew. Stomach lurching, he leapt from the podium and hurled himself at Juno. "No!" he cried. "Don't go! Juno, stop."

But she didn't stop. Instead, she let Keiko fly her into the Pathways and close the Portal.

50
A QUESTION ASKED

Baiyren wilted under his throne's weight. The day had been a long one, hearing requests, meeting with delegates from Haven, and seeing to Sahqui-Mittama's reconstruction. As with the basilica at Tsurmak, Regan and her guardians rebuilt much of the damage; making the citizens feel more secure day to day was now up to him. He stretched, wondering if he could find a better, more efficient way to hear petitions. That would be one of the first things he brought to the council. Yawning, he turned, and was about to start down the steps when he noticed one last figure.

"Come forward," he said, keeping the weariness from his voice. "How may the crown help you?"

"The *crown* can start by helping itself," a voice chided. "You really are an idiot, you know."

A guard appeared from the left, another to the right. They moved a few steps into the room then stopped mid-stride as if frozen.

"Keiko," Baiyren said, exhaling. "Juno said you could do that. I didn't believe her." He ran a hand through his hair. "That seems funny now, considering."

"*Funny?*" Keiko said, walking up to the stairs and climbing. "You know what I think is funny? I think it's funny that a man who's been looking for attention his whole life can miss it when it's right in front of him."

"Juno made her choice, Keiko. She decided to go home."

"She gave you plenty of chances to change her mind. Either you ignored them – which I doubt – or you were totally clueless, which I think is more likely."

"I don't know what you're talking about." Baiyren was having trouble following anything Keiko said.

Keiko rolled her eyes. "Give me a break. Of course you do. This is about you not asking Juno to stay."

"I'm really not in the mood for this, Keiko." Baiyren sat down, not in his throne, but on the first step.

Keiko joined him. "Clueless," she muttered. "Just like I thought." She stood and held out a hand.

"We're going to Earth aren't we?" Baiyren said.

"Naturally. How else are we supposed to fix this?"

"I don't–"

"You do. Just ask her. That's all she wants you to do."

"I don't–"

"You don't have to. You just have to ask. Do you think you can manage that much?"

Baiyren nodded but remained silent.

"Good." Keiko brought her burgundy shield to life and opened the Portal to Earth. "Let's hope you can."

Juno sat at her hotel desk, paging through a sheaf of papers without seeing them. They were all that remained of Baiyren's last expedition: a list of personal effects, the cost of storage, and a voucher from the American consulate in Guangzhou. The other members of her team, the three who'd survived, immediately contacted the nearest American diplomatic post. They'd broken camp as soon as the fighting ended and sought sanctuary behind what was considered American soil. Juno couldn't blame them.

The Chinese were very touchy when something this big happened inside their borders, particularly when fifty or so Chinese had died. Juno put the reports down and rubbed her temples. She wasn't really reading them anyway.

Her mind drifted back to Higo. She missed that world, missed the beautiful vistas, clean air, and strong, hopeful people. Most of all, she missed Baiyren.

Why didn't he ask me to stay? Don't I mean anything to him? He certainly meant a great deal to her.

Standing, she paced about the room for a long time. She stared at the clock next to her bed. Nine forty-five. The man from the consulate would be here soon. He'd promised to drive her to the village where she'd find her things. She told him that wasn't necessary, but he insisted. At least she thought he did; remembering details was difficult. The past few days were a blur of fatigue, tears, and loss. Maybe it was better to have him take her.

She hurried to the mirror, checked her reflection, and headed into the hall.

A quick elevator ride brought her to the hotel's western-styled lobby. Generic stone columns lined a fairly large space, and she made her way over the gray carpets, past the reception desk, and took a seat facing the windows. After about ten minutes, a nondescript sedan – navy blue, naturally – pulled into the circular drive. A man in a suit that matched the car's color got out and headed inside. He was tall, well over six feet, and while his features were Asian, Juno thought he looked more Japanese than Chinese.

"Ms Montressen?" he said. His voice was smooth and deep and only lightly accented. He extended a hand. "I'm Matsuda. I'm sorry we have to meet under these circumstances. I imagine you are anxious to be on your way."

Juno nodded and managed a weak smile. The man's calm demeanor made her feel better. His card, emblazoned with a US State Department logo, didn't hurt either. "Thank you," she said. "I really don't want to inconvenience you. Like I said on the phone, you didn't need to do this."

"After everything you've experienced? It's the least we can do. Come." He gestured at the revolving doors. "We should be on our way."

Juno followed him into the sultry air and slipped into the back seat, staring absently out the window as Matsuda pulled into the street. The ride took the better part of two hours, and Juno was starting to get fidgety when she recognized the tall, sheltering cliffs beyond the windshield. They drove through the same narrow tunnel the crew used to move equipment in and out of the site and emerged on the other side.

Grass already sprouted within the blast craters, and rain and weather had worked over the tumbled rocks to the point that they seemed part of the landscape. *Everything heals*, Juno thought.

A few yards away she spotted the deserted camp. The tents and equipment were gone, the space empty.

Matsuda came up behind her. "Ms Montressen? There's someone to see you."

Juno turned, expecting to see one of the expedition's survivors. She stopped suddenly. "Keiko?" she gasped. "What the hell?" She spun to confront Matsuda, but the man and his car were gone.

"Hello, Juno." Keiko grinned. "It's good to see you again." Keiko wore a short white kimono over a pair of plain pants the same hue as the robe. Burgundy slashes accented the top, a matching obi completing the look. "I had a couple of loose ends to tie up before I go back to my training." She ignited her shield and pointed to the cliff tops. "I'll be up there if you need me." With that, she catapulted into the air and disappeared behind the tall rock.

"Wait!" Juno called, running after her. "Come back!" This wasn't happening. How was she supposed to get out of here? Panic seized her. She looked for some way out: a villager, a child who could fetch a rescue party, even a government official would do.

She didn't see anyone. Fuming, she started walking. How far was the nearest town? Over ten miles from what she remembered. They'd bought supplies there, filled their jeeps and spare gas cans. Her heart sank when she remembered refilling the cars at least once during their trip. Hoping the Chinese had left guards around what was now the place where foreigners attacked, she trudged on. Where was she supposed to find help, and why would Keiko leave her alone.

You're not alone, Keiko said in her head. *Turn around, Juno.*

Juno's feet faltered. *Keiko? This isn't funny.*

Just turn around.

Juno did as Keiko asked and found Baiyren standing before her.

"Hi," he said awkwardly.

"Baiyren?" Juno drew a deep breath and closed her eyes. She couldn't let him know how her heart ached at the sight of him. Slowly, she opened her eyes. He looked the same as he had the day she left, the loose gray shirt, the black pants.

"Juno," he said unsteadily. "I'm sorry. Higo hasn't been the same without you. The... people want you back; they miss you."

Juno arched an eyebrow. "The *people* miss me?"

Sweat dotted Baiyren's forehead. "You still have the Heartstone," he added hastily. "It's one of Higo's most sacred relics. It has to come back."

Juno stepped forward. "The *Heartstone* won't go anywhere until it knows it's wanted. It's perfectly capable of making its own decisions and doesn't like having them made for it."

Baiyren flinched. "I'm sorry," he said again. "I thought you'd want to go home." He sounded small, deflated.

"So instead of asking – instead of talking to me – you simply did what you thought was best. How do you think that made me feel?" Juno pointed a finger at him. "I *told* you how I felt about you and you couldn't do the same. Or wouldn't. Which is it?" She put her hands on her hips. "Take all the time you need." An awkward silence dropped between them. "I'm waiting," she said, timing the words perfectly.

Baiyren shuffled his feet; he couldn't look her in

the eye. "I came back because I knew I was wrong. I'd like you to come back to Higo." He searched her face, his expression pleading. "I miss you. My life is empty without you in it."

Juno tilted her head. She walked over to him. "I'll come," she said. "On one condition." Baiyren didn't say a word; he just dropped his head and nodded. *Excellent.* "I'm not coming back to just hold your hand or hang on your arm." Her body moved close to his, and she felt the furious beat of his heart. "I'm not going to just sit around and play house, and you wouldn't want me to. I know I've changed since the last time we stood here, but I'm still the same person inside, and I want the same things." She placed her hands on his cheeks and pulled him close. "Now that we've settled things, I'll let you kiss me."

Baiyren relaxed, the tension left his body, and he cracked a smile. "That's not very romantic of you."

"I don't suppose that it is. But it'll be worth it, I promise." Juno pulled him closer, guiding his lips to hers. Time came to a stop, and Juno felt as if she was living and dying and everything in between. She let the moment last as long as she could, then reluctantly pushed away from him. "You're an idiot, you know," she said, resting her cheek on his chest.

"I love you too." Though Baiyren's tone was playful, Juno felt the emotion behind it.

A thrill ran through her; she touched a silencing finger to his lips. "Of course you do. Now…" she said, turning away and tapping her cheek. "The only thing left for me to do is decide what I should pack. Is it warm year-round in Sahqui-Mittama?"

The look on Baiyren's face melted her heart. Disbelief mixed with wonder and happiness. "You're sure? You have a life here – a family."

Not this again. "Yes, Baiyren, I'm sure. Besides, traveling between Earth and Higo has been a whole lot easier than most of my trips. I'll have to figure out what to tell my parents; the truth won't work, not right away." She tried to imagine what *that* conversation would be like. "What the hell," she said, tossing her hands. "I didn't pack the last time, and that turned out okay. New life, new start, new... everything." The thought sent a thrill through her. She'd seen so little of Higo. Her curious nature demanded more. Living there, making a life, sharing it with Baiyren. She wanted all that and more. "Okay," she said. "Let's do this."

Baiyren grinned, took her hand, and headed for a low hill. Keiko dropped from the larger mountains and met them at the top, smiling smugly. "Why do you people always have to make things so hard?" she huffed. "You're lucky you have someone like me around."

Juno smiled back as Baiyren pulled her close. A light tingling filled her body and, as before, the world around her dissolved. When it refocused, she found herself looking at Higo. Lush green forests blanketed the deserts, and organized farms stretched from Sahqui-Mittama's gates to the water separating the Ridderroque from the eastern lands. Baiyren squeezed her hand and grinned happily.

"Welcome home," he said.

ACKNOWLEDGMENTS

I'd like to say a huge thank you to all the people at Angry Robot for making *Kokoro* a reality: to Robot Overlord Marc Gascoigne; my AR editors for this one, Paul Simpson and Claire Rushbrook, for taking my words and making them sing; to the incredible Penny Reeve for shouting from the mountaintop until everyone knows about Angry Robot's fabulous books; to Thomas Walker for bringing this world to life with his stunning cover art; and to Mike Underwood, who found me on Twitter and brought me into the Robot Army.

I'd also like to thank my awesome agent, Laura Zats of Red Sofa Literary. Laura is fierce, tireless, and extraordinarily patient with my steep learning curve. A special thank you to my independent editor Lorin Oberweger of Free-Expressions.com, who crammed the initial edit on *Kokoro* into a very small window. Hats off to you, Lorin, and good luck in your new venture.

Finally, to my wife Kathleen for putting up with my daydreaming, to my daughter Caitlin who dreams too much like I do, and to Jeffrey and Justin, who still correct my grammar and storytelling.

Kokoro is a very special work for me – it was the first story I started to write, way back when I was in high school. Chapter two is nearly identical to what I first put to page, and many of the ideas are still there.

This book is a tribute to the first anime shows that fired my imagination as well as a few more recent ones (relatively speaking) that brought me back into the genre. If you pay close attention, you'll notice the *Go-Rheeyo* is part *Space Battleship Yamato* and *Space Pirate Captain Harlock's Arcadia*. The mah-zhin (the name chosen to honor Toho's Majin) represent a throwback to the idea of a god-monster, rather than standard military mecha like Gundam. *Kokoro's* mah-zhin are more *Grendizer*, *Evangelion*, and *Rahxephon* than *Patlabor*.

The story itself revolves around the characters' search for their life's path, no matter how difficult. If only we all had a Keiko to show us the way!

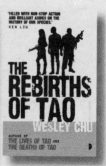

FIND THE GATE. CLAIM YOUR DESTINY.

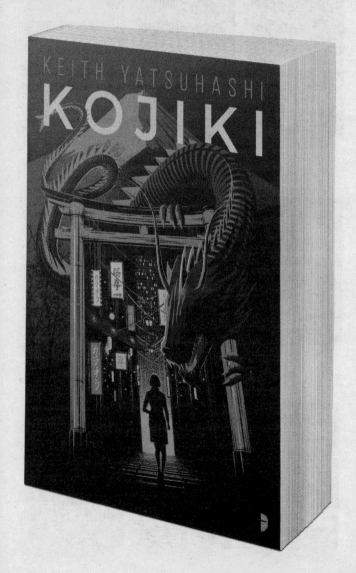

KEITH YATSUHASHI

KOJIKI